WINDBORN

FATED STARS BOOK 1

MARY FAN

Snowy Wings
PUBLISHING

Windborn

Contents

AUTHOR'S NOTE   3

Tell Me My Name

CHAPTER 1   The darkness in my mind   6
CHAPTER 2   This is a dream   30
CHAPTER 3   Of things that make no sense   46
CHAPTER 4   This belongs to you   58

Windborn

PROLOGUE   76
CHAPTER 1   Keep it hidden   88
CHAPTER 2   If the windborn one dies   102
CHAPTER 3   This is the Age of Fire   114
CHAPTER 4   Tick. Tick. Tick.   128
CHAPTER 5   Kill them all   142
CHAPTER 6   You are not alone   150
CHAPTER 7   They are not what they seem   166
CHAPTER 8   We have to get out   182
CHAPTER 9   You're afraid of me   196
CHAPTER 10   Fate of the world   208
CHAPTER 11   For this one moment   226
CHAPTER 12   I know blood when I see it   240
CHAPTER 13   No time for wavering   256
CHAPTER 14   To blazes with prophecies   270
CHAPTER 15   They are not the enemy   284
CHAPTER 16   You don't belong here   296
CHAPTER 17   Reason is beyond him   324
CHAPTER 18   Even into the darkness   336
CHAPTER 19   For the sake of all living   350
CHAPTER 20   All is not lost   360
CHAPTER 21   This is my choice   378

For all those who spun their own bedtime
stories while waiting for sleep to descend.

This was mine.

Author's Note

The story of *Windborn*'s road to publication is almost as winding and full of peril as air nymph Kiri's desperate journey home. I'd had the idea for the world and the overarching plot brewing in the back of my mind since I was a child, but it wasn't until I signed on with a small publisher for a different book that I began piecing together the details. I pitched the idea to the publisher, who was willing to offer on a proposal before I'd even written the first novel. At the time, they were experimenting with a marketing strategy in which a book's prequel would first be published in novella form to drum up publicity for the full-length book.

Originally, I pitched *Windborn* as such a prequel, but it soon became clear that the story was too large to fit inside 25,000 words. And so, working with the editor, I developed the opening few chapters into a separate novella, *Tell Me My Name*, instead. To further set it apart, I wrote *Tell Me My Name* in an altogether different style than *Windborn*.

The main events of *Windborn* pick up about five minutes after *Tell Me My Name* ends. And while it's possible to read *Windborn* by itself, I recommend starting with *Tell Me My Name*, as it gives the reader further insight into Kiri's character and world. For that reason, I have included the novella as part of this book.

Wherever you choose to start reading, I hope you will enjoy delving into the world of *Fated Stars*.

Tell Me My Name

A Fated Stars Novella

The darkness in my mind

IGHT FLOODS MY VISION, BUT THERE'S NO warmth in it, and I shut my eyes, wondering where it's coming from. The darkness returns, and not just the darkness of my vision, but something far deeper, a terrifying abyss that freezes my heart.

The darkness in my mind.

I know I'm lying on a hard surface, and that I woke up here a moment ago, but before that, there's nothing—*nothing.* Just a yawning maw of blackness gaping across my thoughts, a monstrous beast that hollowed out my head, leaving emptiness where memories should have been. Coldness wraps my entire being like an icy blanket; even the air in my lungs chills me. Questions assault me, a million flaming arrows aiming for my heart, and one strikes its target with the greatest impact: *Where am I?*

I sit up and blink, turning my face away from the whiteness that blinded me before. And all I see is ice. Ice and iron. Thick bars stretch up from the ground before me, reaching for the dark ceiling, with frozen water filling the narrow spaces between them. The frosty, pale blue wall glimmers, frightening and mesmerizing at once. It looks so sturdy, it might as well be a mountain, cutting me off from any hope of escape in that direction. Only a small, round window—the source of the light—breaks its otherwise solid form. The cold floor stings my bare feet as I stand and approach it, hoping a glimpse outside might help me figure out where I am. But the window is barely bigger than my hand, and all I see outside is a vast stretch of snow and the pale, empty sky above it. Nothing that tells me anything except this: I don't belong here.

But where *do* I belong? I sense a great shadow looming over me, as if an invisible knife hangs over my head, and hug my bare arms. But the gesture brings me no comfort, for these pale, slight limbs look foreign, though they're parts of me. I realize I haven't even a memory of my own appearance—whether my legs are long or short, whether my face is heart-shaped or round, whether my eyes are black or blue. Who or even *what* I am. The very body I inhabit might as well be a stranger, and the unfamiliarity

sends a new chill racing down my spine. If I don't even know what I look like, how can I hope to discover who I am? Where I came from? Or how I ended up in this icy prison?

A shiver runs through me at the thought, giving my whole body a violent shake, and I clench my jaw in an attempt to stop it. There must be a clue around here somewhere, and I might find it if I can just pull myself together long enough to look. Glancing down, I see that I'm wearing a thin, azure dress that barely reaches my knees, with a top that hangs loosely over my torso from a knot at the nape of my neck, leaving my back and shoulders exposed. I inhale, reminding myself that even this detail is *something*; it tells me that I must have come from someplace much warmer.

But where?

I knit my eyebrows, searching for memories—how old I am, who my family is, what skills I've learned… a cascade of questions tumbles through my head, each yelling for attention and demanding to be answered. What is this place? And why can't I remember how I got here?

But though I scour my mind, only an empty void greets me. I don't even know my own name.

My pulse crescendos with fear, and the shadow of danger grows even darker, closing in around me. I draw a long breath, firmly telling myself to stay calm. I can figure this out if I just focus on one question at a time.

Then something glints at the edge of my vision, and I realize it's my own hair. I reach behind me and pull forward one long, straight lock. It's as pale as my hand, tinted with only the faintest hint of gold. Is it almost white because I'm old? I run my fingers across my face, and the smoothness of my skin gives me the answer to that question: I must be young. Narrow nose, high cheeks, slim eyebrows… I trace each contour with my fingertips, and try to envision what I look like. Part of me says that it's not important—a frivolous detail compared to the larger questions looming over me—but I can't help fixating on it.

I look down and take in what parts of myself my eyes can reach—slight shoulders, small chest, narrow hips. Twig-like legs. Bony wrists. Long, straight hair that reaches my waist. This is *me*, and I shouldn't have to feel strange in my own skin. If I could just find that one thread connecting what I see to what I remember, maybe I could follow it and recover at least one piece of myself.

So I paint a self-portrait, based on what I've observed, and concentrate on the image. The face remains a dark shadow, though, and I focus on that. Surely I must have seen my reflection in the past, in a mirror or a window or even a bucket of water. If I could just recall that single *moment*, I'd have an answer, and maybe that would lead to more.

Because if I can't even recall this simple detail, what hope do I have of escaping the dreaded shadow?

Closing my eyes, I put all my focus on this one simple task and nothing else, trying to sharpen the self-portrait and fill in the blank face with what I puzzled out by touch. The ache returns, and part of me wants to throw up my hands and yell, "This is hopeless!" But I press on, concentrating so hard that I barely feel the coldness surrounding me anymore. I'm so close…

Suddenly an image flashes through my head: a slender girl with sky blue eyes and long, straight hair. And, most importantly, a face. Perhaps… could it be? Is this skinny, bird-like girl, whose wide eyes seem to radiate naïveté, me?

Please let it be, a desperate voice whispers in my heart. *Please say my efforts led to something real…*

A great feeling of familiarity strikes me to the core, and a glow begins to enter my mind, as if a crack has appeared in a cloud-covered sky and revealed a ray of light. *Yes, it's me.* The knowledge feels as certain as the sun shining outside that tiny window, and sudden relief envelops me as I realize I'm one step closer to being whole again. So I *can* recover memories after all. Small as this victory is, it tells me there are more triumphs to be had if I work for them.

And I *must*. I have to know who I am, and where I've come from. How I came to be here. How to get out.

But my sense of victory is short-lived, for the invisible knife, the danger I can't identify but whose presence I feel with every nerve, still hangs over me. If I'm to escape it, I need to uncover more recollections… starting with my name. That could be the next marker in a trail of memories that will lead me home. I know I have one. I feel it in my innermost core—a sense of self whose presence was once as sure as the sun shining outside. But now there's only hollowness within, as if someone stole a piece of my soul.

Still, there must be *something* left, and if I defeated the darkness once, I can do it again. I just need to find a thread, like I did with my appearance,

that will lead me to what I seek. So I whisper random syllables, hoping the sound or cadence of one will somehow trigger the memory of something more. "Tah… Roh… Kee… "

Sudden white-hot pain fills my head, like a burning blade slicing me, and a million tiny daggers lance through my skull, each stabbing me with such force that I feel as if my whole body might shatter.

I cry out in shock and grab at my hair, as if ripping at it might tear away the pain as well. I claw my scalp, knowing it's useless, but unable to keep myself from this vain attempt to stop the great fire. Before I can do anything further, my legs buckle beneath me, and I collapse to the ground.

The impact of the hard metal floor shakes the flames away, and I gasp at the abrupt relief. My knees and shoulders ache from the fall, but their throbbing is nothing compared to the agony I just felt.

I breathe hard, and my heart hammers in my chest. *What was that?*

I look around wildly, wondering if something attacked me, but all I see are the iron bars and the ice between them. Then a thought strikes me: *All I see are the bars and the ice, no matter which way I turn.* Except for the one small window, there's no break in the four frozen walls surrounding me.

There's no way out.

No, that can't be; I must be missing something. I got in here somehow, didn't I? Certain I *must* be wrong, I scramble up to the wall and run my fingers over the hard, freezing mass. Maybe I'm neglecting something with my eyes—maybe there's a hidden door. I sweep my hands across the cold surface, and the chill bites my skin.

But there's nothing.

No matter how I feel along the edges of the iron bars or search the ridges in the ice, I can't find even a single crack. *Maybe I can make one,* I tell myself in a vain attempt to keep my head steady. *Maybe this ice isn't as thick as it looks, and I can break down this wall.* Hoping with all my heart that I'm right, I ball up my fists and pound against it.

The impact sends a bolt of pain shooting up my hand, but the ice doesn't budge. I hit harder and harder, until I'm sure I'll shatter my bones and then, realizing these actions are useless, I flatten my palms and push against it, throwing all my weight forward. My fingers go numb, but I ignore them.

Maybe this wall is stronger than the other three. I turn to the next one

and pound and push until my hands are so sore and cold, I feel like they might fall off. But nothing I do sends so much as a ripple of vibration through the thick ice. My hands look pathetically small against the great surface they're fighting, and while part of me yearns to keep trying, I know I'll break them for real if I do, and still be trapped.

Catching a glimpse of the window, I rush toward it. The wall around the opening is also made of ice—maybe I can widen it. I dig my fingers into its lower edge and tear, desperately using every ounce of strength I have. Though I rip at the ice until my fingers are raw, I can't scrape off a single shard. My breath quickens, until it becomes ragged gasps, and my heart pounds with increasing panic, filling my ears with its desperate drumming. No matter what I do, though, no matter what I try, I can't escape.

I'm trapped.

Exhausted, I collapse against the wall and sink to the ground. My whole body shakes with the cold I can no longer ignore, and I hug my knees to my chest in an effort to warm up. Hot, powerful tears sting my eyes, and dread weighs down with such heaviness that I feel it crushing me. Did someone leave me here to die? Why would they do that? Who could they be?

And who am I?

Just then, a loud clanging noise ripples through the air, and I jump. Realizing that someone else might be outside, and that they might be able to help me, I scramble to my feet and open my mouth to shout.

But then black shadows appear on the other side of the ice, their dark forms vaguely visible through its bluish surface, and my voice dies in my throat. There are at least six or seven figures—tall and shapeless, yet menacing. They draw closer, speaking in low, muffled voices like thunder rumbling in the distance.

Thunder. I remember thunder, roaring in my ears. And lightning, splitting the sky. And rain, both pounding in relentless fury and flurrying in a fine mist. I remember all these elements of the weather—and others, like wind, and fog, and snow… so why can't I remember my name? How is it that I possess so much knowledge about the world, and yet nothing about myself?

Meanwhile, the shadows continue approaching, until they're so near that I could touch them if the wall didn't stand between us. Their looming presence makes me shudder. What are they? What will they do to me?

Then, a deep, commanding voice booms through the barrier: *"Wall of ice, open yourself for me."*

Though the man's words are simple, there's an eerie and supernatural quality to the sound, and the air quakes with its vibrations. The wall responds, somehow, and before me, a rectangular section, stretching from the floor to the ceiling, glows bright green. The rays spread through the entire cell, giving everything an unearthly hue. Where the light appeared, sharp crackling comes from the bars, and lines of white zap through the iron. Only magic could explain these bizarre changes, so this must be some kind of spell.

Then, as abruptly as it all began, everything grows still, and the light fades. Where it glowed, the ice has disappeared, leaving a tall gap almost two feet wide. Yet the bars remain. What I see through them makes me scramble away with fright. A hard surface slams into my back, and, glancing over my shoulder, I realize I've retreated into the wall.

Seven hooded figures stand just outside the cell, robed in black and blue. If it weren't for their chins, barely visible in the shadows, and their hands, which they either hang by their sides or hold clasped before them, I wouldn't even know they were human. All but one has intricate designs embroidered into his or her clothing. The figure closest to me, who must be the man that spoke, wears a magnificent gold chain across his chest, with a thick, circular pendant in the center. Engraved in the pendant are strange symbols for which I can't begin to guess the meaning.

Reminding myself that these are just *people*, I straighten and take a step a step forward, wishing I hadn't been so easily frightened by their appearance. I inhale, telling myself not to let them intimidate me, but before I can say anything, the man with the gold chain throws back his hood, revealing a face so frightening that it stops my breath. If it weren't for the coldness of his narrowed green eyes and the deep frown lines etched between his brows, he might be considered handsome. But his dark expression, his thin nose and sharp cheekbones, remind me of a snake. His lack of hair adds to his reptilian appearance, and his skin, weathered with age, seems wraithlike in its pallor. He stares at me as if he's trying to burn a hole through my head with the intensity of his gaze.

I try to hold my head high and stare back, but my voice betrays my fright as I stammer, "Who—Who are you?"

Instead of answering, he raises his hands, and the wide sleeves of his cloak fall back, revealing the elaborate patterns of black tattoos twisting around his forearms like dead vines. A hot gust surges toward me through the bars, carrying bright red sparks with it, and one lands on my arm. I gasp as its searing heat pierces my skin.

Terrified, I scramble away, trying to escape the other sparks flying toward me. But there's nowhere to go in this tiny cell, and they strike me one by one, each seeming to light a fire as it hits my skin. More of them come at me, and I cry out and cover my face with my arms. Then the sparks seem to connect *under* my skin, and lines of heat blaze through my body, igniting flames in every spot they touch, until every fiber of my being screams with pain. *What's happening to me?* The question tears through my mind like a shriek as fear engulfs me.

I double over and my legs collapse beneath me as a force yanks at my chest, a pair of infernal hands trying to wrench my soul from my body. I scream and scream, unable to form any words or thoughts. All I know is the scorching agony, ripping through my insides with such intensity that I want to cut them out myself rather than let them keep burning. My ears buzz with my own cries, which tear at my throat, and a wave of unbearable hotness flares through my core, oil on an already raging fire. It's consuming every part of me, and dread floods my heart as I realize that soon, there will be nothing left of me.

Stop! You're killing me! I want to shout those words, but can't form them through my screams. *You're killing me!* The idea of death scares me so much that my heart seizes. I feel myself curling into a ball, tears streaming down my face, and press my elbows into my stomach, though for what reason, I don't know. None exists in my mind; there's only anguish and despair as the horror stretches into an unforgiving eternity of endless searing, until I wish I could dissolve into air, or melt into water… *anything* to make it stop.

Then the burning ceases, and though the fire that consumed me just moments ago is gone, I still feel the specter of the torture that wrapped around every muscle, every bone, every vein. How long did I endure it? It might as well have been a lifetime. My pulse hammers so rapidly that it's almost a hum, and sweat clings to my face. All my strength has drained away, as if the pain burned my very life for fuel, and I can barely lift my arm to examine it. Though I expect to see welts or scars, it's as smooth and

pale as before, and I let it drop to the ground. My legs and back sting from the cold floor, but I don't have the energy to move. I'm dying—I'm sure of it. Whatever happened to me just now dragged me to the edge of oblivion, and the darkness beckons.

But some spark inside, perhaps the only one the ruthless magic didn't take from me, tells me I *can't* let death win, and I manage to look up. My gaze meets that of the green-eyed man, whose hands remain raised, red mist swirling around them. A scowl twists his face, and he clenches his fists.

"I *will* discover your secret," he growls, his eyes fixed on mine.

My secret? What could he mean by that?

The question fades as a realization hits me: *He was the one that hurt me.* This man must be a magician, and it was his spell that caused my pain, that nearly drove me mad, that almost killed me. *Is he also the one that trapped me?*

I can't fathom why he'd do either, but if he uses such magic on me again, I have no way to fight him. And I might not have the strength to survive. I feel myself trembling, although I don't know if it's from the overwhelming cold or the fresh wave of fear washing over my heart.

Then a surge of anger rises. What right does this man have to do this to me?

"Who are you?" I demand, managing to speak clearly this time, though the words emerge shakier than I intended. I realize I'm still lying on the ground and quickly stand, hoping I appear stronger than my quaking heart feels. My head rushes from the movement, making the world tilt, and my legs, still weak from the effects of the spell, protest the effort of standing. But I resist the urge to grab the wall for support and, doing my best to harden my expression, say, "What do you want with me?" Though my heart continues to race, my voice doesn't quiver this time.

The man stares at me, but doesn't answer. After a few seconds he turns to the hooded figure beside him and mutters, "I don't understand why it didn't work."

"With all due respect, sir, I'm not surprised," says the other, who has a low, female voice. "We barely gathered any information last time, and we were working on assumptions. We need to know more."

Their words make no sense to me, and I ask, "What are you talking about?"

But I might as well be invisible. The man turns to another hooded companion and mutters, his voice too soft for me to make out any words.

I take a step closer, intending to demand answers, but he shoots me a glare so full of rage that my courage withers. The memory of the pain he caused me — the unrelenting fire I was powerless to fight — causes my heart to pound even faster, and I shrink back. My feeble knees buckle, threatening to collapse beneath me, and I wonder suddenly if I'd survive that torment again.

To my great relief, he doesn't shoot another spell. Instead, he turns his back to me, revealing the brilliant pattern of swirls and shapes embroidered in metallic thread down the back of his cloak. Light flashes off the gleaming embellishments — silver spirals, golden stars, bronze ciphers — that adorn his coat and those of five of his companions. That man used a spell to torture me, and I know that he must be a magician. Could those symbols represent his power? What exactly do they mean?

Who *is* he?

And are the five figures with him, the ones with similarly embellished cloaks, magicians as well?

What about the sixth? He wears no such finery, and I find my attention drawn to this figure in the plain black cloak, wondering if its simplicity places him below the rest in the hierarchy. He stands apart from the others, and all I can see of him are his sharp chin, straight mouth, and the tip of his nose. His smooth, youthful complexion is the color of golden saffron or deep amber, and he holds himself so still, I almost wonder if he's a statue. While the ones in the decorated clothing mutter to each other, step closer, or tilt their heads, he remains motionless and silent.

Hoping that he's not like his companions and won't ignore me, I say, "Please, who are you? What do you want with me?"

His lips part, as if he's about to speak, but then he turns his face toward the man who cast the spell and shuts his mouth. He lowers his chin, and though I can't see his eyes, I know he must be staring at the ground.

That's more of a response than I've received from anyone else. His actions tell me that he wanted to reply, but something about the man

stopped him. *That magician seems to be the leader… does he hold some kind of power over the others? Did he order them to capture me? Why would he do that? And who is this youth in the plain cloak?*

I watch him anxiously for a sign, and a glimmer of hope lights my mind as he lifts his chin and turns his face toward me. He opens his mouth again, but pauses, as if midway toward forming a word. Then he exhales and presses his lips together.

"Please," I repeat, yearning to know what that word might have been. "I… I don't understand why I'm here. If you can't tell me who you are, then I beg you, at least tell me who *I* am."

He remains still for a moment, but then his jaw clenches visibly and he takes a step closer. Desperate hope creeps into my heart, and I keep my pleading eyes on him, wishing I could meet his gaze.

But then the leader abruptly whirls toward the younger man and grabs him by the arm. "Where are you going?" he asks.

The youth bows his head. "I was only going to tell her—"

"I told you not to speak to her!" the magician snaps. He throws me a dark glare and I shrink, terrified that he'll cast his spell on me again. Thankfully, he keeps his arms by his sides. Instead, he whirls to face the other cloaked figures around him and says in a commanding voice: "I forbid *all* of you from speaking to her, am I clear?"

Why? The idea that this man trapped me and then tortured me, without even giving me a reason or justification, rekindles my anger. And now he's destroying my only hope for an ally. A fresh surge of energy flows through me, overpowering my fear, and I give voice to my questions. "Why? What—What do you want with me?"

But nods and murmured assents have already rippled through the small crowd, and nobody even glances in my direction. Except one: the youth in the plain cloak, who briefly turns to me before facing the magician again.

"With all due respect, Master," he says, "she at least deserves to know—"

"Silence!" The magician—evidently the youth's master—takes a threatening step toward him. Though the younger man is taller by several inches, his master's authoritative expression and broad, barrel-chested build make him radiate power. "She may look like a mere girl to you, but

you must remember that this creature is *not* one of us. Have you learned nothing of what I taught you about her kind?"

My kind? What does that mean? Why does he forbid the others from speaking to me at all? What are they hiding? Are they… Could they be afraid of me? But why? I want to ask, but I'm shaking so hard from the cold that I can barely breathe, and my jaw, clenched to keep my teeth from clattering, is no longer capable of obeying my will.

The young man starts to speak, but his master holds up one hand and forms a fist, and the youth's mouth snaps shut as if it's been compelled by magic.

"I make my decisions based on generations' worth of collected knowledge," the magician says in a low growl. "No one here is worthy of challenging its wisdom, least of all a seventeen-year-old apprentice." His expression relaxes, taking on a gentler, almost fatherly look. "You have much to learn, young one. I know this is difficult for you to understand, but what I'm doing is for the greater good. Someday, the fate of the world could rest on our work here. As for the creature" — he shoots me a brief glance — "never forget the destruction her kind has wrought in the past. She's dangerous, and for your own safety, you must not speak to her."

He unclenches his fist, and the young man inhales sharply through his mouth. I'm now certain that this man used magic to prevent his apprentice from speaking. If he can hold such power over one of his own, what would he do to me? And why would he think I'm dangerous? I back into the wall, wishing I could disappear into it. The ice stings my skin, but I barely feel it through my anger.

It has dawned on me that I must have been imprisoned for a reason. Does he mean to use me for some wicked purpose of his? What did he mean by my "kind"?

Suddenly, he raises his hand toward the gap in the wall. Thick ice crawls down from the ceiling and up from the floor, slowly filling the window between us with its frozen crystals. Realizing that he means to close me off again, I rush forward.

"Stop!" I cry, grabbing one of the bars. The metal is so cold it's painful to touch, and I quickly draw my hand back. "Don't leave me here! Please, tell me why you've trapped me! Tell me what I've done!"

The magician ignores me and continues his spell, but his apprentice

turns and faces me. Does he still feel some kind of sympathy toward me? Or have his master's words turned him cold as well? My heart protests the latter thought, telling me that he was the only one with the courage to speak up, instead of thoughtlessly obeying the master, and that kind of courage can't possibly fade so quickly.

"Please," I say for what feels like the hundredth time, and my voice trembles. "Please… "

He firms his mouth, then steps in front of his master. He must block the spell, for the ice stops growing, leaving a jagged, almost square window, bisected by a single iron bar.

The magician scowls at him, and it contorts his face into something so hideous that I almost draw back from it. "How dare you!" He throws his hand toward the apprentice in a forceful gesture, his fingers curved like claws, and the youth slams into the cell's wall as if blown by a hurricane. His head crashes against the metal bar before me, and the sound of the impact rings in my ears.

I cry out as he collapses to the ground, and for several moments he appears to be unconscious, lying in a heap with the thick hood of his cloak covering his face. Finally he sits up, but before he can stand, the master stretches one finger toward him. The boy freezes, caught in an invisible spell.

"What was the meaning of your insubordination?" the magician growls.

"We can't leave her like this, Master." The apprentice's words are strained with forced deference. "She—"

"Weakling!" The man punches his hand forward, hurling the apprentice into the wall again, and a second crash reverberates through the dungeon.

"Stop!" I yell. Though I can't see what happened from my current angle, the sound was more than enough. The punishment seems unreasonably cruel, and my anger rises at the injustice, filling my heart with a crackling force. I glare at the master, wishing I could slam *him* into a metal bar. "He didn't do anything!"

But the magician ignores me, keeping his wrathful green eyes fixed on his apprentice. "Do not question my orders. Or do you really think that your measly knowledge of the magical is a match for mine?"

The mocking lilt in his voice ignites a fresh spark in me, and I shout, "Is

this what you do? Hurt people for no reason? You *monster*!" But my voice might as well be a whispering breeze for all the reaction he gives.

The apprentice picks himself up again, and this time the master doesn't interfere. As the youth stands, I catch a glimpse of a dark bruise creeping down his face from under the shadow of his hood. But if the punishment intimidated him, he doesn't show it, for he holds himself erect, steps toward the magician, and keeps his voice steady. "Master, what good will she do you if she freezes in this cell?"

Guilt gnaws at me, and I bite my lip. Why would he still try to help me, when he's already provoked his master? For a moment I fear that the magician will hurt the young man again, but instead he says dismissively, "Cold does not affect her kind as it would you or me." Before I can protest — for whatever I am, this is most certainly *not* true — he gives me an appraising look and says, "But perhaps this one isn't as strong."

He steps around the apprentice and waves his hand in a circular motion. A ball of yellow light appears, hovering above his palm, and the warmth it emits brings immediate relief. I want to take that warmth and wrap it around me like a cocoon from which I'd never emerge.

The magician draws a long breath, then blows at the ball of light, which flies through the window in my cell. I instinctively reach toward it. A warning rings through my head, telling me that anything this monster sends my way can't be good, but it's too late — the glowing orb is upon me, and I hold up my hands to protect the rest of my body. To my surprise, I'm able to catch the light, and its soft warmth sends a rush of comfort up my arms. Though I feel nothing solid, its presence is undeniable. I tentatively press my hands toward each other, and the force of the magic resists my push.

I pull the sphere close, speechless with gratitude, and let its warmth flow through my frigid arms and chest. For a moment, this source of heat is the only thing I care about.

Then I recall that it was given to me by the same monster who tortured me with his fiery spell, and I almost fling it away, just to spite him. But much as I hate that man, its heat is the one shield I have against the cold. And he only gave it to me after the apprentice said I might freeze… so the magician must need me alive. Why? What does he plan to do with me?

I look up at the window, seeking him, but he and the other cloaked

figures are marching away, toward the stone staircase on the other side of the wide room.

"Wait!" I cry. If they leave, there's no knowing when—or if—they'll return. I have so many questions, and they've yet to answer a single one. I know it's useless to ask, but I have to try. "Just tell me why I'm here!"

The apprentice, unmistakable in his plain black cloak, even when his back is to me, stops. The others continue, but he turns and walks back toward me. I watch him hopefully. He'd meant to answer me before; will he really defy his master again after what just happened?

"Stop!" The leader's voice thunders through the room, and he glares down at the young man from the step. "If you speak even a single word to her, I guarantee you'll regret it."

I suddenly fear what punishment he would inflict upon the youth; if he threw him into a wall because of a protest over the cold—a protest he then *agreed* with—what will he do for outright disobedience? I know how much agony his magic can cause, and I can't stand the thought of that boy enduring more pain because of me. So I bite back my questions, my heart sinking.

The apprentice looks back at his master and pauses. I watch anxiously, hoping he'll choose *not* to provoke the other further. To my dismay, though, he turns and continues toward me. The man keeps his eyes fixed on him and raises his hand in an ominous gesture, as if to cast another spell.

I open my mouth to tell the youth to stop, to obey his master, to leave me—I'll be fine. But then he unhooks the clasp of his cloak and removes it in a single, sweeping motion, revealing his face. Struck by the sight, I forget what I'd meant to say.

The golden light from the ball in my hands glints off his black hair and highlights a pair of well-defined cheekbones, and I almost don't notice the two bruises—one on his forehead and one stretching down his cheek—marring the otherwise even complexion. His eyes are darker than midnight, and the angles of his thick black eyebrows add to their obsidian intensity. The fierceness in his expression is almost frightening, and yet I find something strangely beautiful about it.

Firming his mouth, he throws a glare back at his master, who suddenly looks like a mere shade of a person in comparison. There's something powerful about this boy, something that makes him appear older than his

seventeen years, but at the same time, he radiates a kind of bright energy only the young could hold. Had both faces been revealed before I knew of their relationship, I might have assumed the younger man was the master.

He walks up to the window of my cell, and his expression softens. It hits me that the fierce look it held a moment before was meant for the man giving him orders. It was a look of defiance, a challenge. As he reaches through the bars, the cloak in his hand, I realize that he means to give it to me. Not knowing what else to do, I accept it.

"Thank you," I whisper, closing my hand around the thick black cloth. I don't expect him to respond after his master's threat; in fact, I hope he doesn't.

And though his mouth remains hard, his eyes take on an apologetic tilt, and I can hear what he wants to say as sure as if he'd voiced the words himself: "I'm sorry I can't do more."

Suddenly he twists with an unnatural jolt, turning away from me, and the action snaps me out of my momentary distraction, reminding me that we're both still at the mercy of the master. Behind him, the magician holds up both fists. If his eyes could emit heat, the apprentice would have been reduced to cinders in an instant, and terror darts through me as I wonder what will happen to the boy.

"Don't hurt him!" I cry, wishing I could crash through this wall and protect the only person who's shown me any kindness.

Without glancing at me, the man jerks his fists back, and the apprentice stumbles toward him. The master must have bound him by magic—it's the only answer. "Come. Or will I have to drag you out of here?"

The boy remains silent. A slight, barely perceptible shudder runs through him, and a sense of guilt twists my stomach. His simple white shirt and brown pants appear as useless against the cold as my dress. I would never have asked him to relinquish his source of warmth, and it feels wrong, having taken the cloak from him. At the same time, it would have seemed just as wrong to refuse his kindness when he went through so much to offer it.

Knowing I can't ask any more of him, I turn my attention to his master. How *dare* he act so cruelly, both toward me and toward his own apprentice? What gives him the right to abuse us like this, and for no reason that makes any justifiable sense?

These words teeter on the edge of my tongue, but I can tell by the scowl on his snake-like face that only a thread holds his temper back, and I worry that if it snaps, he'll take out his wrath on the youth. My eyes are drawn to the two bruises on the boy's face—bruises he received because of me—and I'm sure he must have more that I can't see. Rage blazes in the leader's expression, and I can't risk anything more happening to that young man. He may be a stranger, but he's already given me more than I had the right to ask for.

So I just watch, seething in silence, as the magician leads his apprentice and cloaked followers up the stone steps. At the top, he stops and lets the others pass. When the youth arrives, the man unclenches his fists and places a hand on the boy's shoulder.

"You have much to learn, young one," he says, shaking his head. His gentle, fatherly tone sounds so false after the actions I witnessed that it makes me cringe. "I know you must resent me right now, but do not think my actions harsh. Remember, this is our way—the way of endurance and trials, for only the strong are worthy of the kind of power we wield. You knew that when you swore your life to us."

"Yes, Master," the young man says softly, and I don't understand how anyone could have *chosen* this life. What kinds of "great rewards" could be worth serving such a wicked man?

Meanwhile, the magician places his other hand on his apprentice's head and knits his eyebrows in an expression of concentration. At first I think this is meant to be some new kind of paternal gesture, but then I notice the bruises on the other's face fading, and realize with some surprise that the magician must be casting a healing spell. After a few moments, the injuries disappear completely, and he lowers his hand.

"I know you mean well, my young one, but your foolishness will cost you. Never forget how deceptive appearances can be."

The youth gives a slight nod, but his expression is filled with confusion as he draws one hand across his healed face. The master glances back at me and narrows his eyes, then, with his hand still on the other's shoulder, leads him up the stairs. I think back to how he called me dangerous, and notice that he seems strangely protective of the boy, as if he believes that his harshness is for his apprentice's own good. I don't understand how he could think that way, but is there something more to him than the pure

wickedness I see? He locked me up and tortured me with his spell, and yet could he possibly have a good reason? Did I do something terrible to deserve this… something that I can't remember? Maybe *I'm* the monster, and he's keeping me here to prevent me from hurting anybody. But I don't feel like one… Were we enemies? If that's so, why wouldn't he tell me?

I think back to his words and try to puzzle out why he hates me so much. "This creature is *not* one of us," he said. And he kept referring to my "kind." He must mean that I'm an outsider—perhaps I come from an enemy land? Maybe I'm a prisoner of war?

That explanation seems to make sense, and I try to recall what we might have been fighting over. Maybe if I can remember that, it'll help me puzzle out where my home is. The feeling of an invisible knife hanging over my head—the uncanny sensation of omnipresent danger that accosted me when I first woke up—returns, and I shudder. Actually, it's been here this whole time; I just wasn't thinking about it because I was distracted by the magician and his young apprentice.

Now that I'm alone, I sense it looming over me, threatening to fall at any moment. And I realize that the only way I can escape it is to get out of here, to return to a place where I'll be safe. But no matter how much I probe my mind, I find only gaping emptiness. How do I know so much about the world—about storms and magic and war—when I can't recall a single thing about my own life? The magician said he wanted to discover my "secret," but how can he hope to do so when I don't even know it myself?

Whatever it is, I need to find it. If it's important enough for him to desire, it could be the key to my freedom.

Maybe if I look hard enough, I'll find something that can awaken my memories. The sight of my body helped me recall what my face looks like—maybe a familiar word or object from the outside world will bring back more.

I look out the jagged window the magician left in the cell's wall. He and the others have disappeared up the steps, and without them, the large room seems eerie in its emptiness. It's wide and dark, illuminated by only a single iron lantern, hanging on a chain from the low ceiling. The walls and floor are made of dark stone, but not individual blocks such as brick. Instead, the entire place appears to have been hollowed out of a single, enormous rock. A wooden post stands in the center, and I notice a pair of

shackles attached to it. Leaning closer to the wall to get a better view, I look toward the outskirts of the large room.

There's not much, but what I do see tells me that I must be in a dungeon. More shackles dangle from the walls to my far left, and I shudder at the thought of people being bound by them. My cell appears to be one of many, all of which have iron bars frozen over with ice. Do other captives lie within them?

"Hello?" I call. "Is anyone out there?"

Only silence greets me. Hollow, lonely silence.

"Hello? Please, is anyone there?"

I wait, but no one responds. So I retreat into my cell, feeling heavy inside. I'm completely alone here, and nothing stirred any memories. I've looked at everything within sight of my cell, and none of it's done me any good. I need to get out of here — to see more, and to escape before the magician returns and casts his horrible spell on me again. But how? I've already tried, and nothing I did even hinted at working. A rush of anxiety tightens my chest, but I try not to let it overwhelm me. There *must* be a solution, and I feel like I'm missing something obvious…

I glance down at the ball of warm light in my hand, and suddenly an idea sparks. These walls are made of *ice*, and ice melts! This answer seems so clear now, I wonder how I didn't think of it before. The nervous clenching in my heart turns to an excited, elated drumming, and I feel the corners of my mouth tugging into a smile at the revelation. It won't be easy, using such a small piece of warmth to melt so thick a wall, but I can do it. Even if it takes hours, or days, of gradual wearing down, I'll persist until I succeed. And then I'll slip through the bars — I'm sure I'm slight enough to do so — and freedom will be mine.

I press the ball of heat into one of the frozen surfaces and watch intently. Though I remind myself that this will take time, I can't help my eagerness. A drop of water is all I need to see — just a hint to tell me that my plan is working. Time crawls by, and I can't resist pushing the ball harder into the wall in my impatience. *Come on, just show me a drop…*

I lean closer, hoping to catch even the thinnest of rivulets winding down the rough ice. But I see nothing; the wall might as well be made of stone. My excitement fades back into anxiety, and I try not to fear the worst. *I've only just started,* I remind myself.

More time passes, stretching on and on, but I hold the ball of light steady, knowing I need to concentrate all the heat on one spot. Any second now, I'm sure I'll see a sign that my plan is working. *Just a drop… Please…*

My arms and back begin to ache with stiffness from holding the same position for what feels like hours, and I try to ignore them. *It'll all be worth it once I'm free*, I think to myself, but the self-assurance rings hollow. The wall remains as solid as ever, and it occurs to me now that the ice could be enchanted to remain sturdy in the face of heat. I recall the sparks the magician tortured me with — the ones that burned so hot, they nearly drove me mad. There was no sign of water then, and if such fire couldn't melt this frozen mass, how could a small ball of light do anything… especially when it was given to me by the very man who imprisoned me here?

Suddenly the foolishness of my plan descends upon me, and a great swelling of despair fills my chest as I realize that this effort, like my others, is in vain. I let my arms drop, wondering how long I stood here like an idiot, waiting for something that could never happen, and, with tears stinging my eyes, sink to the ground. I don't want to give up, but when I wrack my brain for more ideas, I can't come up with any. I've tried breaking down the walls, widening the window, melting the ice… what more is there to attempt? The ground is solid iron — I could claw at it until I ground my fingers to bone dust, and it wouldn't make a difference. The ceiling is iron as well… not that I could reach it.

It's hopeless. Completely hopeless. I've tried everything I can think of, and I'm no closer to finding a way out. And how can I learn anything if I'm trapped here, with the only other sign of life being those who refuse to answer my questions? Though the ball of light keeps the frigid air back, I still feel incredibly cold. The chill comes from inside me, from the emptiness of not even knowing my own name.

But I can't simply surrender. There must be *something* more I can do — I just need to figure out *what*.

Realizing I'm still holding the apprentice's black cloak, I wrap the material around me. Something about its presence brings me a small measure of comfort. Perhaps it's just knowing that someone — anyone — cares a little about me. *What if I ask him for answers the next time he comes?* a part of me inquires. He alone was willing to help me; he's probably my only hope. But why would he, especially when his powerful master controls him so tightly?

He challenged that authority already, for my sake, that voice in my head whispers. *If I appeal to him, if I let him know how much I'm depending on him, maybe he'll do it again.*

But what would the master do to him if he did? Though the magician healed the wounds he inflicted the first time, I can't forget the horrible way he threw the boy into the wall. I questioned then what right that man had to do so, and now I have to wonder: What right have I to ask the apprentice to face that again? What right have I to ask *anything* of him?

To do what my mind suggested would be to manipulate another for my own gain, and that would be *wrong*. Further, I shouldn't have to depend on someone else in the first place. I *should* find a way to recover my memories and escape this cell on my own. But what if I'm not clever enough? Not resourceful enough? Not… strong enough?

Tears roll down my cheeks, and as I brush them away, I catch a glimpse of the window to the outdoors. The light that previously shone through it has retreated, leaving a bluish-gray shade across the sky. Its darkness seems to reflect how I feel: lonely and lost.

Then a twinkle catches my eye. A star—the first one I've seen tonight. A feeling stirs—not quite a memory, but close. Something inside tells me that stars represent goodness, and I focus on the thought. Maybe it'll bring back the recollection of who taught me that.

Suddenly the stories shine clearly in my head, as sure as my knowledge of the sun and the sky, and I find comfort in their familiarity. I know that the goodness of starlight, given by the benevolent Divinity, glows within all of our souls. She watches over us, Her children, and charged Her heavenly servants, the ayri, with caring for us. They dwell in the Celestial Realm alongside the spirits of the dead, each ayr responsible for a specific aspect of the world—an hour of the day, like midnight; an element of nature, like rain; or a particular virtue, like truth. They embody these pieces of the universe, with the ayri of time ensuring each hour occurs when it should, and those of nature bringing balance to the weather and the earth. As for the ones of virtue—it's said that they whisper their advice into our minds and guide those wise enough to listen. And though they all remain ever watchful, the Divinity forbids them from interfering with our lives in the

Terrestrial Realm. For She loves us, the children She created at the dawn of time, and wants us to have the freedom to dictate our own destinies.

I recall the story of how Her wicked brother, the Fiend, tried to destroy the Terrestrial dwellers—our ancestors—shortly after their creation, and how She and Her ayri fought fiercely to defend us, until finally She cast him into the Firelands—a great cage in the Infernal Realm, from which there is no escape.

But I don't know who told me these things, or where I learned them.

I stare at the star outside, and the knowledge of what it is and what it means sits firmly in my head… yet isn't held there by a single memory of my own. How can that be? Then I concentrate hard on what I *do* know, hoping it'll lead to something more, even if it's just a glimpse of my past.

But an abrupt, searing blaze flares through my skull, and I scream in agony. A hundred red-hot knives cut through me, ripping with such intensity that I would cut off my own head to end the torment. I press my face into the ice, willing to do anything to make the pain stop, and push so hard into the rough surface that I feel as if I'm crushing my skull to powder. But there's no relief from the scorching flames, not even in the frigidness of the wall, and I'm sure the fire will incinerate me. The heat pierces through me in sharp blasts, like someone is firing a volley of infernal arrows, and the air shakes from the cries I have no power to hold back. I slam my forehead into the wall, but the impact hardly registers through the raging, intolerable blaze. No matter what I do, there is only pain, pain, pain.

Then, suddenly, it disappears. I gasp, my forehead still against the cold wall, and my head throbs from the pressure. Every bone has become as heavy as stone, and I sink to the ground. Expecting to find ashes where my hair was, I pat the back of my head, but everything seems fine—on the outside, at least. Inside, I feel like the life has once again been sapped from me, with much of it destroyed in the cursed inferno… just as it was when the magician threw his spell at me.

Is he behind this? Did he place some kind of curse on me that would torture me even in his absence? Why would he do that? What does he want from me? This is the third time I've felt the great heat of a curse overtake me—the first was when I tried to remember my name. What caused it to take effect like that? Did I do something to set it off?

Then, it hits me: I was trying to remember something then, and I was

trying to remember something just now. Could that be the answer? Is the curse meant to keep me from recovering any memories? But why?

What can I do? I haven't the strength to break through these walls. And I dare not search my mind for memories again. I can't stand the thought of facing that pain once more, not when it drove me mad enough to dash my head against the wall this time. And it was all for nothing—I haven't unearthed a single hint about my past. If I could, maybe I would uncover some clue that would help me escape—a skill I've forgotten I have. A piece of information the magician would find valuable enough to trade for my freedom. Or the name of an ally I could call upon for help.

But no matter which way I turn, I see only darkness. It's impossible.

Hopeless.

I wrap the cloak closer around myself and bury my face in my knees.

This is a dream

2

*HIMES RING IN A CASCADING MELODY, BUT ONLY A black expanse lies before me. I follow the sound, hoping to find their source. Silver mist rolls toward me in the distance, and I know it must conceal something important, though what that thing is, I can't begin to guess. Something within me — maybe my heart, maybe my soul — urges me toward it, and I listen.*

The chimes grow louder, yet their tinkling song remains gentle, like the voice of a breeze. I look around for the instrument creating the music, knowing it must lie somewhere in the sea of mist. I don't know why, but an intense need to find it pulls at my core. As I enter the cloud of silver, though, heat assaults my skin, and I jump back with a cry.

Where did that heat come from? I don't see any flames. There's not even any sunlight. Thinking maybe I imagined it, I reach one hand out cautiously. As soon as my fingers brush the mist, a sudden, invisible blaze scorches them. I clench my teeth, breathing hard from the pain, but keep my hand steady. It hurts, but appears otherwise unharmed.

Then, I realize: This is a dream.

No — more than a dream. Those chimes are too familiar… They must be from a memory.

The great desire to know something, anything, about my past overtakes any hesitation I might have, and I press forward.

The mist surrounds me, and with it, the invisible fire. I feel as if someone has taken a sheet of metal that's been sitting under the summer sun and pressed it against my body. But hot as it is, I can tolerate it. I must.

The sounds of the chimes grow closer, and through the mist, I catch a glimpse of green. Knowing it must be the source I seek, I dash toward it eagerly.

The object comes into view, and I stop in my tracks. An old, gnarled tree stands before me. It's not very tall for a tree, and yet its broad, deep brown trunk and myriad of twisting branches give it an air of majesty. Emerald green leaves dance on its boughs, rippling under a slight wind. But I barely notice them, for between them is a sight that makes no sense: clocks.

Where a tree should grow flowers, this one grows clocks. Little silver, gold, and copper timepieces sit nestled in the leaves. A gale sweeps through the tree, disturbing the branches, and the clocks clang into each other. These, I realize, are the chimes I heard. The wind dies down, and I detect the faint tick-tocks created by hundreds of tiny gears.

The heat of the mist continues pressing into me, but I barely feel it as I stare at the bizarre thing before me, dismayed. I thought the chimes would lead me to something that could tell me who I am. Instead, all I see is an image I can't interpret.

Maybe there's something more to the tree. I approach it, hoping to get a closer look, but then a wave of mist crashes toward it, blocking it from my view.

"No!" I cry, sprinting forward. I need that tree. A powerful force inside me is yelling that I must find out what it means, saying that if I don't, something horrible will happen.

Invisible flames bite my flesh, and I do my best to ignore them, but I can't see the tree anywhere. Even the sound of the chimes has vanished. My heart races with anxiety, and I refuse to believe that I've lost it. I must find that tree — and find it soon, before… before what?

The feeling of foreboding tears at my soul, and my anxiety is so great that I can barely breathe. Only mist fills my vision; I sweep my arms, trying to clear it away, but no matter what I do, it keeps pressing against me. A faint ticking sound creeps into my ears, and the great yet inexplicable sense of urgency and fear returns. The noise grows louder and faster, and my heart seems enslaved to its rhythm —

I awaken with a start, my heart still thumping. Sweat clings to my skin, and I push back the cloak I wrapped myself in. I'm almost glad for the chilly air, since it brings me relief in my fevered state. Wondering how a dream could have such a profound effect on me, I close my eyes and try to bring back the images I saw.

A tree that grows clocks.

What does that mean? Or was it just a dream? Now that I'm awake, the vision seems even more bizarre, and I feel like a fool for believing it could be anything more than nonsense. How can a tree grow clocks?

I huff, frustrated at myself. I need to remember something *real*, not the fanciful imaginings of the dreamscape.

A shudder wracks my body, and I wrap the cloak around myself again. The thick fabric brings immediate relief to my frigid shoulders. Looking around, I search for the ball of light the magician gave me for warmth. It sits in the far corner—I must have shoved it in my sleep. I stand, aiming to get it, but find my attention instead drawn to the small window. The rosy dawn brightens the world outside, and its beauty takes my breath away. The snowy vastness glows under the flush of the sky, and golden clouds swirl above in delicate patterns that remind me of lace.

Energy rushes through me, and I feel a smile spread across my face. *The Divinity is in the sunrise.* Whoever told me that was right, and in this one, blissful moment, it doesn't bother me that I can't remember where those words came from. All that matters is that the Ayr of Sunrise, the most joyous of the Divinity's celestial servants, has once again bestowed their wondrous gift upon the world.

A flash of blue, startling in its brightness, appears in the corner of my eye. I glance toward it and see that it's a small butterfly, flitting toward me. It lands on the edge of the tiny window and gently spreads its wings. Though they're translucent, the richness of their color almost makes them glow, and a delicate pattern of black spots line their edges. The presence of this tiny creature is strangely comforting, and I smile.

"Hello," I whisper. I sense a strong affinity to it, like it's an old friend, and wonder if wherever I came from was home to blue butterflies like this one.

It takes off toward the sky, its azure wings twinkling under the dawn light as it floats and darts along, and I watch it, envious of its freedom. The sense of familiarity grows uncanny.

I… I feel as if I've flown beside it.

I recall the cool breeze against my face and the rush of joy from being above the world. It's not the memory of a moment, but of a sensation, unattached to images or sounds. The only reasonable explanation is that I'm imagining what it's like to soar like a butterfly… and yet the strange impression is so potent that there must be more. My nerves hum, and my discomfort grows. What does all this mean? Could I possibly have flown once? But that's not possible, since I don't have wings…

Even though the image in my head clearly depicts an ordinary girl, I

can't resist reaching behind me and feeling my back, just in case there's something to this sensation. But my fingers brush only the bareness of my skin; there are certainly no wings there. Nor the scars that would surely remain if they'd once existed, and I'd lost them.

A rumble in my stomach brings me back to reality, and I suddenly notice how dry my throat is. I turn away from the window, my frustration arising anew. More nonsense! Only fairies, sprites, and ayri have wings. I'm too big to be either of those first two, and to contemplate being an ayr feels like sacrilege. The ayri are holy creatures, demigods who maintain the Terrestrial Realm for the Divinity. Even the most powerful practitioners of magic, combining their forces as one, couldn't capture a celestial being. So how could I even *think* I once flew?

This rubbish is the last thing I should be contemplating, especially when I have more immediate needs, such as hunger and thirst. Why is it that my head can fill itself with ridiculous notions — like clock trees and wings — but refuses to let me recover a single true fact? Instead of imagining that I flew like that butterfly, I should observe the outside world more carefully, in case there's anything new in the landscape, or something important I missed in my panic yesterday evening. I start to turn my attention back to the window, but just then, the distant sound of voices floats toward me from behind.

Someone's approaching the dungeon and, wondering who it is, I scurry across the cell and peer curiously through the bars.

"Remember what it means to be one of us," a stern, familiar voice thunders from the staircase. It's the magician — I'm certain of it. He must be standing at the top, because I see only the tip of his shadow on the steps. "Our loyalty to each other is absolute and unbreakable. You swore that oath when we took you in."

"Yes, Master." The second voice, bright with youthful energy, belongs to the apprentice. I press against the bars of the window and angle my head, trying to catch a glimpse of either speaker, but they're too far away. Chilled by the coldness of the metal, I draw back.

My first instinct is to call out to them, but then, remembering how our last encounter went, I banish the thought. For now, it would be better to listen and hope one of them says something that can help me find answers.

Meanwhile, the master continues. "And remember why you came to

us. Our kind led the world in peace and prosperity for generations during the Age of Magic, and though the present Age has seen us banished to this frozen wasteland, we will rise to power again someday. With all the dark prophecies in the air, that time is drawing close. A great evil is rising, and once it unleashes its wrath upon the world, we will be the only ones with the power to protect the living. But to gain that power, sacrifices must be made, and reluctance is a luxury we cannot afford."

"I understand, Master." Despite this, I sense a tinge of rebelliousness in the apprentice's tone, as if he's saying whatever his master wants to hear without believing a word of it.

The master must sense it too, because he says sternly, "You may think I'm being cruel, or that I'm overreacting to the dangers she presents, but that's not true."

He's talking about me! I lean forward with renewed interest, hoping he'll reveal some information about why he finds me such a threat.

"I never take action without careful consideration," he continues. "You have not dealt with her kind before, and you have no way of knowing the risk you take just by speaking to her. You're not just putting yourself at peril, but opening the gates for danger to attack our entire stronghold. Do not make the mistake of thinking you know better than me."

"Of course not, Master." The apprentice's words are dull, spoken without any real feeling.

Does he not believe the magician? I wonder, hoping that it's true, that I might still have an ally.

Suddenly a great smacking sound, like a fist impacting flesh, snaps through the air, startling me. "*What* must I do to make you understand?" the master asks sharply, and I realize, to my horror, that he must have sensed disobedience in the boy's tone and struck him as punishment. My horror quickly turns to fury, and I wonder again how anyone could be so brutal, and why the apprentice doesn't fight back.

Meanwhile, silence hangs in the air, and my thoughts teeter between two equally demanding ideas: One, that I should intervene by calling the master out on his cruelty again, and the other that I should remain silent, lest I provoke him further and cause him to take his anger out on the apprentice.

Before my wavering mind can settle on a decision, the master gives a

loud sigh and says, "I'm trying to protect you, young one. But as much as I care about you, my responsibility is to the Sorci, and I've already indulged you enough. Our laws have stood for thousands of years, and I won't make any exceptions—not even for you. Now do your job, and nothing more."

"Yes, Master," the youth responds, though his voice is too quiet for me to discern whether any of his previous rebellion remains.

Why do you keep saying that? I wonder, shaking my head. *Why don't you defend yourself?* I yearn to do something to stop the cruelty I've witnessed, but how can I help anyone else when I'm trapped in this cell, and anything I say would only fuel the abuser?

I hear footsteps retreating; the two must be walking away. Why were they heading this way in the first place, if it wasn't to see me? There doesn't seem to be anything else down here.

My stomach grumbles again, and my throat is so dry it itches, but though they both shout for attention, my mind is elsewhere, wandering back to what the magician said: "My responsibility is to the Sorci."

The Sorci. So that's what they call themselves. Noticing how cold my fingers have grown, I crouch by the ball of light and pick it up to warm them. I stare into the golden luminescence in my hands and ponder the name, feeling like I've heard it spoken of before. But I hesitate to try remembering; the memory of the agonizing heat that attacked me yesterday is all too acute.

Then another utterance of the magician's surfaces in my mind—what he said right after he cast his torturous spell on me: "I will discover your secrets."

What did he mean by that? He never asked me any questions; is he hoping to… *extract* information straight out of my mind?

The thought makes me shudder, and I try to banish it by bringing my focus back onto the magician's recent words, the ones that might reveal something. If I can figure out where I am and why I'm here, maybe I can find a way to get out. Whatever curse keeps my memories bound seems to affect only that which is personal, since I was able to recall plenty about the world. It doesn't make any sense—why would someone place such a curse on me? What… never mind. I won't be able to answer any of these questions now, I realize, and I need to keep my thoughts on the ones that I *can.* So I probe my mind tentatively and contemplate what I've just heard the magician say.

He spoke of the Age of Magic, and *that*, I've heard of before. The history of our world is knowledge that shines clearly in my mind. After seventeen thousand years of peaceful existence between all the Divinity's creations in the Terrestrial Realm, humans grew in ambition, and those who practiced magic used their abilities to seize power.

And they were called the Sorci. The fact hits me like a splash of cold water, and I wonder how I didn't recall it the moment the magician uttered the word. Centuries have passed since they were overthrown by ordinary humans who, frustrated after six thousand years of being oppressed by the magical, rose up against them with their armies of knights and weapons of steel, which is how our current era, the Age of Thrones, began. From what the master magician said, the Sorci didn't die out after they fell. I guess a few of them lingered in this snowy part of the world, hoping to regain power one day.

But what did he mean by "rising evil"? Of that, I have no recollections, though I don't know whether it's because I've never heard of it before, or because of the curse. And though the idea of the world being consumed by darkness strikes fear into my heart, I can't help but fixate on something the Sorci master said before that… something about me.

He said that just by speaking with me, the apprentice was putting himself and the entire order of Sorci at risk. How can that be? I'm just a girl, trapped in a cell. I can't even make a chip in the ice. How could I possibly be dangerous?

What did I *do* in my past?

I must know. Even if it means learning that I'm a monster, I have to try remembering — no matter what kind of pain the curse causes me. If I do, I might uncover knowledge that will help me escape this frigid prison.

I squeeze my eyes shut and brace myself for the heat, but before I can delve into my head, the sound of footsteps approaches. Eager for the chance to learn something, I open my eyes and spring up to the window, hoping that whoever is walking toward the dungeon will do or say something to reveal why I'm here.

Outside, the apprentice descends the staircase, holding a brown sack, and I watch in anticipation, wondering what he's coming down here for. His eyes are fixed on the ground, and even though his head is bowed, I find my gaze drawn to his face. What do those knit eyebrows and firm mouth

mean? Is he contemplating his master's words, about me being a threat? Does he regret standing up to him yesterday by trying to help me?

Then I notice that he's wearing only a dark red shirt and black pants, both of which look as thin as paper—nothing warm. His sleeves are rolled up to the elbow, revealing a pair of taut forearms, and his neck and head are exposed to the cold. His tight jaw and balled-up hands betray the fact that the icy air chills him as much as it does me, though his demeanor is otherwise calm.

Glancing down at the cloak wrapped around me, my stomach sinks in dismay. I should never have accepted it in the first place. Why does my comfort matter more than that of anyone else?

The cloak suddenly seems to burn my shoulders, and I tear it off, hating the fact that it warmed me while its former owner shivered. I must return it—I had no right to take it.

The apprentice reaches the bottom of the stairs and crosses the stone room outside, approaching me. He raises his eyes, meeting my gaze with his ebony stare. Not knowing whether it's anger, hatred, or something else clouding his expression, I draw back. Does he blame me for causing trouble between his master and him? Resent me for the punishments he endured? I never meant for any of that to happen, and I sorely wish that I'd never turned my pleas to him.

I reach through the bars with the cloak in my hand, and the black fabric drapes over the window's frozen edge.

"Here." Not knowing what else to say, I whisper, "I'm sorry."

His eyebrows crease even further, and then rise as his eyes take on a gentler expression. He shakes his head and continues toward the cell. "Keep it."

Recalling how his master forbade him from speaking a single word to me, I look around frantically. To my relief, I see no one, and I push the cloak further out to let him know that I mean to return it. He shouldn't go cold because of me.

But he stops before the window, wraps his hand around mine, and gives it a gentle push back. "I'd rather you have it."

His eyes are fixed on mine, and I realize he means what he says. I don't understand why he'd act kindly toward me after everything his master said and did to him, but if I insist on returning the cloak, he might think I'm

throwing his generosity back in his face. The last thing I want is to offend him, so I pull the cloak back in and give him a grateful smile. "Thank you."

He smiles back, and I'm surprised by how much the expression changes his demeanor. When his face was intense with defiance, he seemed like such a fierce young man. Now, with his eyes bright and his lips curved with friendliness, he appears boyish and sweet.

He places the sack on the ledge of the window. "Here. You must be hungry."

My growling stomach agrees, and I tentatively accept the sack. Before I can do anything else, an angry voice explodes through the dungeon.

"Darien!"

I gasp and turn to the sound. The apprentice, apparently also startled, whirls around.

Seeing who has spoken, my insides tighten. It's the Sorci master, standing in the middle of the staircase with one arm raised before him, pointing an accusing finger at the apprentice. The boy named Darien takes a step forward and opens his mouth. But before he can speak, the master shouts, "*Forth!*" and a bolt of red lighting spews from his finger. It strikes the youth square in the chest, and though it vanishes into his body, I know its effects are just beginning, for he doubles over, clasping his arms. He collapses to his knees with his head bowed and his expression contorted with pain, but makes no sound.

"Stop!" I yell. "What are you doing to him?"

The magician pays me no heed and strides toward the other, who remains on the ground in a hunched heap. "I did warn you," he growls.

A muscle in Darien's jaw convulses with the effort of his clenching, and a sheen of sweat forms on his brow. He breathes hard, and I know from the agony in his eyes that he must be suffering a curse as torturous as the one the magician cast on me.

"*Stop!*" I repeat, yet the master continues to ignore me.

Keeping his eyes on the apprentice, he lifts the corner of his mouth in a vague smile. "Good. Very good. You're doing well, young one. Remember, pain is *nothing*. Strength is *everything*. Your endurance is impressive."

What twisted praise is this? I keep screaming for him to stop, wondering why Darien doesn't try to fight back. He just kneels there, still but for the subtle spasms in his tense expression. And the master keeps watching with

those cold green eyes, his mouth curving into something smug.

Then he flicks his wrist and says, "*Cease!*"

The boy exhales as if he hasn't breathed in all this time, and the sudden loosening of his posture tells me he's been released from the curse. I let out a breath of my own, relieved that he's no longer suffering. He glances up at the magician, his black eyes hard with a look of defiance.

The older man meets the youth's glare and says, "Consider that your last warning. Disobey me again, and I will not be so lenient. Now rise, my young one."

Darien stands without a word, and I try to interpret what his expression—with his eyebrows drawn down and his lips pressed together firmly—means. It's somehow rebellion and confusion at once, and I wish I could know what he's thinking.

The master reaches one hand toward him. "Come, my boy," he says, his tone surprisingly gentle. "Punishing you brings me no joy, for it is my goal to watch you triumph, not falter. But it appears the lessons I taught you yesterday weren't enough to still your foolish thoughts, and I hope that you will take my warnings seriously after this experience. Let us go to the library, where the wisdom of our forefathers will set you straight."

He claps a hand on the boy's shoulder and leads him up the stairs. Darien follows without a word, the strange look of confusion still coloring his expression. I watch, guilt gnawing at my heart. This is the third time he's had to suffer because of me, and I didn't do anything to help him. Knowing that I *couldn't* have because I'm trapped in a cell doesn't make the knowledge any less painful. But if he resents me for what happened, he doesn't show it. As he reaches the top of the stairs, he looks back and meets my gaze, giving me a look whose meaning I can't decipher. His eyes are tilted, as if with sorrow, and yet intense with unspoken purpose, though what that is, I can't tell. Then he vanishes from sight.

What did that look mean? I wonder. *Was he trying to tell me something?*

He has a name, a part of me whispers, somewhat accusingly, and I recall what the master had called to him, which I'd almost forgotten in my horror. *Darien.* Knowing that brings me a hint of gladness. His name might not be a particularly useful piece of information, but it matters to me. Because, little as I know about him, *he* matters to me.

He's the only light I have.

A thought whispers: *I could use him. He seems sympathetic toward me – if I plead with him, he might be willing to take the risk and help me, even if it means facing his master's wrath again.*

He's already sacrificed his own warmth for me by giving me his cloak, and then spoke to me even after his master explicitly forbade him to. I didn't even ask for anything; he must have wanted to bring me the comfort of companionship in his own small way. My guess is that he possesses a deep-seated need to help others, to be the hero. It wouldn't be difficult to convince a person like him to take his kindness one step further… to help me escape.

The idea makes my blood pump faster as I realize I *could* make this plan a reality if I wanted to. I could tell Darien that he's my only hope, that I'd be lost without him. I could even weep, and appear every bit the helpless damsel, in need of a strong young man like him to save me. From the way he stood up for me, I don't think he'd be able to resist coming to the rescue. And if we're caught… maybe he'd consider it an honor to endure whatever his master inflicted upon him, as long as he saw himself as the hero.

But if I did that, if I took advantage of him in such a way, what would that make me?

My mind recoils at the thought of intentionally wilting into a tearful fool, of surrendering any dignity I have left to a cold-hearted scheme. It would be all too easy, but every instinct tells me that I can't use another human being purely for my own gain. If I did, I would truly be the monster his master fears I am. How could I even consider it?

A sharp complaint from my stomach yanks my head back to my immediate needs. I pull open the edges of the brown sack Darien gave me and, seeing a bread roll inside, grab it and immediately take a bite. I didn't realize how famished I was until now, and I devour the rest with ravenous speed and wash it down with the entire canteen of water.

My hunger satisfied and my thirst relieved, I place the empty brown sack on the floor and pick up the cloak again. Wrapping it around myself, I start to stand, then glimpse a face glaring down at me and yelp in shock. I instantly recognize the Sorci master, standing outside the cell's window. Terrified that he'll cast his fire-laden spell on me again, I scramble backward. My heart clenches and hammers at the same time, and I inhale deeply to try to calm it.

He raises his hand, and I cower in the cloak and squeeze my eyes.

Nothing happens. I blink and cautiously turn back to the window. He's still there, holding his hand by his face. But his snake-like eyes aren't looking at me—they appear glazed over, as though he's in a trance. His lips move, but no sound comes out.

Then a warm current of air washes over me. It would have been comforting if I weren't certain it came from the Sorci master's spell.

The need for information defeats my terror, however, and I ask, "What are you doing?"

He continues moving his lips, but otherwise remains still. Several moments pass, and I wait. But then my patience grows short. I deserve to at least know why I've been imprisoned like this.

I start toward him, intending to tell him so, but barely make it half a step before his attention turns back to me. He flicks his wrist in a circular motion, and I feel myself thrust backward into the wall, the breath knocked from my lungs. I collapse to the floor, my vision swimming and my body aching.

Before I can even look back at him, pain surges through me. Instead of heat, this time, it's a million tiny claws scratching at my insides, and they're shredding me, like there are innumerable monsters trapped in my gut trying to tear their way free. I writhe in agony, and my own shrieks pierce my ears.

"Stop!" I cry, barely able to manage the word. I want to say that I'll do whatever he asks, as long as he lifts this curse, but my ability to speak is lost in my screams of terror and pain.

The invisible claws rip at my flesh, and I'm sure if I were to open my eyes, I'd see my own blood pooled before me. They slash at every inch of my body, inside and out, as if they're trying to tear the flesh from my bones. The sheer agony erases any other perceptions I might have; the pain has devoured my entire being, leaving nothing but my screams.

Then it disappears. Like before, it vanishes so completely that only the tears streaking my cheeks give evidence to its existence. And though I see no physical wounds on my skin, I feel once again as if the life has been drained from me. My limbs are heavy, my vision swims, and my head wants to sink into the ground.

I wipe my eyes and turn to the window, where the Sorci master is still staring at me.

"If you dare try to bewitch my apprentice again," he growls, "I will bring you such torment, you'll beg for death."

His words impale me as powerfully as his spell did, and I shake so much that not even tensing my jaw can keep my teeth from clattering. When I was under that curse, I would have done anything to make it stop. The thought of facing pain like that again—or something worse—makes tears of terror spill from my eyes.

Then anger jolts me as I realize what he's accusing me of. I never asked Darien for anything—how could the master blame *me* for the actions of another? How could he punish me for a crime I didn't commit? My heart cries out at the injustice, and, forgetting my own weakness, I stand and face him.

"I haven't done anything!" I shout.

He curls his lip with disgust, as if my words are the foulest lies he's ever heard. "You and your kind are a plague upon humanity! You brought disaster to man in the past, and I won't let you do it again here."

"What did I do?" I stride up to the window. My legs quiver, and my head whirls, but I ignore them. "If I'm some kind of monster, then *tell me!*"

But instead of answering, the Sorci master breaks his gaze and stalks away.

"Stop!" Though I know he'll ignore my words as he did before, I have to say them. I have to try. "You can't just lock me up without a reason! Tell me why you've trapped me here! *Tell me what you want from me!*"

The Sorci master continues toward the staircase, and suddenly my anger turns to desperation. I have to know what's going on here, or I might go mad with the wondering. I grab the bar in the window and pull myself forward until the jagged edge digs into my collarbones.

"Just tell me something! *Anything!*" My voice feels hoarse from all my screaming, but I might as well be mouthing nothingness for all the reaction the magician gives me. "Tell me who I am! Tell me my name!" My chest heaves with involuntary sobs, and though I inhale deeply to keep them at bay, I can't stop them from rising. "*Just tell me my name!*"

"Enough!" His voice explodes through the dungeon, and he abruptly spins to face me, then marches toward the cell with his fist raised.

Terror courses through me, but I remain where I am and clench my jaw in an attempt to suppress my sobs. "Please—"

"Silence!" He cuts me off with his great shout, and a hot gust of air slams against me, throwing me back.

My head bangs against the wall, and the world goes black.

Of things that make no sense

SOFT GREEN GRASS COVERS THE GROUND, COOL against my toes. The air is so warm, I can taste the freshness of spring on the breeze. There is joy here. And serenity. I don't know where I am, but right now, it doesn't matter. All I know is that this is a place where I'm safe. In fact, it might be my favorite place in the world. Inhaling deeply, I take a second to savor the feeling of contentment that surrounds me.

Having allowed myself a moment, I bring my focus back to my surroundings, to see where I actually am.

I find myself standing in a small grove. The twisting branches and billowing leaves of tall trees nearly block the blue sky. But these are no ordinary trees. The branches of each one reach toward those of another, intertwining like they're holding hands. At first I think the limbs must be very thick, but as I look closer, I notice that what I took to be heavy branches are actually several small ones, each about the width of my finger, weaving together into intricate braids of brown and gray.

Sitting atop them is an array of hardcover books, with gilt lettering down their spines. That's odd — why are there books sitting outside instead of in a library where they belong? And they don't look like they've been left out by accident, since there are so many of them neatly lined up.

I tilt my head and try to read the titles, but the letters blur and jumble before my eyes, denying me their meaning. What is this place? It feels familiar, like I've been here many times before, but I can't recall why.

An uncanny sensation strikes my mind, and I realize that this too is a dream. Or could it be more?

Something significant must lie between the pages of those books, or I don't think I'd be here. Their words must carry some importance, and I reach toward one, intending to find out what.

Suddenly a wave of mist assaults my vision, and the air crackles with heat as the silver haze I saw in the last dream reaches toward me, searing my skin with its invisible touch. Knowing I have to escape, I turn and run as fast as I can, but the mist chases me, swirling around the trees and climbing over the branches.

Then a thought strikes me: The mist is trying to keep me away from those books. Whatever knowledge they carry in their pages, someone doesn't want me to see it. Which makes it all the more important that I do.

I stop running. The unbearably hot mist engulfs me, but I grit my teeth against the pain. I take a deep breath, which turns out to be a great mistake, for the scorching air fills my lungs, burning me from the inside out. My agony is so great that I want to curl into a ball and weep.

But I can't. I have to find out what's in those books. Something in my heart — something that I don't understand, but know I must heed — tells me that my life could depend on it. I have to listen, if I'm to save myself.

So I turn around, steeling myself against the pain, and start running back.

The mist assails me with renewed force, enveloping my whole body with its blazing grasp, and a scream bursts from my lips. My foot catches on something, sending me to the ground, and when I try to get up, the mist's scorching tendrils wrap around my arms and legs like chains, anchoring me down. Crying out from the pain of a million flames pressing into my skin, I kick and twist with all my might, trying to free myself.

Then I glimpse my own foot, and widen my eyes in horror as it dissolves into ashes before my eyes. I feel nothing where it once was. The ashes creep up my leg, consuming me bit by bit. I desperately struggle to get away from the mist, but it's no use. It's devouring me, and I'm helpless to stop it.

I awaken with a gasp to see the dark iron ceiling staring down at me. The cold floor stings my bare back, and as I sit up, my head throbs with a dull ache. *It was just a dream,* I tell myself, breathing deeply in hopes of calming my racing heart. *Only nonsense.* I glance down at my leg to make sure it's still there. It is — of course it is! Nothing actually happened; that was all in my head. No mist hangs in the air, and even the memory of the nightmare seems distant, now that I'm awake.

I absorb my surroundings with my gaze, reminding myself of what *is* real. This cell of ice and iron. The darkness that fills my mind where memories should be. The Sorci master who imprisoned me, but won't tell me why. I close my eyes. Reality is better than the nightmare of turning to ash, but not by much. I can't tell myself that the mist's infernal touch was just a dream… I've felt it in the real world too, when the magician cursed me.

The last thing I remember before the dream is him telling me to be silent, his eyes so hot with rage, they could have melted glass. The burning mist in the dream must have been my mind forcing me to relive those moments under his spell, and I wonder how I'll ever sleep again.

But there was something prior to that—something that brought me happiness and peace. I think back to what I saw in my sleep, grasping the remnants before they can fade away. A sense of familiarity came over me in the dreamscape, like I was visiting an old friend whose face I knew, but whose name I'd forgotten. I want to believe it means the visions were telling me something… but then again, I had that same feeling about the nonsense I recalled before—the clock tree and the sensation of flying. And now that I think about it, the images I saw this time are just as ridiculous. The sight of branches weaving into shelves and books perched atop them, outdoors where they'd surely be damaged by dew and mist, makes no sense. Even if someone could train branches to form shelves, who would leave so many books outside like that?

I know for certain that my turning to ashes was imaginary rubbish, and I'm glad it was. I have no reason, then, to believe the grove and the books were anything else.

An abrupt shudder down my spine forces my mind back to my surroundings. Glancing to the side, I spot Darien's black cloak just a few feet from me. I want nothing more than to wrap myself in it, but I'm too frozen to move. I look for the ball of light and find it even further away, sitting in the far corner of the cell. Reluctantly, I fight through the stiffness and reach for the cloak. My movements are so slow and shaky that I fear I'll freeze to death before I can even get a grip on the black cloth.

Maybe that wouldn't be such a bad thing. At least I'd leave this world numbly and quietly, instead of screaming in the grasp of the Sorci master's spells. Just recalling the painful curse he placed on me makes me quiver, and it evidently affected me enough to invade my dreams. I know he doesn't mean to kill me—not yet, at least—because he gave me the ball of light and sent his apprentice to bring me food. What, then, does he want from me? Just to torture me? Does he derive some kind of perverse joy from seeing me suffer?

If my living in torment satisfies him, then I'd rather die on my own terms. I start to draw my hand back, but my eyes are caught by what my

stiff fingers were trying to grasp. Or rather, it's my mind that's caught — by the thought of the one who gave me that cloak.

Darien. The image of his smile flashes through my mind, and I feel the corner of my mouth lift involuntarily. His existence reminds me that there is good in this world, and I can't give up on life just yet. There's more than just the four frozen walls of this cell, the painful curses of the Sorci master, the barren loneliness of not knowing who I am. Outside, beyond this dungeon, lie wondrous possibilities — places to see, things to do, and, most importantly, people to know. At one point, I was part of that world. I had a place in it, a life, and I can't abandon that infinite beauty; I must fight with every shred of strength in me to be a part of it again. After all, life is a gift given to us all by the Divinity, and to abandon it would be wrong.

Whatever happens, I *must* hold on as long as I can. My heart tells me so.

So I cover myself with the cloak and move toward the ball of light. Knowing the cruel Sorci master was the one who created it makes me wish I'd thrown it back at him when he first gave it to me, but my desperation was too great at the time. Even now I cling to its warmth, and that I need something so despicable makes me hate myself.

Then I remember that the master only gave it to me after his apprentice protested on my behalf. This enchanted sphere doesn't represent the magician's actions — it represents Darien's.

His smile brightens my mind again, and I hold on to the image. Brief as that moment was, it's the only memory I have of anything resembling joy. I know it didn't mean much, being a smile of sympathy or pity. But still, there was something genuine in his eyes.

The recollection of the master's voice booming behind him invades my thoughts. I remember how he accused me of bewitching his apprentice — why did he say that? I was too terrified then to untangle the meaning behind his words, but now they begin to gnaw at my brain. He must think I'm to blame for Darien's disobedience, but why? What does he think I can do? Is it possible that he's right? Am I… could I also be magician of some sort?

My mind churns with possibilities, some reasonable and others even more absurd than when I thought I might have wings. The most plausible of these is that boys have been known to do foolish things around girls, and the Sorci master thinks I'm intentionally trying to charm his apprentice,

though I have no idea why he'd think a scrawny, pathetic girl like me would succeed. And the most ludicrous is that I once possessed magic like his, including the ability to bend others to my will.

I almost want to laugh at that notion. If I had that kind of power, how could I have ended up captured and cursed?

Then again, maybe the curse was placed on me precisely *because* I have magic, and the Sorci wanted to prevent me from remembering so I couldn't use it to escape. Is it possible that I'm more than just a girl?

I look down at my hands, which seem so fragile. They don't seem capable of doing anything like what I saw the Sorci master do. But he did say that looks are deceiving, and magical powers are unrelated to material ones. A mouse wielding a great spell could defeat a lion that possesses physical force alone.

Perhaps there is indeed more to me than meets the eye. And if there is magic in me, then I *must* recover my memories. They would tell me what I'm capable of, and whether those abilities might help me escape. Perhaps I can conjure the tools to break down these walls, or transform into a creature small enough to escape through the window, or transport myself instantly from one place to another. Even if I can only create illusions, that's still *something*, and *any* ability I have would help. I *need* to remember, before the Sorci magician can do whatever he plans to do.

It's my only chance at surviving.

Part of me tells me to stop thinking like this, since I know that trying to bring back the memories will make that unbearable heat return, and the idea of suffering so much pain again fills me with terror. Besides, how am I supposed to call upon a power I'm not even sure I have? But I silence the warning in my head. I have to at least attempt it, in case there's any truth to the notion.

I wrap the cloak tighter around myself, and, shutting my eyes, probe my senses, trying to get a grasp on the energy inside and hoping something will stir. I concentrate on each breath and each heartbeat, making myself aware of everything within me. I can sense the blood flowing through my veins and the subtle movements of each muscle, and I search deeper, hoping something else lies behind even those.

But I find nothing. I don't know what I was expecting — maybe some kind of spark or force dwelling in me — but after several moments of feeling only the mundane details of my body, I realize that what I'm doing is futile. And foolish — as foolish as trying to fly without wings.

Despite my failure, a perception that I'm onto something nags at me, and my mind refuses to let go of the possibility that I possess something magical. The only way I can know if there's any truth to the idea is to search for memories again. Even though my efforts will likely send that burning pain lancing through me, I have no choice. And I can't let my fear hold me back anymore.

Keeping my eyes closed, I concentrate inward. My shoulders and neck feel tense, and I'm certain that I'll run into the invisible fire soon, but I press on. A strange ache fills my head — one that's not so much physical as mental, like I'm forcing my thoughts into a place they don't want to go. All I see is the blackness of my closed eyelids and the dancing specks of color behind them.

Suddenly, an image flashes before my closed eyes — one so blurred that I can't make out what it is, but present enough that it must mean something. All I know is that it was something green. And it gave me a sensation that it was big, that if I'd stood beside it, it would have dwarfed me. This image must have surfaced from the buried recesses of my mind, and I concentrate hard to bring it back and make it sharper, so I can see what it is.

The green blur returns, and starts to take on a definable shape. It has a narrow base and wide top… like a mushroom. I reach for it, aiming to bring it into focus, unveil the details…

A bolt of heat stabs my mind, and I gasp at its familiar pain. But I keep exploring that green shape, trying to find what it is and what it might mean to me. I know that there's more heat to come, and come it does, blazing through my head with the fury of a lightning storm. I squeeze my eyes and grit my teeth against the powerful hotness, stubbornly holding onto the image.

In spite of the fire tearing through my skull, the shape starts to grow clearer. Excited, I watch as it morphs before my eyes. The narrow base turns the color of wood and reaches lines of brown into the round green top. I soon realize it's the memory of a tree. But what does it mean? Could it be one that grew near my home, perhaps? Is there a sign carved on its trunk that could tell me more?

The image sharpens, the tree's individual leaves becoming clear. The

fiery pain stabbing through my head hurts so much that I can't stop myself from sobbing, now, and tears stream down my cheeks. I try to steady my breaths, but they come in jagged gasps. Part of me wants to open my eyes and make it stop, before this spell turns me to cinders. But a stronger part needs to know what the memory forming in my mind signifies.

So I cling to the image with all my strength, ignoring the infernal pain. I attempt to make out more details of the tree, hoping it will tell me what it means, and why it's the one memory I've been able to bring to the surface. The details of the gnarled trunk become clear, and I see no sign or mark on it. Shifting my focus up to the branches, I notice something nestled between the leaves. A metal item — actually, several metal items. Each is round and made of gold, silver, or bronze. Another surge of heat flares through my head, and a cry escapes my lips. All I have to do to make it stop is open my eyes and stop trying, but I need to know what's hidden in those leaves.

I hear a rhythmic tapping sound, and I know it's coming from the memory, since I'm hearing it in my head and not with my ears. The tapping grows louder and I realize… it's the ticking of dozens of small clocks. That's what those things in the branches are — *clocks*. They clang together as wind disturbs the branches, and a musical chiming fills the air…

It's the clock tree from my dream.

A torrent of anger and frustration sweeps through me; I haven't unearthed a new memory — I've simply brought to mind the recollection of the same nonsense I saw in my sleep. I open my eyes with a wordless cry, fury churning in my stomach.

Though the searing pain from the curse retreats into nothingness, its absence brings little relief to my riotous heart. Stronger than the vexation, than the feeling that my own mind betrayed me, is the heaviness of despair. I inhale sharply, trying to calm myself, and the icy air seems to travel into my head. The tears keep spilling over my fingers, though, and I try to wipe them all away.

I can't believe that I've failed again. Even my greatest efforts have been useless. I thought I was close to uncovering a secret from my past, but I was wrong. The only memories I have are of this cell, and of things that make no sense.

A tree that grows clocks.

A sensation that I once flew.

A grove with books on tree branches.

And surrounding it all, this heat, this pain, this curse that tortures me each time I try to remember something. No matter where I look, I find nothing. Maybe there's nothing to find. I've been going on the assumption that my memories are still *there*, just buried. But it's possible that they're gone entirely, and the reason I can never find anything is because my mind's utterly empty.

How can that be? I *must* have had a life before this cell. It's a sensation as strong as the knowledge of the ground I'm sitting on. How did I lose it? Why did the Sorci trap me here? And what do they want from me?

If they won't tell me, and I can't remember on my own, then what chance do I have?

I curl my knees up to my chest and let my sobs out, knowing I won't be able to hold them back unless they abate on their own. The image of the clock tree lingers in my mind, clear as daylight yet completely absurd. Such a thing isn't possible—that much I know. Trees can grow flowers or fruits, but not manmade machines. Nevertheless, I let the image linger in my mind. The tree may not be real, but it's still beautiful to see, with its grand, reaching branches and the delicate fineness of the little timepieces.

Their soft, insistent ticking echoes through my mind, seeming to grow louder every second. My heartbeat feels bound to their movements, pounding to their rhythm, which is steady but urgent. Suddenly, something inside tells me to hurry, that a great danger is lurking, that I must escape it soon. I know this feeling must be because I'm trapped, and my instincts are telling me to get out before the Sorci master returns and hurts me again. But why is it turning so urgent in my heart?

The ticking of the clocks speeds up, and my pulse follows. I'm breathing so fast now that I'm panting with anxiety. A sheen of cold sweat forms on my skin, and I hug the cloak in an attempt to find comfort. Something terrible is going to happen—I'm certain of it. And there's something more—something dark and powerful looming over me, threatening not just my life, but my whole world. I don't even remember what that world *is*, but my heart holds the feeling of a home I can't remember, and the ominous presence seems ready to ravage it all. It's almost as if… whatever happens to me will happen to my world as well.

And I can't stop it.

Panic rises from the pit of my stomach, and if my heart beats any harder, it will surely rip my chest apart. But I can barely hear its thumping over the ticking of a hundred clocks, each saying that my time is running out.

It's all in my head, I tell myself adamantly. *Those clocks aren't real — it's all in my head!*

But another thought overwhelms my attempt at self-reassurance: *I have to get out.*

I jump up and look around wildly, searching for a way to escape. Yet I shouldn't have to — these walls are made of ice, and ice *is* breakable! I have to try again; maybe I gave up too quickly last time.

I pound at the wall with my fists, but I might as well be hammering at the iron floor. Not even a crack appears, and the only thing I succeed in doing is bruising my hands.

I have to get out.

The thought consumes my mind, as it did when I first awoke here, and I scratch at the ice by the window the Sorci master created, in a desperate attempt to widen it. While I know in my head that this is useless, it's the panic that's controlling me now, dictating my actions.

I have to get out! I have to get out!

My fevered thoughts tell me that if there's an opening, there must be a way to squeeze through, so I press my forehead against the bars, trying to force myself to fit through the gap. Freedom lies just beyond the staircase the Sorci descended, and the sight of its gray stones tantalizes me. But the bars are just too close together, and though the frenzy in my head orders me to keep trying, I push off the wall and stumble backward. My heel catches the edge of the cloak, and I trip.

The impact from landing on the hard ground shakes the madness out of my consciousness, and the ticking fades from my mind. But I'm no calmer, even with it gone. The tension remains, and the great despair returns. My heart turns to lead, weighing me down, and, seeing no point in resisting, I let it.

I lie on the cold floor, staring at the black bars and the frozen walls between them. I'm not sure which is worse — the frenzy that had me pounding at ice or this current despair. I want to die. What's the sense in

living like this, trapped and awaiting torment, without even knowing who I am? If I had a sense of self to cling to, or a home to miss, I might at least have hope. But as I am, I have nothing.

Nothing.

I want to summon the strength to press on, but my willpower is spent. Even knowing that the Divinity would frown upon my thoughts can't keep them away. The coldness of the metal floor bites my bare leg, and I instinctively draw it up into the warmth of the cloak.

The cloak given to me by a kind stranger. *There is good in this world,* I remind myself. I have to hold on to that thought. Without it, I would let the despair defeat me and lose any chance of surviving. But I have to hope, to believe that life is worth living. *There is good in this world…*

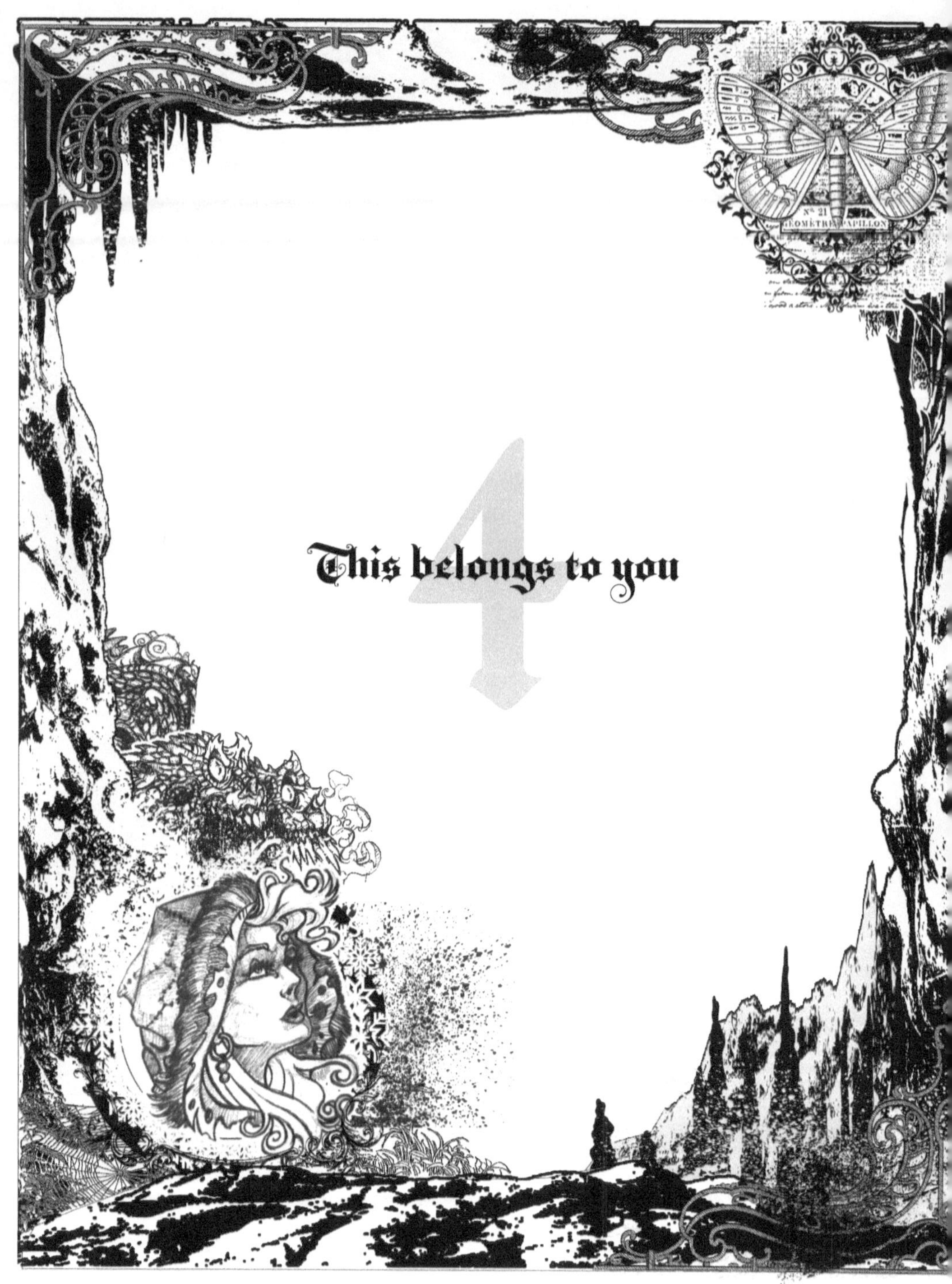

This belongs to you

4

**HE MIST UNDULATES THROUGH THE DARKNESS,** *slow and menacing. I back away from it, frightened to the core. I know that mist. If it catches me, it will burn me to cinders, but not before tormenting me with its fiery grasp.*

A sudden motion catches my eye, and I whirl toward it. But all I see is more of the silver haze, winding through empty blackness.

Another movement. I spin to face it and catch a glimpse of whiteness so pure, it makes the mist look blackened and dirty. Whatever it is, it must lie beyond the smokiness obscuring everything.

Should I go toward it and find out what it is, knowing what the mist will do to me?

A tugging in my heart urges me onward, but fear holds me back. I don't want to feel that fire again, especially when facing it has brought me nothing but pain.

Then the whiteness appears again, glowing through the mist before me, and I draw back, fearing the mist will approach. It doesn't. Instead, the bright object emerges, taking the form of a snowy horse. Only its face is clear — the rest remains a barely recognizable blur in the haze. It regards me with wise, violet eyes, and blinks once.

Its presence is soothing and safe, like it once protected and nurtured me. The desire to go to it and feel the warmth of its sureness overcomes me, and I forget my fear. I force my feet to begin moving, and walk toward it…

Stars fill the tiny window to the outside, and for a moment I just stare at them, hypnotized by their beauty. They represent the good in a world of darkness — someone told me that once, but I don't try to remember who. I know better than that now.

My body aches, and I push off the ground, sitting up. When did I fall asleep? How long was I unconscious? The exhaustion from my panic must have caused me to drift off, and the worldly complaints of my body tell me I've been lying here for a while. My throat itches with thirst, and my stomach feels hollow with hunger. And yet I've no desire to relieve either of them, since I can't allay the deeper thirst and hunger of my mind.

This time, I actually wish I'd stayed in the dreamscape—at least a little longer. That horse—it could mean anything, since it's such a common creature, but its presence comforted me like nothing else could. I felt like… like I was looking into the face of someone who loved me. Not merely as an animal loves its master—as a mother loves its child.

But that's just more nonsense. How could I have a horse for a mother?

I stand with a sigh, gazing out at the stars. If only my dreams would show me something that makes sense, for once. Or, if they must show nonsense, why do they have to seem so real, tantalizing me with the thought that they could be memories, only to yank the hope out from under me when I wake and confront reality?

The stars represent goodness, but they're beyond my reach. And staring out the window just reminds me of how small the opening is, and how impossible it is to escape through it. I turn away and lean back against the wall, then sink to the ground. The sphere of yellow light sits in the nearby corner, but its warmth does nothing to comfort me.

Just then, I hear the sound of footsteps approaching. It must be the Sorci master, coming to torment me again. The thought terrifies me, but there's nowhere to escape to, and so I remain where I am and bury my face in my knees.

Divinity, give me strength, I pray. I wish an ayr would swoop down from the Celestial Realm and carry me away, but know better than to pin my hopes on such foolishness, since, though the ayri watch over the world from afar, they can't interfere with the everyday matters of mortals.

The footsteps come closer, and I hug my knees tighter, knowing I can expect only pain. They stop outside the cell. The Sorci master must be standing outside the window, staring at me, and the last thing I want to see are those snake-like eyes and cruel countenance. I could ask him again who I am and what he wants with me, but he would respond only with more tortures.

Hopeless. All is hopeless.

"Hello?" a voice calls.

It's not the Sorci master's… it's Darien's. I look up and see him gazing down at me from the window. The flame of the torch he holds highlights his angular cheekbones and glints off his broad shoulders, giving him a fiery halo. The sight brings me a measure of relief, and I feel myself relax.

At the very least, he won't hurt me. But knowing that his master would cast his agonizing spell on me if I so much as speak to him taints the comfort his presence would otherwise have brought. And what would the magician do to his wayward apprentice for just that single word, if he knew?

Darien knits his black eyebrows with concern and tilts his head as though examining me. "Are you all right?" he asks.

I automatically open my mouth, but stop. If I respond, the master will accuse me of bewitching Darien again, and inflict his cruel magic on me. The very memory of that pain makes me quiver, and so I close my mouth, drop my gaze, and give a slight nod. It's a lie, answering his question in the affirmative when I'm anything but all right, yet it's the only response I can give. The best thing that can happen right now is for him to decide he's satisfied with that answer and return to his duties, before the Sorci master catches him talking to me again.

But my silence doesn't seem to discourage him, for he says, "Here, I brought you something to eat."

His words, while spoken softly, seem thunderous against the silence, and I cringe. *Please let there be no one listening*, I pray. My body aches with the memory of the million claws tearing through me from the Sorci master's curse, and though I know the pain is just in my head, it feels almost real. I can't stand the thought of enduring that again. And what if he does the same to Darien this time? The only thing worse than suffering myself would be to see the pain inflicted on another.

The practical thing to do would be to get up and accept the food Darien has brought me without a word, but I can't muster the will. What's the point? Eating and drinking are things a person does to stay alive for tomorrow, but I'm not living right now. I'm just existing—without purpose, without hope, without even a name.

Meanwhile, I hear Darien placing something on the icy ledge of the cell's window, and instinctively turn to the sound. It's another brown sack, like the one he brought me before. I try to summon a smile to say "thank you," but even my lips feel heavy, and I only manage a slight twitch. So I give a small nod instead, doing my best to hold my head high and appear all right. Not out of pride—I don't think I've had that since I awoke in this cell—but in hopes of convincing him that it's true. Any concern he has for me would only bring us both more trouble from the Sorci master.

But it's not working. His eyebrows gather with worry, and he leans in, closer to the window. "What's wrong? Are you cold?"

I shake my head. Since he doesn't seem to realize what my silence meant, I whisper, "Please, you can't speak to me." My voice is so soft, it barely reaches my own ears.

His expression darkens. "My master may be wise, but even he isn't all-knowing." He glances to the side, pressing his mouth into a harsh line. After a moment, he shakes his head. "I know he forbade me from talking to you, but you don't have to worry about what would happen if he hears me now. It's my concern."

I turn my gaze to the floor. He doesn't know what his master did to punish me for bewitching him, even when I was innocent of the crime. And I can't tell him—I'd have to speak again to do so, and if the master catches me, he'll torture me again. Each time he's cursed me, I've felt as if a monster latched onto my soul and sucked the energy from it, and that the magician released me just in time to save the last drop I needed to regain my strength. What if next time he doesn't, and his curse leaves me in a state too feeble to recover from? How could I ever escape if I'm too weak to stand?

And what's more, I won't be the only subject of his wrath, since the master said that the spell he cast on Darien the last time he spoke to me, the curse painful enough to take him to the floor, was a mere warning. Even if I had the fortitude to bear the magician's cruelty, I couldn't allow another to suffer like that.

"I'm not going to hurt you." Darien's voice from the window is almost a whisper. "I know this won't mean much to you when you're trapped like this, but we're not trying to be cruel. Our work… it has a very important purpose, and someday the fate of the world could depend on it. The smallest misstep might cause us to fail, and that would lead to disaster."

He sounds like he's trying to convince himself more than me. I hear the echo of his master's words in his; I suppose the magician must have finally instilled his lessons into his apprentice's head. After the brutality I witnessed—the slamming into walls, the curse of pain—I don't care to imagine what else might have happened to Darien, away from here, that I didn't see. Hearing him talk about the Sorci as if he's one of them makes my heart sink. I guess as an apprentice, that's what he's working toward, but the thought of him becoming just like the stone-faced figures — or worse, the cruel master — fills me with sorrow.

My head tells me to say something, or at least ask for a hint as to what this greater purpose could be, but the idea feels so dull that it can't be called a desire. My very mind has grown numb, and my thoughts drift in a dull cloud of "what's the point?" Everything I've tried has been in vain, and the one viable suggestion I came up with — manipulating Darien to save myself — is too abhorrent, even in my desperate state. Though I yearn to hold onto hope, I can't stop the voice in my head telling me that it's just a false promise for something that can never come.

So I just give another nod and keep my eyes on the ground, hoping he'll go away. At the same time, part of me wishes he could stay. His is the only company I have, despite the danger his voice brings me, and I can't help feeling a small measure of comfort in his presence. Once he leaves, I'll be alone again.

Alone with my hopelessness.

A great swelling presses against my heart, and sharp tingling rises toward my eyes. I squeeze them shut, determined to keep the tears back. But for some reason, thinking about my impending return to total solitude brings an upwelling of despair, and the thoughts crash into me from all sides at once.

I don't know who I am.

I have no purpose.

I have no hope.

I don't want to surrender to these helpless thoughts, but they beat against my consciousness like stormy waves upon a stone that, no matter how sturdy, can't escape the wearing down under such repeated, merciless thrashing. Tears threaten to escape my eyes, and I squeeze my lids tighter to hold them back. But it's no use — they stream down my cheeks anyway. I quickly wipe them, then turn my face toward the back wall. I've lost any chance of maintaining the pretense that I'm all right, and I'm ashamed that someone has to see me like this.

I hear footsteps ringing against the stone floor outside my cell and know that it must be Darien leaving. I'm glad he's going; I wouldn't know what to do if he'd stayed. Still, the air suddenly seems hollow and empty in the absence of the one person I can remember ever being kind to me.

I inhale, drawing a gust of cold air into my lungs, but it does nothing to steady my head or push back the desolation that's conquered my mind. I know I should be stronger, should continue searching for a way to escape and focus on my survival, yet I can't bring myself to keep fighting when I don't even know what I'm fighting for.

Opening my eyes, I glance back toward the window, almost hoping he's still there. Of course, he isn't. The small sack of food sits on the ledge where he left it, but despite the hollow hunger in my stomach, I have no wish to retrieve it.

I have no wish for anything anymore.

The despairing thoughts hammer against my mind, and I gaze dully into nothingness.

No chance, no purpose, no hope.

Time rolls by, but I remain still, as frozen and blank as the walls of ice trapping me. Maybe if I sit here like this long enough, I'll turn to ice as well, and never have to feel pain or sorrow or anguish again.

The sound of quick footsteps patters outside the cell, trying to tug my consciousness out of its cloud of depression. But though that may have worked in the past, I'm too numb now to care who approaches. If it's the Sorci master coming to curse me again, let him. I can't stop him anyway. And if it's Darien…

He comes into view before I can finish the thought, striding toward my cell. *What's he doing back here?* I wonder. My curiosity encourages my mind to sharpen just enough to keep my gaze on him instead of dropping to the floor again.

He glances back toward the stairs with a worried, almost fearful look, then picks up his pace. Stopping before the window, he holds up his hand, which clutches something wrapped in a brown cloth made of the same material as the sacks he uses to bring me food. He meets my gaze with a stare so intense, it seems to pierce right through me.

"This belongs to you," he says, placing the package on the window ledge.

What? Surprise jolts me out of my melancholy trance, and I instinctively

stand, my eyes flying to the brown lump. *What is that? How can it belong to me?*

Before I can say anything, the Sorci master's voice thunders from the distance.

"Darien!"

The sound sends a dart of terror through me, and I jump up. At the same time, Darien whirls toward the staircase, then turns back to me, giving the package a slight push forward. "Keep it hidden, or they'll kill us both." He races away without another word.

Shocked and intrigued, I rush to the window and snatch the wad of brown cloth. I back into the corner by the window, where I'm least likely to be seen from outside, and stare at the thing in my hand.

This belongs to me. It must be a relic from my past, some possession I had with me when I was captured. A tremendous wave of joy and awe overwhelms me, and my knees buckle. This is it—the link to my past that could tell me who I am, where I come from, and maybe even why I'm here.

It could hold the answers my life depends on.

With this object in my hands, I can hope again. I can believe once more that there's something worth staying strong for, worth fighting for. My eyes well, but with tears of happiness and relief this time, and one thought sparkles like starlight in my head: *There is good in this world.* And it's not out of my reach—the proof is right here.

Does Darien even know what this means to me? Did he sense that I was so lost, I was ready to let myself die?

Does he know that, just by returning this to me, he saved my life?

After what I've witnessed, and from those last words he spoke, I know he risked his own life to give me this one possession. A twinge of guilt stings me as I realize I didn't thank him. If I ever get out of here, I'll be sure to repay his kindness in whatever way I can.

I tighten my grip on the brown cloth package, almost afraid that it will vanish like an illusion. I don't even know what it is, and yet, it already seems to represent all that I thought I'd lost. Perhaps glimpsing it will bring back my memories, and I can learn who I am and how I got here. And perhaps this knowledge could give me something I need to escape.

My heart pounds with anticipation, and I move to unwrap the package and see what lies within the cloth. Suddenly, I hesitate. What if it's not

everything I hope it will be? What if it's another false promise that tells me nothing? What if the ensuing disappointment sends me into an even deeper sense of despair than the one that nearly consumed me?

Even if that's the case, I have nothing to lose. I can't possibly sink lower than where I was just now. So I tentatively remove the brown cloth, and a flash of silver catches my eye. Then a soft noise, barely audible even in the silence, floats up from the object. I recognize it instantly: It's the sound of a clock ticking.

I push the rest of the wrapping away and find myself staring down at a timepiece small enough to fit in the palm of my hand. A tiny ring holds a chain as fine as thread, and silver metal, engraved with intricate drawings of flowers, rims an iridescent white face. Black numbers that look like they were lovingly drawn by an expert calligrapher encircle the edge: I, II, III, IV… The hour and minute hands, which appear to be slivers of lustrous onyx, point to seven o'clock.

But there's something off about this timepiece—the second hand moves counterclockwise. What's more, when it passes the number twelve, the hand that should have indicated minutes barely moves the width of a hair. *That's so strange. What does it mean?*

Searching for a hint, I turn the clock over in my hand, and my eyes widen at what I see. The clock's silver back, like the rim around the front, is meticulously decorated with beautiful outlines of blossoms and vines that intertwine like ribbons. But lovely as they are, I barely notice them, for they form a ring pattern around an engraving that causes my breath to catch in my throat.

Two words: Kiriall Amdyth.

It's my name. I know it—as certainly as I know that the ground I stand on exists. Just seeing those words is enough to make the memory blaze like the midday sun, pushing back any darkness or doubt that might surround it.

I have a name. And it's Kiriall Amdyth.

Suddenly, an image pops into my mind: A girl in a flowing, apple green dress. I see her as clearly as if she's standing before me. She's about my height and probably my age, but otherwise looks nothing like me. Whereas the lines of my body are as straight as a wooden board, this girl's curve into full hips and a well-matured bust. Her brilliant emerald eyes, framed

by long, dark lashes, dance with joy against a glowing bronze complexion, and her plump, poppy red lips spread into a wide grin. She's beautiful in a way I could never be, and her melodious laughter rings in my head.

"Kiri!" she cries, reaching a hand toward me. Her hair, which fades from deep auburn near her scalp to strawberry blond at the tips, whips around her shoulders, and —

Blazing heat explodes through my head, hitting me with such ferocity that I scream in shock. The image of the girl starts to vanish, blotted out by swaths of darkness.

No, I have to remember. I shut my eyes, clinging to the image with everything I have and refusing to let the searing pain defeat me. The girl called me "Kiri" — that must be what I went by. So she must know me… But who is she? And what else can the memory of her tell me?

Still clutching the clock in my hands, I lean against the wall and let myself sink to the floor. I need *all* of my energy to focus on holding onto this memory and seeing where it leads… and on keeping the strength to press through the flames ravaging my head.

I concentrate on the girl, and, in my mind, she laughs again and says, "Kiri, come on!"

"Slow down!" That's my own voice, responding to hers! My pulse quickens with excitement. This is more than just an image, or a fact — this is an actual *memory* of something I experienced in my past.

A fresh column of heat erupts through me, spreading down into my whole body. The pain is so great, I grab my head and press myself into the frigid wall, trying to find relief in the coldness. But I'm getting so close, I can't back down now.

"Kiriiiii… " The girl with red hair draws out my name in a mocking whine, then closes her mouth into a pillowy pout and crosses her arms. "You're the slowest gust of wind I've ever met!"

Wind? What did she mean by that? Was it just a figure of speech? A protest rises from my heart, telling me that there's more, and I know the only way to find out is to keep remembering. The pain of the curse rages through me, and I bite my lip hard to keep from screaming again.

"Are you sure we should be doing this?" That's my voice again; I'm beside the red-haired girl, wearing the same blue dress I wear now. Next to her radiant beauty, I must look like someone's sickly little sister.

The girl crosses her arms and lifts one arched auburn eyebrow. "We're sixteen, Kiri. We can go wherever we want."

I'm sixteen years old. Despite the anguish from the curse still burning my being, my heart leaps with excitement. Another truth about myself was just revealed—and I *will* remember more.

Then something strange catches my attention: Flames seem to leap from the girl's hair. Not burning it, as if someone had lit it on fire, but flowing down her waving locks. The blaze is… part of her. Slight panic rushes through me—this can't be more nonsense, can it? Those other absurd images I saw came in my dreams, while I was asleep. I'm awake now, and this memory was *triggered*. It came from somewhere; it was brought on by the sight of my name. Are these flames the effects of the curse invading my memory?

I squeeze my eyes tighter, concentrating. *What did the girl do next?*

"Kiri!" My mind flashes back to the first instant of this memory, and I once again see the girl laughing as she reaches out to me. But this time, I see something I must have missed before—she's not standing, like I assumed she would be. No, she's floating in the air. And that's not all; her legs and torso are surrounded by flames. But they're not burning her. She's… she's appearing out of the fire, as if she's part of it. The red and yellow blaze forms a translucent veil around her body, leaping with unfettered energy.

How can this be? I try to keep the panic, now mixed with despair, from taking over, but I can't help wondering: *What if this really is more rubbish?*

"Slow down!" That's me again, and this time, I get a clearer image of myself—and it's not what I assumed, either. Like her, I'm floating, but I look… faded. Translucent. Ghostly, as if I'm made of colored wind. Wisps exude from my legs, and I'm horizontal, like…

Like I'm flying.

Just then, a flood of hotness crashes into me, and the curse seems to double in strength. I feel myself curling up on the floor, writhing in anguish, but I refuse to scream—or to stop. I've come so far, and I can't turn back now. The metallic taste of blood streams through my mouth, and I realize I've bitten my lip too hard.

But I don't care. I need to know more. Impossible as what I just saw seems, it must mean *something*. My soul cries out for the truths in this memory, and I *feel* them lying there, just out of my reach.

I focus on the thought of myself and the red-haired girl, willing to accept anything I see for now and puzzle out the meaning later. The scene repeats again, with the girl appearing out of flames and me floating beside her. But this time, I can see where we are: a lush, green grove, identical to the one in my dream. Even the books are there, sitting on shelves woven from live branches.

The girl and I fly out over the treetops, and she races ahead of me. I slow down with hesitation, and she stops and makes her complaint.

Then the memory flashes forward to our destination, and I nearly open my eyes with astonishment as I see what we're standing in front of: The clock tree. It stands alone in a vast meadow. Waves of grass, speckled with white flowers, ripple as we approach. But the grass isn't green, as it should be—it's purple and blue.

I don't question it. I just keep concentrating, hoping to figure out what my mind is trying to tell me.

The girl reaches up and grabs a branch, bending it toward me. "Just take one," she says with a mischievous smirk. A silver clock dangles between the branch's leaves, and I reach toward it and turn it to look at its face.

Recognition lights my mind—it's the same clock I'm holding in my hands, the one inscribed with my name.

Without warning, a great deluge of thoughts pours into me. The thrill of a hundred forgotten memories returning, of the meaning behind inexplicable images piecing together into a vision, is so clear that I wonder how I ever missed it.

But as suddenly as the thoughts appeared, the curse's heat attacks with a vigor more than I ever could have imagined, so painful and hot, it seems the Firelands themselves have opened their infernal gates and consumed me. Searing blades pierce through me from every direction, and I feel like I've fallen on a bed of sizzling swords. The shock is so great that I can't stop my scream this time, and my ears buzz with my own cry. Unadulterated instinct takes over, and I open my eyes before I realize what I'm doing.

The pain instantly fades, but it doesn't vanish as it did before. I still feel as if a dozen swords, hot from the forge, have stabbed me at once. I remain on the floor, weeping.

But my tears aren't from the pain—not entirely. No, despite everything, I feel a smile spreading across my lips, because I've won. The curse may have ejected me from my memory, but I already found what I was looking for. Somehow, that one memory, of flying beside a girl of flames and approaching the clock tree, awakened elements of my very self that had been locked behind the curse's gates. I don't have *everything*—far from it. There are still barriers in my mind, blocking me from much of what I once knew.

But I have enough. I know who I am, now. Though I still don't know how or why I'm here, I've found a reason to keep fighting to recover more. And I *will*. I'm too exhausted to try again immediately, but with time, I *will* defeat this curse once and for all.

I turn onto my back and stretch across the floor, finding relief in its coldness. Meanwhile, the truths I've just learned file through my head one by one, brilliant in their clarity.

My name is Kiriall Amdyth, and I'm called Kiri. I'm sixteen years old. And I have a friend with red hair and a melodious laugh. But she's more than a girl—she's a being born of flames. Who can race through the air as a blaze races through dry wood, but without damaging even a scrap of paper.

She's a fire nymph.

And I… I'm not a girl either. As she was born of flames, I was born of wind. And I *can* fly, even without wings. I can transform myself into a gentle breeze or a forceful gust and soar through the sky as a cloud does.

Because I am an air nymph.

That's why the Sorci master called me dangerous. Though nymphs now reside only in certain enchanted forests, they once wandered the Terrestrial Realm with humans, and there are tales of men—and sometimes women— being lured to their deaths by a nymph's hypnotizing call.

And *that's* why the Sorci master said he'd discover my secret. He must want my abilities—my powers over the air and over the human will. It's an explanation based on assumption, but one that makes too much sense to deny.

Other answers come to light as I contemplate the revelation. Remembering the white horse with violet eyes from my dreams, I recall the question that arose then: How could I have a horse for a mother? *This* is how: Because nymphs aren't truly born, as humans are, but formed by the unicorns from elements of nature. Unicorns were created by the Divinity to be guardians, and they would, of course, care for and nurture their own. The unicorn I saw must have been the one who made me from the air, and she must have raised me.

The grove with books must have been a part of the forest I lived in, and knowing that it resided in a place of magic makes it seem like anything but nonsense. How did I never think to consider that I came from a world of unlimited enchantments? With all the charms in the air, one could easily leave a book outside without worrying about it being damaged by rain or mist.

Mist… I understand now what the mist in my dreams was: The curse, trying to keep me from comprehending my memories. No wonder it burned as it did. It wasn't just a memory of the spell binding me. It *was* the spell.

And this same spell must be why I couldn't summon my powers when I thought I might have magic. But then, I didn't know if my abilities were real or imagined. I'll try again—and this time, I'll know what I seek.

The last embers of the pain from recovering my memories fade, and the chill of the floor no longer seems comforting. Though I'm still exhausted, I force myself to get up and approach the ball of light. Glimpsing Darien's cloak nearby, I pick it up and wrap it around myself.

"Thank you, Darien," I whisper.

I huddle by the source of warmth and, staring at the small clock, feel the joy of remembering fall away. Because I know now what that clock tree meant—and why each time I saw it, I felt like something terrible was about to happen.

A nymph's life force is bound to her homeland. When she leaves her borders, it starts to drain away. And if she doesn't return in time, she will die.

I will die.

This clock, which I took from a magical tree in my home, tells me how much time I have left. Which is why it runs backward—it's counting down. Each hour represents a day, and the short hand is pointed at seven.

Which means I have seven days left to live.

My heart hammers with fear as I realize that even though I no longer wish to die, I might not have a choice. The clock's second hand moves with unbearable speed, and each tick strikes new fear into my heart.

Seven days.

Seven days to find a way out of this cell, to recall just where my homeland is, and to return to its safety. But how can I do so when all my past attempts at escaping have resulted in nothing but despair?

I'm an air nymph, I remind myself. *I can transform into wind. And if I do, these bars will mean nothing to me.*

Drawing a deep breath, I repeat the thought to calm myself. The power is within me, and I *will* recover it, no matter how much pain I have to endure to break past the spell's magical chains.

Because I *must* — before the clock strikes midnight.

Windborn

Fated Stars Book 1

Prologue

F SHE DIDN'T ACT NOW, THE TERRESTRIAL REALM would dissolve into ashes under the Fiend's wrath. He would kill every creature—enchanted and human alike—created by the Divinity and trap their souls in the Infernal Realm, where they would suffer for all eternity. For after the Divinity, full of joy and inspiration, had blessed the world with life and free will, the Fiend, Her wicked brother, had grown jealous of how Terrestrial dwellers loved and worshipped Her. And so he had attacked with his dark forces, seeking to destroy his Sister's creations.

All nineteen years of Nameed's life had been spent preparing for this moment, when she found herself face-to-face with the Fiend himself and at last had the chance to destroy him.

And yet, she hesitated. Because to save the world, she would lose her beloved forever.

It wasn't the hideous face of a powerful monster she stared into, but the beautiful brown eyes of Denár, the young man who'd stolen her heart, who'd shown her the kind of devotion she'd never thought she'd deserve. Having been driven to the edge of the Firelands, a deep pit within the Infernal Realm from which there was no escape, the Fiend had hidden himself in her beloved's body, no doubt hoping to escape the Divinity's ever-watchful gaze.

Despite the tears burning her eyes, Nameed held her blade steady against Denár's chest. The flames below bathed her hand, copper in hue and unrelenting in its grip, in a light as red as blood. One blow would be all it took to end his life—and the war that had been raging since before she was born. If she struck him down, the Fiend would be forced to leave his dying host, and the Divinity, upon seeing him, would drive him into the fiery cage.

The fate of everything the sun touched would be decided at last.

"Lower your blade!" Denár's voice rang in her ears, bright and clear as when he'd told her he'd die for her. "It's me!"

Behind him, flames danced within the chasm, throwing a foreboding light upon his fine features and giving his dark complexion a golden glow. The hellish blaze glinted off the crimson sash he wore over his bare chest, a sash she herself had woven to honor his previous victory against the Fiend's monstrous henchmen, the guié. How could she destroy the person she loved most in the world when she would gladly have given her own life for his chance to live?

This is not Denár.

Nameed hardened her expression and looked straight into his eyes, doing her best to see the evil hiding behind his face. "Leave my betrothed's body," she growled. "Or I shall force you to leave."

A dazzling white light blazed above, but she resisted the urge to look, for she knew what it was: the Divinity, watching over this final battle between Her forces and Her brother's. Though She'd sworn never to interfere in the matters of the Terrestrial Realm, allowing Her children the freedom to create their own destinies, handling the Fiend was a different matter. On Her side were the ayri, celestial immortals who soared on feathered wings and who each embodied a particular aspect of the world, from the cultural — like music — to the elemental — like moonlight. Also on Her side were the strongest representatives of all Her creations, from the great — like dragons, whose emerald scales were harder than metal — to the small — like fairies, whose gossamer wings scarcely seemed strong enough to withstand a raindrop, and yet whose fortitude drove them to battle monsters a thousand times their size. And, of course, the humans, like the warriors of Nameed's own tribe.

On the Fiend's side were his dark creations, beasts he'd designed solely for the purpose of inflicting pain and destruction. Most numerous among them were the guié, who resembled humans only in that they had two arms and two legs. Beings of darkness, their blazing eyes were the sole features amid the blank black shadows that should have been their faces. Talons protruded from their fingers, and jagged black wings spread from their backs. Alongside them were greater monsters still — blazing beasts who towered over the trees and relished the taste of blood.

These were the world's future masters unless Nameed acted. Already, too many villages had succumbed to the Fiend's forces, and she'd heard the screams of the fallen as their souls were ripped from their bodies to burn, burn, burn in the Infernal Realm.

Nameed dug the point of her blade into Denár's chest. *This is not my beloved — this is the Fiend.*

A crimson rivulet wound down his dark torso, but if he felt anything, he did not show it. Denár — or rather, the Fiend — twisted his mouth into a sneer, as if he took great pleasure in her pain. In the corner of her eye, the white light blazed on; the Divinity hovered overhead, watching and waiting. Had the Fiend possessed any — *any* — other, Nameed would have gritted her teeth and done what she had to.

But not Denár.

To her, he represented everything good in the world, all the virtues of the stars above — courage, honesty, kindness, generosity. She would have thrown herself into the Firelands before letting anything happen to him. And yet there she stood, with her blade against his heart.

How did it come to this? One moment, they'd been fighting side-by-side against the guié, driving the enemy closer and closer to the chasm. And the next, she'd spotted a glint of red in his dark eyes and seen a ferociously gleeful look twist his expression. Though anyone else might have denied the sight, thinking it a trick of light, Nameed knew her beloved like no other, and she'd been warned that the Fiend might try to possess the living. So she'd turned her blade on him in a movement so quick, she didn't remember making it.

A mere instant must have passed since that moment, yet it felt like eternity. All around her, the battle raged on, but it seemed muted and blurred behind her agony. Time slowed, and tears spilled down her cheeks. *There must be some other way.*

Denár — no, the *Fiend* — met her eyes. "Nameed —"

Hearing her name spoken by the impostor jolted her out of her hesitation, and fury overwhelmed her. With a primal scream, she plunged her sword into his chest. Though delivering such a blow must have taken all her strength, she felt nothing — no steel in her hands, no pressure against her arms, not even the blood that splashed onto her face. In that instant, she was no longer the warrior Nameed, but a being of sheer rage.

Denár's eyes widened, then turned from brown to red. Flames exploded from them as the Fiend rushed to escape his dying host. The young man's

body collapsed against the hilt of her sword, and Nameed suddenly felt the weight against her hands. She released the weapon to catch him. He fell onto his knees, and she knelt down with him, holding him up, as if that would somehow keep him alive.

"Denár…" She meant to tell him how much he meant to her, apologize for her failure to save him, and let him know that she'd make sure his sacrifice would be remembered forever. She ached to hear him tell her that everything would be all right, that she'd made the right choice, that he forgave her. She wanted—no, *needed*—a tender goodbye, in which she'd hold him in her arms, clasp his hand, and give him one final kiss.

But it was too late.

His head slumped, with eyes still and unseeing. Robbed of even one last moment of solace, Nameed screamed a scream that could have shattered the stars. His blood soaked her long black braid, and the hilt of her sword, still embedded in his chest, dug into her ribs.

The flames that had burst from his body—the Fiend in a half-formed state—swirled into a dazzling wash of white as the Divinity bore down upon him. The great light engulfed the entire world with its astonishing luminescence, and thunderous rumbling filled the air.

But Nameed hardly noticed the ground quaking beneath her as she pressed her beloved's lifeless body to hers. Only one thought existed in her mind, circling endlessly: *I'm sorry, I'm sorry, I'm sorry…*

What little of the world she could make out through the Divinity's almighty light was nothing but a haze behind her relentless tears.

But then came a sound so powerful, it shook her out of her grief-stricken state.

"Hear me, Sister!" The Fiend's voice enveloped her with its booming power, penetrating her core with its terrible vibrations. "You may have triumphed for now, but our war is not over! Everything You created, everything You love, will one day be mine!"

Through the whiteness of the Divinity's light, Nameed glimpsed his horrible face, made of flames and twisted with cruelty, grinning with malicious glee. He opened his mouth, revealing the depths of Inferno within, and the light of the Divinity spiraled into the abyss…

AMEED OPENED HER EYES, HER FACE STILL WET from the tears she'd shed in her sleep. Though forty years had passed since that fateful day, she'd never forgotten a single detail of the moment that had changed her life — and the entire world. Because she of what she'd done, Terra was now a place of peace and freedom for all the Divinity's creations. After liberating the innocent souls trapped in Inferno by the Fiend, the ayri had returned to Celeste, the divine realm beyond the clouds. Meanwhile, the Fiend's servants had been driven back to their dark dimension, where their master lay trapped forever in the Firelands.

The thought that he now inhabited the cage he'd built himself — meant to hold his divine Sister — never failed to bring a dry smile to Nameed's face. But though the corner of her mouth lifted, she found no joy.

The moment between when she'd drawn her sword on Denár and when she'd struck him down had lasted mere seconds, but it was a moment she would never escape.

Sitting up on her thin straw mattress, which lay flat on the stone floor, she brushed her cheeks, now lined with age, and wiped her eyes. Outside the entrance to her small cave, the bright morning sun stretched its golden rays across the pale horizon, gilding the flat, grassy plain below the mountain she dwelled in. She'd lived alone here for twenty years, and she intended to remain alone for twenty, thirty, forty more, until her body surrendered to the weariness of age.

All the advice people had given her, telling her that Denár would have wanted her to move on, had been useless; even the Ayr of Reason couldn't sooth her guilty conscience. She knew she'd done the right thing, that if she hadn't killed him, Denár would have died anyway at the hands of the Fiend, along with everyone else. And she did not regret taking action. But that didn't lessen the pang of loneliness that came with living every day with half of herself missing. Or quiet the relentless question of "what if" that never ceased to plague her, asking whether she'd acted too hastily.

The rewards and praises she'd received for her deeds had done nothing to assuage her pain, even when the Ayr of Tomorrow had chosen her to be the first Sibyl. Only the bravest and wisest had been considered for the

honor, and the celestial being had bestowed it upon Nameed, who could now foretell those parts of the future that her gift allowed her to see.

Though her prophecies could have earned her the finest dwellings and richest foods, she'd chosen to remain a hermit, for every prize seemed soaked in her beloved's blood. She would have traded it all for the farewell she'd been denied, the chance to tell him her final, "I love you."

An uncanny feeling washed over her: a wordless, visionless prediction that left her with basic knowledge of what would come, but no specifics. Someone would enter to seek her prophecies, and whoever it was would not be a danger to her. With her psychic abilities, such a simple prediction was as clear and familiar as the light outside.

And yet…

Something more profound loomed too—something much darker and deeper. An inexplicable dread descended, chilling her despite the warm summer air.

Before she could untangle the meaning behind the abrupt disturbance within, a glimmer of light caught her eye. The air in the center of the sparsely furnished cave glittered with blue sparks, and an instant later, a burst of white filled her vision. When it cleared, a unicorn, one of the great immortal creatures who kept the peace, stood before Nameed, her white coat gleaming so brightly, she made everything else in the cave appear filthy and tainted. The tip of her silver horn shimmered like the light of the stars, and her long silver mane flowed down her muscular neck.

Recognizing her as Amdyth, a guardian of Terra, Nameed bowed. But the feeling of comfort and security she usually felt in the presence of a unicorn was absent.

Amdyth's words, always communicated telepathically, slipped into her mind: *What's troubling you, Nameed?*

I'm not sure, Nameed replied. *Have you come with a question?*

Amdyth's deep purple gaze met hers, and though the unicorn's placid expression did not change, Nameed sensed her worry. *What I seek is more than I have the right to ask for, but the fate of all may depend on it.*

Nameed nodded. *Then ask.*

Inferno has been restless since our day of victory, but lately the rumblings have grown more ominous. Tension clung to each of Amdyth's words, which floated through Nameed's head in a soft yet resonant whisper. *They want*

nothing more than to free their master.

And you've come to ask if they will succeed. Nameed drew a breath, dreading the visions she would have to face to find the answer.

Amdyth lowered her head, and her long mane glinted. *Yes.*

Nameed didn't want to contemplate the possibility that the Fiend could fulfill his final threat, but if there was a chance, then the world had to prepare. So she closed her eyes and raised her hands high above her head to begin the ritualistic gesture that would call her visions, then crossed her wrists in the air and brought them slowly down to her chest, lifting her chin to the skies. It did not matter how many layers of rock stood between her and the physical sky, for such barriers hardly mattered to the Celestial Realm. Already, its wondrous power tingled in her nerves.

She concentrated on the darkness, allowing her mind to reach beyond its ordinary capabilities. Just three years ago, she'd required all manners of rituals and potions to enter the tranquil, transcendent state that would allow divination to occur, but at last, she'd mastered the ability. Still, what Amdyth was asking for went beyond the usual entreaties of the everyday, requesting that she predict earthly banalities such as when the Ayr of Rain would next visit a village. No, this question surpassed anything Nameed had dared try before, and if it hadn't been for the great fear that had struck her heart at the memory of the Fiend's final words, she might have turned even the great unicorn away.

Nameed reached out with her gift, expecting to strain herself to the brink of death in order to answer such a mighty question. To her shock, the vision flooded her mind on its own accord, filling her head with images so vivid, she had to press her wrists together until they felt like they would crack in order to keep her grip on reality. They were not unpleasant thoughts — visions of human villages growing crops, of playful nymphs dancing in meadows, of graceful mermaids diving through serene seas. But a dark cloud loomed, ready to consume them all.

"*Listen well, unicorn,*" she said, the words pouring from her mouth with such power and ferocity, she didn't recognize her own voice. Something was using her tongue to convey its message, and she was powerless to stop it. A terror unlike anything she'd known before gripped her. Was this how Denár had felt when the Fiend possessed him?

"*Enjoy your little world while you can. The Divinity has indeed triumphed,*

and for three Ages, the Terrestrial Realm will prosper. First, in the Age of Unicorns, during which you and your kind will act as guardians of the world, and the enchanted will walk alongside the human. Next, in the Age of Magic, during which the humans will seek powers beyond their natural abilities and rise to dominance over Terra. And then in the Age of Thrones, in which knights and kings will overthrow the magicians, and the enchanted will live separately, far from human civilizations."

A low chuckle rose from her throat. But when she tried to stop it, she found herself unable to move.

"Though you and yours will enjoy peace for millennia, it will be no more than a flicker of light in the eyes of the universe. Before the Age of Thrones reaches its sixteenth century, a human child will be born with the power of Inferno. Though the child's Terrestrial parents will be human, his soul will belong to his true father, the Fiend. He will be known as the Starless Prince, for none of the virtues of the stars will glow within this being of pure evil. He will release the Fiend, and together, they will conquer not only the Terrestrial Realm, but the Celestial as well. And this will be the Age of Fire, which will last for all eternity."

Images flared through Nameed's mind. Legions of guié descended upon a village, led by the Starless Prince, who appeared as the winged silhouette of a man. Screams of terror and pain rang in her ears, and she watched helplessly as the infernal creatures tore countless innocents to shreds. From their lifeless, mutilated bodies, their shimmering souls arose, reaching for the Celestial Realm, but the guié caught them and dragged them down into Inferno.

Even if they had escaped, it would have been no use, for in lieu of the white haze of Celeste floating in the sky, great black clouds, laced with glowing red flames, rolled over the land. And the face of the Fiend looked down from them with his flaming red eyes, watching with glee as his servants ravaged his Sister's beloved world.

Overwhelmed by the horror, Nameed tried desperately to end the vision, but the force still held her.

"Fear not, unicorn." The voice spoke through her mouth again, its deep tone crackling with mockery. *"The Fiend will not seek to destroy your precious Terra as he did in the last war. No, he will allow life to continue, but all those living will exist only to suffer under his wrath. And the Divinity will weep as everything She created, everything She loves, writhes within his grasp."*

Recognizing the echo of the Fiend's final words, Nameed realized that an infernal force had penetrated her through the channel she'd opened for Celeste.

Leave me! Her entire body trembled from the effort as she tried to open her eyes, to close her mind, to do *anything* to escape.

Suddenly, the force released its grip, and her legs collapsed beneath her. Opening her eyes, she drank in the ordinary surroundings of her cave. Yet the visions remained in her head with painful clarity. Though they were of the future, they felt as real as the stone beneath her.

Amdyth gazed down at her in silence, violet eyes as serene as ever, but Nameed felt the waves of worry rippling beneath her thoughts.

"It cannot come to pass." Tears filled Nameed's eyes. "Amdyth, I will be long dead by the time the Starless Prince is born, but you and the other unicorns are eternal. Promise me that you will do everything in your power to stop the Age of Fire."

Amdyth nodded, and the unicorn's soft voice floated through her mind: *I promise.*

But Nameed barely heard the words through the memory that pounded in her head: the voice of the Fiend repeating his final threat in endless echoes, each filled with hatred and wrath.

Everything You created, everything You love, will one day be mine.

25,000 YEARS LATER

YEAR OF THRONES 1,504

1

Keep it hidden

Could no one erase the stars and rewrite their fateful messages? Could no one rip those pages from the book of the universe and insert a new story?

Kiri knew it was no use praying, for even the Divinity could not change what had already come to pass. And if she didn't make her move, the next pages of that book would be written in fire, written in blood.

TODAY...

EEP IT HIDDEN, OR THEY'LL KILL US BOTH.

Darien's words, hastily spoken and shaded with fear, rang in Kiri's head, and her heart pounded as loudly as the footsteps outside. From the sound of it, the Sorci—the dark magicians who'd captured her—were fast approaching the staircase leading down to the dungeon. In the few days she'd been their captive, she'd witnessed more cruelty than she'd thought possible. Not only had they imprisoned her in this small, frigid cell, which had enchanted, unbreakable ice filling the space between its dark iron bars, but they'd stolen her memories, her magic, her very self. For what had felt like an eternity, she'd shivered alone and terrified, not knowing who she was, or why she was there, or where she'd come from. If Darien, the Sorci's young apprentice, hadn't defied his dark master and stolen back the one item she'd possessed when she was taken—a small silver clock she now clutched in her hand—she would still be lost.

Thanks to him, she knew who she was—and *what* she was. For the clock had her name, Kiriall Amdyth, engraved on its back, and the sight had caused a single memory to flash through her head: that of a red-haired fire nymph calling her "Kiri" and telling her to pluck that clock from a magical tree. The recollection had scarcely lasted a few moments, yet it had been enough to tell her that she was no ordinary sixteen-year-old.

She was an air nymph, created from wind by one of the great unicorns.

Because of what she was, the Sorci had stolen everything from her. And they weren't done yet. She could only guess at their motivations, since they refused to speak to her, but from what she'd heard them say to each other, they evidently wanted to harness her powers — her abilities to transform into the wind, fly like the breeze, and control the gust. And one more, which she shared with all of her kind: the ability to lure humans and bend them to her will.

But each time she tried to unleash her magic or recall her past, unbearable heat consumed her entire being, inflicting a kind of pain she'd never imagined possible. Not only that, but the Sorci master, who led the others and controlled Darien with absolute authority, had cast further spells upon her in his attempts to discover the secret to her powers, each one weakening her and nearly driving her from sanity. And when he'd caught Darien speaking to her once before, even though it had only been to tell her that he'd brought her food, the cruel magician had accused her of bewitching him and tortured her for a crime she hadn't committed — that she *couldn't* have committed because of the very curse he'd placed on her.

Kiri trembled at the thought of the excruciating death he would surely deal her if he knew she possessed the clock. Worse, the boy who had risked his life to give it to her would suffer the same fate. Kiri had already witnessed the master inflicting brutal punishments upon his apprentice for the slightest signs of defiance. Whatever happened, she couldn't let allow another to die because of her.

Keep it hidden, or they'll kill us both.

She stuffed the clock in the brown sack he'd used to deliver her food and looked around, her long, pale blond hair whipping across her face. Not knowing where else she could hide it, she crouched down beneath the tiny window of her cell, the one facing the rest of the dungeon, and crammed the forbidden object into the corner. That was the spot least likely to be seen from the outside, but was it enough? Glimpsing the enchanted ball of heated light the Sorci master had given her to keep her from freezing to death, she seized it with both hands and placed it over the package. The ball's golden brightness engulfed the rough cloth.

The footsteps rang louder against the stone staircase outside, and she

stood, knowing that soon, the Sorci would cross the wide room between the steps and her cell. No one else was imprisoned here — only silence had greeted her when she'd called out — and so they had to be coming for her.

What will they do to me this time? What more could they do? They'd already tortured her so harshly, she'd wanted to die rather than continue suffering, and ensured her death by keeping her trapped. Because all nymphs were bound to their homelands, her life force had begun to drain the moment she'd stepped out of hers.

Kiri didn't remember leaving her home — or where her home even was — but she recalled taking the clock from the enchanted tree because its magic would tell her how much time she had left.

Seven days.

Each of the beautifully drawn numerals ringing the clock's shimmering white face represented not an hour but a day, and the slender black hands, which ran backward as they counted down, currently pointed at seven o'clock.

Once they struck the midnight hour, she would die.

Darien must not have known what the clock signified, or else surely he would have done something more than give it to her. Unless he didn't care she was dying, but that thought clashed violently with the way he'd acted, enduring his master's wrath again and again to help her. Not to mention the last words he'd spoken.

Keep it hidden, or they'll kill us both.

He'd sworn his life to the way of the Sorci, and he might have forfeited it to bring her a piece of herself that had been lost to her. In doing so, he'd unknowingly pulled her out of the pit of despair that had nearly driven her mad. She wouldn't doubt him.

Fear sat like icy dew on her skin, and a sharp shudder wracked her body. She pulled the thick, black cloak she wore tighter over her shoulders. Its presence was the only comfort she had in this dismal place — not only because of its warmth, but because it reminded her that despite the evil she'd experienced, the goodness of the stars still glowed within humankind. Darien had taken the garment off his own shoulders and faced his master's fury to give it to her, even though he hadn't known anything about her.

He still didn't know her. And she didn't know him. Scarcely a dozen words had passed between them, and the only information she'd gathered,

other than his name, was that he was seventeen years old and bound by oath to serve the Sorci as he trained to become one of them. The idea of that brave, kind-hearted boy becoming just like the wicked magician who'd tortured her twisted her stomach, and she wondered what lies they'd told to lure him into their fold.

The Sorci master came into view, his face hidden beneath the hood of his ornately decorated black cloak. Its swirling embellishments—brilliant symbols and ciphers in metallic threads—and the gold medallion hanging across his chest glinted in the firelight of a lone iron lantern hanging from the dungeon's stone ceiling. Behind him, five other magicians followed, each wearing cloaks similar to his but with their own unique glimmering figures.

Blood drained from Kiri's face, though she wasn't sure it was possible for her to grow any paler than her already snowy complexion. She inhaled deeply in hopes of calming her quivering heart. Each time the master had come to her cell, he'd brought her unrelenting torment.

Still, he would *not* defeat her.

She strode to the small, jagged window—the lone break in the ice. Though she couldn't see his eyes beneath his black hood, she knew what they looked like from past encounters. Picturing the cold green gaze hiding in the shadows, she met them with the hardest glare she could muster.

"You have no right to keep me here," she said, surprised by how her words reverberated against the walls. "I am not an experiment for you to toy with! Release me!"

Her own fortitude shocked her, for just moments ago, before receiving the clock, she'd been a trembling mess curled up on the floor. Something about knowing who she was had awakened a strength she hadn't known she possessed, an inner fire that had flickered before but now blazed with full force. Perhaps it was because she now knew for certain that she didn't deserve her fate; previously, she'd wondered if she was some kind of monster that had to be trapped. Or perhaps it was because she finally felt like a *person* again, and not a meaningless object existing without a purpose.

No more pleading, no more cowering; she would face her tormentor and deny him the satisfaction of seeing her vanquished.

The Sorci master didn't answer as he drew closer, but a subtle sneer curved his lips.

Anger flashed through Kiri. *"Release me!"*

He stopped inches from her cell, lowering his chin and folding his pale, weathered hands before his stomach. For several seconds, he remained completely still.

His head snapped up. *"Wall of ice, retreat!"*

His thunderous voice boomed with a strange thickness, unnatural and terrifying. Kiri jumped. The icy surface before her turned from pale blue to bright green and glowed with such otherworldly intensity, it hurt to look at. Bolts of white light streaked up each of the iron bars, and the sharp crackles of magic snapped in the air. Kiri tensed, doing her best not to let her dread creep onto her face.

The light faded, and the crackling ceased. The ice disappeared from between the bars, and she couldn't help considering the spaces between them. They were narrow, but so was she, with her bird-like legs, slender hips, and small bust. But with the Sorci master standing right in front of her, flanked by his followers, she didn't stand a chance of escaping even if she could slip through them.

The Sorci master threw back his hood, revealing the cruel face she knew so well. A face whose prominent cheekbones and high nose hinted at having once been handsome, but whose coldness cemented his reptilian appearance. Deep frown lines, etched by years of scowling, streaked his wraithlike face, and his shaved head gleamed under the dim yellow light of the lantern. His merciless green eyes bore into hers with such harshness, she wanted to pull her cloak over her head to hide from their heat.

The master raised both hands, and the wide sleeves of his cloak fell back to his elbows. Lines of black tattoos, whose jagged angles gave them the appearance of thorny branches, wound around his forearms, and Kiri could almost hear the dark magic humming beneath them. She recognized the gesture and knew what was coming, yet had no way of escaping. A powerful part of her wanted to try anyway, wanted to run to the back of the cell and tear at the tiny window to the snowy outdoors in a vain attempt to get out, wanted to duck into the corner and make herself as small as possible, wanted to weep and plead and swear to do anything he wanted as long as he spared her.

But she'd faced this man before, and she could do it again.

The other five Sorci, standing behind the master in a triangular formation, threw back their hoods and raised their hands as well, imitating the leader's motions. Though they varied greatly in appearance, from a tall, broad-faced woman to a small, pointy-chinned man, they acted with such uniformity, they might as well have been copies of each other. Each of the three women and two men had similar black tattoos snaking around their bared forearms, and each stared at Kiri with icy, pitiless eyes.

They *all* meant to cast the spell the Sorci master had inflicted upon her before. Her breath stopped in her throat. Previously, the master's single curse had tormented her within an inch of her life; how could she survive the power of six?

The Sorci held their gesture, silent as the iron bars. The air quaked from an invisible force rippling toward her, and a low hum vibrated in her ears.

A great upwelling forced its way up her chest as tiny red flashes appeared before each of the Sorci, dancing like infernal fireflies. A strong gust blew toward her, hot as the Fiend's breath, carrying a swarm of blazing sparks that quickly engulfed her.

No matter how hard she breathed, no matter how tightly she gritted her teeth and squeezed her eyes, she couldn't keep the tears from flowing down her cheeks. A thousand flaming daggers stabbed her from all sides with unrelenting force. A sudden burst of agony dug into her chest, like a great claw plunging into her heart.

She screamed and doubled over, collapsing to the ground. The impact from her fall barely registered as the invisible claw squeezed her insides, as if trying to dig its talons into her soul, and she wondered if it was the hand of the magicians, trying to steal her powers over the wind. The sparks kept coming, each lancing her with a new force. Her knees curled to her chest, and her hands scratched at the ground in vain.

All she knew were flames—scorching, excruciating flames, wrapping her entire body in a cocoon more agonizing than anything she'd suffered before. She writhed, kicking and flailing in a useless attempt to fling the pain away, and ripped at her chest, trying to tear at the horrible force yanking at her core. But there was nothing for her fingers to grasp.

Red filled her vision through her closed eyelids. She became vaguely aware of several voices chanting in rhythm but couldn't hear much through her own cries. The invisible claw continued yanking and yanking and yanking, ripping her apart from the inside.

Her screams softened to whimpers, and her limbs weakened until they were too heavy to lift.

She would die here. Not in seven days, as her clock foretold, but in seven minutes if she was lucky.

The all-consuming fire raged on, but her body had lost the strength to fight back. The claw scratched at the rope binding her to life, until only one thread remained, and she wished the silent Ayr of Death would take her into their embrace.

But then the flames vanished, and where there had been heat, cold air rushed in and wrapped her in a blanket of iciness. The claw faded away, leaving her with a strangely empty sensation, as if it had hollowed out a piece of her soul. In that moment, the chill actually brought relief. Her body sank into the hard, iron ground. She wanted to disappear into oblivion and forget all she'd learned and all she'd leave behind.

"Fiend take you!" The Sorci master's voice jolted her back to attention.

She managed to open her eyes, but even that small effort felt monumental. Embers of the curse lingered within her bones. The magician glared down at her, his face contorted with fury and his eyes snapping with the raging hunger of a starved beast.

That look could only mean one thing: The man had failed. Again. He'd done his worst, even multiplied his curse with the power of his followers, and yet he still hadn't found what he was looking for. Which meant that even though she lay within his cell, *she* was the triumphant one.

One of the other magicians—a tall woman whose powerful cheekbones offset large brown eyes—approached the master. "Do you understand now, Worak?" she asked in a low voice. "It is the *method* that we lack, not the force."

"How dare you?" The master spun to face the woman. "I felt her power in my grasp!"

If Kiri had held any doubts about the Sorci's intentions, those last words swept them away. Worak—she presumed that was the man's name—wanted to steal something that not only belonged to her, but that was a *part* of her.

The woman shook her head, brown hair sweeping against her chin.

"You know as well as I do that an enchanted creature's power is woven into the fabric of her being. Trying to take it would be like attempting to rip the beating heart from a person. You can tighten your grip and strengthen your pull, but if you separate the one from the other, both will die, and both will be useless to you. We already went through all this with the last nymph, and it got us nothing."

Kiri started at those last words. *The last nymph.* So she wasn't the first to suffer this cruelty. *Whoever the other was, no one deserves this.* She wanted to stand and shout, but she barely had the strength to keep her eyes open.

The master glared at the woman. "Are you finished?"

The other held her firm expression. "You may be our leader, Worak, but that is a right *we* gave you, and I will not stand by while you continue to waste our efforts on this one little nymph!"

"I agree with Limali." A boy's voice rang out from the direction of the staircase.

The sound sent a jolt through Kiri, strong enough to make her sit up. Black spots invaded her vision from having moved too quickly, but the sight of the one descending the staircase made her pulse quicken. *Darien.*

The first time she'd seen him, he'd been wearing a plain black version of the elaborately decorated cloaks the rest had, but that garment now lay on the cell floor beside her. The white shirt and brown pants he was dressed in made him stand apart from the rest as much as his youth did, and as always, she couldn't help feeling a pang of guilt at the sight of him. He may have denied that the cold affected him, but she could tell that it did.

Worak whirled toward him. "What are you doing here? I told you to stay in the library!"

Darien strode toward his master, and firelight glinted off his thick, ebony hair and deep amber complexion. His were the blackest eyes Kiri could have imagined, and she found something beautiful about their obsidian fierceness. They were almost frightening in their intensity, especially coupled with his well-defined cheekbones and hard jaw, and yet she'd seen them melt into friendliness when he smiled. But there was no trace of that boyish sweetness as he stopped before Worak, his expression so firm and authoritative, she would never have guessed he was an apprentice.

Darien, who was taller than Worak by half a head, squared his shoulders.

"I said, I agree with Limali. We've kept the nymph long enough."

His eyes flicked past his master and met hers. Kiri hadn't thought it possible to feel both joy and fear at once from the same source. Joy because Darien's was the only kindness she could remember, and just seeing him warmed her heart. And fear because she'd seen how powerful Worak's wrath could be, and she dreaded seeing Darien suffer again for speaking up.

But if his master's past abuse had intimidated him, Darien didn't show it. "Master, this was your greatest experiment, the culmination of all your studies, and yet it didn't work. You have nothing more to gain from keeping her—"

"*Silence!*" Worak swept one arm toward Darien.

The youth flew backward into a nearby post, thrown by the master's spell. Kiri gasped as he impacted the wood, but though his legs faltered, he didn't fall. Instead, he grabbed one of the shackles chained to the post and steadied himself.

"You said you'd release her when you were finished." Quiet anger simmered in his voice. "These experiments cannot—"

He broke off and collapsed to his knees, doubling over in pain. Worak strode toward him, holding one hand out in front of him like a claw and slowly twisting. A faint red shimmer filled the space between them. A curse, possibly one as terrible as what Kiri had endured.

"*Stop!*" She tried to stand, but her feeble legs shook the moment she tried.

The other Sorci, including the woman Darien had agreed with, watched with cold indifference.

"What gives you the right to challenge me?" Worak took a step toward Darien. "Have you forgotten that you are a mere novice? Do you really think your six meager months of training are enough to make you my equal?"

"I've kept silent long enough." The strain in Darien's voice betrayed his pain, and yet his eyes remained undaunted. "You can do whatever you want to me, but that won't make me wrong."

Worak gave his wrist an abrupt twist, and Darien grasped his stomach as his body folded forward over his knees.

"Leave him alone!" Kiri cried.

Worak glanced back at her, and Kiri met his gaze with the darkest glare she could muster.

The master let out a harsh laugh. "Ah, I understand." He dropped his hand, and the red shimmer vanished.

Darien exhaled, slumping as the tension left his body.

Worak crouched beside him and put a hand on his shoulder. "You have so much to learn, young one, but how can I teach you when you won't listen? Have you forgotten what I told you when you joined us? About our ultimate mission?" He let out a disappointed sigh, and Kiri recoiled at the fatherly tone his voice had taken. Surely, Darien must have heard its falseness as clearly as she did.

But the master seemed to hold some kind of spell over the boy, for the anger in Darien's eyes turned to confusion. "You said that when the Age of Fire arrives, we'll be Terra's last defense against Inferno. But I don't understand—"

"The Fiend is the greatest evil this world has ever known," the older man interrupted. "We may be mighty among humans, but that won't be enough. Only by combining our powers with those of the enchanted creatures can we wield enough force to stand against the Fiend. To save the world, sacrifices must be made."

The confusion on Darien's face deepened.

The Age of Fire… Though Kiri had lost her personal memories to the curse, her knowledge of the world and its history remained. Was the dreaded Age of Fire really drawing close? If the Fiend really was on the cusp of his prophesied return, if her life were truly a price that had to be paid to defend all of Terra, then she could almost believe that her suffering was justified. Yet it seemed impossible that Worak could fight for the side of good when he represented everything wicked.

The magician held out a hand. "Rise, my young one."

Darien let the other pull him up, but his mind seemed as distant as the moon.

Worak gave him a hard look. "Never forget what she is and what she's capable of. She's been wielding the seductive power of her kind since she awakened here, and it struck you with full force. Remember, when you're around her, your thoughts and emotions are no longer your own."

An arrow of outrage shot up Kiri's chest. "It's not true!" she yelled.

"Silence!" Worak held up one fist, and her jaw clamped shut.

A cold tingling sensation rushed down her throat. She glared at him, her anger overwhelming any doubt or fear. Not only had that man imprisoned and tortured her, not only was he lying to turn her one ally against her, but he'd taken her ability to speak. The injustices piled on top of one another, churning up a rage she hadn't known herself capable of. *Let me go, you monster!*

Her vision suddenly narrowed into two points of light, fixed on the magician's eyes. A low humming filled her head, muting the world, and a shimmering energy vibrated before her, connecting her mind to Worak's. Though ribbons of fire coiled through her insides, the pain hardly registered beneath the awakening energy. Her thoughts vanished, blank but for one: *Let me go.*

The order felt as natural and effortless as lifting her finger, and as her finger wouldn't resist a command from her mind, neither did Worak resist. His face became slack, and he dropped his hand. Immediately, both the tingling in her throat and the force holding her jaw vanished.

Exhaustion descended, and she realized of how powerful a heat burned at her core. In those last few moments, she'd felt like someone else, someone who'd known exactly what she was doing even though her present self had no idea how that was possible.

Worak's face contorted, and he punched both hands toward her, sending bolts of red lightning streaking from his fingertips. "*Enforce!*"

A million tiny invisible ropes wrapped around every inch of her body, each hotter than the sun. She screamed and crumpled to the ground. The ropes tightened, as if trying to squeeze the life from her, and she struggled to breathe between her cries. She dug the heel of her hand into her arm and slid it down her skin, trying desperately to free herself, though there were no actual ropes for her to push away.

Worak turned and strode away from her, as if he'd unleashed a monster in the form of a spell and left it to attack her on its own. Limali stood before the cell with one hand extended, and swath of thick ice filled the space between the bars, crawling toward the ceiling. Kiri wanted to cry out for the woman to stop, but another scream escaped as the blazing coils continued digging into her.

Limali completed the wall of ice between the cell's bars, leaving only a

small, square window. The heat of the invisible ropes began to subside — or perhaps it had burned away so much of Kiri that she could no longer feel — but she still sensed them binding her.

She caught sight of Darien staring at her, his black eyebrows drawn low. Where there had been anger, bewilderment now reigned, and he didn't resist as his master clapped one hand on his shoulder and led him away. No longer did he appear to be her defiant ally; he seemed to have reverted to being the obedient apprentice.

He can't have turned against me so quickly… He can't have believed what Worak said about my powers.

Yet for a brief moment, she'd held Worak's mind in her grasp. *How is that possible?*

If she'd had any strength left, she would have searched for a hint of that magic, would have attempted to harness it again or test her other abilities. But she could barely keep her eyes open. Feeling the cold air biting into her skin, she tried to tell her body to get up and wrap itself in Darien's cloak, but it wouldn't obey.

As darkness descended, a faint ticking sound emitted from the corner where she'd hidden the clock.

Seven days, it whispered. *Seven days…*

ELSEWHERE...

"Great Fiend, my master! Aren't the ways of humans most laughable? Why worry about one little nymph when the entire enchanted domain lies at our fingertips? The unicorns are powerful, yes, but we now possess the knowledge to defeat their magic. However rare or difficult the spell is, we will find ways to make it work. Behold, the first pillar is complete! A mirror touched only by starlight, as the magic calls for. Once the power reflects off its glass, it will pierce the borders, and the unicorns themselves will be at our mercy."

2

If the windborn one dies

TOMORROW...

Too late for regret, too late for hope, too late for anything but quiet acceptance, and every protest was useless, every resistance pointless, every living thing caught in the grip of fate helpless.

And yet, Darien fought.

For he alone stood between Terra and the merciless hands of Inferno, and he would not let them pass.

TODAY...

OO MANY TRUTHS CROWDED DARIEN'S MIND, and he try as he might, he couldn't line them up. Until a few days ago, he'd been certain of the path he'd chosen when he'd sworn his life to the Sorci, but the arrival of one nymph had shaken his faith in the order. Adding to the chaotic jumble was the terror that had shadowed him since he'd stolen the nymph's clock from the chest in which Master Worak stored enchanted artifacts.

If the theft were discovered, no power on Terra could save him, for the Sorci Code was absolute, and he'd broken it. The penalty was death.

Worak's hand on his shoulder felt as binding as any manacle, and Darien wondered where his master was leading him. The magician hadn't spoken a word since telling the other Sorci to leave.

Does he suspect something? Darien barely heard the echoes of his and Worak's footsteps against the high stone walls over the nervous drumming of his heart. His eyes darted to the enormous wooden doors, carved with intricate symbols whose meanings he'd barely begun to understand, on the other side of the hall. They led to the outside, to freedom, and part of him yearned to run for them. But he quieted that foolish instinct, for the doors could would only open for an intricate spell he had yet to attempt, let alone master.

And to leave the Sorci after swearing the oath was also punishable by death.

The fortress that had been his home for six months suddenly felt like a dungeon. But this wasn't his first time facing death, and if he'd survived once, he could do it again. Funny, Worak had been the one who'd saved his life then, but now, the Sorci master was the one who would take it away.

Six months earlier, Darien had found himself bleeding out from a knife wound after being attacked on a dark, rainy stretch of road. Who the assailant was, he didn't know — all he'd seen was a large shadow lunging at him. Lightning had struck the ground nearby right after the blade had plunged into his ribs, and some force of fate must have intervened, because that bolt had scared away the assailant and called Worak's attention to the spot.

"I can save you," the magician had said, after materializing in a burst of yellow light. "But you're teetering on the brink of death, and the one spell powerful enough to bring you back can only be cast upon another member of the Sorci order. Swear yourself to us, and I'll call upon it."

Soaked in his own blood, Darien hadn't hesitated to agree. At the time, he'd been glad for the way things had turned out, as he'd been on his way to seek the Sorci's guidance. He'd seen how they'd used their supernatural abilities to help humankind, and Worak himself had been the one to save Darien's brother after a riding accident, responding to their parents' call after all the doctors had been helpless.

Which was why, for months, he'd never regretted the oath he'd sworn. But now, he wondered just how clouded his judgment had been.

"Something is troubling you, young one."

Darien jumped at the sound of Worak's voice. "What do you mean?"

"You understand exactly what I mean." The magician's piercing eyes flickered between green and gold under the flaming torches.

He knows what I did, a part of Darien warned, but another part reminded him that Worak was not the kind of man to hold his anger back. "I must have missed something."

Irritation flashed across his master's eyes.

He shrugged. "You always said I was a slow learner. Enlighten me, Master."

Worak entered the long hallway at the top of the stairs. "You allowed the nymph to charm you with her wicked powers. You defied me for her sake under the mistaken belief that you were helping an innocent creature. But now that you've seen what that her lure looks like when cast upon another, you wonder how you could have been so wrong."

If only that were true. At least that meant his crime hadn't been discovered—yet.

"Yes, Master." The reply had become such a natural reaction to anything and everything Worak said that it had lost all meaning for Darien. It was the mask behind which he hid, the shield with which he protected himself.

And yet despite the safety they offered, they tasted foul, and he longed to cleanse his tongue with words that were true. But in this case, he didn't know what those words were, for he didn't entirely disagree with what his master had said. *Who are you, Kiriall Amdyth?*

In the days preceding her arrival at the Sapphire Bastille, as the Sorci fortress was called, he'd spent hours reading about her kind, and he knew how dangerous someone like her could be. Thousands of years ago, during the Age of Unicorns, the fair daughters of nature had walked alongside ordinary humans, who were so enchanted that they remained ignorant to the nymphs' dangers until it was too late. Deception was woven into the very soul of each lovely creature, as they all knew how vulnerable humankind was to the charms of the beautiful. Lured by their songs, sailors would smash upon rocky coasts and riders would steer their steeds off cliffs. People would burn alive trying to reach fire nymphs, drown in watery depths trying to reach river nymphs, and perish in frozen expanses trying to reach snow nymphs. As for air nymphs—they were known to drive people mad with their ethereal allure, swirling around them in the form of wind, inviting yet untouchable, and then, with one great gust, send them flying to their deaths. History was filled with tales such as these, and it was well known that a nymph could steal a person's willpower just by speaking, bending their minds to serve her purposes.

This was who she was: a dangerous beauty whose wide blue eyes hid treacherous powers. Darien hadn't wanted to believe it, but now that he'd seen her take hold of Worak, the most powerful of the Sorci, he couldn't be sure of anything. In order to hypnotize the magician, she would have had to break through the protective enchantments the master surrounded himself with, and if she could do that, then what chance did a novice like

Darien have? For all he knew, his desire to help her had been due to an illusion she'd cast.

In silence, he followed his master to an arched doorway, which led to an enormous library with a magnificent vaulted ceiling and a star-shaped chandelier made of enchanted ice. The bluish-white illumination cast a watery glow on everything it touched. Thousands of tomes bound in everything from dark leather to white cloth crowded the four marble walls, their lines broken only by two tall windows that revealed the snowy treetops and gleaming stars outside. Rows of dark wooden shelves, each inlaid with angular mother-of-pearl designs, stood neatly from one end to the other. In the aisles between sat long stone tables decorated with carved swirls.

This place housed five thousand years' worth of collected knowledge. Though Darien spent a significant portion of his time there, it never failed to fill him with awe. During the day, he could reliably find at least five or six magicians researching one subject or another, but now, and the space was empty. *What are we doing here? I doubt it's to look up another obscure history…*

Worak released Darien's shoulder. "I believe that you, in your fascination with the nymph, have lost sight of our greater goal, and the best weapon against foolishness is knowledge. One of these volumes contains the first Sibyl's vision of the Age of Fire. Not merely an account, but the memory itself, preserved by spells within the pages of a book. Find it, and do not leave until you've viewed it a hundred times." Worak let out a weary sigh, and his eyes took on a gentleness wholly in conflict with the stern master he'd seemed a moment before. "I *want* you to succeed. Remember what I told you when you first joined the order?"

"'A life of great power and great reward, but for that, great prices must be paid. A life of truth and clarity for those strong enough to lead it.'" Darien would never forget those words, nor how he'd trusted them. After years of searching for a path he could believe in, of seeking his place in a world that didn't seem to want him anywhere, the Sorci's way of absolutes had been too enticing to resist. He owed them more than his life; he owed them the sense of purpose he'd so craved. The sense of belonging. The sense that for once in his life, he was doing something right.

The hint of a smile played on Worak's lips. "Do you still believe in those words?"

Darien opened his mouth to give his customary "Yes, Master," but the words, as if exhausted from having been misused so many times, refused to come. He wished he could mean them, since, for six whole months, he'd enjoyed the relief and certainty that came with knowing just what he was supposed to do. Not only were the Sorci powerful practitioners of ancient and fascinating arts, but they used their magic to help the people of Eryu, the kingdom in which the Bastille resided. He'd seen them heal the sick and conjure necessities for the needy, rebuild homes destroyed in fires and do away with diseases that threatened crops.

What was more, the Sorci were among the few forces in the Terrestrial Realm—and the only *human* force—capable of fighting the powers of Inferno. Cannons and crossbows would do little to defend against supernatural fire, and with knowledge of magic all but wiped out during the early years of the Age of Thrones, the ordinary armies of kingdoms would not stand a chance. Whether in one year or a hundred, the Age of Fire *would* come to pass, and Terra would depend upon the Sorci to defend them. If it happened during his lifetime, then Darien wanted to be among those who would save the world. And if it didn't, then he wanted to help prepare the next generation so that humankind might stand a chance.

A life of developing great powers and achieving great things—*that* was what he'd thought he'd sworn himself to. But Kiriall Amdyth had shattered his certainty.

"Yes, I still believe in those words," he managed.

"Good." Worak narrowed his eyes. "Do not push the limits of my patience. Your life belongs to the Sorci, and if you break your oath, I will not hesitate to carry out the consequences."

"I understand." Darien's pulse raced. Even if Worak wasn't aware of the clock theft yet, he definitely knew that *something* was wrong. It was apparent in the magician's expression and tone, and only a true imbecile would have ignored it. *But knowing that doesn't make me any less of an idiot,* he thought dryly. *Swearing myself to this order then breaking the oath on an impulse... What the blazes is wrong with me?*

Worak swept out of the library, leaving Darien alone with the high stacks of books and the even higher stacks of questions.

How could Kiriall Amdyth have turned his world around so quickly? Or, at least, that was what he assumed the air nymph's name was, based on the engraving on the back of her clock.

Worak had told him time and time again that her heart-wrenching screams and pitiable tears were as fake as a clown's performance, that the spells he cast on her caused her no harm, and that she was only acting helpless in hopes of manipulating someone into opening the cell for her. Darien had tried to believe those statements, but he couldn't shake the idea that his master was wrong and she really *had* been suffering while he'd stood by and watched. The thought made him sick. Yet, if she were merely a convincing actress whose magic amplified her power to manipulate, that would mean he'd broken the Sorci Code for nothing.

Darien wished he could go back to the sureness and security he'd known before. Too many ideas, equally powerful in weight yet pulling him in opposite directions, crashed down upon him.

The Sorci used their powers for the greater good of the kingdom.

That was true.

They were the only ones among humankind who could save Terra from the Age of Fire.

That was also true.

Yet, they had captured an innocent nymph and experimented upon her against her will.

Again, true.

Even if her screams and tears weren't real, even if, as Worak had said, the cold didn't affect her as it would a human, no one could deny that she was trapped. But though Darien had convinced himself that he'd rather risk helping a wicked creature than doing nothing while an innocent one suffered, he couldn't help wondering if his master had been right all along.

Either way, someone had lied to him. And either way, he'd doomed himself.

Lit only by the haunting blue light from the ice chandelier, library shelves stretched before Darien with intimidating vastness. Unsure of what else

to do, he decided that his best hope was to carry on as if nothing were wrong while continuing to search for answers. If Worak wanted him to find a preserved prophecy, then that was what he would do. He scanned the myriad spines, wondering how he was supposed to find a book whose title he didn't know. *I'll have to use a spell.*

Glad for the distraction, he turned all thoughts to this one simple task. When he'd first joined the Sorci, he'd thought that magic could only be called upon by memorizing incantations or mixing ingredients or conducting rituals. The actuality, it turned out, was both simpler and more difficult. All humans possessed the potential for magic, but it took training and practice to access and control it, and not everyone was born with the same level of power. The rituals and enchanted devices were simply conduits for a force that already existed within each practitioner. In a way, magic was like combat. Every fool possessed the physical ability to fight, but it took years of training and studying techniques gathered across generations to become good at it. And while it was possible to win a battle without weapons, blades and arrows made that a lot easier.

While Darien could not call upon his powers with the same ease as the others did, at the very least, he possessed enough aptitude to cast a simple object-finding spell. So he closed his eyes and felt the magic stirring within him, rising from his core, then reached inward to coax the power to the surface. A great bolt of pain flared through his chest, and he clenched his fists.

This was what he had been training for, and why the Sorci enacted such harsh tests of endurance upon their students. The more powerful a spell, the more pain it caused the wielder, and if one did not learn to bear it, one could lose control, with disastrous consequences. Though the magic he called upon was basic, it still tore through him like a scythe.

"Bring me the vision of the Age of Fire," he muttered through gritted teeth. While more experienced Sorci could work magic in silence, verbalizing one's intentions was the simplest way to stay on target.

The magic churned up his chest like a wave of miniscule knives, and every breath became excruciating as his expanding lungs pressed into the invisible points. But having felt its sting countless times in his training exercises, he knew he could handle it. A million tiny, invisible hands—the

reach of the magic—extended from him, aiming for a tome they recognized even if he didn't. *Getting close…*

"If the windborn one dies, the Fiend will triumph!" A girl's desperate voice ripped across his mind.

Startled, Darien lost his grip on the spell. The hands became a frenzied mess of tangled fingers, grasping anything they touched. He tried to regain control, but heat exploded within him. Unable to hold on, he released the magic and opened his eyes. The pain vanished, and dozens of books fell from the shelf.

He looked around wildly. *What was that?*

His thoughts flew to Kiriall Amdyth, for "the windborn one" could only mean the air nymph. What did it mean that if she died, the Fiend would triumph? Worak had promised to release her once he was finished, so her life wasn't in danger—was it?

He wondered if she'd somehow sent the thought using her power over human minds, but her soft, airy voice was altogether different from the rich tones that had entered his head. If she'd sent it, wouldn't it have sounded like her? But who else could it have been? Perhaps an ayr, delivering a warning from the Celestial Realm? Or a ghost, trapped in the Ether between realms? It was said that the first Sibyl wandered that mysterious expanse, and his spell had been calling to something she'd left behind…

If the windborn one dies, the Fiend will triumph.

But Worak had assured him that his magical experiments wouldn't harm the air nymph. Still, it was possible the master was wrong, or that the iron lining the cell, which weakened the powers of enchanted creatures, was poisoning her. He would surely want to know of the warning immediately.

Darien dashed out of the library and down the Bastille's stone corridor.

By the time Darien reached the door to Worak's office, which resided in a tower at the top of a narrow spiral staircase, he could barely breathe. A tall wooden door stood before him, and he raised his fist to knock.

A high, discordant screech, surrounded by the crackle and whooshing of flames, pierced through the thick door. Darien froze. Having watched

countless visions of its kind brought to life in the Sorci's magic mirrors, he recognized the sound at once.

A gui. An infernal minion of the Fiend.

Skies above! The gui were meant to be trapped in the Infernal Realm, only capable of breaking out under the rarest of circumstances. How could one have not only escaped, but penetrated the Bastille's layers of protective spells? And it was in Worak's office—that meant the master was under attack.

Darien grabbed the door handle, aiming to fight with whatever power he had. But then, he heard something that doused him in an even colder horror.

Worak's voice, saying: "It is good to see you again, though your presence comes as a surprise. What can I do for you, my wicked friend?"

Friend? Darien's heart clenched.

"My lord grows impatient," came a voice that was almost a hiss. Acute snapping sounds, like wood crackling in a fire, punctuated each word.

The voice of a gui. The ropes of fear bound Darien so tight, he could scarcely breathe.

"I doubt that." Worak sounded as cool as ever. "A few days are but a blink of an eye to one who's been waiting for twenty-five millennia. I think, my friend, that it is *you* who are growing impatient. Tell your master that we are all working on harnessing the powers of the enchanted creatures, and that while it will take time, our work will be complete before the Starless Prince rises. You may rest assured that when the time comes, Inferno can count on the Sorci to do our part."

Confusion swirled through Darien's head, pulverizing every idea about the Sorci he'd once thought certain. Worak's words couldn't have been clearer: he was working for the Infernal Realm. Yet that seemed impossible. He'd made it his—and the Sorci's—mission to defend *against* the Age of Fire.

"The Starless Prince already walks the earth," came the unnatural, hissing voice of the gui. "Before the year is up, my master will claim his Terrestrial son, who will unlock the Firelands and, at long last, release him."

What?! Though Darien had known that the Age of Fire might come

soon, the notion hadn't felt quite real. But now, one of Inferno's own was saying that the Fiend would escape the Firelands in a matter of months. Weeks, maybe. Or even days.

This can't be. Darien's pulse staged a mutinous riot in his chest. *This must be a trick.*

But his instincts screamed that his worst fears were true: That his dark suspicions regarding the order he'd sworn himself to were true, and everything he'd believed in was a lie.

Behind the door, Worak said, "Before you leave, I have one more thing to report. The boy we took in—I fear we may not be able to tame him after all. His potential is great, yes, but he's a wild one and could easily turn into a threat."

"I will inform my master," said the gui.

Darien drew a deep breath but couldn't calm his thumping heart. That meant… That meant the *Fiend* had an eye on him.

He raced back down the stairs.

Too many truths crowded his mind, but now, they no longer conflicted each other. Everything he'd trusted, everything he'd believed in, everything he'd devoted himself to, had been false. In his head, he'd started building a home here, one where he could at last belong. Now, the walls came tumbling down.

How could he have fallen for such lies? If his master could deceive him about the very foundation of the Sorci order…

Oh skies, her screams were real.

Whatever it took, whatever it cost, he had to get out. And he would take Kiriall Amdyth with him.

ELSEWHERE…

"Oh Master, oh Lord, oh great Creator of Inferno, we have triumphed in full! The Sorci no longer belong to your unworthy Sister, who watches mutely from Her starry throne. Where once was good, now wickedness reigns, for each magician's mind belongs not to themselves, but to us. And those who walk upon green Terra still think them the benevolent order they once were. Meanwhile, my eye remains ever watchful over the boy's movements. He saw exactly what he needed to see,

and it is not difficult to know his thoughts, for he is still pure and incapable of the trickery that plagues humankind. This makes him predicable — and vulnerable. The powers could not have chosen a better vessel in which to converge. Soon, he will come to me, and I will bring him to you."

3

This is the Age of Fire

All the dreams Arrin had built for herself lay shattered. She wanted to fight the forces of destiny that had brought her here, to scream and kick and wrestle her way free. Yet she couldn't, and she'd known that from the moment she'd started down this path. Too much depended on her for those desires to stand in her way.

Someone had written her story for her. And she was powerless to defy it.

IF THE WINDBORN ONE DIES, THE FIEND WILL TRIUMPH! Arrin focused on the words with all the mental power she possessed, hoping against hope that they would reach someone who could save the girl made of air, who she'd seen in her vision, before that one death set off a terrible sequence of events leading to Inferno's eventual victory. Squeezing her eyes, Arrin tried to reach out with her mind as she imagined a psychic would, but she had no idea if she was accomplishing anything other than giving herself a headache.

If someone had told her yesterday that she'd be attempting something like this, she would have scoffed, saying she had too much sense to do something so foolish. Only experienced psychics, who'd spent years studying the mystic arts, could send messages using only their minds. The most Arrin had done was read a few books on the subject. The probability of her succeeding was negligible, practically nothing, but mathematically speaking, even the smallest fraction was infinitely greater than zero. And as long as a chance existed, she had to try.

She mentally repeated the words yet again, picturing the windborn one who had appeared in her dream, only to die. A girl who looked to be about Arrin's age, but whose appearance could not have been more different. Skin as pale as Arrin's was dark, figure as delicate as hers was sturdy, hair as straight and white as hers was curly and black. An ethereal, otherworldly being who appeared as colorful wisps of air. Beautiful, yet fragile.

Who—or even what—this wind girl was, Arrin didn't know. Nor could she fathom how exactly the girl's death would lead to the Age of Fire. The vision had been too blurred and feverish for her to comprehend the details. But she needed to *act,* and that was why she was gripping her head with both hands, concentrating as hard as she could on an ability she wasn't sure she possessed. *But I received a prophecy… surely that must mean I have other abilities of the mind.*

While ordinary humans such as her were sometimes born with psychic powers, Arrin had never experienced anything close to a vision before. Part of her still insisted that everything she'd seen in her nightmare, from which she'd awakened, trembling and gasping, about twenty minutes ago, was merely a random terror from the dreamscape.

Yet, her heart warned that it was more.

The sound of a twig snapping jerked her mind back to her surroundings, and her eyes popped open. She looked around wildly, fearful of having been followed, since she'd snuck out in the dead of night—a major offense in the eyes of her mistress. The mountain air, always cold at this altitude, stung her through her short wool jacket and loose-fitting pants.

Though the moon and stars shone brightly, with only a thin spattering of clouds standing in the way of their light, she could barely see anything. The dirt path she stood on, the field full of tall stalks to her left, the broad tree to her right—they might as well have been made of shadows. And the servants' quarters, which should have been a familiar sight considering she'd spent the past eight months living there as one of Lady Bolliore's indentured workers, appeared black and menacing, like monsters waiting in ambush.

Don't be ridiculous, she chastised herself. She was fifteen blighted years old, after all—practically a woman and far too old to indulge such childish fantasies, especially when there were real dangers to worry about. Like the chance that one of Lady Bolliore's guards would catch her running away.

I really shouldn't be standing here out in the open. She rushed down the dirt path, keeping her steps as quiet as possible. Moments ago, she'd paused in her journey to because a sudden flashback to her nightmare—which had shown the entire kingdom of Nikhilim, her homeland, burning under the Fiend's wicked rule—had jolted her with a fresh sense of urgency, leading her to try warning someone who could save the windborn girl in case Arrin was too late to do it herself. But what had possessed her to stop in her tracks when she was in the middle of breaking the law? *Curse me! When did I become such an idiot?*

Though Arrin was not a slave—Nikhilim had outlawed that practice a century ago—she often felt like one. Until her twenty-year contract, stating that she had to work unconditionally and for almost no pay, with Lady Bolliore was up, the noblewoman as good as owned her. The penalty for breaking the agreement was dire—at least ten years in prison, after which Arrin would *still* have to finish out however many years were left in her contract. When she'd signed the document in exchange for her parents' freedom from Lady Bolliore's dungeons, to which they'd been sentenced after being unable to repay the money they'd borrowed from her, Arrin been almost glad, because it had meant trading her labor for her family's safety. The injustice of a world that would put her in such a position—by striking her little sister with an illness curable only by expensive medicines—ate at her, but she'd taken comfort in knowing that her actions meant her parents could go back to taking care of her two younger siblings. The four of them could live on happily without her.

Heart pounding, Arrin picked up her pace. The farther she could get before sunrise, the greater her chances of stopping the prophecy from coming true. The vision had shown her the famed Sapphire Bastille, the last bastion of the ancient Sorci order—that had to be the girl's location. What happened next had been a chaotic mishmash of terrifying images. Though Arrin had spent the first few minutes after waking scared out of her wits, certain that the nightmare had been a prophecy but unable to explain how, she'd decided that she wouldn't just sit there pondering it.

The only solution, besides attempting a psychic warning, was for Arrin to save the windborn one herself. Thank Celeste she'd ignored her father's admonitions about spending too much time reading books, because her fascination with the bygone Age of Magic meant she knew how to reach the

Bastille. The border between Nikhilim and Eryu was only a day's journey from Lady Bolliore's lands, and the Sorci fortress was just beyond that, in the same mountain range.

Arrin threw a glance over her shoulder, half expecting to see a guard's torch, but to her relief, glimpsed only the tall shadow of Bolliore Castle towering over the servants' quarters. Focusing hard, she tried to find a landmark that might tell her how far she had until she escaped the noblewoman's domain, but she might as well have been running into an abyss for all she saw. The leather bag slung over her shoulder bounced against her hip. She hadn't brought much—just a change of clothes, a canteen of water, a bit of food, and what little money she had. And, of course, her notebook. It wasn't important to her quest, but it represented years of research and calculations, and she wasn't about to leave it behind.

She wished she had a knife in case she had to defend herself, but the only weapon she possessed was the throwing crescent tucked into her belt, a simple tool she'd made to scare birds away from the crops. Too bad she'd had to return the blade she'd borrowed to carve it.

A sharp squawk rang out. Arrin looked up in time to see a large bird flying off from a tree branch. Suddenly, the bluish-gray clouds turned pitch black, and a scarlet blaze leaped up toward them, burning them as if they were firewood.

Arrin froze.

The flames spread across the atmosphere, consuming everything in their paths, until the heavens themselves turned crimson, and the clouds dissolved into ashes that rained down like hail. It was one of the images she'd seen in her nightmarish prophecy, except she was fully awake, with her eyes open.

This can't be real. Arrin squeezed her eyes. When she opened them again, everything would be back to normal. The sky would be starry again, and the fire would be gone.

But what she saw instead made her scream aloud.

Her mother, bound in chains, writhing on the ground. A monstrous gui held her neck in its flaming, taloned hand, its black wings spread behind it as it stared down with blazing eyes. From where it held her, bolts of light shot down her body, setting fire to her clothes and turning her dark brown skin to white ash.

"Mahtim!" Arrin rushed forward, but her foot caught on something, and her face smashed against the dirt. She scrambled to her feet, but when she got up, a new horror appeared before her.

Her father, dangling in the air, each arm held by a flying gui that pulled him toward the burning sky. Red gashes covered his dark, muscular arms, and his head hung limply to one side, blood pouring down his chest from where his throat had been slashed.

"Tahtih!" Tears filled her eyes. She flung her throwing crescent at the monsters in a desperate attempt to save him. "*No!*"

"*Arrin!*" a high-pitched voice shrieked.

Arrin whirled, and her heart seized. Her little sister, Myla, crawled toward her, stomach flat against the ground, pulling herself forward with her one remaining limb: her left hand, a blistered mess attached to a blackened and bony arm. Where her other arm and her two legs should have been, scorched stumps protruded. Her face was no longer full-cheeked and bright-eyed, but thin and haunted, with a great gash running from her forehead to her chin. Beside her, Tam, their baby brother, lay face-down and unmoving, his tiny limbs covered in burns. Three guié hovered above, flapping their wings and baring their fangs as they spat fireballs.

Arrin sprinted to her siblings, tears of despair streaming down her cheeks. Any logic or reason she might have possessed flew out of her head. All she knew was that she had to help Myla—

A wall of flames burst from the ground, blocking her path.

This is the Age of Fire, a voice whispered. *This is the Age of Fire…*

Something hard smacked into Arrin's shoulder, and she stumbled, landing hard on her back.

The flames were gone—she was sprawled on the dark dirt pathway beside the orchards of Bolliore. *Another vision… It hasn't come to pass yet…*

The Age of Fire had always been a distant possibility, an apocalypse that would occur long after she was dead. And yet, in her vision, she'd seen undeniably that the Fiend's forces would not only rise during her lifetime, but very, very soon. Because while her parents might look the same in ten years or twenty, Myla was only eleven, and she hadn't looked any older in the grisly prophecy.

Arrin's pulse thundered, a stampeding herd of panicked beats. Trying to focus on the immediate world, she glanced around. The throwing crescent

lay a few inches away. She must have tossed it for real, only to have been too distracted by the vision to catch it when it returned. Though her head throbbed, she was glad the blow had knocked her back into reality. She grabbed the modest weapon and stared up at the stars. Never before had she been so glad to feel the earth, wonderful in its ordinariness, firm and secure beneath her.

But though the horrors had unraveled in her head, they hadn't merely seemed real—they'd *been* real. She couldn't explain it, but she *knew*. A prophecy… of a time that would someday come to pass.

Unless she found a way to stop it.

Lying on her back, Arrin inhaled to her lungs' full capacity and then let it out slowly. Eventually, her pulse slowed, and reality settled around her. It hit her that she was still in the middle of running away, and she cursed herself for having indulged her panic. Stuffing her crescent into her belt, she started to stand.

A firm hand gripped her wrist.

She spun and found herself face-to-face with a square-jawed guard, whose gray uniform looked yellow under the firelight of his torch.

He frowned. "What are you doing out here?"

"Let me go!" Arrin twisted as hard as she could, but couldn't escape with his whole meaty hand wrapped around her arm.

The guard snarled. "You're running away, aren't you?"

"Well spotted." A vicious instinct shot through her, outweighing her fear. She was trying to stop the blighted Age of Fire, and this thick-skulled curbrain had no right to stand in her way. With a fresh surge of energy, she tried again to yank herself free.

"Oh, no you don't." Tightening his grip, the guard pulled her down the path toward Lady Bolliore's castle. "Do you know what the penalty is for runaways?"

"Putting up with your stench?" Arrin considered explaining that she was trying to save the world—including his sorry hide. But she had no way to prove that she'd even received any visions, let alone that they were real. *Skies, I can't even prove that to myself!*

She quickly assessed what she was up against: a man twice her size whose broad strides she had to jog to keep up with. Also, he was armed with a dagger strapped to one side of his belt and a sturdy club strapped to the other. And what did she have? A wooden throwing crescent, with which she might have struck his head if she'd thought she could knock him out. But she barely reached his shoulder and wouldn't have been able to get enough leverage.

She glanced around for anything she might use, but saw only the thick trunks and round leaves of the moonfruit orchard along the path. If only she'd run into it! He would have had a harder time catching her with so many trees in his way.

Her eyes fell to his torch. *Size doesn't matter when you're dealing with fire.*

She stopped walking, planting her feet firmly on the dirt. Though the guard gave her arm a hefty yank, she managed to stand her ground. He faced her with a glower, but before he could say anything, she swung her foot and kicked the torch's base. The guard's arm snapped back, sending the flames shooting toward his eyes. With a cry, he dropped the light and released Arrin to grab his face.

She kicked her heel into the back of his knee, sending him to the ground, and sprinted into the orchard. Leaves smacked her face and stung her cheeks despite the arms she held up to shield herself.

A shrill whistle tore through the night. The guard had called for reinforcements.

Cursing, Arrin pumped her legs as fast as she could, wishing they were longer. But where was she even going? She knew how to reach Eryu by road, but she had no idea what lay on the other side of the trees. *I should've paid more attention to this lightforsaken place!*

Maybe if she'd actually run after the blighted birds she was supposed to chase off the trees instead of making the crescent to do the job for her, she'd have a clue as to where she was heading.

Shouts filled the air—guards yelling things like, "Runaway!" and "After her!"

Arrin shoved through the branches, wishing she could see anything other than blackness ahead. She must have glimpsed a map of Bolliore at some point... How was it possible that she knew where the Sapphire Bastille resided, but was unfamiliar with the place she lived? Wracking

her mind, she flipped through the possibilities. Perhaps she'd end up in the neighboring village of Brena… unless that was adjacent to the orchards on the other side of the castle, making this the orchard beside the untamed Clohi Forest. Or—

Her foot plunged through empty air, and she stumbled forward, a shriek bursting from her lips. Grabbing the closest branch—a thin, springy one—she clung on for dear life.

A deep ravine yawned below, one whose bottom was too dark for her to see. Terrified, she scrambled back, kicking a few chunks of dirt off the cliff's edge. But she didn't hear them land.

So this was what she'd been running toward: a giant expanse of nothing. She'd gone into the third orchard—the one on the edge of a cliff overlooking the valley. *Blazes!*

The guards' shouts grew louder, and the nearing sounds of rustling leaves told her they were getting close.

Thinking maybe she could run along the edge of the cliff, she looked to the right. But then a second whistle shrieked from that direction. There would undoubtedly be more guards over that way, and she wondered if the entire Bolliore army was after her. She thought about going to the left, but her pursuers had probably spread out. Whichever way she went, they could be waiting.

Stay calm, Arrin. She may have been trapped on the edge of a cliff, but every situation had a logical solution. *These cliffs aren't barren rock. They've got brush and things growing out of every crevice. I could climb down…*

She crouched down, gripping one of the branches near the edge of the drop-off, and leaned forward. The bright moon cast its silvery light on several rocky protrusions below—plenty of handholds and footholds for one bold enough. And, as she'd hoped, several bushes and small trees stuck out sporadically.

Still, doubt filled her head. She'd never done anything like this before, and one wrong move could send her tumbling to her death.

"I think she's over here!" came a man's shout, too near for comfort.

The consequences of capture spiraled through her mind. She'd be thrown into the dungeon, but worse, no one would stop the Age of Fire.

The image of her sweet little sister screaming in agony brought a surge of tears to Arrin's eyes. *I won't let it happen, Myla. I'll do anything to keep you safe.*

It seemed the universe was testing her, daring her to risk falling into an early grave for a chance to keep the prophecy from coming true.

Challenge accepted. The shouts and noises grew nearer, and a third whistle confirmed that she had no other choice. No matter which way she ran, this orchard was crawling with guards. She had to move before it was too late.

Arrin inched toward the edge of the cliff. Spotting a bush growing near it, she wrapped her hands around two branches and tugged back to test its strength. When it showed no signs of moving, she crouched and extended one leg over the cliff. Her ankle brushed something jagged but wide, and she planted her foot on it, checking its solidness. *Seems firm enough.* Trying not to think about how deep the ravine was, she lowered her other leg and felt around until she found a similar surface.

So far, so good. She mustered her confidence, released her grip on the bush with one hand, and grabbed a sliver of rock near the edge.

But when she released her other hand from the branch, her left foot slipped. Panicked, she reached back up but grasped only thin air. She teetered, desperately searching for the foothold she'd lost, but her flailing only cost her the other. The next thing she knew, she was plummeting, the roar of whooshing air and her own panicked scream filling her ears.

She grasped at the air for anything, anything, *anything.*

Blackness surrounded her, pierced only by vague silvery shapes illuminated by the moon. Icy air whipped around her.

She was going to die.

She was going to die.

She was going to die.

Something impacted her back, and a shock punched up through her like a fist. Her head snapped back, banging into something that crunched beneath her. Great buzzing noises hummed in her ears, and the world spun, the stars becoming white swirls. For several moments, she couldn't understand what had happened.

Then, she it hit her: She wasn't falling anymore. She was lying on something—a surface that was solid yet springy and that rustled when the wind blew. Not daring to move, she shifted her gaze and glimpsed the silhouette of a long, leafy branch.

Her fall had been broken by a tree—or maybe a large bush, or perhaps a shrub, to be botanically correct—sticking out of the cliff face. A laugh bubbled up her throat, and she pressed her lips shut in time to suppress it. *Skies above! What's the probability of that?*

Too small to attempt the math for. Some force beyond the Terrestrial Realm must have saved her. Closing her eyes, Arrin silently thanked whoever it was. She couldn't believe her great fortune and had to wonder if there was a reason. First the visions, and now this—maybe she was some kind of chosen heroine, destined to save the world.

Speaking of which, I should get back to that…

The elasticity of a tree—or a bush, or a shrub—was not always reliable, which meant the natural cradle could snap beneath her. Reluctantly, she sat up into a tangle of leaves. It hurt to move, but at least she'd survived.

"I'm telling you, she's dead!" a male voice yelled above. "I heard her scream! She must have gone over the edge."

That's right, she thought, as if she could project the thought into the guard's head. *Arrin Velindale fell off a cliff while trying to run away. No way for her to fulfill twenty years of servitude now. And no need to send anyone after her or bother her family for information. You all witnessed what happened.*

Arrin tried not to think about how her siblings would weep and her parents rage over her presumed death. She didn't want to imagine how they'd mourn her, or how angry with her they'd be when they learned she'd fallen because she was trying to run away.

It's for you that I do this.

"Poor thing," said a woman's voice. "We'll never find her body down there."

Arrin's mouth quirked. By nearly falling to her death, she'd actually saved herself.

A wide surface, a ledge of sorts, protruded to her left, several feet in length and as wide as she was tall. If she could make it, she'd at least have something solid to sit on until she could figure out how to get down.

With slow, deliberate movements, she pulled herself into a crawling position, then inched carefully over the branches toward the cliff face. Her muscles quivered, and she made sure to always have at least one hand gripping something. The guards' voices grew softer.

By the time she made it to the ledge, she was a breathless, sweaty, shaky mess. But she was safe. She squeezed her eyes, trying to calm her racing pulse. Once she'd had a moment to collect herself, she could figure out how to reach the bottom. There were plenty of plants to grab onto—she'd seen their ragged silhouettes beneath her. She'd be fine.

A terrible cry, distant yet piercing, cut through the night. Hot air blasted her face, and something so bright, it looked fiery orange behind her closed eyelids, streaked past.

Wondering what that could have been, she opened her eyes and looked down into the ravine.

Her heart stopped.

Where there had been darkness, now everything was as bright as daylight, illuminated by something that filled her with a kind of terror she hadn't known herself capable of—the kind that left her too frozen to breathe, staring unblinkingly at the image below and hardly able to accept what it meant.

A fire, burning furious and yellow in the dense forest below, in the shape of a symbol she'd seen a thousand times in books but never once outside their pages: The mark of the Fiend. A perfect circle with a jagged symbol slashing across it, its three angles protruding from the circumference.

Stretching across the burning emblem, in a pattern of white ash upon the treetops, was the silhouette of an enormous person with feathered wings. Arms sprawled, legs bent, head lying on a profile—the figure was too indistinct from where Arrin was to make out clear features, and yet unmistakable in its shape.

This was the imprint left by a fallen ayr.

And its presence at the center of the Fiend's symbol could mean only one thing: A battle had occurred between an ayr and the forces of Inferno— and the ayr had lost.

For a moment, she thought this might be another vision, but then she heard the guards' exclamations.

"Did you see that? Skies above!"

"Somebody alert Lady Bolliore at once!"

"An ayr… they killed an ayr…"

The last time one of the great beings of the Celestial Realm had fallen, the Fiend had still been terrorizing his divine Sister's creations thousands of years ago. And the collected knowledge from across the Ages stated that nothing other than the infernal master could destroy the immortal ayri with only one exception: if the wicked being channeled his power into another.

Which meant he was getting close enough to escaping the Firelands that his powers could pass through its gates and manifest within his minions.

Which meant they could also incarnate within the prophesied human known as the Starless Prince.

Which meant the Age of Fire was even closer than Arrin had expected.

An ayr had fallen. The first wave of desolation had begun.

ELSEWHERE…

"Ah, who doesn't enjoy unexpected good news? Though with four other Ayri of Deep Thought—Contemplation, Musing, Rumination, and Deliberation—remaining, the loss of the Ayr of Reflection will not impress upon the Terrestrial much… for now. But without their guidance, minds will jump to conclusions faster, and such impulsiveness will make them less effectual against us. Celeste has now heard our battle cry and prepares herself for war, though she will not provoke it. She is waiting for us to make the first move, and oh, what a move that will be!"

4

Tick. Tick. Tick.

TOMORROW...

The maw of Inferno yawned before her, ready to pull her into its fiery depths. And from it poured legions of monsters, unleashed upon an unsuspecting world, a world that, until now, had been a land of joy, a land of peace.

Kiri's heart shattered at the sight. All hope had died the moment she'd seen the black wings of the Starless Prince stretch across the sky, and yet she'd clung to one last shred, one last wish, one last prayer.

But now, even that had broken, and there was nothing left to hold on to.

TODAY...

HE SKY OUTSIDE FADED FROM THE BRIGHT BLUE of daylight to the lilac hues of sunset. Shivers raced through Kiri, turning her blood to ice.

Tick. Tick. Tick. The second hand of the silver clock kept turning without mercy. She clenched the timepiece, knowing what it would read even though she couldn't bear to look at its face: six o'clock. Six days left. And she was no closer to escaping than she'd been last night. Though she'd spent every moment of the past several hours trying to call upon her magic, all had been in vain. She longed to get back the time she'd lost when, exhausted from her efforts, she'd fallen asleep on the cell's floor, but that was impossible. Almost as impossible, it seemed, as transforming into wind and escaping.

The powers that had been at her fingertips the previous day now seemed lost and unreachable; Worak's last spell must have reinforced the binds of the curse. Nevertheless, she had to keep trying.

But even if she succeeded, she'd still have to find her way back to the homeland whose name she couldn't remember. The few flashes from her lost memories hadn't given her anything specific enough to piece together an answer. Tall, majestic trees, reaching toward the heavens with sinewy brown branches and crowned with gleaming leaves of emerald and amethyst. Rushing streams falling into silky cascades, the water streaked with rainbow hues. Glittering sparks and iridescent bubbles dancing through the air, coloring the whole world with their whimsical charm. Everything was beautiful, safe, familiar... It was *home*. Yet she didn't know where it lay.

While Worak hadn't returned since last night, he could at any moment. She wasn't sure if she'd survive his tortures next time. The only person she'd seen since the Sorci master's last visit was a cloaked magician she hadn't recognized, who had come to drop off a sack of food and canteen of water. That it hadn't been the person she'd expected, the one who had delivered her last few meals, made her heart skitter with worry.

"Where's Darien?" she'd asked, but the other hadn't responded.

Warning herself not to jump to conclusions, she tried to reassure herself with mundane explanations—that Darien had simply been assigned to other duties, or that he'd been sent out for supplies, or that that he was assisting Worak.

When she got out, she couldn't just take off and save herself. She had to find Darien first and persuade him to come away with her to a place where no one would hurt him again.

Tick. Tick. Tick. Steady as the timepiece sounded, the minute hand seemed to jerk arbitrarily when she wasn't looking. The little silver clock both terrified and comforted her. On the one hand, it served as a constant reminder that her days were running out. On the other, it was a piece of her and had restored her sense of self.

Holding it close to her heart, she closed her eyes, as she had a thousand times before, and reached within, searching for any sign of the magic that once lived there. Still and silent, she cleared her thoughts, becoming aware of every breath. Her pulse crescendoed, keeping in perfect time with the ticking.

Picturing herself floating as a being of colored air, Kiri called upon the memory of flying in hopes that it would help bring her latent abilities to the surface. A great, agonizing heat shot through her chest. She clenched her jaw. Grasping with her mind, she detected a distant spark crackling in her soul. Something was stirring, awakening.

This is it. Her powers, struggling to escape.

A brief burst of elation made her forget the heat. She'd never come so close before, and she clung to the slippery threads of her abilities, determined to pull them to the surface.

Invisible flames tore through her, bringing a cry of pain churning up her throat. This time, she couldn't stop it. With a million searing blades piercing her from every direction, she stumbled to her knees, but she managed to keep her concentration. With her eyes still shut, she gripped the flickering spark with her mind, kindling it with her thoughts.

A faint current of air swirled around her, warm and inviting. It was… It was *hers*. No, it *was* her. She knew it, just as she knew her own hands. Oh, wondrous breeze! It was a mere hint of what she'd once wielded, but it gave her the hope she needed to press on.

An explosion of fire, scorching her from the inside out, blasted through her chest, her stomach, her head, so strong that it brought her crashing to the ground. She held on to that precious spark nonetheless, keeping her focus inward. This torture was Worak, denying her the power that was rightfully hers, and she would not let him win.

Her fingertips tingled, but not from the heat of the curse. No, there was something else at work, nipping at her. The feeling was strange, yet familiar. Was she… Was it possible she was transforming into air?

An image flashed through her head—a new memory, breaking past the curse. The first thing she saw was herself, leaping from a grassy field. Her dress—the same she one she wore at present and a thin garment that tied at her nape, leaving her back almost entirely bare—whipped around her knees as she rose. Her legs became translucent, and the lines of her hips blurred, becoming a blue-and-white swirl vaguely shaped like a girl's figure. She was weightless and free, unfettered by whatever forces kept the rest of the world earthbound.

Suddenly, that sensation vanished, and her body became solid again. Her own weight crushed her, and she tumbled toward the ground. But right before she reached it, an invisible force caught her and righted her, until she was standing on her feet once again.

The curse's fire blazed through her with its raging fury, and she squeezed her eyes harder, needing to know what her past was trying to

tell her. In her memory, she spun in the field and found herself facing a pure white unicorn with a gleaming silver horn, blinking down at her with warm violet eyes. The sight filled Kiri with comfort, because she recognized this unicorn immediately as the one who had created her, nurtured her, protected her. In many ways, the great enchanted being was her mother.

"Amdyth!" The voice in the memory, tinged with anger, was her own. "Why did you do that?"

She was the reason I fell, Kiri realized. The unicorn called Amdyth—after whom she must have been named—had used her powers to stop Kiri from flying away.

In the memory, Kiri strode up to the majestic white creature, which gave off a soft glow, mesmerizing against the field of aubergine grass. "Why can't you let me go?"

Because I love you, my child. The words floated through Kiri's head, deep and resonant, in a kindly yet exasperated tone—Amdyth, speaking to her through her mind.

"I only want a look!" Kiri protested. "All the others—the fairies, the sprites, the merfolk—come and go as they please, so why are the nymphs the only ones who can't leave?"

To keep the peace. The unicorn blinked once, a slow, graceful movement representing infinite patience. *Our reign over Terra ended generations ago, for humankind desires dominance over this world, and had we not retreated into the enchanted domains, they would have driven us here. Too much life would have been lost in a fight, and we have enough. As nymphs are parts of the elements you are created from, the borders confining our lands confine you as well.*

"I know that!" Kiri crossed her arms. "Everyone knows that!"

Then you also know that the enchanted must stay away from the human. Amdyth took a step toward Kiri. *Even the Great Ones went into exile. Only the merpeople remained as they were, for their undersea world was already separate. The humans have their territory, and we have ours.*

"Yet others can wander the human lands while I'm trapped. How is that fair? I want to see the world too. Every day, I hear more stories of the wonders that lie beyond our borders—the great human cities with their machines and arts…" Kiri trailed off. The unicorn would never understand how much she yearned to go on an adventure like the ones she'd read about, to explore the magnificent unknown and experience its exciting

newness. She'd always been the odd one among her people for dreaming of such things. It had to have meant something, her desire to —

A sudden noise jolted Kiri back to the present, and all the magic around her — the pain of the curse, the thrill of her stirring powers, the flash of the memory — vanished. Quick footsteps approached from the dungeon's staircase. She cursed the disruption, but then her thoughts flew to the stolen clock in her hands. She scrambled for the brown sack she'd used to hide it.

The footsteps grew closer. They probably belonged to Worak, coming to torture her again. She shoved the clock into the corner and dropped the sack on top of it. There was no time for anything else; a man's dark figure rushed toward her.

Kiri faced the cell's small window, expecting to see Worak's cruel face on the other side. Instead, her eyes met Darien's obsidian gaze. He stood just beyond the bars, breathless from running.

Relief poured through her at knowing that he was all right. Or, at least, he looked unharmed. But a strange energy simmered beneath his furrowed brow, taut eyes, and clenched jaw… She couldn't tell if he was terrified, determined, or both.

"I'm getting you out." His whispered voice carried the force of the wind before a storm. As he grabbed the strap of the leather bag he carried on one shoulder, his gaze fell. "I'm sorry, I…" He shook his head. "I'm so sorry."

Kiri's head spun. Not knowing what to say — or whether she'd even heard him right — she stared in bewilderment.

"I won't ask you to forgive me. I didn't know…" He drew a breath. "Worak told me you were pretending, that the spell wasn't hurting you. I realize now that it was *he* that was lying. I-I'm sorry. I shouldn't have listened to him — I should have stopped him."

Hardly daring to believe her ears, Kiri watched him warily.

Darien looked up, fierceness crackling behind his eyes. "I know you have no reason to trust me, but if you'll let me, I'm going to do what I should have done days ago: I'm setting you free. If they hadn't been watching me so closely, I would have come last night."

The light of a thousand stars seemed to radiate from his core, and, unable to resist any longer, Kiri dared to let hope peek through.

Darien drew closer. "I beg you, say something. Say you'll let me help

you. Or, if you can't, I understand—tell me I don't deserve your trust. Curse me for all I care, just please… say something, Kiriall Amdyth. Tell me what you're thinking."

Still reeling from the great gusts of emotions whirling around her, Kiri found herself speechless. The panic of knowing her time was running out, subdued by the determination to survive. And the agony of being trapped, tempered by knowing that someone cared about her. Now, that someone, that lone hope in the darkness, was here, risking his life for her though he hardly even knew her. She didn't know how to express her gratitude, her admiration, her wonder. And so she spoke the only words her frenzied mind seemed capable of forming.

"I'm called Kiri." An involuntary smile tugged at her lips, and she let it blossom.

Darien returned it, and in that instant, all the shadows surrounding him vanished, melting into boyish sweetness. "Kiri. My name's Darien."

"I know." For an instant, there was no cell, no Worak, no danger. Just two people saying hello for the first time. Warmth tickled her heart, and she momentarily forgot where she was.

His smile vanished, and he reached into his bag. "I'm going to open wall of the ice. Stand back."

"*Don't!*" The word burst from Kiri's lips as it hit her just what he planned to do.

Darien gave her a puzzled look.

"They'll kill you," she whispered.

A wry smile quirked his lips. "I already broke the code when I gave you that clock. As long as I'm doomed, I might as well do as much as I can before they find out."

"I can't ask you to do this. Get out before your master catches you."

"I'm not leaving you here. I've left you long enough." He held up a clear crystal the size of her fist, which he must have taken from his bag, and pointed it at the wall between them.

A voice exploded through the dungeon. "*What is the meaning of this?*"

A cry tore past Kiri's throat.

Worak stood at the top of the staircase, a menacing figure more terrible than any nightmare. He threw back his hood, revealing a pallid face twisted with monstrous rage.

Darien whirled to face him. "Master—"

The master thrust his right fist at the apprentice, who fell to his knees and caved forward at the waist. Great crackling noises filled the air, and red bolts of magic wrapped around Darien's crumpled form. Though his face contorted with pain, he made no sound. But Kiri had felt the power of the magician's tortures enough times to know what he had to be enduring.

"*Stop!*" she screamed.

With his fist still clenched, Worak strode toward the youth. Glancing at the floor, he flicked his left hand. The crystal flew toward the magician, who caught it and examined it with narrowed eyes.

"You were trying to break her out." His face settled into a look of cold, deathly calm. As he tucked the crystal into the folds of his cloak, his eyes fell to the bag. "What do you have in there? More stolen items? The silver clock, no doubt?"

He squeezed his fist tighter, causing the bolts of magic to brighten. Still curled into himself, Darien spasmed.

"Let him go!" Despair filled Kiri's heart, but a powerful fury ignited behind it. She glared at the Sorci master. "Your fight is with me, Worak. Whatever rage you must unleash, aim it at me!"

Darien's eyes flicked in her direction, then raised to meet his master's. Trembling with effort, he lifted one hand as if about to attempt a spell of his own.

Worak twisted his fist. A horrible convulsion wracked Darien's body, and he grabbed his stomach with both arms as he fell forward, banging his head into the stone floor.

"*No!*" Anger pulsing through her, Kiri recalled how she'd taken hold of Worak's mind the previous night. If only she knew how she'd done that! She reached within herself, desperately searching for the magic.

Towering over his fallen apprentice, Worak growled, "You broke the Sorci code. How could you betray us, after everything we've done for you?"

"You lied." Darien's voice was choked with pain. "You lied about *everything.*"

"Worak!" A new voice burst through the dungeon.

Kiri whirled to face the staircase. An old man in an embroidered, twilight-blue cloak approached so quickly, his hood fell back, revealing a leathery face bearded in white. Behind him, two other magicians followed: the woman called Limali and a man the size of a bear.

"What are you doing?" The old man's crinkled gray eyes filled with horror.

A surge of hope swept over Kiri. Though she held the others in no high regard, maybe they would at least intervene to help one of their own.

Worak glanced at the old man. "Ah, Vimunax." His gaze moved to the other two. "And Limali, and Gilonar. I am glad you three are here to bear witness." He unclenched his fist, and the bolts surrounding his apprentice disappeared.

Darien glanced up at the other three magicians. "He's working for Inferno!" With pained movements, he stood and pointed at Worak. "I heard him speaking to a gui—everything he's doing is for the Fiend!"

The Fiend? Terror sliced across Kiri's heart. Ruthless as Worak was, she'd never imagined he'd go so far. Her blood churned. The magician had betrayed every one of the Divinity's creations—human and enchanted, Terrestrial and Celestial. He'd betrayed the Divinity Herself.

The rage in Darien's eyes matched her own anger, but none of the others appeared troubled. Instead, they stood in stone-faced silence.

They already knew. New horror lanced through Kiri.

Darien's expression darkened as he took in the others' lack of surprise. "You're all working for Inferno too. Does this entire order belong to the Fiend?"

Worak extended one arm at him. "*Bind!*" An unnatural resonance amplified his voice, and a volley of yellow bolts flew at the youth, who stumbled back then jerked upright as if yanked by an invisible rope.

Darien's wrists snapped together, bound by invisible chains, and he lurched forward as the spell pulled him toward the thick wooden post at the dungeon's center.

"*Stop it!*" Kiri must have screamed those words a thousand times since waking in this cursed place. *I have the power to end this… If I can look into*

Worak's eyes... That was how she'd unleashed her mind-bending powers last time. She could do it again.

Angling herself by the window, she searched for Worak's glare, but the magician's attention was fixed on directing his apprentice toward the post, from which two black manacles dangled.

"You *monster!*" she cried. "Let him go!" She just needed him to look her way, even if it was to silence her, but no matter how she called, he ignored her.

Worak flicked his finger, and the manacles opened, metal jaws ravenous for their next victim. They snapped shut around Darien's wrists.

Kiri's panicked breaths quickened. Frustrated, she continued searching for the power, but nothing stirred.

"Darien Jekh Zakar, you have broken your oath." Worak punched his hand forward, and a white-blue bolt of magic lanced through Darien's chest. Gripping the chains that bound him, he crumpled toward the post with an expression of agony.

Tears stung Kiri's eyes. *Look this way, Worak.* But she felt no whisper of latent magic, nothing to indicate that her command was anything more than an empty wish.

Though the master's face remained frigid, his eyes snapped with rage. "The Sorci code states that any person who breaks it must die. I am sorry, young one, but you are no exception. The sentence will be carried out immediately, for I will not suffer a traitor to live."

"*No!*" Kiri banged her fists against the cell's wall.

"Worak, *enough!*" The old man called Vimunax strode up to the master, his lined face tense with worry.

Hope fluttered in Kiri's heart.

Vimunax grabbed Worak's shoulder. "You've made your point. Now—"

"The code is absolute!" Worak threw off the old man's grip and glared with eyes that could have boiled steel. "The apprentice has betrayed us!"

"He's a *child.*" Vimunax's wrinkled eyes pleaded. "You said it yourself—the nymph bewitched him!"

He flung one hand in Kiri's direction, and for once, she had no desire to deny the false accusation. In fact, she couldn't believe she hadn't thought of it herself.

"I did!" she yelled. "It was my fault! I-I forced him to help me!"

Darien glanced at her and shook his head. His lips parted, but before he could speak, a great *boom* shook the air.

Kiri jumped back as green smoke exploded around Worak and Vimunax. When it cleared, the old man lay on the ground, eyes shut and body slack. For a moment, she thought he was dead, but then she noticed a faint breath rustling the white hairs of his beard.

Worak looked down at him coldly. "Our code has stood through a thousand generations. It must be upheld, and I will not let anyone stop me." He turned to the other two followers, who remained as still as statues, then spun back to Darien. "A life of great power and great reward, but for that, great prices must be paid. A life of truth and clarity for those strong enough to lead it. The way of endurance and trials, for only the strong are worthy of the power we wield. But you, young one, are no longer one of us. Even if what Vimunax said is true, your weakness proves that you are unworthy of our order."

"I defy you for what is right." Darien's eyes blazed. "There will be a reckoning, and when the forces of Inferno are defeated, you, too, will fall, *Master*." He spat the last word.

Worak let out a dry laugh. "I'm afraid you won't live to see that day. For your crimes, you will die as the Sorci live — in pain."

He threw off his cloak with one quick, sweeping gesture. With a malicious gleam in his eyes, the magician held out his arm and flexed his hand. Staring at his palm, he whispered something inaudible, and a thick line of golden light materialized above his arm, snaking through the air. When the brightness faded, it left behind a long leather whip interwoven with metal wires whose sharp, protruding ends glinted. It looked as thick and solid as a club, and a pointed hook jutted from the tip like a metal fang.

What lightforsaken weapon is that? Kiri turned away, unable to watch Worak murder her one ally.

No, not just murder. Torture him to death.

I can't give up. Maybe if she escaped the cell, she could attack Worak and force him to engage her. She'd awakened a hint of her power over the wind just moments ago — she had to try again.

Closing her eyes, she reached and reached within, not caring if her efforts awakened the excruciating curse. She'd rather face it a thousand times than stand helpless.

A great crack shattered the air, followed by the horrible impact of leather and metal meeting flesh.

Resisting the instinct to open her eyes, she tried to recall the sensation of flying. Imagining the thrill of soaring above the world, she pictured herself as colorful wisps and —

A second crack. It seemed to land on her heart, and tears burned her eyes. Though Darien made no sound, she'd seen the weapon. Such a monstrosity would cause its victim unbearable agony, breaking flesh, spilling blood, cracking bone, and, if allowed to complete its gruesome task, ending life.

Focus! she ordered herself. But her head rushed with the horror of what was happening and the terror that she couldn't stop it in time and the guilt that it was all somehow her fault and the anger at the injustice and —

She wanted to scream, cry, break things. Clenching her fists, she tried to push back the invading thoughts, but they kept filling her mind, crowding out the memories she needed.

Another crack. And then another. And then another. How many did it take to kill a person? She was running out of time, and her cursed mind continued to mutiny, denying her the concentration she needed. Despair encroached, wrapping its leaden hands around her, and, try as she might, she couldn't fight it off.

Darien was going to die. Because of her — because she'd called on him for help, and he'd answered.

Another crack, this time followed by a tortured scream.

Her eyes flew open, and what she saw sent tears cascading down her cheeks. Darien had been stripped of his shirt, and his back was latticed with blood. Red dripped from the whip in Worak's hand as he wound back for another blow. Meanwhile, the other two magicians stood behind their leader, silent and still. Each had one hand extended toward the bound apprentice, with strands of white smoke extending from their fingers.

The sight of Darien's anguished face sent a tornado of rage careening through Kiri. White-hot wrath blazed in every corner of her mind, burning away everything else.

A tremor rumbled within her. Her magic, straining against the cursed bonds.

The spiked lash came down again, and Darien collapsed against the post. Her anger flared, and the tremor within doubled in force.

Fiery pain erupted in her chest, its tendrils stabbing her head and piercing her legs. But she embraced the curse, for it told her she was getting close.

The rumbling grew stronger, until she was sure her bones would shatter, and a million sparks crackled within. Recognizing their energy, she grasped them with her mind. Scorching flames bloomed through every bone, but the part of her that would once have collapsed in agony remained mute, drowned by the determination fueling her. All the fires of Inferno leaped through her, so hot, even the Fiend himself would have howled at their touch.

Then, a great upsurge of power burst forth. It was *hers*, within her control at last. She punched her hands forward, and a blast of wind, stronger than any hurricane, slammed into the wall, splintering the ice. The shards exploded into the room outside, filling the dungeon with frozen projectiles.

Kiri glimpsed Worak's startled expression in the instant before several chunks smashed into his body, sending him flying. A great *thud* cut off his holler of surprise as he plunged into the floor. For an instant, a flush of satisfaction coursed through her veins.

Unable to hold on any longer, she lost her grip on her magic. The rumbling ceased, and the air stilled. Her legs melted beneath her.

The floor's frigidity felt welcome against Kiri's fevered cheek. Blackness crashed down. With no strength left to fight, she let it take her.

ELSEWHERE...

"Who is this strange beauty who's blown into our path? My apologies, oh Fiend, for failing to regard her more closely. But she seems simple enough to decipher. Another noble heart, another kind spirit. These are things that, when presented in a package so lovely, draw the affections of others all too easily. She will be no hindrance; on the contrary, she is exactly what we need."

5

Kill them all

TOMORROW...

For as long as he could remember, Darien had stumbled down the tangled pathways of possibility, wondering what destiny awaited him at the end of each and yearning to find one that would lead him to a place where he belonged. But now, a force stronger than will, fiercer than love, and darker than wrath had decided his fate for him, erasing the questions of "what if" and pulling him down the lone road that remained.

And he had no power to stop it, for all his efforts had been futile, and all choices mere illusions.

TODAY...

HE CHILLED AIR DID LITTLE TO DULL THE STINGS stretching across Darien's back, and though the blows had ended, he still felt the lash ripping, shredding, tearing him to pieces. Blood streamed down his skin, and he drew a sharp breath. His hands remained clenched around the chains, the manacles still binding his wrists, but at least the invisible cords from the Sorci's spells had vanished. They'd restrained more than his body; they'd kept him from calling upon his own nascent powers. Each time he'd tried summoning a spell to free or shield himself, vicious flames had devoured the waking magic, thwarting his efforts and draining his strength.

Now, with Worak and the others unconscious, the sorcerous binds were gone, leaving only the physical ones. The magicians had fallen so quickly, he still couldn't believe what had happened. The air nymph—Kiri—had sent forth a mighty gale, splintering the wall of ice and striking down the Sorci. Yet the shards had missed him entirely.

Shivering, Darien turned to look at her, but even that slight movement sent a flash of agony surging through his frayed skin. Though he'd been training to grow immune to pain, nothing could have prepared him for what Worak had done. His blood simmered at the very name of his master—*former* master—and the powerful desire to crush the man's skull flared through him.

But then, his eyes fell on Kiri, and all thought of the magicians evaporated. The nymph lay sprawled on her back, having collapsed from the effort. With her silver-blond hair fanned out beneath her head and her willowy arms spread by her sides, she almost looked like she was floating in water rather than lying on a bed of iron. Hauntingly beautiful even in sleep, she lay so still, even her breath failed to move her chest. *Skies, what if the effort killed her?*

Remembering the mysterious prophecy that had invaded his mind, he shuddered at the realization that in his effort to prevent it, he might have ensured its occurrence. *If the windborn one dies…*

An ache stabbed his heart, sending forth a sudden wave of tears. He squeezed his eyes to bar them passage. *No. She's alive.*

He started toward her, but with the manacles still digging into his wrists, barely made it a step. Before he could help her, he had to free himself.

Eyes shut, he focused on the binds and thought only of them unclasping. The familiar feeling of waking magic churned in his chest, sending a volley of razors darting through his insides. "*Open*," he whispered.

He gritted his teeth as the spell hacked its way into his shoulders and through his arms, seeming to tear muscle from bone with every rolling movement. Hearing a low hum from the direction of the post, he opened his eyes but was careful to keep his concentration inward.

Tiny yellow sparks materialized around his wrists, blinking like fireflies. One by one, the glittering magic shot into the cuffs, until the metal glowed as if fresh from the forge. The binds vibrated against his skin.

"*Open*," he commanded. "*Open…*"

With a sudden *clink*, the manacles obeyed. He hadn't realized he'd been clinging to their chains for support, and the movement, slight as it was, was enough to unbalance his unsteady legs. He grabbed the post in time to keep weakness from dragging him to the ground. His body yearned to recline on the floor and let sleep wash over him.

But there was no time for that, with Worak lying mere yards away.

Darien couldn't have fought the Sorci master if he'd had all his strength, and at the moment, he was feebler than a newborn foal. Moreover, there were two others who wanted him dead. The third had tried to help him, and gratitude flooded his heart as his eyes fell on Vimunax. *If ever we meet again, old man, I won't forget that you alone defended me.*

He released the post and tried to straighten, but a deluge of burning, stinging pain overwhelmed him, and he had to grip it again to keep upright.

Blazes! How will I get out of here when I can barely stand? Especially since he'd have to carry Kiri; even if she no longer breathed, he refused to leave her in the dark dungeon. Though she'd blown apart the wall of ice, the iron bars remained, and he'd need to remove at least one to reach her.

His mind flew back to what he'd been doing before Worak had caught him, recalling how the magician had stuffed the clarion stone — an enchanted item he'd stolen to aid their escape — into the folds of his cloak. It was one of several crystals mined from the land under a magical nexus, where supernatural powers converged on Terra, and it could both focus and augment a magician's powers. However, its usage was limited, for each spell cast through it turned a bit of it back into ordinary rock.

Without it, he'd never reach Kiri. Protective magic ran through every wall, every door, every window of the Sapphire Bastille. Spotting Worak's cloak on the floor, Darien staggered toward it. Even those few steps took more strength than his body was willing to give, and he didn't so much crouch beside it as collapse to his knees. Wincing from his still-bleeding wounds, he rummaged through the thick, embellished cloth until his fingers met the crystal's faceted surface.

As he closed his hand it, the enchanted stone hummed. A low, otherworldly sound, more felt than heard, unnerving and powerful at once. The sensation sent a trickle of warmth up his arm. For a moment, the burn of his lacerated back dulled, and the leaden heaviness of his limbs retreated. Just holding a clarion stone granted its wielder a small, temporary rush of strength, and it felt especially potent in his present state.

The warmth vanished, and he flinched at the sudden influx of pain. His head drooped, and darkness encroached his vision. No matter how he tried to persuade himself that he could muscle through with enough willpower, he couldn't deny that his strength was fading fast.

Darien considered the stone. Healing himself seemed like such an indulgence when Kiri was hurt—possibly dead—and there might be precious little time before the Sorci awakened. Not to mention, it would consume some of the stone's limited magic.

He tried to stand, but his legs refused to hold him, and he barely caught himself as he fell forward. His whole body felt cold from the inside out—not just from the frigid air, but from the weakness bearing down upon him.

I won't do Kiri much good if I black out. So he tightened his grip on the enchanted crystal and looked into its gleaming surface, hoping he wouldn't need to use too much of its power to restore himself to a functional state.

His thoughts latched on to the memory of what it had given him, and he pictured the rush of warmth as a golden light. Then, calling upon the magic within, he beckoned, asking the stone to grant him that sensation once again—and let him keep it.

A tiny white light flickered in the crystal's center, and its hum grew louder, as if whispering, *As you wish.*

The abrupt feeling of a fanged jaw clamping down on the hand grasping the stone nearly made him drop it. He let the pain sink in. *As far as magic goes, this isn't so bad.*

The rush of warmth returned, flowing from the crystal and spreading through his body with shocking speed. He'd never felt such power or such ease before. Was this how Worak felt when he wielded his spells? Part of him wanted to seize the force and blast it into the wall, just to see what it would do. But magic was not to be toyed with, and doing so would be wasteful. Already, one of the stone's edges was fading from its pellucid clarity into a dull gray.

Deciding he was well enough, Darien broke his thoughts away from the magic and opened his hand. The warmth faded once again. He wasn't fully restored—far from it, since blood still trickled from some of his wounds—but he no longer felt ready sink into the ground either. The crystal's glow died away, and the power's invisible maw released his hand.

Shivering, he stood. His eyes fell on the leather bag packed with a handful of supplies for the escape. He grabbed it and retrieved a spare shirt. Though the crimson garment hardly guarded against the frigid air, it was better than nothing. As he shouldered the bag's strap, he contemplated taking Worak's cloak, but the idea made his stomach twist. *I want nothing to do with that infernal cur.*

The thought that he'd spent half a year serving such evil made fury smolder in his core — both at the Sorci and at himself for having sludge for brains. He glared at Worak. *The Sorci were once great protectors and healers. How could you have betrayed thousands of years of goodness and led the order into Inferno?* Sorrow surged beneath the wrath, but that only made it grow hotter. *You were supposed to guide me along a higher path, and for that, I would have given my life for you had you asked. Instead, you deceived me.* Tears of rage burned his eyes. *I can't believe I was foolish enough to trust you.*

Unconscious, Worak no longer appeared to be the awe-inspiring magician who'd spun a false world from melodious lies. No, he looked like just another man.

He's as helpless as a sleeping child. A dark voice slipped into Darien's mind. *Take the knife from your bag. Cut his throat. Rid the world of a monster.* There lay the one who had lured him into a wicked order and tried to kill him for leaving. Such evil had to be destroyed.

Shaking with anger, he felt his hand automatically reach for the weapon. *Kill him,* his thoughts urged. *And the others too. Kill them all.*

It would be easy, with his enemies asleep. It would be smart, since he would eliminate the threats they posed. And it would be justified.

His grip closed around the handle of his knife. With the blade in one hand in the clarion stone in the other, he wielded the weapons of both thrones and magic. Nothing could stop his revenge. He moved toward Worak, aiming to start with him, then finish the others.

Kill them all… Kill them all…

His arm raised the knife on its own. He barely felt the movement; it would be so easy… so, so easy…

Worak is evil… He kills with no thought… Cut his throat now, before he wakes…

Darien froze, suddenly aware of how close his blade was to the unconscious man. He didn't recall crouching down. *If I do this, wouldn't that make me as evil as him?*

It doesn't matter, the voice whispered. *He deserves to die.*

Yes, he does. Yet a feeling of wrongness pervaded. Perhaps it was because he'd never taken a life before and had never thought he would. Perhaps it was cowardice. Or perhaps it was the Ayr of Mercy trying to guide him…

A soft groan interrupted his thoughts. Behind the iron bars of the cell, Kiri stirred. "Darien? What are you doing?"

Darien glanced at the knife, and horror flooded him as he realized that in his rage, he'd completely forgotten about her. *What* am *I doing?*

There was no honor in killing a man, even a wicked one, in his sleep—only sheer malevolence, like the kind the Fiend delighted in. And the kind his followers undoubtedly embraced.

I won't be like you, Woruk. Darien shoved the blade into his bag and rushed to Kiri's cell. "Are you all right?"

Her eyes fell shut.

Spurred by urgency, Darien aimed the crystal at one of the iron bars and called upon the magic. *"Bar of iron, retreat."*

He gritted his teeth as what felt like a thick spear plunged into his back. A rush of heat raced down the arm that held the crystal, which grew warm and quaked in his hand. The force twisted slowly through his ribs, seeming to rip his bones. The air around his hands rattled, and he sensed it reaching toward the bar, then gripping it.

An explosion of power flowed through his fingers from the crystal, charging at his target. The iron bar briefly glowed white, then vanished, leaving enough space for him to step into the cell.

The air stilled. Stars filled the small window opposite him, but none of the Estal Magora—the brightest and most prominent stars that represented the main virtues—were visible. He couldn't imagine what it must have been like, being trapped in here with only that sliver of the outside world.

"Kiri?"

She didn't respond. He knelt beside her. The mild contours of her face sloped with gentle perfection, and her rosy lips curved with beguiling softness. No wonder why there were so many tales of men dying in vain attempts to reach her kind. But she was more than the physical beauty she shared with her elemental sisters—so much more. She was courage, and strength, and selflessness, and a million other things his mind couldn't find the words to describe.

He placed one hand on her shoulder and shook her gently. "Kiri?"

Her face remained slack, and her body limp. Her blue dress looked thinner than paper, and her skin was cold under his touch.

The plain black cloak he'd given her lay at the cell's edge, and he ran to get it. As he picked it up, a thought struck him: *The silver clock... she'll want it.*

Though he'd told her to keep it hidden, there weren't many places she could conceal it within the tiny cell. His gaze fell on a brown sack in the corner, and when he lifted it, he found the little engraved timepiece, whose slender black hands pointed at five o'clock, even though it was well past that in reality. *Strange device.*

After dropping it in his bag, he returned to Kiri's side, placed the cloak over her, and tucked its edges under her. The nymph's delicate frame seemed too fragile to house the great power she'd wielded, and a pang of guilt stabbed him. He'd come to help her, yet she'd ended up saving him. How could he ever repay her?

I can't. Such a debt was beyond any price; he could walk through the blazes of Inferno at her behest and still owe her. *But I can take her home.*

Carrying her in his arms, he made his way out of the cell.

ELSEWHERE...

"My Master! You ask to know what's happened? A victory — that's my answer. He thinks he's won a battle against his foes, that he's the commander of his fate, but in truth, he's only taken another step down the road we've laid out for him. And he is ignorant to the truth. He thinks I'm asleep. He thinks I'm his defender. In due time, he will think of me as a friend. That, oh Lord, will be the key to his undoing."

6

You are not alone

So there she stood, at the edge of Inferno, feeling the chaotic fury of thousand knives shred her within. Who was the monster before her, and where was the Darien she had trusted with her life, with her heart, with her very soul? Had the flames of Inferno truly consumed the brave young man she'd known, leaving only a tantalizing shell? Those were the same obsidian eyes that had once given her courage when hope seemed out of reach, and yet the hollow darkness behind them belonged to someone else: the Fiend.

TODAY...

*"*KIRI! DOWN HERE!" THE FIRE NYMPH *beckoned, her emerald eyes dancing. Elaia… that was her name. A friend. More than that — a piece of Kiri's lost past. One look at the girl, and she was home.*

Flames leaped around the other's thick, flowing locks, which faded from deep auburn at the scalp to reddish blond at the tips, as playful as the energy in her voice. Her lively green dress rippled around her curved hips, flowing from a breeze Kiri realized she was causing.

She didn't know where Elaia was headed, but a tugging in her heart urged her to go with her. Wherever this beautiful, vibrant girl led, she would follow. And so she flew toward her, a bright smile on her lips.

The fire nymph reached one shapely bronze arm toward her, and Kiri took the hand she offered. She though the other meant to fly beside her, but instead, Elaia gave an abrupt tug. Startled, Kiri couldn't stop herself from crashing into the girl, and the next thing she knew, both of them were tumbling into the soft, turquoise grass.

She yelped in surprise as she landed on Elaia, who giggled melodiously.

Realizing she'd done this on purpose, Kiri smacked the girl's shoulder. "Elaia!"

"You should have seen the look on your face!" With her bright grin, Elaia looked like the very picture of merriment, and her high, musical laugh radiated joy. All the brightness of the sun twinkled in her eyes, catching Kiri in their spell.

For several moments, she just watched her friend laugh, mesmerized by the beauty and delighted by the comfort of the fire nymph's presence. She wanted to stay in this moment forever, happy and safe — and with someone close to her heart.

The flames of Elaia's hair leaped at Kiri, scorching her with a hotness so sharp, she screamed. She threw her hands before her face and scrambled to get up. This was strange — a fire nymph's blaze wouldn't burn a twig... unless she wanted it to.

But though Kiri rushed to back away, the flames followed, swallowing her and sending pain erupting through her. Still covering her face, she cried, "Stop! Why are you doing this?"

Elaia only laughed in response. This wasn't like her... something was terribly wrong...

Steeling herself, Kiri uncovered her face. To her surprise, the only flames she saw danced from the tips of Elaia's red, wavy locks, which remained tangled in the grass several feet away. Thick silver mist filled the space between Kiri and the fire nymph, making the other appear ghostly pale. And that laugh — it wasn't the girl's anymore, but a precise imitation, repeating the same few cadences without true life.

Then it struck her: This was a dream.

And the mist — Kiri knew its touch. The invisible fire was the same as the one that had attacked when she'd tried to call upon her powers or recover her memories.

Suddenly, Elaia appeared before her, wrapped in the full glory of her flames, which surrounded her in a translucent veil of red and yellow.

"Come with me." Her red lips tilted in a mischievous smile, and she ran into the smoky expanse.

Though the mist and fire obscured her vision, Kiri caught a glimpse of the other nymph's bare back, exposed by the style of her dress. There was something drawn across it — a tangle of curved mahogany lines. An uncanny feeling struck her, telling her that whatever it was, that image was important. It was a piece of Elaia, a piece of home, a piece of Kiri herself... The thoughts dominated her head, but she couldn't understand why. All she knew was that she needed to see it, to understand what it meant, but already the mist was swallowing Elaia —

A sudden *bang* crashed through Kiri's ears, and her eyes flew open, but all she saw was blackness. Fear gripped her heart. Even during the night's darkest hours, she should have seen *something*, illuminated by either the golden ball of warmth or the firelight of the dungeon's single lantern.

Meanwhile, her entire body, heavy with weakness, seemed ready to melt into the hard floor she lay upon. She drew one arm beside her to press against the ground and realized that the thick cloth of a cloak surrounded her. It had to be the one Darien had given her, but how had she ended up wrapped in it? The last thing she remembered was unleashing all the forces of the wind she could muster and shattering the wall of ice. Though she found the garment's warmth comforting, it hindered her movement, and she shrugged it off as she sat up.

"Kiri!"

A whispered voice called from behind, and she spun. A line of yellow-brown light ran along the ground. *What's that?*

Darien's face came into sight, lit by a luminous sphere of white hovering above his palm. Evidently, he'd escaped. A relieved sigh escaped her, yet her confusion remained. Where were the iron bars that should have stood between them?

A memory surfaced—she'd glimpsed him crouching over Worak, holding a blade to the unconscious man's throat with a strange, almost feral look in his eyes. Had he slain the master? Though she told herself the killing would have been justified, she shuddered at the possibility.

She opened her mouth to ask what had happened, but Darien pressed his finger to his lips. "Keep quiet," he whispered, kneeling beside her. "Worak and the others are searching for us."

That means the master's still alive. She didn't know why, but she felt relief.

The sound of muffled footsteps approached, and Darien's gaze flew to the line of yellowish-brown on the ground. Pressing his mouth into a tense line, he closed his hands around the floating sphere of light. A few rays slipped through his fingers, highlighting the anxiety in his eyes.

We're in a dark room. Kiri realized what the light on the floor was: the gap between a door and a threshold. Had the banging that awakened her been the sound of the door closing? In the time she'd been unconscious, Darien must have found a way to get her past the iron bars, and now they were hiding from the Sorci.

Gratitude and gladness glowed in her heart. No more walls of ice blocking her from the world. No more bars of iron standing between her and the freedom she so craved. No more huddling in terror, wondering when her captors would return and torture her again.

But reality soon doused her joy with a cold splash of fear. The masters of dark magic were surely seeking revenge against those who had defied them, and they would show no mercy. Her eyes fixed on the crack. Any moment, she might see a shadow stop before it — that of Worak, coming for them. She shuddered.

A gentle hand clasped her shoulder. She glanced over and caught Darien's gaze, which somehow spoke to her without words.

It's going to be all right, he seemed to say, his eyes glinting from the escaped rays of the enchanted light he held.

The sensation of his skin against hers was at once comforting and strange, filled with the warmth of companionship, yet foreign.

Darien withdrew, but she wished he hadn't, for his touch had told her, *You are not alone.*

Outside, the footsteps drew closer, and her breath stopped.

Then, it came: the dreaded shadow. Small at first, blocking just the end of the gap, but growing, growing, growing, until it covered half the light. Someone was standing right outside. Any moment, she would hear the rattling of the doorknob and the creaking of the hinges.

I'll fight him, she thought firmly. Beside her, Darien tensed.

A quiet voice came through the door: "Run, my boy!"

What? Kiri's gaze snapped toward Darien.

The shadow disappeared in a burst of bright yellow light. For several moments, silence hung in the air. Darien's drawn brows told her that he was as puzzled as she was.

"That voice belonged to Vimunax," he muttered, still staring at the door gap. "I don't understand."

Neither do I. The aged magician was surely risking himself to help Darien, yet he was also among those who served the Infernal Realm, and, though Kiri didn't remember his face specifically, likely one who had helped Worak torture her.

"Despite who the old man serves, some compassion must remain," she mused aloud.

"The world can't just be simple, can it?" Darien uncovered the enchanted light. Brightness splashed across his face, throwing shadows under his sharp cheekbones and highlighting the confusion in his eyes. "Worak saved my brother's life—and mine. Every word I've ever heard spoken about the Sorci told me that they were peaceful and sought only to use magic to aid humanity. I've seen them cure disease and assist the needy without asking for any reward. I thought they were quiet heroes, helping humankind in ways that weren't glorious to tell of but vitally important to those whose lives they touched. And someday, I thought, they would be Terra's defenders against the Age of Fire. *This* was why I swore myself to them: I wanted to be a hero too." He glanced away, clenching one fist. "How could I have known it was all a lie?"

Kiri's heart ached for him. She couldn't imagine what had to be going through his head, knowing that everything he had devoted his life to had been a falsehood.

"Never mind." Though he relaxed his expression, a cloud of anger shaded his eyes. "That's yesterday's concern, now, and it's tomorrow I'm worried about." His face warmed. "Don't be afraid. I swear, I won't abandon you again. Until you're safe, I won't leave your side."

Safe…

Kiri scarcely recalled what that word even meant. Her only memories were of being confined and tormented. *That's not true*, she reminded herself. She had recollections—precious few as they were—of another place, another life. A world of enchantment she had once called home. Beautiful. Serene.

Safe.

She suddenly realized that she'd forgotten all about the silver clock. Her pulse raced, and she could almost hear the *tick, tick, tick* of the little timepiece.

Darien's eyes filled with worry. "What's wrong?"

"What land is this?" she asked.

"Eryu, near the border with Nikhilim." He might as well have been speaking a code for all the sense she could make of his words.

"I… I'm afraid I don't know human domains."

"It's all right. I'll help you get home—I know the layout of these kingdoms pretty well. Where do you need to go?"

Kiri shook her head. "I can't remember where my land is or what it's called."

"That complicates things." Darien frowned. "It's because of the curse, isn't it? If I lifted it, you would recall."

"You can do that?" she asked, not daring to believe it. An end to the curse—the powers and memories locked away by the Sorci would be hers once more, and she would be whole again.

Concern crossed his eyes. "I wasn't there when Worak cast the spell, and so I don't know what he used, but the power to perform all types of magic resides within every human, including me. And I have this." He reached behind him and retrieved a clear crystal. "If there is a way, I will find it."

Despite his reassurance, doubt clouded her thoughts. She trusted his intentions, but could someone who'd apprenticed a mere six months really undo the master's sorcery? Nevertheless, she had to let him try.

"Go ahead," she said.

Darien tipped the hand above which their source of light glowed, and the floating sphere drifted toward the ground, stopping an inch from the stone surface. Aiming the crystal in her direction, he closed his eyes.

A white light ignited in the stone's center, throwing an otherworldly tint upon the room. Only then did Kiri realize where they actually were: A closet, no more than a few square feet in area, with green stone shelves lining it from the floor to the high ceiling. Outlandish gadgets decorated with strange symbols, ranging from tiny, angular ciphers to grand, swirling emblems, crowded each, and she couldn't begin to guess what they were for.

An invisible force clamped down on her. Gasping, she looked to Darien, who remained still but for the lines forming between his eyebrows. From the crystal, which he now clasped with both hands, a glittering white mist reached toward her. She instinctively drew back, then reminded herself that this was *Darien's* magic and wouldn't hurt her as Worak's had.

The mist spiraled around her. Cold, tingling sensations rushed through her wherever it touched, and soon, it enveloped her face as well, throwing a thick, icy shroud over her vision.

"*Release her,*" Darien whispered, and the sound hissed with the eeriness of a lonely winter wind, resonating with magic.

Scarcely had the words left him when great pain exploded in Kiri's chest. She barely managed to stifle a shocked cry, and panicked thoughts filled her head as the spell bit her with the same fury Worak's curse had. Countless needle-sharp arrows darted through her body, bringing agony with every movement, and it was all she could do to contain her screams. Had Darien made a mistake? Or was this part of the magic needed to free her?

Heat burst through her. The flaming swords of Worak's curse spread through her entire body, and she clenched her jaw hard. The pain was becoming too much, and she felt it eating away at her already meager strength. Her life was breaking down—she could feel it.

"Stop!" she said through gritted teeth, but the sound emerged as hardly more than a whisper.

The blaze continued raging. Leaden weights bloomed around her head and limbs while blackness splattered her vision. Every corner of her mind screamed one thought: *You're killing me!*

Her gaze fell on the glowing crystal, and with a desperate blow, she knocked it out of Darien's grasp.

It hit the floor with a *thud*, and the glow vanished from its center. She barely caught the confused look in Darien's eyes before she collapsed toward him.

He caught her shoulders, his breaths short and his face glistening with sweat—an incongruous sight in the chill. "What's wrong?"

"The curse," she whispered. "It was trying to kill me. If you'd continued, it would have."

A horrified look filled his eyes. "I-I didn't know. I'm sorry. I didn't mean to hurt you. I thought… If I'd known… "

"I know." She managed a vague smile. "I'm grateful for your efforts."

Darien glanced at the crystal. In the faint light, she noticed that it was not entirely lucent; one its facets appeared to be gray rock. "I don't understand. Perhaps if I—"

"No!" She tried to continue, to tell him that she was sure any repeat effort would claim her life, but her tongue was too weary to form the words. Her head drooped against his chest, and she struggled to keep her eyes from falling shut.

Darien wrapped his arms around her. "Please, forgive me. I would never hurt you… not on purpose."

I know, she repeated in her head, but she couldn't find the strength to speak.

"Worak must have designed the curse to kill its victim if anyone tried removing it," he muttered. "I should have known. I… I should have known a lot of things."

She wanted to say, *You were not the one who captured me and cursed me. This is Worak's doing, not yours.*

For several moments, she lay against him in silence, waiting for the effects of the magic to wear off. It seemed to be taking longer than it had in the past, though she didn't know if it was because she was still exhausted from using her abilities or if it had something to do with the way the curse had attacked her. Either way, one thing was certain: She couldn't let him try lifting the curse again. Next time, she might not survive.

But with her memories still bound, how could she find her way home? The Terrestrial Realm was a vast, vast place.

A thought tugged at her mind — the sense of urgency she'd experienced as she'd run through the mists of her dream. Once, she might have dismissed it as nonsense, but she knew better this time. The first dream she'd experienced after finding herself in the Sorci's clutches had shown her the tree from which her enchanted silver clock grew, and she'd thought it an impossible image. But it was because she'd assumed herself to be a human girl, though why that would be her default identity when she'd probably never met one before remained a mystery. Perhaps it had been part of the curse; if Worak hadn't wanted her using her abilities, then he wouldn't want her knowing she had them at all — so she couldn't even try.

Elaia's smiling face flashed through her mind. Though Kiri didn't possess more than a glimpse of their past together, her heart recognized the other even if her mind didn't. But right before she'd awakened, the curse had attacked that memory. There had been something more… something the dark magic had been trying to keep from her. A mark on her friend's back, etched into her skin. She'd needed to see it; there was something it could have told her…

"The mark," Darien whispered, interrupting her thoughts.

Kiri glanced up at him, startled. Some of the strength was trickling back into her limbs, and she slowly tried to sit up. He was so close she could feel his breath upon her face, and as he helped her, a feeling of warmth trickled through her.

"What did you mean?" she asked, finding it an odd coincidence that he'd spoken the very word she'd been thinking of.

"I remembered something I read once." He drew back. "All nymphs bear the mark of their homeland somewhere on their bodies, drawn by magic when they come of age. I think you have one on your back—I thought I saw a white tattoo there."

The image of curved mahogany lines running down Elaia's skin returned to her mind, along with the uncanny feeling that had accompanied it. *A piece of Elaia, a piece of home, a piece of myself…*

She twisted her neck in an attempt to glimpse her back, but all she was her own hair tumbling over her shoulder. Then, she realized the foolishness of the effort. She couldn't spin her head around, after all.

She glanced at Darien. "Can you check?"

He nodded, and she turned away from him. His hand brushed her skin as he swept her locks over her shoulder, and the heat of his touch sent a sudden shiver down her spine. She'd grown so accustomed to having her waist-length hair covering her back that their absence left her feeling exposed and vulnerable. Yet the fear that ordinarily accompanied such sensations was absent.

As his fingertips grazed the small knot of her dress at the base of her neck, she wondered whether the reason her clothing left her back bare was in order to display the tattoo. "Is something there?" she asked.

"Yes!" Darien sounded excited. "A white tree."

Catching a glow in the corner of her eye, she glanced back to see a faint light emitting from his hands. He stared into them, his brow drawn with concentration, and she realized he was casting another spell. *"Show what the light shows."*

One of the lights stretched into a round mirror, hovering inches above his palm. But the angle was off, showing the opposite profile of the one it should have reflected. Then, he turned his other hand, which held only shimmering glow, and the image shifted, displaying the edge of her arm and the floor. The mirror wasn't reflecting what it was turned toward, but what the light fell on.

Holding the first hand in place, he reached around her with the mirror, raising the reflection before her eyes. "Look."

The mirror's image shifted again, displaying a crescent of azure cloth along the bottom edge and a girl's back rising above it—her own. And stretching across the pale skin was a white tree, whose roots disappeared into the dress and whose gently curving branches reached up to her shoulders. But in place of leaves, a spattering of feathers danced on the otherwise bare boughs. Though the tattoo covered her entire back, its whiteness almost disappeared into her own pallor. With her long hair falling over it, most would have missed its presence.

A sense of familiarity struck her. In her dream, Elaia must have possessed a similar image in mahogany brown. No wonder why that tangle of obscured lines had seemed so important.

"It's the symbol of one of the unicorn domains," Darien said. "I've seen it, along with the other four, drawn in several books and more than a few pieces of art. The feathers weren't there, and some versions had other embellishments, such as flowers or jewels, but the shape of the branches is always the same."

The unicorn domains… When the Age of Unicorns had ended, the mighty enchanted creatures had forged an agreement with the humans to stay out of each other's lands. But she'd known already that she'd come from a land of unicorns. What she hadn't known was that there were *five*. "Do you know which one it represents?"

"Let me think… " He furrowed his brow, as if trying to remember something out of reach.

She stared at the tree, trying to derive some further meaning from it. A blurred shape appeared in her head, too vague for her to discern anything but a few points of purple light glowing against a mottled swath of black and blue.

Closing her eyes, she concentrated on the lights and tried to make sense of them. The black splotches narrowed, becoming straight lines connected by thin wisps…

Heat lanced through her head, confirming what she'd suspected: This was a memory, triggered by the symbol on her back. She steeled herself against the familiar pain. Whatever she found, every shred of her past was important. She held on to the vision, determined not to let the fire stop her, and watched in anticipation as the black lines sharpened into the silhouettes of trees while the lights danced around them.

A second wave of hotness surged through her head, and she gasped. Then, a deep, female voice floated through her head, whispering, *Kristakai…*

"Kiri!" Darien's voice interrupted her thoughts, and he gripped her shoulder.

Startled, she opened her eyes. The image splintered, leaving her with only the hazy impression of a shadowy forest. But though the heat rushed away, she found no relief in its absence. "Why did you do that?"

Before he could answer, a shroud of heaviness enveloped her. She fell forward, sinking into the hand with which he still clasped her shoulder. A warm drop splashed on her hand, and she felt a line of wetness down one cheek. Realizing that she'd been too focused to notice her own tears, she understood: He must have believed he was rousing her from a nightmare.

"What happened?" he asked, releasing his grip. The mirror was gone, along with any sign of the magic that had powered it.

"The mark triggered a memory." She attempted to straighten her posture, but her head drooped. "Kristakai…"

Darien's eyes widened. "That's the domain bordering Nikhilim."

A rush of hope flooded her heart. Her home—she'd found it! "How far is it from here?"

"Seven to ten days by horse, depending on which route you take. I know the kingdom well. I can guide you through it."

But as his expression brightened, hers fell. "I don't have that long."

Darien tilted his head. "What do you mean?"

"My life is bound to my homeland. As soon as I left it, I started dying a little, and unless I return before my time runs out…" She trailed off, blinking back a sudden influx of tears.

A stormy look descended upon Darien's face, and she could almost see his thoughts through his eyes. Surprise at the revelation. Anger that he hadn't known. Anxiety because he might fail to prevent her death.

Then, firm determination. "We'll find a way. I swear to you, I won't let you die."

That wasn't a promise he could keep, given the realities they faced, but

she appreciated it nevertheless. She wished she didn't have to rely on his help, but she had no choice. No matter how slim the chances, she had to fight for her own survival. Had to run as fast as possible, in case she could make it.

"*If the windborn one dies, the Fiend will triumph.*" Darien's words, barely audible even in the silence, made Kiri's heart jump.

"What do you mean?"

Apparently, he hadn't meant to speak the words aloud, for he seemed startled by the question. "I'm not sure. I heard a voice in my head speaking those words, and it wasn't of this world. I think it was a prophecy, but I don't know what it signifies."

A shudder wracked her body. The foretold Age of Fire was a tale everyone knew, but it had always been an abstraction, something too distant to be real. Who could have spoken those mysterious words? The Ayr of Tomorrow?

How her one, seemingly insignificant life could be connected to the destiny of the whole world, she couldn't begin to guess, but it made her need to return home all the direr. Whether her death was only a harbinger or whether it was the impetus for a darker chain of events, she had to survive.

"Six days," she murmured. "That's all I have."

"It's enough." He grabbed the enchanted crystal from the floor. "Although…" He held up the stone. "I might be able to use magic to take us there."

"How?"

"It's a skill every Sorci possesses — they can transport themselves across vast distances in the blink of an eye. With a clarion stone to help… It's worth a try."

She nodded. "All right. What do I do?"

"Take my hand."

She did as he asked, trying to keep the hope from shining too brightly. The warmth of his hand around hers momentarily melted away her fear, and she wondered if he could feel her quickening pulse through her palm.

"*Take us to Kristakai,*" he murmured. The crystal glowed, humming with energy.

Bolts of pain shot down her limbs and through her torso, as excruciating

as the curse had been. She bit her lip hard and squeezed her eyes. Something was tearing her apart within, shredding her bones. Her shaking hand tightened around his.

She glanced at Darien, whose expression was tense with anguish—the spell had to be affecting him similarly. His head drooped over his chest, and his eyes fell shut. Her own body weakened; it was all she could do to remain upright. Darkness encroached her vision, and a wave of coldness rose as exhaustion overtook her. The pain of the magic felt so similar to her curse, she feared it would have the same effect—draining them both of life as well as tormenting them.

Without warning, Darien collapsed. The crystal tumbled from his grip, and his hand slipped from hers.

"Darien!" She rushed to him and, when he didn't respond, shook his shoulder. "Darien?"

He was as cold as ice, his body completely still. Fearing the worst, she touched his lips, feeling for a breath. To her relief, a soft wafting of warmth brushed her fingers.

After a moment, he blinked up at her, and a great weight dissolved from her chest.

"Are we…?" He sat up abruptly—too abruptly, for he fell backward.

She caught him. "Slow down."

He leaned back on his elbow. "We're still in the fortress, aren't we?"

"Yes." Kiri tried to keep her head up, even though her weakened body wanted to sink into the ground beside him.

"Blazes!" His mouth hardened. "If I try again—"

"No!" She shook her head rapidly. "That spell had the same effect as the curse." Worse even, for it had harmed him as well.

"I thought it was just me… It hurt you too?"

"Yes."

He stared at the ground, his expression grim. "I… I didn't know. I must once again ask your forgiveness."

"It's all right."

"I guess we'll have to travel like ordinary people then." He picked up the crystal. Almost a quarter of it was gray. "How could I have used so much of it when both spells failed?" Frustration clung to each word. Looking at Kiri, he explained, "Each time I use it, a little more turns back

into ordinary rock. I can't believe how much I've wasted already. If I were more powerful… But nothing's ever easy is it?" With a wry smile, he reached behind him and retrieved a leather bag. "If there's no one outside, we can leave this place now. The main door is on the other side of the Bastille, and it's the only way in or out because the rest of the building is enchanted with magical barriers."

Kiri's stomach sank. "Won't Worak wait for us there if he knows there's no other exit?"

"Perhaps, but we have no choice. I'll find a way past him." Anger edged his voice.

Though she doubted he could win such a battle, she refrained from saying anything. He was right—they had no other options.

Her gaze fell on the bag, and she suddenly wondered why she'd never asked him about the silver clock. She'd assumed that he'd simply grabbed her and run, but he'd had the crystal… She voiced her question, and he responded with a nod.

"Here it is," he said, pulling it out of the satchel.

She took it, grateful that he'd thought to find and bring the little timepiece. Though she didn't really need the information it held any longer, it was precious to her.

But when she glanced at its face, terror jolted her. The hands had changed since the last time she'd seen them—they now pointed at just before five o'clock.

Five days… less, even. She couldn't have been unconscious for a whole day…

"How long has it been since I fainted in the dungeon?" she asked.

"Not long." Darien looped the bag's strap over his shoulder. "Worak awakened moments after we left, so I had to find the nearest hiding place. I made it just before you opened your eyes."

It wasn't time that moved the clock's hands. A flurry of ice swirled in her stomach. She'd lost an entire day—but how?

Then, she recalled the erratic movements of the minute hand that had occurred when she'd tried using her powers in the cell. She'd thought at the time that because the hours actually represented days, the movements were simply uneven, but now, she realized she'd missed something terribly important.

The clock didn't only count time; it measured her life. Now, she knew why each time the curse attacked her, she'd felt herself draining. It was more than pain and weakness; it was because she was expending her days. And the harder she fought to free her abilities and her memories, the more she exhausted. In fact, the powerful blast of wind she'd used to save Darien had been why she'd lost so much this time.

Despite what it had cost her, she didn't regret what she'd done. Still, she couldn't afford to go through anything like that again. The possibility of reaching Kristakai in five days when a normal journey would take at least seven was slim enough, and they hadn't even started.

She forced herself to stand, listening for movement outside. With a whispered word, Darien extinguished their enchanted source of light. Total blackness, broken only by the door gap, pressed on her vision, but from the slight rattling sound from Darien's direction, she knew he'd placed his hand on the doorknob. Any moment, he would throw it open. Fear still clasped her, trying to hold her back, but she prepared to burst through its grip.

Time was running out.

ELSEWHERE...

"The shadow dwells within him, though he does not yet know of its presence. For seventeen years, it has slept, unseen by all around him while the veils of assumption concealed his true nature with minimal effort. But no longer. I sense it stirring inside his soul. As it grows, it will consume the starlight within, leaving only darkness in its wake. And then — oh, and then, my Master — it will be the end for your Sister and all Her children."

7

They are not what they seem

Now that she'd embraced the gift and opened her eyes to its wonders, Arrin felt as if she held the entire universe in her hands—a colorful sphere with the beauteous Celeste floating at the top, the lively Terra sitting in the middle, and the fiery Inferno churning beneath.

But then the flames of the lower realms crept up the sphere's edges, devouring the Terrestrial Realm with unrelenting rage. And they didn't stop there—no, they continued up into the Celestial Realm, consuming even the stars and the sun, until all she held was a ball of flames.

TODAY...

LAZES, BLIGHTS, AND BLUNDERS!

Brrin tore through the dark trees, unable to believe her own idiocy. The footsteps and shouts of her pursuers rang out through the night, closing in behind her. What on Terra had possessed her to take a well traveled road when she was a lightforsaken *fugitive*? After finding her way down from the cliff face the previous night, she'd caught a few hours of sleep in an abandoned barn, thinking that would give Lady Bolliore's goons enough time to give up on finding her body. But she'd underestimated the noblewoman's vindictiveness—when she'd reached the village of Brena, she'd seen numerous signs offering a reward for her return, even if she was a corpse. Evidently, her former mistress wanted proof that she was dead.

And so Arrin had spent the past day making her way toward the Eryu border, taking a confusing, roundabout way in order to avoid areas with people. As a result, the journey was taking much longer than it should have. With her agitated heart drumming with impatience, reminding her that if she didn't save the windborn one in time, the Age of Fire would destroy everyone she loved, she'd returned to the road after sundown, since that was the fastest and most direct way to the Sapphire Bastille. The wide path of compacted dirt had been empty, and she'd thought that no one would spot her in the darkness.

But she'd scarcely made it two miles before a unit of Lady Bolliore's riders came barreling toward her, and she'd fled into the trees, hoping that would force them to dismount. Though she was fast, no human could outrun a horse. That her strategy—if one could call it that—had worked was a small consolation next to the bigger problem at hand: The fact that there were *armed guards chasing her.* From the rustling leaves and cries of "She went this way!" or "After her!" or "She won't get away this time!", there had to be at least five or six of them.

She ducked under a branch and dashed through the darkness, wondering where the blazes she was going. Though the moon was bright, it barely broke through the tangle of leaves, and she could barely see enough to avoid crashing into a trunk. One thing she was thankful for, though: She was running through the dry forest of the high mountains, where only the hardiest of plants could survive. That meant fewer bushes for her to crash into, more space between trees, and no mud to slow her down.

A quick analysis of her situation impressed upon her the urgent need for a new strategy. She could only run for so long, and already her pounding heart and ragged breath were ordering her to stop before they gave out. Her best bet was to find a place to hide and hope the goons would streak past her, then go off in a different direction.

Her foot caught on something, and she crashed to the ground. Cursing, she picked herself back up, hoping nothing had spilled from her bag. She needed every scrap of food in there, since she had barely enough to last a day as it was, but she didn't have time to check.

After a few more sprints, she found herself face-to-face with a vertical cliff face, stretching up toward the star-filled sky. *Blazes!*

No escape in that direction; she spun and dashed in another. How long would she have to run without seeing? The mountains rose in unpredictable peaks and valleys—what if she found herself at the edge of another drop-off? She couldn't count on another miracle tree breaking her fall.

Think, you curbrain! Arrin's mind whirred. She could never outrun or outmuscle a pack of trained combatants. Her only hope was to *outsmart* her pursuers. *They're all thick-skulled buffoons anyway… come on, Arrin! You're an inventor — invent a solution!*

"Spread out!" The man's voice sounded too close for comfort. "You, continue this way. You two — over there. The rest of you, follow me!"

Good, she thought, racing around a thick tree. If they caught up to her, at least she'd only have to deal with a few instead of the whole group.

But their scattering also meant she had a greater chance of running into one of them. There was no way to run in a straight line with all the plants and rocks to circumvent, and her encounter with the cliff face meant she had to double back and zigzag away. The sweat covering her made every chilly breeze feel like a blast of icy wind. She wasn't sure how much longer she could run before she made herself sick.

Ahead, the moon reflected off another craggy surface, and her first instinct was to pivot away and change directions. But then, an idea struck her. The rock ahead wasn't completely vertical — the curvature of the shadows indicated that it was more of an enormously tall yet shallow cavern, as if a giant had taken a bite out of the mountain. Maybe one of those shadows was actually a cave.

Deciding she had to chance it, she headed in its direction. The plants stopped growing about ten yards before it, where the ground was almost entirely rock, leaving a bit of a clearing before the cavern. Horizontal bands streaked its rough, concave surface, and layers of stone jutted out. The giant formation towered over her, and she estimated it was at least twenty times her height.

Her eyes fell on circle of black about a quarter of the way up. Since only a particularly deep crevice would cast that kind of shadow, she headed toward it, aiming to conceal herself in its darkness. The slope of the cavern wasn't very steep, and the rock provided enough friction that she had no problem scaling it. The anticipation of relief, of getting a chance to stop and breathe, spurred her toward the beckoning cave.

A coarse voice shot toward her: "You! Stop where you are!"

Terrified, she spun. Two men, each holding a flaming torch, emerged from the trees. *What now?*

She was in the middle of a giant, concave cliff face. Any way she went, she'd wind up having to run into the woods again, where the men would

surely follow. Furthermore, one had a crossbow.

She'd gotten herself cornered. And there was no way out.

If I can't run, I'll have to fight. But all she possessed were her two small fists and booted feet, against a crossbow, a sword, and whatever knives the guards had tucked into their belts.

And my crescent! It wasn't much, but it was better than nothing. Blood humming, she reached into her bag and grabbed it.

The man with the crossbow raised his weapon. "Stop what you're doing!"

Ignoring the command, she whipped her arm out, sending the crescent flying down at him, then ducked, knowing he'd shoot. The arrow whizzed over her head, its wind blasting her hair, and smashed into the rock.

A *thwack* and a quick grunt from below told her the crescent had met its target. She jumped up as its dark, spinning form flew back toward her and snatched it out of the air. To her relief, the man who'd fired lay unconscious. The torch flickered on the rocky ground beside him, scattering the shadows with its orange-gold light.

A second torch sat abandoned not far from it. Her chest tightened. Where was the man who'd held it?

A slight movement caught her eye, and she whirled. The man scaled the cavern's shallow slope, coming for her with sword in hand. She gasped as she recognized his square-jawed face—it was the same brute who had nearly caught her when she'd run away. The darkened, raised flesh on his left cheekbone indicated that she'd burned him when she'd kicked his torch. A minor wound, but enough to explain why he had such a vicious look in his eyes as he raised his blade.

"It's a *corpse* we were sent to find." He snarled. "I figure I should deliver one."

With both hands on the weapon, he swung at her. Through the jumbled chaos of her panicked brain, Arrin instinctively raised her crescent, one hand at each end. Turning it at an angle, she caught the flat of the blade in the crook of her wooden instrument.

The man's scowl deepened as he pressed down on her rudimentary shield. Her arms trembled as she struggled to keep him back.

Then, she noticed that, rather than towering over her as he had previously, he appeared to be her height—because they were standing on a sloped surface, and he was below her.

She kicked his gut with all the force she could muster.

With a cry, he lost his balance and went tumbling down the rock. His sword clanged, having fallen from his grip, and she jumped over it as she ran down after him.

He stopped and sat up, but before he could get any further, she leaped at him. Using her whole body for leverage, she twisted and brought the end of the instrument crashing down onto his head. His eyes rolled back, and he fell.

Arrin sneered. "Blighted sludge-eater. Don't you know that the higher ground has the advantage?" Standing, she peered down at the two unconscious men, and an immense feeling of satisfaction swelled in her heart.

Rustling noises from the woods ahead meant the rest of the search party was still out there, and it sounded like they were getting closer. She briefly contemplated returning to her original plan of hiding in the cave, but then someone yelled, "I heard something this way! I think they found her!"

Blazes! She searched for new ideas. Hiding was out—the cave was the first place they'd look once they found their knocked-out companions. She considered taking the high ground again and repeating her performance but quickly swatted the notion away. She was no fool—she knew she'd gotten lucky.

I have to throw them off my trail. Spotting the crossbow, she snatched it up. A glint caught her attention; the man had a dagger tucked into his belt. She grabbed it as well. At least she was armed now. She considered going back for the sword, but dismissed the idea. Not only did she have no idea how to use such a weapon, but it looked too big for her to handle. She was no weakling, with her sturdy, compact frame, but she wasn't exactly strong either, being barely taller than a fence post and unconditioned for combat.

After shoving the knife and her crescent into her bag, she yanked the arrows from the man's quiver and pulled back the crossbow's lever to draw the string. Though she'd never fought with one, the weapon's engineering had always fascinated her, and she was familiar with how it worked from

having spent hours dissecting its mechanics.

Arrin loaded the arrow and stuck the rest, which numbered at only three, in her bag. Their pointed tips protruded over the leather edge. Wondering how close her pursuers were, she listened carefully to their approaching footsteps and dragged her eyes across the shadows for any sign of movement. The light of the two dropped torches danced against the rocky clearing but barely broke the blackness of the trees.

That was when she realized how much of a disadvantage she had—they'd be able to see her, but she couldn't see them. And they might have crossbows too. Even assuming the best possible scenario, she could still only fire one arrow at a time while they had numbers on their side. Whichever way she looked at the situation, she couldn't think of a way to work it to her advantage.

Time to run again. She took off into the trees, still clutching the crossbow. Her pulse hammered. There *had* to be a better way to escape than sprinting recklessly like a panicked animal.

"Listen!" A woman's voice rang through the woods. "She's going that way!"

If only I weren't so loud! The darkness offered her cover from their sight, but there was nothing she could do to keep their ears from locating her footsteps.

An idea flashed through her head, and she paused. *The crossbow!*

Kneeling, she located the longest corridor of moonlight between tree trunks and fired close to the ground. The arrow crashed through the brush, rustling leaves and branches—just like she would have if she'd run in that direction. To give the guards more reason to think she'd run that way, she grabbed another arrow and fired again.

The footsteps stopped. Then, someone yelled, "That way!"

To confirm their erroneous suspicions, she fumbled for the third—and final—arrow, figuring she might as well use it, since one shot wouldn't do her much good. She fired one last time and was rewarded with a shout of, "Did you hear that? She's over there!"

The noises moved away from her, and her muscles melted with relief. *Thank Celeste, it worked!*

After waiting a few moments for the sounds of their footsteps to fade

into the distance, she turned in the opposite direction. Leaving the crossbow behind, since without arrows it would only be a burden, she crept through the woods as silently as possible.

Arrin wasn't sure how long she'd been moving, stepping carefully around branches in an effort to keep Lady Bolliore's guards from hearing her, but she hadn't detected any noises or footsteps for several minutes. She desperately hoped that meant they were far enough away that they wouldn't find her, because she wasn't sure how much longer she could remain upright. A full day of walking with hardly any breaks, followed by the mad chase that had nearly landed her an arrow through the skull, and all on a crust of bread and half a canteen of water—no wonder she was worn out.

She wished she had some inkling as to where she was actually going, but her sole concern when she'd run off the main road had been to get away. As far as she could tell, the forest was uniformly comprised of brush and trees, with no features to set one clump of plants apart from the other.

Her stomach tightened as she realized how hopelessly lost she was. The forest was enormous—for all she knew, she wouldn't even be able to find her way out, let alone make it to the Sapphire Bastille.

If it weren't for her physical needs—the aching of her muscles, the lightness of her head, the dryness of her throat—she might have fallen into full-blown panic. But she was too tired for even that. Her vision swam, making the tree trunks appear to sway, and a vaguely visible swirl of steam wafted from her burning face. She was sure she would pass out soon unless she found some respite.

A glimmer caught her attention—a flutter of glowing white on a glassy texture. Immediately recognizing it as water reflecting the bright moonlight, she dashed toward it, too eager to care how much noise she made anymore.

As she drew closer, she found a calm river, the widest she'd ever seen, flowing serenely along a winding path. It was so clear, she glimpsed the smooth stones resting beneath its placid surface even in the dark. Cupping

her hands, she shoveled water into her mouth, not caring how its iciness sent shivers down her skin.

After satisfying her thirst, Arrin sat back on the embankment and finally let her tired body rest. But her mind remained alert, listening for any sign of the guards. Assuming they'd continued in the wrong direction, they were probably well away by now. She must have walked for at least twenty or thirty minutes after loosing the arrows, which meant, given her average walking speed of one-and-a-half to two miles an hour plus theirs in the opposite direction…

Skies, I'm too wiped out to even solve that elementary problem.

If she was lucky, then the guards would give up and tell each other that she wasn't the fugitive they sought, that Arrin Velindale did indeed lie dead somewhere in the ravine, and they'd been chasing a lookalike vagabond. Doing so would be in their best interests if they wanted to avoid their mistress' wrath. Once news reached her family, though, they'd be devastated.

I'm sorry, Mahtim, Tahtih, Myla, Tam. If I succeed… when all this is over… I'll go home and apologize. It won't be enough, but at least you'll be safe.

The images from her prophecies still burned vividly in her mind, but where they had driven her before, they now filled her with despair.

What did I think would happen — that I'd just race to Eryu and stop the Age of Fire? I don't even know what part of Terra I'm on anymore.

It seemed like foolishness to believe she could be the one to save the world. That was the role of a true hero—a royal, or a warrior, or a chosen one with great abilities. And who was she? Just a carpenter's daughter, indentured to do menial work, with impossible dreams of building great things someday.

Still, the stars had picked *her* to receive the vision, and they didn't make mistakes. She'd read as much in countless books written over the millennia by the master thinkers of their times. Whatever Celeste's reasons, it would do her no good to wallow in self-pity.

A light caught Arrin's attention—a pale blue glow, the color of the sky at daybreak, shimmering beneath the river's surface in the distance. Knowing it had to have an enchanted cause, for no human could produce a light underwater, she edged forward, trying to make out its source. *Some kind of magical fish? The aquatic equivalent to a fairy, perhaps?*

The light drew nearer and brighter as it rose from the depths, rapidly moving upstream until she was able to make out its shape. Her eyes widened. Under the glassy river, a mermaid swam toward her, holding a spherical lantern in one hand. The girl's elegant tail, whose colors were difficult to make out in the darkness, swayed quickly from side to side, and grand translucent fins rippled like silk. Long straight hair flowed behind her, glistening with ornaments that rivaled the stars.

Arrin stared, mesmerized. Though she'd heard much about the mermaids since their politics often intertwined with Nikhilim's due to their shared shore, she'd never seen one in person before. What was this one doing so far upriver, anyway? As far as she knew, they kept to the ocean.

As the mermaid drew closer, Arrin was able to make out the details of her appearance. Hair as smooth and black as polished onyx. A long torso, clad in a glimmering silver garment that covered her bust and upper stomach but left her naval exposed. Lithe arms decorated with spiraling silver bracelets. Upswept eyes, black in color, accentuated by sharp cheekbones and a pointed chin. Her moon-pale skin gleamed with a smooth, pearly luster; she was young, probably around twenty.

The mermaid's eyes darted to the surface. Embarrassed to have been caught staring, Arrin glanced away, reminding herself that mermaids were people like herself and not animals to be gawked at. As the other approached, probably to tell her just that, Arrin suddenly realized that she'd been so hypnotized by the mermaid's appearance, she'd forgotten that she was a fugitive with several unfriendly people after her. For all she knew, the aquatic girl was an ally of Lady Bolliore's.

Since she couldn't afford to take any chances, Arrin scrambled to her feet and spun toward the forest.

A splash, followed by, "Wait, don't go!" The girl's voice, deep yet vibrant, sounded more desperate than demanding.

Unable to help her curiosity, Arrin turned back around. The other had surfaced and was now treading water near the riverbank, holding the blue lantern by her side as water lapped around her waist. Now that she was just a few feet away, Arrin could see that her tail was a pattern of rich

purple and green hues, curving as a human woman's hips would and then tapering and culminating in two grand emerald fins. A silver diadem, no wider than a finger, encircled her head, and from it, thin chains decorated with small violet gemstones ran down her hair. Everything about her was so graceful and put-together; Arrin was suddenly aware of her own rumpled appearance, with rips all over her clothes from getting snagged on thorns and enough twigs and leaves to build a bird's nest caught in her unkempt hair.

"Have you seen any guié around these parts?" The mermaid swept her arm to indicate the mountain range.

The question took Arrin by surprise, but she warned herself not to become complacent. She narrowed her eyes. "Do you know Lady Bolliore?"

The other lifted one arched black eyebrow. "I don't trouble myself with the petty nobility of humankind. Why do you ask?"

I'll take that as a no. Arrin approached the water's edge. "Never mind, she's just someone who doesn't like me very much. Aren't you a little far from the ocean?"

"It's by necessity, I'm afraid." The mermaid's eyes darted around. "Tell me, have you seen any guié or not?"

The command in her voice sparked Arrin's irritation. *Who just goes up to a stranger and asks for something without offering an explanation?*

"Hello, my name is Arrin," she said sarcastically. "Last name's Velindale, if you care. Nice to meet you."

The mermaid knit her eyebrows, then let out a sigh. "Apologies for my coarse manners. I'm Ilaerii." As she spoke her name, her eyes searched Arrin with suspicion.

Is she a fugitive too or something? Deciding it was better not to ask, she tried saying the other's name. It was the strangest one she'd ever heard, probably derived from an ancient marine dialect far the common tongue.

"Ih-*lair*-ee?" she said.

"That's right." The girl called Ilaerii lowered the lantern until it floated on the river's surface. "I'm here because rumors are spreading through Marae about Inferno growing more powerful. From what I've heard, more guié are infiltrating the Terrestrial Realm than ever before, and people are scared."

"That's… a bad sign." Arrin tried not to let her fear show on her face. "It's been decades since the last recorded gui attack." *And millennia since the last ayr fell…*

"I wanted to see if there was any truth to it, and so I consulted one of our oracles. She said there'd been a great upsurge in dark magic in these mountains, so I came to find out what it was about."

"And you came alone?"

"I had to. If anyone knew I was taking those rumors seriously, they'd panic, and my kingdom would be overwhelmed by chaos. But *something* must be going on. I've seen Nameed's prophecy of the Age of Fire. The events leading to it have already begun."

Perversely enough, Arrin was almost glad to hear someone else speak of the Age of Fire because it meant she wasn't alone in knowing it was imminent. Perhaps this mermaid, whoever she was, knew something that could help Arrin on her quest.

"What exactly do you mean?" she asked.

"This is what the prophecy states." Ilaerii shifted her gaze, staring blankly into the river as she recited, "'Before the Age of Thrones reaches its sixteenth century, a human child will be born with the power of Inferno.'" She looked back at Arrin. "That means the Starless Prince already walks the Terrestrial Realm. So far, our efforts to locate him have failed, for neither we nor our human allies have found a strong enough convergence of dark magic in any single person. And he could be *anyone*—a child of five, or an old man of eighty… We have no way of knowing."

Terror darted through Arrin's heart. At least someone else was seeking a way to prevent the world's doom, which brought her a drop of comfort.

"I haven't heard of any guié in these parts," she said, to answer the mermaid's initial question. "But last night, I saw an ayr fall." She recounted the terrible sight she'd witnessed: the mark of the Fiend burned into the trees, the winged silhouette in ash at its center. As she spoke, the horrifying future she'd seen seemed to draw even closer, and so she told Ilaerii of that as well.

By the time she concluded her account, Ilaerii's expression was taut with worry. For a moment, the mermaid didn't speak, as if digesting what she'd heard.

"I heard reports of the ayr's death, but since the witnesses were so few, I'd hoped they weren't true," she said. "Who is the windborn one you speak of?"

"I don't know," Arrin confessed. "The vision didn't tell me, but it did show me that she's at the Sorci fortress. Say… do you know where that is?"

Ilaerii shifted her gaze upward, searching the sky, then pointed. "Do you see the Prudence Star?"

Arrin looked up. The Prudence Star was one of the Estal Magora, the night's brightest stars. Each twinkled a different color — blue for patience, pink for kindness, green for charity. *And amber for prudence.* They remained in the same place no matter what the season, silent sentinels of all that was good. During her many reading adventures, Arrin had encountered plenty of stories about sailors or travelers using the Estal Magora for navigation.

Following Ilaerii's lead, Arrin found the glinting Prudence Star shining prominently above the riverbank, unmistakable. "Yes, I see it."

"During the Age of Magic, the Sorci built their fortress under it because prudence is the virtue they value the most." Ilaerii lowered her arm. "If you follow that star, you'll find the Sapphire Bastille."

"Thank you." A great pressure lifted from Arrin's heart. That was a direction she could follow no matter how turned around she got. She glanced at the terrain ahead. The river curved out of sight, and a mountain rose above it, its peak pointing directly at the Prudence Star. Perhaps the Bastille was on the other side. "Do you know how far it is?"

"I'm afraid not." A warning gleaming in Ilaerii's black eyes. "Be careful. You may think you know who the Sorci are, but they are not what they seem."

"What do you mean?" Arrin had only heard good things about the last remnants of the Age of Magic. In fact, just a few months ago, the heralds had sung the magicians' praises because they'd saved the king's nephew. The value they placed on knowledge matched her own, and she'd often fancied that, if she'd been inclined toward the magical rather than the mechanical, she might have sought an apprenticeship with them.

Ilaerii flicked back one strand of black hair. "I'm unfamiliar with the details, but I know there's corruption within their ranks. Perhaps they were once a force for good, but now…" Her expression darkened. "I suspect

they may be the reason behind the infernal stirrings in this region."

Skies above! Arrin shuddered. She'd hoped the magicians would help her with her quest — maybe they knew the windborn one and would protect her — but now, she wondered if they were the reason the girl was in danger. Though she reminded herself not to trust Ilaerii's word too quickly, she detected no lie in the other's voice. And it couldn't hurt to be careful.

"I appreciate the warning," she said nervously.

Ilaerii gave a polite nod. "I must return to my investigations. If I don't return to Marae by sunrise, people will know something is wrong, and I don't want any more rumors to get started. Farewell, Arrin Velindale."

She dove back into the water before Arrin could respond, sending up a small splash. Taken aback by the mermaid's abrupt departure, Arrin watched her swim away and found her gaze drawn to a gleaming jewel in the girl's hair. It glittered so brightly, the only explanation for why she hadn't noticed it earlier was that the mermaid's long locks had covered it. Black like onyx but flashing with every color of the rainbow, glowing with its own luminescence — a stargem, rarer than rubies or diamonds or any other earthly jewel… This was a piece of the Celestial Realm. Legend had it that stargems had been created during the final battle against the Fiend, when the powers of the ayri had struck the earth and solidified starlight into a few precious stones.

Arrin's mind flashed back to the moment Ilaerii had given her name — the odd, suspicious look that had crossed her face. Only someone extraordinarily powerful would wear a stargem, and the mermaid must have wondered if Arrin would recognize her.

Skies, she's royalty! Arrin gaped, staring after the mermaid's retreating form as it disappeared around the river bend. No wonder why Ilaerii had been so knowledgeable, and why she'd kept referring to *her* people. *Ilaerii of Marae… Wouldn't be hard to find out exactly who she is. Probably a princess.*

Arrin couldn't believe she'd actually spoken to a royal from any kingdom; she'd always imagined that Lady Bolliore would be the most powerful person she'd come into contact with.

Adjusting the strap of her bag, she found the Prudence Star in the sky. The one disadvantage about traveling by it was that she could only do so at night, and time was limited. She'd have to get as far as she could by daybreak. Up to the mountain, at least. Perhaps even over it.

With that in mind, she marched down the riverbank, trying not to think about the dangers that would await once she reached the fortress of magic.

ELSEWHERE…

"See how the mortal fools pursue without rest, little realizing how pointless their actions are! Well, let them run. Let them believe that killing him is the answer. The direr his circumstances, the more desperate he'll grow, and that will pave the way for Inferno to enter. But though they've lost sight of their goal, I have not, and I shall carry on with the process so that this delay will not set the plans back. Kristakai will be ours, sooner than they think."

We have to get out

TOMORROW...

Kiri wanted to believe he was possessed. She wanted to believe this wasn't *him*, that this was an illusion, a trick, a nightmare she would awaken from. Yet she knew it couldn't be, and the Fiend's corporeal form stood behind Darien, a beastly shadow against the blaze.

Though it hurt to look at him, she held Darien's gaze, searching and searching for some sign that she was mistaken — that the entire *universe* was mistaken — and that at least one ray of starlight still glowed within his soul. And she couldn't help but wonder: Was this her fault?

TODAY...

IRI RACED DOWN THE WIDE HALLWAY, SO FAST THE flaming lanterns on the walls streaked into blurred yellow lines. Cold air nipped at her skin even beneath the thick cloth of Darien's cloak, and she wondered how all that running had failed to warm her.

"*Find them!*" Worak's voice, distant yet loud enough to pierce through stone walls, crackled with rage. "I want them alive!"

So he can torture us first and then kill us himself. As she sprinted past the wooden doors along the corridor, doing her best to breathe steadily, she tried not to think about the ever-ticking clock she wore around her neck.

A few steps ahead, Darien rounded a corner. Dark splotches stained the back of his shirt, creeping slowly across the crimson material. Though he'd insisted that he'd cast a healing spell on himself and didn't feel any pain, she couldn't believe that when her own eyes told her that several wounds remained open. The memory of his cries haunted her, and she didn't dare imagine what Worak would do to him if they were caught.

She glanced behind her, but, to her relief, saw only the flickering firelight. With each step, her weary legs wanted to cave beneath her, and

only through sheer determination did she push them to keep moving. Her head felt light, though she didn't know if it was because she was unaccustomed to running or if she was still weakened from her last attempt to break through the curse. She prayed that willpower alone would keep her going until they could find a way out of the enormous fortress. *If only I were stronger!*

Darien stopped in his tracks and held out an arm. She halted in time to keep from crashing into him, and followed his gaze. At first, all she could hear was the pounding of her own frantic heart, but then her eyes caught a bright green glimmer from the hallway adjacent to the one she stood in. As the unnatural light grew in size, undoubtedly nearing, the sounds of footsteps became audible.

She looked around wildly for a hiding place, searching the corridor and wondering if any of the doors were unlocked—and whether opening one would cause too much noise.

Darien furrowed his brow. Something about him—maybe it was the way he clenched his fists, or maybe it was the anger tinging his expression— told her that he was contemplating confronting their pursuers outright. The idea of a fight filled her with dread, for two fugitives already weak with injury could not possibly win against numerous powerful magicians.

Kiri spotted a recessed arch with the large bronze statue of a cloaked woman standing at its center. It was only a few paces ahead, and there appeared to be enough room to hide behind the sculpture. If fortune favored them, the Sorci would only glance briefly down the hallway as they passed by.

She tapped Darien's shoulder, pointed at the statue, and ran to it. He followed.

As she squeezed into the narrow space between the bronze cloak and the wall, she tried to calm her riotous pulse with long breaths. Though the statue was decently wide, being at least three feet in breadth, it felt like flimsy protection against searching eyes. Darien edged in the area beside her, pressing his shoulder against hers, and she wondered how he could feel so warm when the whole fortress seemed engulfed in winter. Something about his presence softened the block of fear sitting in her chest, reassuring her that whatever came next, at least she wouldn't have to face it alone.

"This is abrupt," a woman muttered, and Kiri recognized the voice as belonging to Limali.

"Indeed it is." Worak's voice, soft as a growl, sent a tremor through Kiri.

Darien wrapped his arms around her, and she glanced up to see a reassuring smile flicker across his face. *Don't be afraid*, he seemed to say. *I'm right here with you.*

She leaned into his embrace, which warmed her in a way the cloak had failed to, and hoped desperately that the Sorci would not come down the hallway.

"Do you have any idea why he summoned us?" Limali asked.

"He gave no indication, but he would only seek us now if his reasons were important." Worak sounded contemplative. "It pains me to delay the search, but his request cannot be ignored."

Who are they talking about? Kiri wished she could have found some comfort in knowing that the magicians were not currently looking for her or Darien, but she dreaded whatever had the power to draw them away.

"I've ordered the others to continue while we are occupied," Worak went on. "The traitor and the nymph must be outside the Bastille's walls by now."

A measure of tension released Kiri, and she felt Darien relax somewhat, the heat of his relieved sigh tickling her cheek. Still, she warned herself not to grow overconfident in their chances. She wondered if the only reason she and Darien hadn't been discovered was because Vimunax appeared to be on their side and may have thrown the other Sorci off their trail.

"Do you really think they could have escaped, though?" Limali asked. "Gilonar has been keeping watch on the door, and surely he would have seen them approach."

"There are other ways out," Worak said.

"Yes, but I doubt Darien could even perform the spell necessary to open the main gate. How could he break through our barriers around the windows and walls?"

"Do not underestimate the boy's abilities. His potential is great, and had the nymph not interfered, he might have broken through our binding spells in the dungeon. Did you not feel how strong the pull of his magic was, even against the power of three? That is why I had to weaken him

first—if I had tried to kill him outright, his defensive instincts might have unleashed a force too great for us. And it is the reason we *must* eliminate him; he is too dangerous to be allowed to live."

Kiri's gaze flicked to Darien. From the perplexed expression written in his dark brows, he was as puzzled by the claims as she was. It didn't seem possible for him to hold as much power as Worak claimed, for she'd witnessed him overpowered by his master numerous times. Or had that been because, until he'd tried to free her, he hadn't fought back? And though the magician seemed to think his former apprentice could break through the fortress's protective spells, Darien had believed such a thing impossible.

Though Worak's and Limali's were the only voices she heard, from the multitude of taps against the ground, there had to be more magicians walking with them in silence.

"Inferno will want to know about our progress with Kristakai."

At Limali's words, Kiri covered her mouth to stifle a gasp. What did the Sorci want with her homeland? The magicians had trapped her for her powers, and she apparently hadn't been the first—perhaps they planned to capture more of her kind.

Needing to know more, Kiri angled her head toward the edge of the bronze statue and glimpsed two cloaked figures at the intersection of the hallway she stood in and the one perpendicular to it. Green light from the glowing crystals they held glinted off the elaborate designs embellishing each. Neither wore the gold medallion she'd always seen around Worak's neck; the master and Limali had to be further ahead.

They disappeared from sight, and Worak's voice faded into the distance as he spoke of how impatient Inferno could be. She waited for the sounds of their footsteps to fade. Though she loathed to leave the safety of the shadows and the comfort of Darien's embrace, she couldn't stay in the hiding spot forever.

The corridor she stepped into felt exposed and dangerous. Steeling her nerves, Kiri started toward the direction in which the Sorci had departed in.

Darien grabbed her arm. "We can't go that way."

She whirled toward him. "I need to know what they meant when they spoke of Kristakai."

He raised his brows. "Somehow, following the people out to kill you doesn't seem like the best plan, especially since whatever they're doing, it's keeping them from hunting us. For now, at least." But there was doubt in his eyes, and she could tell that he, too, longed to know.

"They're going to talk to Inferno. What if they say something that reveals what the prophecy meant?"

The doubt spread like a shadow over his face. He didn't argue when she spun away and followed as she marched toward the intersection.

Each heartbeat pounded harder than the one before. Once she rounded the corner, she'd be out in the open, possibly with the Sorci still ahead. Part of her warned that following them would do her no good if they recaptured her before she could act on her discoveries. But for her homeland's sake, she had to try.

She paused. "Do you know where that hallway leads?"

"There's a ritual room in that direction—they're probably heading for it to cast whatever spell they need to talk to their fiery friends." Soft as Darien kept his voice, the bitterness in his tone was impossible to miss. "It's not far. They're probably already in there."

An abrupt explosion thundered from the corridor ahead, which flashed with green light, and Kiri jumped. Though the sound was muffled by distance and probably a door, it nevertheless sent a tremor through her.

A humorless smile crept onto Darien's mouth. "If I had to guess, I'd say they're not only in the room, but have begun knocking on Inferno's door." He strode into the next corridor with a confidence that seemed bizarre considering the danger they were in.

"Wait!" Kiri grabbed at him but missed. If he was wrong, he might have walked right up to their pursuers. She rushed to catch up.

The new hallway she entered, the one she'd last seen the Sorci walking down, looked no different from the one she'd just left, except the door at the very end differed from the plain wooden slabs that stood along the walls of gray. Hexagonal in shape and made of glittering white marble, inlaid with colored stones that leaped and twirled across its flat surface in patterns similar to the symbols and ciphers she'd seen on the Sorci's cloaks—the sight was magnificent to behold, and Kiri couldn't help marveling at its intricacies. All six edges glowed green, illuminated by the spells brewing behind it. Only magic could explain how Worak and his followers could

have opened and shut such a great—and probably heavy—slab without her hearing so much as a bump. With no visible hinges, the door likely could only be moved through otherworldly means.

The threat of discovery rippled in the air, but though her heart seemed to shout *run, run, run* with each frenzied beat, she pressed on until she reached her target. Hoping to catch a hint of what was going on inside, she peered into the crack on one side of the door. But only glaring green light filled her vision.

She turned to Darien, who stood in the center of the hallway, facing the door and holding with both hands the crystal he'd used to amplify his powers. His eyes were shut; he had to be casting a spell. He wouldn't be so foolish as to fling open the door and confront the Sorci—would he? She rushed up to him, but before she could say anything, a look of agony contorted his face, and he gasped.

"Are you hurt?" she asked, alarmed.

"It's the magic." He tightened his grip on the crystal, his hands quivering.

"What do you mean?"

"Humans aren't gifted as the enchanted are. Magic doesn't come to us naturally, but must be coerced to the surface, and our bodies don't like that. Casting spells is about as pleasant as falling onto a bed of blades."

"Why didn't it harm you before, then?" She recalled how he'd cast the mirror spell to let her see the mark on her back, and he'd seemed all right then. Also, she had never seen any signs of pain from Worak or his followers. "And why didn't it harm the Sorci?"

"It did." His whispered voice was tight, strained. "You simply learn to bear it. That's why apprentices are treated so harshly—to teach them endurance. But I don't think anyone can really become accustomed to being gutted by flaming daggers. This spell is stronger than the mirror one, and it caught me off guard." A sheepish grin crept onto his lips. "I'm sorry if I scared you."

Though she was relieved that he wasn't injured, it troubled her to know that beneath his calm face, a part of him was screaming. His mention of flaming daggers led her to wonder if he was experiencing the same agony she did each time she tried to recover a memory or use her powers. Except she'd been trying to break through a curse and retrieve what had once been hers — it seemed absurd that he'd harm himself voluntarily, and repeatedly, for a power, it seemed, that humans weren't meant to have.

"*Reveal what lies behind that door.*" Darien's voice glowed with a supernatural quality.

Glad that he wasn't planning on infiltrating the ritual room, Kiri looked around to make sure no one was approaching. The green light gleaming from the cracks of the hexagonal door made her wonder again what the Sorci were doing behind it, and why she hadn't heard anything from them. Was it because the door was too thick? Or were they waiting for something?

A white flash caught her attention, and she whirled toward its source. The crystal in Darien's hands was now surrounded by an incandescent white mist. Curious, she reached toward it, touching it with just the tip of her finger. Her skin tingled, but not in an unpleasant way.

"It's called a clarion stone," Darien said, his eyes still shut. "Learning what the Sorci are doing with Inferno seemed important enough to use it, though I wish I didn't have to. Unfortunately, I couldn't even cast a simple spell to open the cell without it… I don't understand why Worak believes I'm so powerful."

That does seem strange. Perhaps the Sorci master had a way of reading the stars and divining the destinies written in glittering patterns across the sky; perhaps Darien was fated for greatness, and the magician hoped to exploit that. The idea rattled her heart, and she couldn't tell if she hoped it was true… or if she hoped it wasn't.

A deep voice resounded through the hallway from the direction of the door, so loud that even the solid stone was insufficient to block it. Snapping noises sizzled at the sound's edges, but despite the distortion, she instantly recognized it as Worak's. The words he spoke were in a strange tongue, garbled and foreign to her ears, as far from the common language as a snake's hiss. More voices joined in, slithering in quieter tones around that of their leader, whispering yet loud enough to shake the ground upon which she stood. They spoke the same odd syllables in perfect unison, and the sound chilled her. Though there were probably no more than ten inside, the sound could have represented thousands. *Is this the language of the Fiend?*

The green glow ringing the carved hexagon brightened into glaring yellow and pulsated between fiery gold and deep amber so rapidly, it

made her dizzy. But radiant as it was, the flash of a greater luminance caught her eye, and she whirled to see the crystal in Darien's hands ablaze with white light.

Shadows formed at its center. Amorphous black splotches at first, they soon took the shapes of seven silhouettes of cloaked humans, standing in a circle at the center of a vast rotunda with their arms outstretched before them.

Above the image, Darien's mouth quirked into a satisfied smile. "The spell worked."

Intrigued, Kiri approached the image, which shifted when she changed the angle she viewed it from as a real object would. It was more than a window into what lay within the mysterious room, but an imitation, giving her a miniature version of what was going on. The details, initially obscured by the white rays, soon became sharp, until she saw not just shadows, but seven Sorci, and even the gleaming details embroidered into their garments became clear. Each held, with both hands, a glowing object emitting two bright beams, which connected to form a coruscating seven-point star with a magician at each point. Upon closer inspection, the items turned out to be human skulls with rays bursting from their grinning mouths. All but one of the magicians kept their hood up; only Worak had thrown his back. The black tattoos entwining his forearms undulated in the flickering light as he moved his lips to a dark incantation, accompanied by the others.

At the center of the formation, a cloud of black smoke, laced with flame and lightning, danced to the rhythm of their chant. It grew larger with each word, and the fiery cracks in the billowing fog widened. Kiri couldn't take her eyes off of it, even though it filled her with dread to think about what would emerge.

"What are they saying?" she asked. "Is this the spell to summon a gui?"

"It's not the one to summon an ayr," Darien said dryly. "I've never heard anything like it before."

As the spell continued, ominous rumbles shook the ground, and the foul stench of burning flesh wafted toward her. The smoke, now a thick column that stood ten times as tall as the Sorci surrounding it, grew thinner, while the bolts of lightning sparking around it grew larger. Plumes of black shot out and then snapped back in, as if something inside was trying to push its way out, only to be thwarted by the stiffness of what encapsulated it. But the egg was cracking; soon its monstrous spawn would break through, and Kiri's breath quickened. Though the idea of being so near such powerful forces of Inferno frightened her, she silenced any notion of running. She had to know what they wanted with her homeland.

A great explosion burst through the rotunda, engulfing everything in an impenetrable wash of red. She jumped at the thunderous roar. The scarlet light retreated into the center of the seven-point star, taking the form of an enormous, towering man made of flame with jagged black wings that spanned the entire room. Two featureless yellow eyes stared down at the circle of magicians, and his giant arms were crossed tightly over a circular symbol etched in fire across his chest.

Kiri wanted to scream, for she recognized the mark of the Fiend. Only the ruler of Inferno himself bore it.

The Sorci had not summoned a henchman of wickedness; they'd brought the very master of evil into the Terrestrial Realm.

Horror rushed through her, and her instincts ordered her to flee at once. Only a stone door stood between her and the being who had tried to destroy everything at the dawn of time, a being said to have once been as powerful as the Divinity Herself before She locked him in the Firelands. How could the Sorci have called him to Terra?

"Well, it's not a gui." The lightness in Darien's tone belied the anger in his eyes, and pain flickered behind both—of failure, of loss, of betrayal.

Kiri could almost hear the thoughts churning beneath his forced calm: *I should have known. I should have acted. I should have stopped them.*

She longed to banish those notions from his mind, but what words could soothe a mind so furious?

In the image, the flaming Fiend slowly stretched his arms out beside him. Cuffs of brilliant white light materialized on his wrists, and his arms snapped back into their crossed position. The fiery face contorted into a hideous scowl as he turned his gaze to the heavens.

"Curse you, Sister!"

His roar of fury vibrated in Kiri's bones, and ground shook so hard she feared the walls would topple.

"Your prison won't hold me much longer. And once I escape, everything You created, everything You love, will be mine."

She grasped her arms, trembling at the sound of the voice.

The Fiend's voice.

A voice darker and more frightening than anything she'd imagined possible. Booming with thunder, simmering with heat, crackling with flames.

"The Starless Prince will rise before the seasons complete their turn, and the Age of Fire will begin."

Fear shot Kiri through the heart with a million shards of ice, sending a horrible shudder down her frame. She gripped her arms tighter, but it didn't help. What could, when the master of evil claimed that the end was so near?

"Don't be afraid," Darien murmured. "The Fiend can't have escaped the Firelands… This must be a projection, or some kind of communication portal the Sorci opened."

Kiri nodded, but the information did little to comfort her.

The Fiend tilted his head toward Worak.

"Those who fight for me will reap the rewards, but any traitor must be destroyed, and his dead, mutilated body displayed as a warning to those who would challenge me."

A surge of horror enveloped her. If Worak was receiving such orders from the Fiend himself, then surely the man wouldn't rest until he'd captured his former apprentice and killed him in the most vicious way imaginable.

Struck by urgency, she grabbed Darien's arm. "We have to get out!"

"Not yet." His eyes fixed on the image.

"Now."

"What about your homeland?" The corner of his mouth twitched. "This was your idea, remember?"

Annoyed, she gave his arm a hefty tug. "Come!"

"Now, tell me of your progress with Kristakai."

Kiri froze.

"Within days, we will have a spell that can infiltrate the domain's enchanted borders." Worak's face remained expressionless as he looked up at the towering giant. "Once we enter, all enchanted creatures under the unicorns' protection will be at our mercy, and we will rip the magic from them and harness it for ourselves. Including that of the unicorns."

Her eyes widened. The agony she'd endured as Worak's prisoner—he wanted to inflict the same upon everyone in her homeland.

"*You speak with much confidence,*" the Fiend said.

"The unicorns have not been great in many millennia." Worak sneered. "They believe their domains impenetrable by humans and will be unprepared for our attack. Caught off-guard, they will not be difficult to handle."

I have to warn them! Kiri's heart pounded so hard, she felt dizzy. If the Sorci succeeded, they would gain vast amounts of power in the name of the Fiend while draining it from those who would fight him. Once the Starless Prince freed his infernal father, they would be an unstoppable force: magic and evil against ordinary creatures of Terra, deprived of the few beings who might have defended them. They wouldn't stand a chance, and the Fiend would triumph…

This is what the prophecy meant. She had to warn her homeland of the planned attack; she was the only one who could, since, as a human, Darien wouldn't be able to enter the domain.

Worak had said they would infiltrate Kristakai within days, which meant he and his followers were already closing in on the unsuspecting forest.

There was no time to lose.

"Darien, I must warn Kristakai, or the prophecy will come to pass!" she whispered urgently.

A look of realization dawned on Darien's expression. "*Cease,*" he said into the crystal. The image of the ritual room vanished, cutting off Worak's words as he spoke of the Sorci's loyalty to the Fiend. The glow around the clarion stone disappeared. Almost a third of the crystal had turned to rock.

Darien shoved it into his bag, turned away from the hexagonal door, and ran, motioning for Kiri to follow. She raced after him, trusting that he would find the quickest route to the fortress door. But what if the Sorci waited there in ambush? She couldn't call upon her powers again. Even if she could endure the pain, it would cost her time, moving the silver clock's hands further toward the dreaded midnight hour. Already, she might not have enough days to make the journey. She couldn't afford to lose any more.

The moment she and Darien rounded the next corner, she found herself face-to-face with a sight that made her scream aloud.

Worak stood in the center of the hallway, a glower in his eyes and a sneer on his lips.

ELSEWHERE...

"Yes, she is an unexpected force of fate, and I, too, fear she may blow him off his destined path. The stars are tempestuous, it seems. But though she may bring us complications, she could also be a powerful asset, whether she knows it or not. What moves a young man more than the charms of rare beauty? Love can be the most powerful weapon of all when wielded by expert hands. Indeed, she will be most useful to us."

You're afraid of me

9

High above the earth, with limitless space surrounding him in his unfettered glory, he should have reveled in his newfound liberty and delighted in the infinite possibilities of the immeasurable universe. And yet he knew he might as well have been chained in the lightless dungeon again, unable to fight and unable to flee, for any perceptions of freedom were false.

Inferno had claimed him, and no power of Terra or Celeste could save him now.

LL THE CURSES IN THE WORLD COULDN'T EXPRESS the terror that assaulted Darien's mind at the sight of his former master. He whirled, aiming to grab Kiri and flee into the next hallway, but scarcely had he turned around when Worak materialized in front of him, flanked by Limali and one other. A quick glance back revealed that four other Sorci had appeared, blocking any hope of escape in that direction.

He looked around wildly, searching for a way out—*any* way out—and reached for the clarion stone. The bag containing it flew from his shoulder, yanked by a spell. A bolt of heat wrapped around him like a scorching chain. Recognizing the force as the same kind that had bound him in the dungeon, he tried to break through.

"Kiri, *run!*"

Magic quaked within, lancing him with piercing blades as he fought, but it was no use. The power slipped from his gasp as a second bolt attacked him with all the rage of a firestorm. Before he could attempt to counter it, a third enveloped him, and then a fourth, then fifth and sixth and seventh, until the might of many working as one held him tight. Every

nerve screamed with white-hot pain, but he refused to cry aloud or admit defeat. He reached inward, scrambling to reignite his abilities, but found nothing.

An invisible force jerked him down, and he fell to his knees. The Sorci surrounded him in a tight circle, each with both hands outstretched.

"Let him go!" Kiri's cry reverberated through the hallway. She shoved Worak's shoulder.

"Don't!" Darien exclaimed. "Get out of here!"

Limali thrust one hand at Kiri and slammed her into the ground with a wave of green magic.

"*Kiri!*" Darien tried to get up, but the Sorci's curse held him too tightly.

Raising a hand, Limali took a step toward Kiri, who lay unconscious.

"Forget the nymph!" Worak snapped. "Concentrate your force on the traitor."

With a nod, the woman resumed her previous position.

The scorching blaze coiled around every iota of Darien's existence—not just his body, but his mind and soul as well. A scream clawed at his throat, but he refused to release it and instead met Worak's cold green eyes in silent defiance.

"What a waste," the magician said, a mocking lilt in his voice. "I had such high hopes for you."

Through the heat surrounding him, a shard of ice slithered down Darien's spine. Having heard what the Fiend had said about traitors, he knew there was no hope for mercy. Still, there had to be a way out. He had nearly broken through the binding curse the last time the Sorci had tried to kill him—Worak had admitted so himself. But there had been only three then, and now, there were more than twice as many.

You will survive… The thought floated through his head, drowning out his fear with its cool serenity. But it felt foreign—as unfamiliar as the one that had spoken the prophecy. Yet whereas the latter had invaded his mind with someone else's voice, this one came from within and sounded like his own. He couldn't comprehend the sensation—it was somehow a part of him and not at once. And it was powerful.

Something stirred within, and not the magic he was accustomed to, the unnatural power coerced into existence through might and endurance. This new force was quiet, yet strong—perhaps a previously untapped ability, rising to the surface now that his survival depended on it. A whisper, crescendoing with each second.

Unable to move and unable to fight, he chose not to question its nature, but to nurture it and hope it could somehow save him and Kiri. *I need time… I have to stall them.*

"I used to think you were a great leader," he said to Worak. "But now, I know that someone holds your leash."

Worak let out a harsh laugh. "Is that supposed to insult me? The Age of Fire cannot be stopped, and only those who side with the victor will survive."

"Are you sure?" The rumbling magic within pushed against the sorcerous bonds holding Darien, but unlike his previous efforts, which had taken great effort, this one moved on its own. And other than its growing presence, he felt nothing from it. No agony, no strain—only power. "The forces of Celeste and Terra defeated Inferno before. What makes you think they won't again?"

"Your foolishness is great, young one." The magician glowered. "Even trapped in the Firelands, able to speak only when a communication portal is open, the Fiend knew you lingered outside the ritual room's door, spying with the clarion stone, for he sees all, knows all. He remains more powerful than you can possibly imagine."

"I don't know about that. I *am* quite imaginative." Darien managed a smirk. "I imagine you're afraid of me. Isn't that why I'm not dead yet?"

Face contorting with rage, Worak twisted both wrists, sending a burning flare through Darien's stomach. He doubled over, and a sound escaped his lips, but it wasn't a scream—it was a laugh.

"Coward!" he exclaimed. "What kind of craven fears a mere novice like me?"

"If you only knew what you squandered," the other growled.

"Enlighten me, then." Though he said it partially to stall and give the strange magic building within him time to bud, he also yearned to know what the Sorci master had meant earlier, when he'd spoken of great potential. "Tell me what I could have been."

Worak angled his head. "You regret your betrayal, don't you? You're searching for something that might be worth sparing you for."

No, but you are. Darien detected something akin to hope in the other's voice, which seemed bizarre considering what the Fiend had said about traitors. He would rather leap into the Firelands than return to Worak's command, but if this line of thought would keep the man talking, so be it. The magic within continued pushing back against the Sorci's binding spells, like crashing waves beating against a weakening wall. *Just a little more time...*

"No one likes dying," he said.

"Indeed." Worak gave Darien an appraising look. "If given a second chance, would you swear your loyalty to the Fiend?"

Darien suppressed a shudder. "I would consider it. Why didn't you tell me about him from the beginning?"

"All you wanted was to do good. After I realized that, I made sure you believed the best about us."

Worak's casual tone kindled Darien's anger. The stirring magic grew stronger, as if lapping up his rage and using it for fuel.

"I'd been watching you, young one," the magician went on. "We needed to grow our ranks, and so we divined which humans possessed the greatest potential for magic. Yours burned brighter than anything I'd ever seen before, so when your parents asked for our help in healing your brother, I made sure to respond myself. That way, when you saw me next, you would trust me." An amused lilt lightened his voice.

He's laughing at me. The rising tide within Darien pressed against the fiery bonds, so close to breaking them, he could sense their threads snapping. Yet those holding him didn't seem to feel it.

He longed to erase the smug expression on his former master's face, to shatter it into a bloody pulp and burn the remnants. His mind went back to that night, six months ago, when he'd been traveling alone in the darkness. He hadn't seen much of the robber who had attacked him—only the broad silhouette of a man wielding a knife. In fact, he hadn't even known it was a robber at the time, since those who stole normally demanded things, and this assailant had appeared out of nowhere and begun his attack without speaking a word. Everything had become a blur of blows and struggling, until the blade had found its way into his stomach... and Worak had conveniently appeared moments later.

"You orchestrated the attack on me." The realization hit Darien as he spoke the words. "Did you hire someone to kill me, just so you could save me?"

"Of course not," Worak scoffed. "I created him from smoke. And to smoke he returned once your oath was sworn."

Fury coursed through Darien. The burgeoning power within, until now an uncontrollable force of magic, was suddenly within his grasp, as if someone had built a mighty weapon and slipped it into his hand.

He unleashed its full force against his enemies in a sudden burst of energy. The invisible chains shattered around him. Before the Sorci could react, he thrust his hands out, sending a great gust of red magic crashing toward them. Sweeping his arms in a circle, he directed the glowing spell at the Sorci and watched with satisfaction as they collapsed one by one, blown by the enchanted gale.

Worak alone remained on his feet, but only because Darien had purposely avoided him, to ensure that the master witnessed his minions fall—and saw who'd done it.

Standing, Darien gave the older man a satisfied smirk. The supernatural forces hummed at his fingertips. The scowl on Worak's face was more of shock and fear than outright fury. Though the man punched out his hand with a spell of his own, Darien dodged it with a swift sidestep, then threw the ruby gust at the other, hitting him square in the chest.

With that, it was over.

And it had been all too easy.

His mind was blissfully blank, and the whole world seemed colored by the harsh red light of the strange magic still crackling in his grasp. Now that it was here, it felt as natural as his own hands. He could do with it whatever he pleased, whether it was to destroy, or create, or change, or move; he only had to think about what he wanted, and the power would obey. With it, he was no longer a mere human, but a creature of tremendous might—a deity who could destroy a person with an effortless flick.

But the force was fading… Strong as it was, it wasn't infinite, like a mighty bow with all but one arrow spent.

Use the last to kill him, a part of him whispered. *He's at your mercy.*

Darien stared down at the fallen Worak. Blood pounded in his ears, muffling the world in a strange buzz. Before him lay a deceitful monster

whose evil knew no bounds. Who had twice now tried to kill him. Who had lured him into this hateful place with lies and tricks. Who served the Fiend.

Kill him… Kill him… Kill him…

The words repeated in Darien's head, a rhythmic chant summoning the will to take a life. And in that moment, he saw no reason to resist.

A distant shout echoed through the hallway. It was only then that he recalled there were more Sorci out there. From the pattering off footsteps, they had to be approaching.

The buzzing in his ears faded, and the redness tinting his vision dissipated like steam. He hadn't realized how thick the fog around his mind had been until it had thinned, but now everything suddenly seemed sharper, louder, clearer. Yet he still held the last piece of that great magic, churning and waiting to be released.

Kill him…

He looked up to search for the source of the noises, but wherever the other Sorci were, they hadn't come close enough to be within eyeshot. Even without this strange force, he still possessed the clarion stone, which sat in the leather bag on the floor. With a quick swoop, he picked up the satchel and threw it over his shoulder. The crystal was back within his reach, and after he destroyed his former master, he could use it to direct his ordinary magic at his would-be attackers.

Kill him…

A glimmer caught his eye, and he looked down to see the reflection of firelight dancing in Kiri's silver-blond locks. The magic he held was strong enough to transport him anywhere in the world. If he chose to, he could use it to travel to Kristakai in an instant, and their journey would be over before sunrise. But if he did that, he would have to let Worak live—again.

She doesn't matter… Kill him… Kill him now…

He turned his glare back to Worak, and the rage frothed within him, demanding that he act while he had the chance.

Kill him!

Jolted by a sudden upsurge of wrath, he raised his hand and took a step toward the Sorci master. No more excuses, no more hesitations, no more waiting—

But then something in his heart tugged him back, and he once again glimpsed that flicker of light in Kiri's hair. Choosing not to resist, he spun away from his enemy, knelt beside her, and took her hand.

"*Take us to Kristakai!*" he shouted, channeling all his thoughts into that one idea.

A rush of magic swirled around him, enveloping him and Kiri in a bright red gale. Closing his eyes against the enchanted wind, he felt that last fragment of power disappear, leaving him an ordinary human once more. Tiny sparks pricked his skin, sending tingles up his arms, and loud whooshing filled his ears.

Then, the world went quiet. Yet everything felt the same — the ground was still hard and stone beneath him, not plush with grass or rough from the litter of forest floors. He opened his eyes. A mix of disappointment and anger shot through him at the sight of the same hallway, strewn with unconscious Sorci.

Blazes! Why didn't it work?

Now that the mysterious force was gone, he realized just how bizarre it had been that something so powerful had appeared out of nowhere, and that he hadn't questioned it. What if it hadn't been, as he'd believed, a part of him? What if it had come from some outside source and had now betrayed him?

"Worak!" came a man's voice.

Darien whirled to see Gilonar speeding toward the scene, followed by a hooded man. His pulse quickened, and he instinctively reached for the clarion stone. But there was something off — the two approaching figures shimmered with ripples of distortion, as if he were watching them from underwater.

"What happened here?" Gilonar came to a halt just a few feet away but didn't look at Darien. He threw back his hood, revealing eyes wild with confusion. "How could he have cast a transport spell? No novice can accomplish that!"

Transport spell? But I'm still here. Puzzled, Darien watched the large man and his companion crouch down beside their leader, apparently oblivious to the presence of two fugitives within arm's reach.

"He's no ordinary novice." Darien recognized the voice of the second Sorci as belonging to Vimunax. "Perhaps it wasn't a transport spell."

"How else could both he and the nymph have vanished?" Gilonar placed one hand on Worak's forehead and screwed up his face in concentration, a look signaling that he was about to cast a spell.

Vanished? Darien suddenly realized what had happened. *We're invisible! But how?*

Though the magic hadn't done as he'd told it to, neither had it failed completely. Bewildered, Darien dropped the clarion stone and stared at his hand, wondering where the power had come from. He didn't know who he could turn to for answers, but one thing he was sure of: Worak must have known about this mysterious, latent force. And he must have feared it.

We have that in common, Worak. A disturbed feeling twisted Darien's gut. If the magic had taken him to Kristakai as he'd intended, he might have rejoiced over his newfound abilities. But it had come on its own, cast a spell he hadn't meant for, and then left without explanation. He'd thought he'd controlled it, but, given a moment to reflect, it seemed more likely that it had controlled him.

A sharp cry interrupted his thoughts. Worak bolted up, knocking Gilonar aside.

"*Where is he?*" the master demanded, glaring at the other two. "Where is that cursed Darien?"

Darien was looking straight into the magician's cruel eyes, and yet the other showed no sign of acknowledgement. Nevertheless, tension gripped his heart, for he had no idea how long the invisibility spell would last. If he had to fight Worak again, he couldn't rely on some mysterious force saving him again. And Kiri was still counting on him.

Enough time had been wasted—he had to get them out while he had the chance. He started to stand, then realized he still clasped Kiri's hand. Would she become visible if he let it go? He couldn't take the risk.

"*Find Darien Jekh Zakar!*" Worak shouted, holding his arms up to the air and releasing bright swirls of green. A seeking spell—it would locate something even if it couldn't be seen or heard. Whatever cloak of invisibility Darien wore at present would be useless against such magic.

Alarmed, he scooped up Kiri and bolted down the hallway, aiming for the fortress's door. His footsteps seemed thunderously loud against the stone, but that hardly mattered when Worak was using magic to chase him.

Green light tinted the walls; the magic was approaching. Any moment, it would catch him, and any victories he'd won before would be meaningless.

A flash of light filled the hallway ahead, and he stopped in his tracks. Worak stood directly before him, surrounded by green mist. The seeking spell — it had found him.

But confusion was written in every crease on Worak's brow, and his unfocused eyes indicated that he still didn't see Darien. The strange shimmer told him that the shield of invisibility still protected him, but would that be enough?

He held his breath.

Worak strode forward and walked right past Darien without a glance in his direction. "He's not in the fortress!"

The seeking spell must have failed. Either that, or Darien's shield was powerful enough to block Worak's magic. But everything Darien had learned about the supernatural arts told him that what had just transpired was not possible. Yet there he stood, hidden by a power he shouldn't have possessed. Something greater must have been at work — greater than him, greater than the Sorci, greater than the very nature of human magic.

Keep moving, he reminded himself.

He sprinted through the fortress, the leather bag bouncing against his hip as he made his way to the main door. How he would open it when spells he didn't understand guarded it, he didn't know. Kiri seemed weightless in his arms, though he wasn't sure if it was because she was such a slender girl or if the rush of urgency numbed him to any such strain.

By the time he reached the great hall, his breaths no longer seemed capable of filling his lungs, and he wasn't sure if the world appeared blurred because of the invisibility spell or because his head was swimming with weariness.

He stared at the enormous door, which towered over him with its strange symbols and ciphers. *Now what?*

"*Open!*" A man's voice, thick with the eerie quality that accompanied a spoken spell, filled the air.

The doors obeyed and banged against the walls with thunderous crashes. A powerful, icy gust flew in from the black expanse outside. Darien whirled, wondering how he'd failed to hear someone approach or see the flash of light that would have accompanied a Sorci's appearance by magic.

Vimunax strode across the hall, the hood of his embroidered cloak bouncing against his back. He stroked his white beard with a whimsical glint in his eyes—which were fixed right on Darien. Not looking past him, as Worak's had, but *at* him.

He sees me… Darien stood frozen, watching the old man.

"Any sign of him?" Limali's voice rang out from above, and Darien looked up to see her standing on the staircase overlooking the great hall. But though she faced his direction, her question meant that he was still invisible—to her, at least.

"Not an inkling." Vimunax's eyes remained fixed on Darien's, and the corner of his mouth lifted into a knowing smirk. "If I were him, I'd be long gone by now." He raised his eyebrows, as if to say, *Go, you fool.*

Questions raced through Darien's mind. How did Vimunax see him when no one else could? Had he opened the doors on purpose? Why was he aiding the escape?

Someday, after Kiri had safely returned to her home, he'd figure out what had happened to him tonight. But with an unconscious girl in his arms and an entire order of magicians hunting him, he didn't have time to investigate at the moment. And so he pushed the thoughts out of his head and ran out into the frigid night.

ELSEWHERE…

"Behold, oh Fiend, behold! The moment we've waited for! He's loosed the darkness, yes, yes, and thus begun his descent down a road slicked with the temptations of power. I shall cut away every bond he might cling to, so that he will have no choice but to fall down and down and down, right into my awaiting grasp. Oh, glorious night! The shadow is risen!"

10

Fate of the world

TOMORROW...

All her life, Arrin had been sure of what was right and what was wrong. The morality of each possible path had seemed so obvious, she'd never doubted her choices. As the stars always knew their places in the sky, so had she always known what she had to do, even if it came at a great cost to herself.

Yet now she stood at a crossroads, unable to choose between two paths, each too horrible to contemplate. And no matter which way she looked, there was no third way.

TODAY...

***M I THERE YET?***

With the fate of everyone in the Terrestrial Realm resting on her weary, drooping shoulders, Arrin should have had more meaningful thoughts drifting through her mind. Perhaps a rousing, self-motivating speech about how she must have been chosen by one of the great ayri for this task. Or a profound reflection about the value of life and how precious each of the Divinity's creations was. Or even a tactical, blow-by-blow strategy as to how she would reach the Sapphire Bastille—she was usually good at breaking things down like that.

But she'd gone through each of those more times than she cared to count in the last several hours of trudging through the unkempt brush cluttering the mountain. Remnants of a previous day's snowfall sat in small, uneven clusters and made the ground slick. Having run out of—or simply grown tired of—important ideas, her mind had slipped into the mundane, such as *How much further is that blighted fortress?* and *Skies, I'm tired!*

If only she had a map or a clock! Then she might at least be able to figure out how far she'd gone since taking the mermaid Ilaerii's advice. The amber Prudence Star peered down at her from between the dry branches of tall trees, and she wished she could ask it one simple question: "Where the blazes is the lightforsaken Bastille?"

With only it for navigation and no hands-on knowledge, she didn't even know whether she'd crossed the border between Nikhilim and Eryu yet. Lines on maps were one thing. Actually walking across the terrain was another. How much longer would she have to trudge uphill before she reached the mountain's summit? For all she knew, the fortress didn't even lie on the other side—there could be yet another mountain she'd have to cross before she reached it. The windborn one could be dead by then.

Now, now, Arrin. Mulling on what-ifs will do you no good. That was something Mahtim had always told her, and the words had never seemed wiser. She could whine and wonder and groan to herself all she wanted, but it wouldn't get her any closer to her destination. So the only thing to do was keep putting one foot in front of the other and recalling why she was doing this in the first place.

Save the wind girl. Save her family. Save the world.

Noble thoughts, all of them, but her body's protests—the unbearable dryness in her mouth, the burning aches in her legs, the labored complaints of her lungs—now screamed louder than the brave proclamations of her conscience.

More tired than she'd ever been in her life, Arrin dropped to the ground. She needed a *break*; she was only human, after all.

Considering her present altitude, the temperature couldn't have been much above freezing. And yet sweat dripped off her forehead. *The air's probably thinner up here too—that certainly isn't helping my situation.*

The heaviness of sleep pressed down on her eyelids, and she wanted nothing more than to curl up on the ground and drift off.

Maybe that's not such a bad idea. Reaching into her bag, she grabbed her canteen and took a long, satisfying swig. *Even chosen ones need to sleep.*

The thought made her laugh aloud, but she instantly regretted it. She wasn't out of danger yet, after all. Lady Bolliore's goons might still be searching for her, and who knew what predators lurked in the tangle of shadows? Still, the idea of being a "chosen one" was more than presumptuous; it was downright bizarre. Logically speaking, it was the thing to conclude, since someone in the Celestial Realm had literally

chosen her to receive the prophecy. But it puzzled her that they'd picked an indentured servant with no magic abilities, no combat skills, and no mystical experience. As far as she could tell, the only thing that set her apart was her superior intelligence. *Maybe that's reason enough.*

Partly to remind herself that she *was* worthy and partly because she desired the comfort of a familiar presence, Arrin took her notebook out of her bag and held it close. There, between the worn covers of her leather-bound journal, lay all her dreams and ambitions, sometimes scribbled in a frenzy of inspiration and sometimes painstakingly drawn over hours of pondering. Each page, once pristine with newness, was now covered in layouts for castles, designs for weapons, and calculations for new machines she hoped to build someday. More than anything, she yearned to fly, which was why half the pages were covered in sketches of artificial wings.

But did anyone see in her a future creator of magnificent things? An architect, an engineer, an inventor? Lady Bolliore certainly hadn't. If she'd asked, Arrin could have fortified the Bolliore forces with stronger weapons, or discovered ways to make the land's agriculture more efficient, or magnified the noblewoman's status with plans for a glorious new fortress. But all those visions remained trapped in her head and within the pliant covers of her beaten journal.

Neither, it seemed, did whichever supernatural force picked her for the vision care about all Arrin hoped to be.

Whoever you are, you really should have picked someone else. What this quest needs is a brave, trained warrior who can fend off enemies. I'm not that person. All I have is a little wooden crescent not meant for combat, a knife I don't know how to use, and the stubbornness to try fighting anyway.

Sighing, she drew her knees up to her chest and gazed up at the glittering sky. *The stars don't make mistakes,* she reminded herself.

She closed her eyes and, with a long breath, drew in the night, savoring its cool crispness and quiet rhythm. The air wrapped her in its fresh, invigorating blanket, and the soft songs of distant creatures cooing and calling through the darkness pierced the silence.

A rustling noise caught her attention. The imprecise *crunch-crunch-crunch* of feet upon dry leaves and twigs sounded from uphill, drawing closer with every step.

Arrin jumped up and shoved her journal back into her bag. Given how long she'd walked without finding any sign of human existence, odds were that the footsteps belonged to a particularly large and lumbering animal. But she wasn't about to take any chances, especially when she was too exhausted to put up a proper fight if it turned out to be Lady Bolliore's minions—or worse, a bloodthirsty robber who would slit her throat for the handful of coins in her bag.

Looking around frantically, she spotted a large tree a few paces away. Tall yet dense with numerous thick, inviting branches—perfect for climbing.

With a few well-placed maneuvers, she scaled it in seconds.

A quiet voice wafted toward her. "It's all right, Kiri. Don't be afraid."

"Darien?" A second voice floated through the night. "What happened?"

There are two of them? Arrin was certain she'd only heard one set of footsteps. She scanned the darkness but couldn't make out anything.

"We escaped," said the boy called Darien, in a voice that seemed like it was meant to comfort the girl, yet whose curtness instantly alerted Arrin's suspicions.

Escaped? From what? She leaned down against the branch, eager to hear more.

"What? How?" The girl—whose name had to be Kiri—sounded puzzled. Then, in a completely different tone, she said, "Let me down. I can walk."

Ah, so he's carrying her. That explained why Arrin heard two voices but only one set of steps.

A short pause, in which a brief crunching noise suggested that something—or someone—was being placed on the ground, followed, and then Kiri asked, "Where are we?"

"Hard to tell when we're in the middle of the wilderness, but I was aiming for the Nikhilim border." Darien's voice was light with nonchalance, but the way his words rushed between shallow breaths revealed that he must have been exhausted.

"The wilderness?" Kiri sounded confused. "But… how?"

"Worak isn't the only one with surprises," Darien muttered darkly. Then, in what sounded like another attempt at offhandedness, he said, "I do know a little about magic, you know. Perhaps not as much as the Sorci,

but enough to catch them off-guard. It's been a while since I last saw any sign of them. If we're lucky, they might even have given up on finding us — at least for tonight."

That means they escaped from the Bastille — I must be getting close! A rush of excitement flood Arrin's veins.

"You carried me all this way?" Kiri asked.

"Well, you were unconscious, it seemed rude to leave you behind." The casualness in Darien's tone sounded so false, even he probably didn't believe it. Behind the careless words lay a tender note, and Arrin bit her lip to stifle a giggle.

Aw, he's sweet on her! It seemed as if, instead of encountering some danger, she'd stumbled upon a classic pair of star-crossed lovers. Maybe the Sorci, famous yet secretive, weren't as magnanimous as they seemed, and the two were runaway indentured servants like her.

When Kiri didn't respond, Darien said, "I made you a promise, Kiri. And no matter what, I intend to keep it."

Arrin wrinkled her nose, unsure of whether she found the statement sweet or maudlin. It occurred to her that, as an invisible witness to a pair of lovebirds, she might end up hearing — or worse, seeing — an intimate moment or two. The thought made her cringe, and she wondered if she should jump down and make herself known before it was too late.

"Thank you," Kiri whispered. Her tone suggested that she longed to say more, yet couldn't find the words.

"We should keep going," Darien said. "As lovely as this random patch of forest is, stopping here probably isn't a good idea."

"They're still looking for us, aren't they?"

"I wouldn't count on them giving up. Though it would be nice if they did."

"Darien…" She drew an audible breath. "I'm sorry."

"Why?" He sounded perplexed.

Good question, Arrin thought.

"If it weren't for me, none of this would have happened," Kiri said so quietly, Arrin could barely make out the words. "I should never have involved you in this."

"It's not your fault," Darien said. "In fact, you saved me… I owe you so much. More than you can realize."

There was a pause, and then Kiri repeated, "I'm sorry."

Why are girls always apologizing? Annoyed, Arrin twisted her mouth. *Lucky for Kiri, her boy seems decent enough not to take advantage of it.*

"Sorry for what?" Darien said. "Saving my life? Opening my eyes to evil? Forgiving me when you had every right to hate me? Kiri, it is *I* who am sorry. And I swear, I will atone for it."

Hm… There's a story here. Though Arrin had read many wise words about avoiding the pettiness of gossip-like notions, she couldn't help her interest. Despite all the book learning and savviness with numbers, she was still an average person in many ways, and average people were fascinated by other people. *Maybe I'm not as smart as I thought. Well, technically, I'm evaluating a potential threat. That's justification enough, right?*

The crunching sounds resumed as two pairs of footsteps drew closer, and Arrin leaned further down from the branch, searching for the source of the voices. *Maybe I should say hello and ask if they can point me to the Bastille. They sound harmless enough.*

But a warning bell rang in her head, reminding her that they could be more dangerous than they seemed. She had no idea who they were, after all, other than that they sounded young and sappy. With everything riding on her mission's success, she couldn't afford to take any chances. *Fate of the world,* she reminded herself with an internal sigh. *Never thought that kind of incentive would get old, but it's starting to grate on me…*

For several moments, the approaching pair didn't speak. The silence hinged on awkwardness, though Arrin had no way of knowing if the two were indeed uncomfortable or if they were accustomed to being in each other's presence without talking. Couples were known to do that, after all—her parents could spend hours in the same room without exchanging a word.

The rustling sounds were so near, the pair had to be right in front of her, but cloaked in shadow. Patches of moonlight brightened the forest floor, and she hoped—to satisfy her curiosity, if nothing else—that either Kiri or Darien would step into one.

Her wish was granted a few moments later, when a young man emerged from the darkness, entering the silvery pool created by the moon and stars. An uncanny feeling struck her at the sight of his sharp, handsome features, as if she'd seen him somewhere before, but she forgot about him a moment

later, when the other followed him into the light—it was the wind girl from the vision. Though she looked human at the moment, there was no mistaking that face.

The words *I found her!* lit up like sunlight in Arrin's head, and excitement jolted her heart. Before she realized what she was doing, she swung down from the tree branch and landed solidly on her feet. "You're her!" she cried, the words tumbling out. "You're the windborn one!"

Kiri's fearful gasp made Arrin realize how stupidly she acted. A flash of light caught her eyes—a short blade glinted in Darien's grip.

"Whoa!" Arrin threw up her hands in the universal gesture of surrender. "I mean you no harm! I don't even have anything I *could* harm you with! No weapons, I swear!" That wasn't true, but with a knife pointed at her, it seemed like the thing to say.

"Who are you?" Kiri demanded.

Arrin opened her mouth to answer, but Darien spoke first.

"It's you!" His eyes widened, and he lowered his weapon. "Yours was the voice I heard! 'If the windborn one dies, the Fiend will triumph'… *You* sent that message!"

Arrin gaped. "Skies above, that *worked?*" Seeing his eyes narrow with suspicion—and keenly aware that he still held a knife—she rushed to explain. "I had a vision of the Age of Fire. Hard to explain the specifics, since most of it was a roaring jumble of flame and despair, but one thing I saw for sure." She gestured at Kiri. "*She* died, and that set off a chain of events that led to the end of… everything. I had to stop it, but wasn't sure if I'd reach her in time, so I tried to send a warning. Since I was getting messages like a psychic would, I thought maybe I could send one as well. Had no idea whether I was right or not, though. Until now."

"You're not a prophet, then?" Kiri asked.

Arrin crossed her arms. "By definition I am, since I did receive a prophecy, after all. And don't ask how I know it's real and not a hallucination. I just *do.*"

"I believe you." The girl pursed her lips, clearly worried.

A pensive look crossed Darien's face. "I was trying to summon the first Sibyl's vision of the Age of Fire when I heard the warning… I must not have been focused enough, and that left an opening for our magic to converge."

Arrin shrugged. "Sounds reasonable." The uncanny feeling struck her again; she was *sure* she'd seen him before. "You look familiar… Are you from Nikhilim?"

"Yes." His short answer made it clear that he didn't want to elaborate, but she ignored the cue.

"I think I've seen you somewhere—"

"Mine's a pretty common face. You're probably thinking of someone else."

She raised her eyebrow. *A "pretty common face"? Where? On the Island of Improbably Attractive People?* He had to be hiding something. But though he'd sparked her curiosity, who he was didn't really matter. It was the wind girl she needed to worry about.

Turning her attention back to Kiri, she said, "Who are you, exactly?"

"An air nymph from Kristakai," the other replied. "I know what your vision means… The Sorci are working for the Fiend. They're looking for a way into the unicorn domains, to steal the powers of every enchanted creature and use them to fight for the Infernal Realm."

"The Sorci are allied with *Inferno?*" Arrin shook her head, dismayed. So this was what the mermaid had meant by her warning. She wondered if Ilaerii knew the extent of the Sorci's corruption. *So much for peaceful scholars of magic.*

Something must have poisoned their ranks. From what she'd read about the magicians, they could be ruthless when it came to gaining power. Of course, that was hundreds of years ago, back when they dominated the Terrestrial Realm, but she imagined certain philosophies would carry across the generations. And, logically speaking, aligning themselves with a powerful—if evil—enemy to the world *was* the surest way to secure their own survival. But it was still… *wrong.*

"We have to stop them," she muttered.

"That's the idea," Darien said. "Do you know how far we are from Nikhilim?"

"Not a clue—I was just following the Prudence Star and praying the Bastille wasn't too far." Recalling what she'd overheard them say earlier, Arrin cocked her head. "How exactly does running *away* from the Sorci thwart their wicked plans?"

Kiri's mouth tightened. "You're right—instead of warning my

homeland, perhaps I should stop those who would attack them." She turned, looking up the mountain.

Darien put his hand on her shoulder. "It's too dangerous—it was enough of a miracle that we even escaped. They'd capture you, and we'd be right back to where we started."

"And where's that?" Arrin asked. Though she'd picked up pieces of their story, she still hadn't formed a clear picture of who they were. "Actually, start with who you are."

Darien arched his brows. "You never told us who *you* are."

Oh, that's true. "Arrin Velindale." She put her hands on her hips. "Also known as the girl who crossed miles of blighted wilderness while running from passels of benighted curbrains in a noble attempt to find a girl I saw in a vision. To stop the Age of Fire. Which seems pretty important, especially since the battle has already begun… Yesterday, I saw an ayr fall."

Kiri's hands flew to her mouth, and Darien's brow furrowed.

"Are you certain?" he asked.

"Dead sure." Arrin shuddered, wondering what it meant for the world that one of its guiding lights was lost. Already, everything seemed darker. "I don't know which it was, but it's the most definite sign there can be that Inferno's rising." She glanced at Kiri. "All I know is that I have to keep you alive, or the world will burn. If the Sorci are after you, that makes them my enemy too. And you know the old saying: 'The enemy of my enemy is my friend.' So I guess we're friends now."

Kiri smiled. "I'm glad. My name's Kiri."

"I know. I overheard you talking when you approached." Arrin turned back to Darien. "Your lady seems to trust me. How about you, lover boy?"

A flurry of protests and denials rushed from both Kiri and Darien's mouths, bombarding her with expressions of shock and embarrassment, such as, "Oh, we're not lovers!" and "No, no, we're not a couple!"

Startled, Arrin raised her hands. "Whoa! My apologies!" Not that she believed them; she didn't have to be a prophet to know those two would wind up kissing eventually. But she wasn't here for gossip. "Now, back to more important things… *What* is going on?"

She listened with consternation as Kiri explained—how the Sorci had captured her, how they'd bound her powers and her memories, and how she and Darien had barely escaped with their lives. But upon hearing

about the silver clock, Arrin's mind instantly went back to her vision. Kiri's hypothesis with regard to the prophecy sounded logical, but it felt incomplete.

"So it comes down to this," she said, when Kiri had finished speaking. "You have to get home within the next few days. But what about the Sorci? Who knows what they'll be doing in the meanwhile?"

"Chasing us, for one thing," Darien said. A nervous look crossed his eyes, and he turned to Kiri. "We should keep moving. The further we can go before exhaustion forces us to stop, the better. Hopefully, we can make it into Nikhilim, where, at least, the Sorci hold no official power. Unless granted special permission from the king or one of his advisors, they're forbidden from practicing their supernatural arts within its borders. Once we're there, we can cut through the capital and take a ship across the gulf… That will shave days off our journey and put us within a few miles of Kristakai."

"I don't know this land, but you do," Kiri said. "Wherever you go, I'll follow." She spoke in a voice so sweet and trusting, Arrin had to resist hard to avoid rolling her eyes.

Oh, she's got it bad. Well, at least it sounds like they know what they're doing. But what about me?

Her plans had begun and ended with finding the windborn one, and she hadn't possessed enough information to formulate anything further. Now that she'd encountered Kiri, the next step seemed to be to ensure that she returned to the unicorn domain. But would accompanying the two on their journey actually help? One extra person wouldn't make it go any faster, and the idea of traveling with two strangers did not appeal to her… especially since they were bound to realize they were in love at some point, which would make her the awkward third party. The very thought made her want to gag.

If she'd been particularly skilled in some aspect that might help Kiri reach her home, Arrin would have swallowed her discomfort and volunteered to go with them anyway. But as her own recent experiences proved, she was no travel expert. If the Sorci managed to catch up to them, she was more likely to hinder than help in a fight.

Meanwhile, the Sorci were still cooking up whatever diabolical magic they planned to use to infiltrate Kristakai. While she understood why Kiri

and Darien were fleeing, she felt uncomfortable about leaving the agents of Inferno to do as they pleased. *Someone* should keep an eye on them. And sabotage their efforts. And thwart them in whatever way possible.

That someone would be her.

"How far is the fortress?" she asked, looking to Darien, since Kiri would have been too unconscious to know how long he'd walked.

"Probably about two or three miles behind by now—not nearly far enough." He adjusted the bag on his shoulder. "Which way are you headed?"

"Apparently, two or three miles that way." Arrin pointed uphill. "It's on the other side of the mountain, right? I'm going to figure out what exactly those blackguards are up to."

He let out a dry, incredulous laugh. "And I'm going to sprout wings and fly."

She gave him a funny look. "What are you talking about?"

He shrugged. "I thought we were making ridiculous statements that had no chance of coming true."

"Arrin," Kiri said, sounding worried. "The fortress is guarded by layers and layers of magic, and the Sorci will kill anyone they deem a threat."

"Fortunately, they're not looking for me." Arrin crossed her arms, popping her hip out with defiance. She didn't need their—or anyone's—permission to go through with her plan, but since they all had the same ultimate goal, she felt they should be allies. And they had information she needed for the next leg of her quest. "I've *seen* the Age of Fire, witnessed what it will do. I've watched my family burn. And I would do anything, *anything* to prevent it. I take it you have the same goal, or if you don't, you should, because when the Fiend rises, he will spare no one. So don't lecture me on something I already know. Just tell me whatever you can about that place—unless you want me to go in clueless."

For a minute, no one spoke. Then, Darien said, "I can draw you a diagram of the fortress. It won't be exact, but I've memorized enough of its features to give you a rough idea. Do you have anything on which I can write?"

"I even brought something to write with." She retrieved her notebook from her bag. Though she hesitated somewhat, since she'd hoped to keep it pure, in a sense, and have it contain only her plans and calculations, her

immediate needs outweighed such lofty ideas. After a bit of rummaging, she located her pencil, a thick rod of graphite wrapped in string. It had snapped near the middle—probably because the notebook had landed on it at some point—but it was still long enough to use.

Darien cupped his hands by his mouth and whispered, "*Shine gently.*" A soft blue glow appeared, illuminating the hands that held it but barely reaching his face. Tinted by its enchanted light, he seemed otherworldly and strange, almost like a spirit whose piercing black eyes could see into a person's soul. Yet Kiri, bathed in the same watery luminance, looked as if she were in her natural form, and Arrin realized that it was because, in her visions, this was how the air nymph had appeared: an ethereal being both familiar and unearthly at once.

He released the light, which floated in the air, and held out his hand for the notebook.

She reluctantly gave it to him, along with the pencil. "There are some blank pages at the back… Don't draw on any with writing already there."

"You brought your journal?" he asked, lifting the cover.

"Something like that."

She bit her lip as he flipped through the pages. Kiri watched over his shoulder. Though they probably weren't paying any attention to the sketches that occupied the crinkled paper, she still felt nervous about someone seeing her work. All the fellow servants who'd glimpsed her diagrams had either laughed, calling her a delusional dreamer with ideas too big for her head, or attempted to be "helpful" by reminding her that penniless girls didn't become architects and inventors.

"Did you draw these?" Kiri asked, eyes fixed on the pages.

Arrin straightened. "Of course."

"They're beautiful."

"Thank you," she said, though the compliment was undeserved. Her scribbled notes, numbers, and equations were, at best, messy and, at worst, incomprehensible to anyone other than herself. As for the sketches of buildings and weapons and machines—they were pragmatic blueprints, not artistic endeavors. Rough, hastily drawn outlines with angles and measurements marking, theoretically, how each piece should fit together. "I'm not sure 'beautiful' is the right word."

Darien's dark eyebrows gathered. "You're right—the proper term is 'brilliant.'" He glanced up from the page. "Are you a student at the Royal Academy?"

"Only in my dreams," she scoffed. But she didn't miss the notes of admiration in how both he and Kiri had spoken, and the looks on their faces could only be described as "impressed." The warmth of pride filled her chest. "I'm glad I'm good enough to fool you into thinking so."

"Have you considered applying?"

"I would if I weren't contracted to haul water buckets for the next twenty years of my life." Realizing she'd left the Lady Bolliore part of her life out of the introduction she'd given, she said, "By the way, I'm a fugitive, too," and briefly explained how she'd ended up an indentured servant, and how that meant if she ever returned to Nikhilim, she'd be arrested.

"That's terrible," Kiri said. "I'm so sorry."

"I was trapped anyway." Arrin sighed as the realities of her future weighed down on her. She'd tried not to think about them, since she couldn't change her circumstances, but the fact was that she'd probably spend the rest of her life on the fringes of society, scraping by on whatever odd jobs she could find and avoiding the kingdom she'd once called home, lest the outstanding warrant land her in a dungeon.

"It's a shame," Darien murmured, turning his gaze back to the pages. "Once I get Kiri home… You belong at the Academy, Arrin. I might have a way of getting you there."

Don't make promises you can't keep, Arrin thought cynically. It was nice that he wanted to help, but she knew better than to mistake good intentions for future actions. *First, he betrays dangerous magicians to save an air nymph, and now he wants to give a stranger a shot at her dreams. There's a hero complex if I ever saw one.*

Darien reached the first blank page of the journal and, balancing it in the crook of his arm, began sketching a rough floor plan. The drawing was probably out of proportion, especially given his apparent inability to produce straight lines or right angles, but it was better than nothing. How she would enter the fortress in the first place, especially if it was indeed guarded by "layers and layers" of spells, was a problem she'd yet to solve, but she decided not to worry about it until she was closer to her destination.

"If you could make one of your drawings come to life, which would you pick?" Kiri asked with a smile.

"The flying machine." Arrin didn't hesitate—she'd known the answer to that question for as long as she could remember. "Can you imagine what it must be like to soar above the world?" Then, remembering who she was talking to, she chuckled. "Of course—you're an air nymph. But for those of us who are merely human… Every facet of the world seems designed to contain us. We're kept on the ground, and each time we try to reach higher, we're pulled back down, sometimes with deadly results. All around us are barriers, both of distance and of substance. I want to rise above them—literally. I want to be free."

"That's a lovely dream." A wistful look crossed Kiri's face, and Arrin, recalling that the girl was cursed and no longer possessed her abilities, suddenly regretted having spoken.

She searched for another topic to fill the silence while Darien continued his rough map of the Sapphire Bastille but couldn't come up with anything that wasn't either prying or self-centered. Deciding that the latter was less likely to offend, she said casually, "I built a miniature of the machine once and threw it off a cliff, hoping to watch it glide out of sight, but it plummeted into the valley. I later realized that I was building on the assumption that merely the *size* would need to be shrunken, and that I had completely forgotten to account for needing lighter building materials." It was a dull statement, but it beat standing around awkwardly.

"I hope you build the real one someday," Kiri said, but the mournfulness remained in her eyes.

Luckily, at that moment, Darien concluded his drawing, saving Arrin from having to make further small talk—a skill she had never been particularly adept at.

"I hope this helps." He handed her the closed notebook with the pencil tucked between the pages.

"So do I." Arrin placed it into her bag.

"This might help too." He pulled out the knife he'd nearly stabbed her with. Well, perhaps that was an exaggeration, but he *had* aimed it at her.

"Thanks, but… I lied before. I *am* armed—sort of. I have a blade of my own."

"Can't hurt to have a spare."

Deciding she could use as much help as she could get, she chose not to protest and accepted it. "Won't argue with that, though I hope I won't need either weapon."

"So do I. Oh, and there's one more thing." He rummaged through his bag again and pulled out an egg-sized stone, which looked like a clear crystal growing out of a plain gray rock. "*Cleave*," he murmured, closing his fist around it. The transparent part glowed white as a rushing wind swirled around him, ruffling his hair without disturbing the branches that hung behind him. His eyes were closed and his face tight, and he looked to be under some kind of duress, though she wasn't sure if it was physical discomfort or mental strain that caused it. Glittering blue sparks flurried like snowflakes around the stone. A sharp noise, reminiscent of glass cracking, sounded from its direction, and the whooshing ceased.

When Darien opened his hand, a piece of the crystal, roughly the size of a coin, had broken off. But it retained its supernatural luster until he whispered a word that extinguished them both.

"What is that?" she asked.

"A clarion stone." He picked up the shard, then explained how the crystal—and others like it—could amplify a magician's powers. "And if it's ever broken, the pieces remain connected to each other. Sometimes, the Sorci use them to communicate." He handed the shard to Arrin. "I don't like the idea of leaving the Sorci to do as they will any more than you do. Whatever they're up to, I want to know."

Arrin didn't like the thought of reporting her observations to someone but reminded herself of the need for allies. "How does it work?" She examined the transparent disc, though she couldn't see much of it in the darkness. "I don't know magic."

"You don't need to. The shard is, in a sense, already speaking to the larger piece. Using its magic for spells turns parts of it back into rock, but communicating through it does not. Just ask it to bridge the distance, and it will. Like this." He clenched the stone and said, "*Link.*"

White mist rose from the small stone she held, swirling and glowing as it thickened, until soon, it took the form of Darien's face in shimmering silver. Arrin watched in fascination as the facsimile imitated his movements when he smiled.

"And to break the connection, just say, *cease.*"

At that word, the mist disappeared, leaving her once again with a piece of rock that looked like broken glass.

"Though don't fret if you forget the precise terms," Darien went on. "When it comes to magic, it's your intention that matters."

"I'll remember." Arrin tucked the crystal shard safely into a small pouch sewn into her bag to carry coins. She glanced up at the sky, where the stars still twinkled against otherwise unadulterated blackness, and found the amber Prudence Star shining above. "I'd better go on my way. Be careful."

"You too," Kiri said.

As Arrin trudged through yet more untamed tangles of forest flora, her heart drummed nervously behind her heaving chest.

She couldn't shake the feeling that she was walking toward her doom.

ELSEWHERE...

"Here lie the firegems, touched by your own power, my dark Master. These sorry magicians would not complete their own spell were it not for my assistance. But I am happy to report that we are drawing close to completing the concoctions needed to enter Kristakai. The nymph believes she can warn her people and stop us — laughable, is it not? Let her run, let her hide, let her attack us, for all I care. Nothing she does can stand in our way."

11

For this one moment

"Who *are* you?" Kiri cried, blinking back the tears of fury, of pain, of sorrow. "What have you become? Where's the one I fell for?"

His lips split into a humorless grin. "He's dead. I killed him."

TODAY...

ELICATE LEAVES TWIRLED ON A GENTLE BREEZE—miniscule dancers of green against an azure sky. And yet they were bound to their branches, unable to frolic with the same freedom as the white butterflies flitting above. They strained at their stems, twisting and flapping, until one broke off and flew triumphantly into the atmosphere.

Lying back on the soft bed of grass covering the forest floor, Kiri watched the leaf flash like an emerald as it ascended toward the clouds. She smiled at its newfound independence, but then sorrow filled her heart. It wouldn't be long before that leaf, separated from the tree that was its home and lifeblood, faded and died.

The same would happen to her if she ever left Kristakai.

Hot sunlight spilled through the loose canopy above — too hot for her taste — thickening the air until a silvery fog floated all around her. Yet despite her discomfort, she didn't want to leave.

"…And so, despite her family's warnings, she set forth on her quest, determined to let nothing stop her…" Elaia's voice, melodious and soft, drifted toward her.

Kiri twisted to face her friend, who sat beside her reading aloud from a thick book in her lap. If the heat bothered Elaia at all, she didn't show it. Behind her, multitudes of colorful tomes sat on shelves woven from the branches of majestic trees. The song of a distant choir, intoning a mournful ballad, surrounded Kiri in dulcet, cascading tones. Whose voices they were, she didn't know, but they felt as familiar as the air they filled.

This was Kristakai. This was home.

And yet, this was also a prison. A beautiful, comfortable one, where she would always be safe, but a prison nonetheless.

"…Not two days into her journey, she came across the magnificent city of Bahinei, whose palaces of white stone stood as tall as any mountain…" Elaia's voice rose with excitement as she described the gleaming human metropolis the story's heroine had encountered.

Kiri closed her eyes and tried to imagine what it would be like to walk among such grand manmade structures. If only she could spend just one day outside the domain's enchanted borders, just one day exploring the wonders of a world she'd heard about countless times, yet had never seen with her own eyes.

She lifted her hand to flick a stray hair out of her face, and her fingers brushed something smooth on the ground beside her. Glancing toward it, she found a small wooden bird with a cylindrical body. Red cloth stretched over the frame of its wings, and a small crank protruded from beneath its painted tail.

She picked it up and admired its craftsmanship, wishing she knew who had made it. A human — that was all the sprite had said when he'd given it to her. Like nymphs, sprites were closely connected to their land, except they had the freedom to leave if they chose to. The ones who could pass for human — whose skin was a shade of brown or beige rather than purple or blue or some other floral hue — often journeyed outside and later returned with trinkets and tales. Other inhabitants of Kristakai would at times accompany them, despite the unicorns' warnings about possible dangers, though they seldom traveled as far as their better-disguised counterparts. Only nymphs were bound to their homeland forever.

Bound like a leaf to its tree, doomed to die if she ever left.

Kiri glared at the sky. If she'd been created during the Age of Unicorns, she could have wandered as far as she pleased.

Still lying back and holding the wooden bird above her, she aimed it at the sky and twisted the crank, causing the wings to flap as whatever mechanism lay hidden behind the painted body clicked with each turn. Then, she released it, and the artificial creature took off, its red wings flashing in the light. Even that trinket, a child's toy from another world, could cross Kristakai's borders without consequence.

"Kiri? Are you even listening anymore?" Elaia's face appeared, staring down with an expression of annoyance. Her thick, flaming hair tumbled over her shoulders, so close that Kiri could feel their heat pressing into her, and yet she didn't mind. "If you find the tale so boring, you should have told me to choose *another instead of letting me go on." Elaia's auburn brows tilted. "What's the matter?"*

With a sigh, Kiri sat up. "I wish I could visit a city like the one in the story." The artificial bird landed in the grass near her outstretched legs, and she grasped it. "I wish I could meet the kind of people who can look at a block of wood and see a bird."

"Then go." Elaia crossed her arms. "There are no chains binding you to this forest. If you want to see what's outside, just leave."

Kiri shook her head. "You know I can't."

"As long as you return in time, what's the harm?" Elaia leaned forward, staring into Kiri's eyes with her sharp green gaze. "You should go."

The heat radiating from her hair became scorching in its intensity, and the look on her face suddenly seemed malicious, as if she were purposely wielding her flames as weapons.

Kiri drew back. "Elaia?"

A blaze erupted around her, emanating from the fire nymph's locks, then her hands, then her body, surrounding Kiri in unbearable heat.

"Stop!" she cried, scrambling to get away.

Only Elaia's face remained visible through the red and yellow conflagration. She stared at Kiri with eyes that snapped with inexplicable hatred.

Out of nowhere, three figures cloaked in black appeared from behind the fire nymph, reaching toward her with hands surrounded by silver mist. Kiri spun and ran, only to find herself faced with three others, shadowy beings whose faces were swaths of blackness beneath their hoods.

Before she could flee, they grabbed her wrists so tightly, she thought they might crush her bones. She twisted and kicked, but then more hands clasped her shoulders, and then her ankles.

Crying out for help, she struggled uselessly against their iron grips as the fire continued burning…

Kiri gasped, blinking rapidly as the vestiges of her dream faded into the recesses of her mind. For a moment, she wondered where she was, for the wooden crates surrounding her seemed entirely unfamiliar, as did the brown cloth stretching over her in a wide arc. The ground beneath her shook, and the muffled sounds of horses neighing drifted past her ears.

Then, she recalled: This was the back of a wagon, one of at least a

dozen in a long caravan journeying through Nikhilim. She and Darien had walked through the night, until the first hints of dawn had peeked over the horizon, throwing its pale gray light over a wide road. Upon spotting the caravan, ambling slowly yet steadily in the direction they wanted to travel in, they had slipped into one of the many covered carts, which, as Darien had explained, were carrying various types of merchandise—from food to cloth to furniture—from the outlying villages to sell in the city.

Pushing the black cloak, which she'd used as a blanket, off of her shoulders, Kiri sat up and stretched, a smile tugging at her lips. Though the wooden wagon bed was no softer than the floor of the cell had been, this was the first time she could remember waking up someplace other than that frigid dungeon, and the feeling was wonderful. But then, her ears caught a quiet ticking sound emitting from the folds of her dress, and a wave of fear washed away the momentary relief.

Perhaps she was no longer a prisoner to the Sorci, but neither was she free. The specters of danger, recapture, and death loomed still.

She thought back to her dream, wondering how much of it was memory and how much was a fevered imagining. There had been hardly any of the threatening silver mist this time, and, until the very end, no heat from the curse either—unless that was why the air had felt unnaturally hot, and why pale fog had swirled above the grass? But the magic hadn't attacked her until the very end. Perhaps it was possible that, when she'd unleashed her powers to save Darien, she'd unbound a few memories as well.

Some aspects of the dream she knew to be nonsense—mostly the end, when the scene had stopped making sense. Yet certain elements she knew to be real—the fire nymph, the grove, and her own longing to see the world beyond Kristakai.

In a way, her wish had come true. She *had* left the unicorn domain and witnessed some of the new and unusual things that lay outside. The Sapphire Bastille in all its dark magnificence, as awe-inspiring as it was evil. Arrin's drawings—sketched manifestations of ideas Kiri could never have dreamed of. The caravan she was presently traveling with in secret, which Darien might have viewed as mundane, but that, to her, was among the many fascinating aspects of human life.

Though her memory was far from complete, she at least had enough pieces to understand how she had ended up the Sorci's prisoner. Her curiosity — and perhaps a sense of defiance — had driven her to seek escape from her home. But she couldn't recall what had happened between venturing outside and finding herself in the cell. She wasn't sure if she wanted to remember being captured and cursed, though she did wonder how far she'd traveled before the magicians had targeted her.

Tugging on the chain she wore around her neck, she pulled the silver clock out from under her dress collar, where she'd tucked it to keep it safe. The gleaming black hands pointed to four o'clock.

Four days. And they'd barely begun their journey.

She dropped the timepiece back into her top and hugged her knees to her chest. At least she was heading in the right direction. Her only hope was to trust in Darien, who knew this land well enough to have strategized a shortcut.

She spotted him on the other side of the wagon, leaning against a large basket filled with gleaming bolts red and green fabric, with his eyes shut and his hands resting on the bag across his lap. He'd told her he would stay awake to keep watch, but she couldn't blame him for succumbing to weariness.

This was the first time she'd seen him at peace — without the ferocity of anger, the darkness of fear, or the anguish of pain both outside and within. As soon as he awoke, all those things would return, and she wished she had a way to chase those shadows away.

You've spoken so much of how you'll help me, but what will become of you? The Sorci were still after his blood, and they would not easily give up their pursuit. And she couldn't bring him into the protection of Kristakai when the enchanted barriers made it impossible for any human to enter. Could the laws of Nikhilim protect him? It was his homeland, after all — surely the kingdom would not allow one of their own to fall into the clutches of evil.

It suddenly hit her that, once she returned to Kristakai, she might never see him again. The thought filled her with melancholy, and she quickly reminded herself that it was possible for her to find him once the curse was lifted and her life force restored as long as she was careful. But what would she do, fly to whichever town he'd made his new home in and say hello? Assuming he hadn't vanished to stay out of the Sorci's sights.

A deep, aching sorrow curled through Kiri's chest, and heat rushed to

her face as she realized how long she'd been staring at him. Yet she couldn't deny that something was stirring in her heart—strange and frightening and wonderful at once. Had it really been less than a day since he'd defied the Sorci in an attempt to set her free? So much had happened, it seemed an eternity had passed in the night.

There was an old saying that stated one could never truly know a person until one witnessed their most desperate hour. Well, she'd seen Darien face his darkest moments and watched him stare unblinkingly into the abyss, broken yet unconquered. If the adage were right, then she had no reason to doubt that she knew him.

Distant drumming sounded from outside, accompanied by metallic crashes and wordless singing. Entranced by the hauntingly beautiful sounds, Kiri moved to the back of the wagon and pushed aside the cloth flap to get a look outside.

The caravan passed a wide hill covered in green grass and tiny yellow flowers, which glinted like gold in the late morning sun. At the crest, musicians sat with percussion instruments, eyes shut as they sang close intertwining harmonies of luminous altos and sonorous baritones. A dozen people surrounded them, spinning in place with their arms stretched to the heavens. The long skirts of their glitteringly embroidered, brilliantly colored robes—crimson, marigold, pine green, cobalt, and more—whirled around them. The looks on their faces were of beatific serenity, calm and joyful as they turned, turned, turned.

What are they doing? she wondered, fascinated.

Hearing a movement behind her, she glanced back. Darien blinked with a perplexed look on his face. Catching her eye, he smiled sheepishly. "I meant to stay awake, but I guess my eyes had other ideas."

"Your eyes were wise," Kiri said. "Everyone needs rest."

"Including the Sorci, I hope." He tilted his head. "What's that sound?"

"There's some kind of dance happening outside." She turned back to the scene and gestured for him to join her. "Look."

Each whirling dancer held themselves completely erect, with legs as straight as wooden flutes. Meanwhile, their flaring skirts dazzled with flashes of red, glints of gold, bursts of green, flickers of blue, and a myriad of other glittering colors.

Darien crouched beside her and peeked through the opening. "Ah, I

see. It's a devotional ceremony, an ancient Nikhilim custom to praise the Divinity. See how they're holding their arms out? It's to represent how they're opening themselves to all Her wisdom, and how they're thankful for everything She gives."

"It's beautiful." Kiri wished she could join them and lose herself in the mellifluous melodies and pounding rhythms. A smile bloomed across her face.

"Wait till you see Yessalem, the capital." Darien leaned out of the wagon, peering around the cloth covering to get a look at which way they were going. "We're getting close."

Hoping to catch a glimpse of the city, she followed his gaze, but saw only the other carts of the caravan, fastened together and drawn by a large team of oxen at the front. Black and brown horses carrying individual riders walked beside them. One woman, garbed in a long coat, started to turn back, and Kiri quickly ducked back inside.

"I wonder how Arrin's doing," she mused aloud.

"Let's see." Darien retrieved the clarion stone from the depths of his bag. "*Link.*"

The crystal glowed, and white mist rose from it. Moments later, it took the shape of Arrin's face, imitating every detail of her full lips, round eyes, and thick brows, which were arched with skepticism.

"I'm not sure I like this thing," she said. "All I saw was something that looked like smoke rising from my bag, and at first, I thought my notebook was on fire."

"Next time, I'll find one that rings a bell before activating," Darien replied sarcastically. "I take it you're still outside? You wouldn't be talking to us if you were sneaking around the fortress."

Arrin gave him a dry smile. "And what was I supposed to do if I *had* been sneaking around, and your blighted rock interrupted me?"

"Magic works by sensing intentions. If you hadn't wanted to answer, the spell would have ceased before making a sound."

"You could have told me that before." She shifted her gaze, looking at something in the distance. "I haven't reached the Sorci yet, but I will soon. How are you two doing?"

"We haven't run into any trouble," Kiri said. "I hope that means we've lost them."

"Me too." A nervous look crossed Arrin's eyes. "As much as I like looking at your pretty faces, I think I should get moving before my luck runs out… not that I had much to begin with."

"Be careful."

"You too. *Cease.*"

With that, the mist dissipated, and the glow vanished. Darien put the stone back in his bag, his mouth pressed in a hard line.

"What's wrong?" Kiri asked.

"I can't help feeling as if something terrible will happen to her," he said. "I should have stopped her."

"It was her choice to make, not yours."

"I know, but… She's just a girl, Kiri. And the Sorci are not the forgiving type." He shook his head. "You're right, though… I'm not responsible for her. I just hope that, by drawing her that map, I didn't send her to her death."

A sense of foreboding filled her, and she shivered. "So do I."

The wagon came to an abrupt halt, and Kiri seized the edge of a crate to keep from tumbling across it. The rhythm of wheels turning and hoofs clopping stilled; the caravan must have stopped, and the sound of distant shouting made her nervous.

"We should go," she whispered. "Before they realize we're here."

"Good idea." Darien slung his bag over his shoulder. "The city's not far — we can walk the rest of the way."

Kiri grabbed the cloak and pulled it over her shoulders. After checking to make sure no one was watching, she jumped out the back of the wagon and, spotting a large tree, rushed to duck up against it. She glanced up the road ahead, wondering what lay in store.

The frenetic rhythm of human life swirled through the streets, and Kiri rushed to keep up with Darien's hurried pace, the cloak flapping behind her. Brightly painted houses and shops, with walls of periwinkle blue, sea foam green, sunshine yellow, and rose-quartz pink, lined the stone roads, which bustled with pedestrians and horse-drawn carts. The sounds of the city — people shouting, hoofs clopping, doors opening and shutting —

drowned out the soft ticking of the silver clock tucked into her dress. In the distance, a merry horn melody bounced along a joyous scale, inviting all who heard it to dance. So many delights surrounded her, she wanted to stop and savor them, but she reminded herself that time was short.

Darien strode forward in a manner so assured, he had to have been familiar with Yessalem's layout.

"Did you live here once?" she asked.

"Yes. The harbor is on the other side of the city. I'm still trying to figure out how to get us passage across the gulf when I don't have anything to trade… Maybe we can stow on board as we did with that caravan." Doubt shaded his voice. "If all else fails, I might know someone who can help us."

"Do you have family here?"

"I used to." At those words, a dark look descended on his expression, but it wasn't anger. It was something more akin to sorrow and loneliness, and she wondered if he'd lost his family to some terrible circumstances. Though she wanted to ask more, she decided it was better not to pry when the past seemed to hurt him so.

She soon found her eyes drawn to a tall rotunda of white stone capped with a rounded blue dome, a magnificent structure she'd never imagined she'd see. As they continued through the streets of Yessalem, they passed stores that sold everything from fresh flowers to live birds to gleaming baubles. The smells of baked goods and sweet spices and crisp fruits perfumed the entire city. Every turn held a new surprise. Statues of ancient rulers, imposing in their great capes and glorious crowns, towering over the populace. Burbling stone fountains of green, pink, and white with artificial waterfalls cascading from the mouths of marble mermaids. Ornate buildings covered in brilliant mosaics depicting dragons, phoenixes, griffins, and other Great Ones who had long ago vanished.

And the people—oh, the people! Kiri's eyes seemed drawn to every shouting vendor, every giggling child, every posturing street performer they passed. Here, a dancer swirling long red scarves around her lithe body. There, a flute player whose cheeks puffed with each skittering note. Women in bright ruffled skirts. Men in long flowing coats. Babies in joyously dyed bonnets. Hawkers showing off their wares, bragging about their specialties, and offering deals. Each moved with purpose, hurrying along to the ebb and flow of their lives.

What must it be like, to live in such a place? If it weren't for the ticking of the silver clock, she could have stayed in this city for months, years even, just to explore all its fascinating details. Everything whirled by too fast, and she tried to drink in as much as she could of what had to be the most wonderful place she'd ever seen.

Darien paused several steps ahead and waved his hand in a beckoning motion. "Kiri, come on."

Reluctantly, she rushed to catch up, feeling foolish for having slowed their pace to indulge her frivolous curiosity.

As they sped down a narrow alley, an effervescent song, played on bright fiddles, soared over a vivacious percussion orchestra, intertwined with the airy countermelodies of flutes. The music skipped and frolicked with endless ebullience, growing louder as she approached the next intersection.

She stopped in her tracks. Rising before her was the most resplendent structure she'd ever seen: a fountain depicting three magnificent ayri with their great feathered wings outstretched behind them. Each stood at least twenty feet tall; the one on the left held a fiddle, the one on the right carried a drum, and the one at center clasped their hands to their heart with their mouth open in song. Wild horses and untamed birds surrounded them, all flowing manes, kicking legs, flapping wings, and calling beaks. Though they were stone, there was movement in the lines of each carved being, and she thought they might spring to life at any moment. Water tumbled down from the mouths of the animals, descending into a wide circular pool. The fountain towered over a vast city square paved with colored stones arranged in curving patterns: red and green flowers, yellow and white stars, blue and orange interlinked rings.

And upon it, laughing couples, giggling youths, and squealing children danced to the beat of the band, who stood in glittering costumes upon a platform at the center.

"We call it the Heart of Yessalem." Beside her, Darien gestured at the square. "A hundred years ago, Queen Vakma declared this place to be an everlasting tribute to the three Ayri of Music: Melody, Rhythm, and Harmony. And so every day, from mid-morning until twilight, the best musicians in the world perform upon this stage. Travelers journey from the far-flung kingdoms of Terra to visit this place." His face brightened,

as if catching the first light of dawn after a long, dark night. "I couldn't let you leave thinking those dull houses and huckster stands were the best our city had to offer."

"You… you brought me here on purpose?" Kiri gave him a surprised look. "We weren't just passing by?"

He glanced down sheepishly. "I… saw the way you were admiring everything and felt bad that I had to rush you when you so clearly wanted to explore. If we were two ordinary people, I could have spent a whole year taking you around my city. As it is, I thought that at the very least, I could show you the best of it. I hope you like it."

"It's…" Kiri trailed off, unable to find an adequate word to express the happiness and awe that filled her heart. Her mouth seemed stuck in a grin, and she was sure she must look like a wide-eyed idiot, but she didn't care.

"I know our time is short, but… It's still on the way to the harbor. A few minutes can't hurt, right?"

She nodded, still speechless with wonder.

"I might add that most visitors don't come only to watch." He held out his hand to her with an inviting smile.

Kiri instinctively reached out to take it, then paused. Though she yearned to join the merriment before her, she was sure she'd make a fool of herself. But then she thought about how she'd feel looking back, knowing that she'd squandered this chance. And so she put her hand in his and followed as he led her into the square. A bolt like lighting zapped up her chest, and she shivered with excitement and delight.

The next thing she knew, she was whirling and twirling with the others, caught in the music's exuberant spell. Her skirt whipped around her knees as Darien spun her out, then pulled her back in. With her hands in his, she let the sounds and energy carry her away.

Then suddenly, he grabbed her waist and lifted her in the air. Startled, she yelped and gripped his arms, terrified that she'd tumble to the ground. But his grasp was sturdy, and all her reservations fell away. She released her grip and spread her arms out beside her like wings, feeling the rush of wind against her face.

She was flying, higher than she ever had before. Higher even than in her stolen memories of being one with the wind. No treetops or mountains or clouds could compare to her stratospheric joy as she lost herself. For this

one moment, stolen in the midst of a never-ending nightmare, there was no Sorci threat, no ticking clock, no looming danger. *For this one moment, I'm free.*

All the terror and pain of the last few days vanished into the exhilarating music and the animated laughter shimmering in the air, including her own.

What would she give to remain like this forever? In a land of wonders, with someone whose very presence made her heart sing as gloriously as the instruments filling the air?

Even after Darien lowered her and her feet touched the ground, she still felt as if she were floating above the world. She looked into his eyes, which shone with elation as pure as her own, and longed to close the space between them and disappear into his embrace. Her very soul called for him, and she sensed him answering its song. His warmth against her body, his breath upon her face, his energy flowing into her being—she yearned for it all, and she leaned toward him.

A glint of red caught her eye, and an ominous feeling gripped her, pulling her out of the blissful trance. She looked past him in time to glimpse a cloaked magician, clasping a bow made of flame and drawing back its fiery string as he aimed a blazing arrow—right at Darien's back.

"Darien!" She grabbed his shoulders and pushed him to the ground just as something exploded above them, showering them with scorching yellow sparks.

The music broke off, and a cacophony of discordant screams replaced the laughter. Knowing the magician would fire again, Kiri grabbed Darien's hand, sprang up, and sprinted through the crowd.

Throwing a glance back, she searched the chaos for any sign of the man but couldn't see anything other than frantic people scrambling to get away. *How did they find us?*

A second explosion tore through the sky, high above the people yet close enough to prompt a new wave of screams.

"This way!" Darien gave her hand a tug and headed into a narrow alley.

She followed, flinching as a third explosion thundered, sending searing sparks flying into her back. Ignoring the pain, she scanned the crowd for the enemy. Could she call upon her powers again? Did she dare try when doing so might cost her what little time she had left?

A cloaked man appeared in a burst of yellow light before her, and she gasped. Whirling, she started to run back toward the square but froze when a second magician appeared, blocking off that route as well. To either side of her lay the solid stone walls of two houses, with no windows or doors within sight. She glanced up, hoping to find a balcony or something she could climb onto, but found only the empty sky above.

They were trapped, and the Sorci were closing in on them.

But she would not let fear overwhelm her—no, she was not helpless anymore. Closing her fists, she drew a breath and reached for the power within.

ELSEWHERE...

"How sweet the flutterings of love! How bright the glow, how charming the song, how delightful the warmth! Come together, young lovers, and fall into each other, like all your tales and arias said you would. Swear undying faith to each other—the more unshakable your bond, the more excruciating it will be when I rip it apart. Ah, fair nymph, thank you for your unexpected entrance into our plans. The fonder he grows of you, the better a weapon you will be—for Inferno."

12

I know blood when I see it

Darien tried to avoid her pleading gaze, but even when he looked away, her eyes still burned in his mind. Her words became muffled in his ears as he tried to block them out, but the very presence of their buzz was too much. He couldn't tell himself that he had no choice; there was always a choice.

Not two feet away, the blade glinted, mocking him with its silvery wink.

HICHEVER WAY DARIEN TURNED, HE FOUND NO escape, and he closed his fist around the clarion stone, wondering if he could cheat death for a third time. Too late, he realized that the explosion over the city square had gone off far too high above the crowd to have been meant to hit him. The Sorci must have purposely driven him into a trap… and he'd been foolish enough to fall for it. Recalling the strange force that had saved him back at the Bastille, he wondered if he dared attempt to call upon it.

Though it had been too much to hope that the Sorci would give up at Eryu's borders, entering Nikhilim, where their magic was forbidden except under special circumstances, should have slowed them down. By casting the spell that had exploded over the Heart of Yessalem, the Sorci had violated peace treaties that had stood for decades. It seemed bizarre that they would risk plunging the entire kingdom of Eryu into a war with the most powerful nation in the land. *Am I really so dangerous? Or is it Kiri they want?*

With walls to either side of him and two hooded magicians blocking the alley in both directions, the only option was to fight. But Darien had never

wielded magic as a weapon before except that one time last night—and that power hadn't been the kind he'd been training to use. And it didn't stir in him now, which meant he could only rely on his ordinary powers. With so many innocent people around, he hesitated to try, lest he misfire.

A subtle tremor shook the air with a low, otherworldly hum. Kiri stood with her eyes shut and her fists clenched, a look of intense concentration on her face. She had to be calling upon her abilities again. *The last time she used them, the curse nearly killed her…*

"Kiri, don't!" he exclaimed, but she didn't respond.

Both magicians raised their flaming bows, aiming at him, but did not unleash the projectiles. What were they waiting for?

A shudder wracked Kiri's body, and a small breeze stirred. She kept her mouth pressed in a thin line, but though she didn't wince or cry out, he knew she had to be suffering as she attempted to break the bonds of the curse.

At a loss for what else he could do, Darien called upon his magic. The familiar churn of blades tumbling over each other rose within him, much faster than anything he'd experienced before. It was the clarion stone, calling to those supernatural forces with a voice much louder than he alone could have mustered. The magic bubbled up from the depths of his being, threatening to overflow and tear him to pieces if he didn't direct its energy somewhere.

"*Forth!*" He thrust his hand toward one of the magicians.

A burst of red energy sprang from his fingertips, exploding toward his target. But the magician vanished in a blink of yellow before the spell could hit, and it impacted the wall instead, sending chunks of stone flying into the street. Screams pierced the air, and Darien wondered with horror whether anyone had been hurt. Fast hoofs clopped nearby, though he couldn't tell from which direction.

He looked around wildly, wondering where the magician had disappeared to. The second Sorci remained, apparently unfazed.

"Stop in the name of the king!" A man's voice shot through the cacophony.

Ignoring him, Darien he called upon the magic again and, with a shouted word, sent another red blast barreling toward his second target. The magician disappeared as the first had, leaving behind only a flash of light.

Something whizzed by his ear and impacted the wall behind him. He whirled and found himself staring up at a mounted guard aiming a crossbow right at him.

"Drop the stone, or next time I won't miss." Though the shadows of the man's domed silver helmet—pointed at the top with chainmail draping down the back and a piece covering the nose—obscured his eyes, Darien sensed a glare. The azure cape flowing behind the guard, the similarly colored tunic over his chainmail armor, and the golden eight-point star embroidered across his chest indicated that he was a member of the Yessalem Guard. Behind him were two others, also aiming their weapons at him, and their black stallions pawed at the ground, eager to charge.

"Darien?" Kiri opened her eyes in bewilderment. "What's happening?"

"The Sorci are gone, thanks to our new friends here." Darien nodded at the three horsemen. Had they appeared before the Sorci vanished, he might have been glad to see them. But, it appeared, they took *him* to be the wicked one, and he couldn't really blame them when he had fired spells in the middle of the street. He considered attempting his powers again, but with three crossbows aimed right at him, chances were that he'd find himself riddled with arrows. Also—and perhaps more importantly—these guards were not his enemies; they were simply doing their jobs.

"The stone or your life, boy." The guard leaned down threateningly.

"You drive a hard bargain." Darien let the crystal slide from his grasp, and it clattered against the pavement.

"You, keep your weapon on him," the guard barked at one of the others, then spun toward the third. "And you, watch the girl." He disarmed his crossbow and slung it onto his shoulder by its strap, then jumped off his horse in one swift movement.

"Please," Kiri said, her eyes wide. "We don't want any trouble. The Sorci—"

"Save your breath," the guard snapped. "I don't care what kind of witchery you were attempting or what your excuses are."

"She didn't do anything!" Darien exclaimed. "Arrest me if you must, but let her go."

"Are you saying *this* is nothing?" The guard gestured angrily at the wall shattered by Darien's blast. "There were people inside!"

"*I* did that. She's just a bystander." Gritting his teeth, Darien met the

other's glare. "Didn't you see the Sorci? They were the ones who attacked!"

"Enough lies!" The guard retrieved a pair of manacles from the pouch hanging off his horse's saddle.

Darien glanced at the clarion stone lying at his feet, wondering if he could grab it before an arrow met his skull. Or maybe didn't need it—he'd cast spells without its aid before. But if they suspected anything, they'd shoot him down without hesitation. That was what they were trained to do: Act first, think later. He found it kind of funny how he now feared them when once their presence had made him feel safe. Were he alone, he might have been willing to take the risk, but if one of those arrows hit Kiri…

He let the guard cuff his hands without a struggle.

"We were attacked!" Kiri protested. "We were only trying to defend ourselves!"

"You can tell that to the court." The guard gave her a cold, unsympathetic look.

Court? Darien suddenly realized that he'd been so busy worrying about how to avoid getting shot, he'd neglected to consider what would happen next. There was no time for the Nikhilim justice system—Kiri had only days before her time ran out.

"Make way for the captain!"

A beautiful white stallion, powerful and pristine, galloped toward the scene. Its rider wore the same blue tunic and cape as the other guards, but the azure jewel gleaming on the hilt of his sword indicated his position. Though the captain's helmet obscured his face, something about him gave the appearance of youth. Perhaps it was his lack of a beard, or maybe it was the manner in which he carried himself. Either way, in Darien's experience, young officers were the most difficult to deal with, for they were always out to prove themselves. This one would probably take credit for his and Kiri's arrest and claim he'd heroically saved the day.

Just what we need, he thought dryly.

But, to his surprise, the captain's first words were: "Lower your weapons!"

The guard looked at the captain in bewilderment. "Sir?"

"Do as I say! *Now!*"

The two mounted guards obeyed, glancing at each other with uncertainty.

There was an uncanny familiarity in the captain's voice, and Darien tried to get a better look at the face beneath the helmet. *Could it be…?*

The captain stopped the horse a few feet from him, jumped off, and strode up to the guard.

"Unhand him!" He pulled off his helmet, revealing a riot of thick black hair.

There was no mistake: Darien was looking into the face of his brother.

Even a stranger would have seen the connection, for they'd both mostly taken after their mother, whose dark features and copper skin were typical to Nikhilim. But whereas Darien had also inherited her piercing eyes and high cheekbones, Nythen more closely resembled their narrower-faced, finer-featured father from the southern kingdom of Gattalo. Some went as far as to claim that had Nythen been born with Father's paler skin and lighter hair as well, he would have been the man's very image. Perhaps that was why Nythen had always been the clear favorite; Father had made no effort to conceal his preference for his eldest, and Mother, who hadn't had much time for either of them, had taken his word for it when he said that while Nythen showed great promise, Darien was a worthless troublemaker.

And so while their parents had showered his brother with affection and praise, Darien had been left to endure constant reminders that no matter what he did, he would never live up to their standards. But none of that was Nythen's fault, and his one regret when he'd set out in search of a new life was that he'd left behind the one true friend he'd ever known.

Nythen pointed at Darien's bound hands. "Didn't you hear me? Remove the manacles at once!"

"Yes, my prince," the guard grumbled. The sound of a key undoing a lock clinked behind Darien, and he felt the cuffs release their metal grip.

Both surprised and relieved, Darien rubbed his wrists.

"You two!" Nythen said to the men on horseback. "Stop wasting your time here and join the hunt for the cloaked ones! *They* are the culprits here. And *you*" — he glared at the guard — "report to headquarters and let them know what has transpired here. Feel free to leave out the part where you nearly shot my brother, but if you lie about anything else, you'll answer to me."

"Yes, my prince," the man repeated, his voice low with disgruntlement.

As the three guards rode off, Nythen strode up to Darien with a look of disbelief. In his armor, he was the very picture of what one would expect a captain of the guard to look like. Tall and sturdy with a face that resembled the heroic statues decorating the city squares, carrying himself with such pride and confidence that most would never have guessed he was only eighteen. But all Darien saw was the boy he'd grown up with, the one he'd cajoled time and time again into abandoning his dull studies to play with the practice weaponry, steal a ride on the family horses, or explore the city in disguise.

"It's good to see you, brother," he said with a slight grin. "You're looking shiny—did you steal that outfit from a bronze statue?"

"You muckhead!" Nythen punched him in the arm. "Where the *blazes* have you been? You couldn't have left some hint in your letter?"

"Letter?"

"Your farewell letter, you sludge-eater! You know, the only sign of you I could find after waking from that blighted spell? Do you know what it's like to come to after a month and learn that your brother has vanished? And did you really think that writing 'don't look for me' would suffice? I would have torn the Terrestrial Realm apart trying to find you! Skies, I almost *did!* All Mother and Father would say was that you'd abandoned us to go on some kind of spiritual journey, to search for your true purpose in life or some sludge… You could have at least waited until I awakened before gallivanting off!"

A pang of guilt stabbed Darien's heart at the look on his brother's face, which held an expression that was somehow anger, joy, relief, and confusion at once. He didn't know what their parents had told Nythen, but they must have planted the farewell letter, because Darien had been far too frenzied to have thought to write such a thing.

The memories he'd spent months avoiding rushed into his mind.

"Come on, you stiff!" he'd said, more than two seasons ago, before he'd gone searching for the Sorci. Nythen had buried himself in his studies, preparing for the annual university entrance exams, and Darien had grown tired of seeing his brother stressed and miserable. "You could burn down the palace and still be everyone's favorite, so why waste a perfectly fine day? The world won't end if you skip a few hours of cramming those books into your skull!"

That was how he had goaded Nythen into abandoning his responsibilities for an afternoon and stealing their uncle's two fastest horses. Darien had thought it would be a harmless bit of fun for his brother, who had been driving himself mad with anxiety. But then the horse Nythen was riding had panicked in the forest, miles from home, and thrown him from its back. None of Darien's shouting and smacking had been able to wake him, and, fearful that moving him would cause further injury to his brother's broken bones, he'd raced back to get help.

"You *left* him there?" Father had hollered, his face purple with rage, and refused to listen to Darien's abject apologies. "Make no mistake: *You* are the one to blame for this, and if he dies, I'll see that the law treats you like any other murderer!"

You won't have to execute me, Darien had thought, misery burying his mind and consuming his soul. *If Nythen dies, I'll do it myself.*

Though he couldn't forgive himself, he'd hoped for just an inkling of reassurance, but found none. That was the day he'd realized his father truly hated him. It wasn't mere disappointment or disapproval—those he could have lived with. No, something about the thundering storm clouds in the man's eyes had made it clear that he would never see Darien as his own again—if he ever had.

He'd said so himself: "You are no son of mine."

As for Mother… Her refusal to acknowledge Darien's existence had been even worse than his father's raging. She'd always been distant—too busy attending to national affairs to spare much time for her second son— but after Nythen's accident, she'd given up any pretense of caring.

For as long as Darien could remember, his parents had always acted as if he were some unfortunate burden they'd been saddled with. He'd never known why, and to this day, still couldn't puzzle out what he'd done to deserve their coldness. After realizing that none of his efforts would appease them, he'd given up entirely. From a young age, he'd contemplated striking out on his own, forgetting that he'd ever had a family. Only his brother's companionship had kept him from doing so, and his own idiocy had nearly cost him that.

With Nythen caught in an enchanted sleep, Darien had found himself totally alone. No, more than just alone—hated and unwanted in a place he could no longer call home.

It couldn't have been clearer: He had no place there. He never had, and never could. So he'd done the only thing that had made sense: He'd left. One night, he'd grabbed a few possessions and run off into the night, without knowing or caring where he was going. Certainly without leaving behind any kind of letter.

His parents must have deceived Nythen with a counterfeit one, and the idea made him seethe. They must have been glad to be rid of him; instead of searching for him or pretending to worry, they'd lied to the one person who'd cared at all about his abrupt disappearance.

But knowing how much Nythen loved and respected their parents, Darien couldn't bring himself to reveal the truth. Besides, if he did, his brother would come up with a hundred excuses for their actions; to the family favorite, Mother and Father could do no wrong. That was the last thing he needed when the past he'd tried to leave behind was now returning with full force.

So, in response to Nythen's tirade, Darien simply shrugged and said, "As the letter stated, I went to find myself. Turns out, I can be rather scarce."

"You might have been *dead* for all I knew!" Nythen's hands shook, and tears glimmered in the corners of his eyes. "You couldn't have sent a note? How long would it have taken to write 'Hello, Nythen, I'm not dead. Signed, your curbrain brother'?"

Darien couldn't recall the last time he'd seen Nythen lose his temper like this, especially in public. But stronger than the anger in his voice was the pain in his expression.

I'm sorry, Darien wanted to say. *I shouldn't have left without saying goodbye. I love you too, and if I'd realized how much leaving would hurt you, I would never have gone.* But the words wouldn't come; to speak them would have been to reveal too much. "I thought about it, but I couldn't find a courier who'd deliver to the palace for a reasonable price," he said instead.

"Palace?" Kiri, who had been watching in confused silence, gave him a questioning look. "Darien, why did that guard call your brother a prince? Are you… royalty?"

He gave her a humorless smile. "Only a little."

Though he had been born in a palace to the king's sister, he'd never considered himself among the elite and powerful of the kingdom—partly because it had been made clear to him that the succession ended with Nythen, who was fifth in line for the throne after their mother, Princess Brisyas, and the king's own three children. The justification had been that no more than five named successors were needed, and he'd never had any aspirations for the throne, but still, the omission had always felt like yet another reminder that he was unwanted. According to Nikhilim tradition, the title of "prince" or "princess" was bestowed upon not only the reigning sovereign's own offspring, but upon his or her siblings and their sons and daughters as well. But being associated with the word "prince" had always felt wrong to Darien, and even now, Kiri's question made him uncomfortable.

"What does that mean?" she asked.

That I may have a few drops of blood in common with the king, but I don't matter enough to count. Especially since my parents disowned me after I left. He'd learned that little piece of news from the gossips; not long after running away, he'd overheard a few Yessalem busybodies, one of whom knew a palace cook, talking about how Princess Brisyas and her husband had stricken their younger son's name from the family records, attempting to erase him from existence. Though such sources were little better than rumor, he hadn't doubted this particular information. It hadn't been entirely unexpected, but still stung. The knowledge had solidified his determination to never look back; if they wanted to forget him, then he would forget them as well.

But there was no way he could give Kiri the honest explanation without sounding like a pathetic pity-monger, so he tried to summon another nonchalant response.

"He renounced his family and title when he left home." Nythen spoke before Darien could, and the words sent a new flare of anger through him.

I suppose that was in "my" letter as well.

"By the way," Nythen said, apparently noticing Kiri for the first time, "I don't believe we've been properly introduced. Apologies for the rudeness, my lady. I am Nythen Jekh Zakar, Prince of Nikhilim and Captain of the Yessalem Guard."

He angled his mouth into the crooked grin that always appeared in

the presence of pretty girls. Judging from the fits of giggles that usually followed, many found it charming, but Darien had always thought it made his brother look like a lopsided idiot.

From the way she raised her eyebrows, Kiri probably thought the same. "I'm Kiri," she said in a tone that couldn't have been less impressed.

"You should probably mention that you didn't earn either of your titles," Darien said, unable to resist an easy chance to mock his brother. "Unless you miraculously compressed the fabric of time and, since I've been gone, completed the years of training and service it usually takes to become an officer, let alone the captain? While forgetting to mention that you call the king 'Uncle'?"

"Muckhead!" Nythen's lips twitched. "This position is strange to me as well, but though I only requested to join the Guard, no nephew of the king's could be seen as a mere foot soldier."

"I'm sure the city rejoiced when they heard their favorite prince would be in charge of protecting them."

Nythen wrinkled his nose. "More likely they wondered why I couldn't have requested to join the Carpenter's Guild instead."

Darien made a derisive noise. For someone who had been told all his life that he was the finest example of Nikhilim's future, Nythen could be awfully dense about just how beloved he was, both by the royal family and by the people. Perhaps that was the reason behind his popularity — he never seemed to let his potential go to his head.

"This is all your fault, in a way." Nythen pointed at the jeweled sword indicating his rank. "I missed the university entrance exams because I was too busy almost dying, and then I missed the extended deadline because I was out hunting for your blighted head. I had to do *something* to fill the next year."

"You searched for me? Didn't you say the letter—"

"You didn't think I'd listen, did you? Of course I searched! It took me weeks to accept that you didn't want to be found. And even then, I gave you six months to surface or send word before I tried again. If you hadn't shown up today... Skies, I've missed you!" Whatever pretense Nythen might have retained vanished, and he embraced Darien — or, rather, he clamped his arms around Darien's neck so tightly, it might have been more accurately described as a backward chokehold.

Despite having the wind knocked out of him—and a sound slap delivered to his wounded back—Darien welcomed the gesture. Guilt burned at his conscience. Not only had he nearly gotten Nythen killed, but he'd abandoned him without explanation, without apology, and, until now, without regret. It seemed like a rotten thing to do, in retrospect.

"What on Terra happened to you?" Nythen released his hold and drew back, eyes filled with concern. "Why is your shirt covered in dried blood?"

"It's mud." The lie leaped onto Darien's tongue by instinct.

"The blazes, it is! I know blood when I see it!"

Darien suddenly realized that he'd been so distracted by his brother's arrival that he'd stood there like a fool for several minutes when the Sorci were still after him and Kiri. "Nythen—"

Nythen grabbed Darien's shoulder and gave it a yank, forcing him to turn around. "Skies, it's everywhere!" He turned to Kiri. "If I ask him, he'll lie, so *you* tell me. Who did this?"

"The Sorci," Kiri replied in a pained voice. "They nearly beat him to death."

A look of rage and horror spread across Nythen's face. "That's who those cloaked men were, wasn't it? Blazes, Darien, what have you gotten yourself into?"

Darien was so accustomed to hiding any sign of weakness that to confess how much trouble he was in felt wrong. But with powerful enemies after them and hardly any resources to speak of, he couldn't afford to let his pride stand in his way.

"I need your help," he said reluctantly.

"Finally, the muckhead confesses!" Nythen threw up his hand in mock praise to the skies.

"Don't be a curbrain," Darien grumbled. "Yes, the Sorci are after us, and if they catch us, they'll kill me and lock Kiri away until she dies." He gave as quick an explanation as he could—his oath to the Sorci, Kiri's identity, the silver clock, their escape. He left out the parts about the Fiend and Arrin's prophecy, since he didn't want to cause a panic. And he never considered speaking of the strange power he'd called upon at the fortress; until he figured out what it meant, that was something he would keep to himself. He concluded with, "She has five days to live. We can make it, but only if we cut across the gulf."

"Four," Kiri murmured.

He spun toward her. "What?"

"The clock… I have four days." She placed her hand over her chest, where the top of her dress covered the small timepiece around her neck.

"I thought you said—"

"I was mistaken."

There was something more going on—he was certain. She'd told him *six* days just the previous evening, and the sun hadn't even made a full circuit since. She couldn't have deceived him on purpose—some force of magic must have shortened their time. "Why didn't you tell me before?"

A small shrug lifted her shoulders, but otherwise she didn't respond.

Jolted by urgency, Darien decided he wouldn't press her; there was no time for that. "Four days, Nythen. And the Sorci are still after us."

"It couldn't have been a simple gambling debt you needed me to pay off?" Nythen let out a dry laugh. "A death sentence and a dying girl—how could I refuse?" Turning to Kiri, he lowered his head in a slight bow. "Don't worry, my enchanted lady. I shall—"

"There they are!" A man's voice shot through the alley.

Darien whirled as the sounds of galloping hoofs pounded toward him. Four members of the Yessalem Guard approached on horseback, including the guard who had shot at him earlier. Though they were nearly impossible to distinguish visually, since they all wore the same pointed helmets and blue capes, he recognized the man's voice. The guard dismounted and—once again—aimed a crossbow at him.

"Lower your weapon!" Nythen shouted. "How dare you? I ordered you to—"

"I'm afraid Lord Hidrith's orders supersede yours, my prince." The man threw him a mocking smirk. "The fugitive may be your brother, but the law is the law."

"What in the—"

"Nythen!" A voice boomed from behind, but Darien didn't need to turn to know whose it was. He'd heard it a million times in the nearly seventeen years he'd spent as an unwanted royal, always either cold with indifference, stern with disapproval, or harsh with anger.

"Hello, Father," he deadpanned, without looking at the approaching rider. He had little desire to see his father's steely blue eyes, which would

only soften for his eldest, or the sharp lines etched into his face from years of scowling.

"I'll take it from here, son," Father said, and Darien knew he wasn't the one being addressed.

I suppose I should think of him as "Lord Hidrith" now, like everyone else.

"Seize him!" The order came as a merciless bark; a stranger would never have guessed that the one giving it was related to the fugitive.

And neither would I, Darien thought bitterly. He briefly contemplated running or fighting, but quickly came to the same conclusion as he had before: There were too many arrows pointed at him and Kiri. So he remained still, clenching his fists, as the guard once again manacled him.

"What are you doing?" Nythen strode up to their father, his brown eyes — which could have been a mirror image of the older man's if it weren't for their color — flashing with anger.

"I received a very interesting notice earlier today." Father — or rather, Lord Hidrith — dismounted and landed heavily on his feet. "Darien Jekh Zakar, a citizen of Nikhilim, is wanted in Eryu for various crimes committed over the past few days, including theft, assault, and attempted murder."

Attempted? Indeed. Darien curved his mouth into a wry smile as his mind flashed back to the two chances he'd had at killing Worak. Though sparing the magician had seemed like the right thing to do, he almost wished he shared a shred of his former master's evil.

"They're lying!" Kiri cried. "They're trying to kill *us!*"

"Who are you?" the older man demanded.

"She's innocent!" Darien spun and found himself face-to-face with a man he had always admired, feared, loved, and hated at once. If only he could remove the past and see the lord as nothing more than the self-righteous official he was! But Darien couldn't help searching for some sign of sympathy — or even just recognition. "Whatever problems you have with me, leave her out of it."

"This has nothing to do with me." Father — *Lord Hidrith* — looked down his nose with disdain. The man had always made Darien feel like a small, worthless rat, even though he'd outgrown the man by an inch or so. "Evidently, you've graduated from childish transgressions to actual crimes."

"You can't believe them," Nythen protested. "Listen—"

"We must uphold the Gattalo Accords."

Though Darien had not expended any particular effort in learning international law, the Gattalo Accords were famous enough that even *he* was familiar with them. Among their many articles was one stating that if a criminal fled one nation was caught by another, then that other was obligated to return the fugitive to the prosecuting kingdom for justice.

If I had to guess, I'd say that's what Father's referring to, he quipped to himself. *Curse it, he's Lord Hidrith to me! I'm clearly just "the fugitive" to him.*

Nythen crossed his arms. "To blazes with the accords!"

The lord raised his eyebrows. "You believe your opinion matters more than a two-hundred-year-old peace treaty signed by all the human nations of Terra?"

"I do when my family is involved." Nythen glared at the older man, jaw set with stubbornness.

The other sighed. "Your devotion is touching, my son, but unwarranted. Lest you forget, he is the one who left our household."

And you disowned me for it. Darien looked away, trying to push down the sudden surge of sorrow threatening to invade his heart. *You never even tried to bring me home, because you always wanted me gone. Why? Why was I never good enough for you or Mother? That is — Princess Brisyas.*

"Please, sir," Kiri said. "You don't understand—"

"She's his accomplice!" the guard holding Darien exclaimed. "She should be arrested as well!"

"No!" An avalanche of raging words teetered on the edge of Darien's tongue, but then, reason clawed its way past the anger, giving him a better argument. "She is no ordinary girl—she's a nymph of Kristakai. And if she doesn't return, I'm sure the unicorns will come looking for their daughter of nature."

Lord Hidrith regarded Kiri. "A nymph? She looks human to me." Before Darien could explain that her enchanted abilities were bound by a curse, the other turned to the guard and continued, "But in any case, the notice only named one criminal. It said nothing of a girl, and, as we have no evidence of wrongdoing on her part, I see no reason to detain her." He glanced at Kiri. "You may go on your way."

Darien exhaled, glad that, coldhearted as his father was, the man wasn't malicious. At least Kiri could continue her journey without him… Though she couldn't do it alone.

"Nythen!" he called, turning to his brother.

"I'll see that she gets home." Nythen replied before Darien could ask his question. He reached out to lay a hand on her shoulder, but she stepped away from his grasp.

"You have to release him!" Kiri shouted at Lord Hidrith. "They're going to kill him!"

"Enough hysterics." The man gave her an exasperated look. "He will receive a fair trial and be sentenced according to the law."

"Please—"

"Kiri!" Darien interrupted. No amount of pleading could sway Lord Hidrith where the law was involved. "Don't worry about me. Just return to Kristakai before it's too late."

"If you think I'll let them turn you over to the Sorci—"

"*Kiri!*" He inhaled sharply. "The clock won't stop because I got myself into a bind."

"Let's go!" Lord Hidrith jumped onto his horse.

The guard jerked the chain attached to the manacles around Darien's wrists, forcing him to move forward. But he held Kiri's gaze, shaking his head.

"Go, Kiri," he said. "This is bigger than you and me."

Kiri bit her lip, then looked away with a dejected expression, and her ensuing silence told him that she would protest no more.

Unable to stand the sight of her misery, he turned his eyes forward and walked away.

ELSEWHERE...

"Well, Master, it appears I was mistaken about Worak Uinar. He can be useful after all, even if unconsciously. I had thought to use the boy's family against him — it would be all too easy, given how his parents shun him. I just didn't realize the idea could be put into motion so soon. This is an opportunity with great potential, though it seems a mere flutter in the winds of fate today. Tomorrow, though, that flutter will grow into a gust that will push him further down this course, and nothing will stop him from fulfilling his destiny."

13

No time for wavering

"Is this some kind of joke?" Arrin screamed to the stars, wishing she could aim her crossbow at their mocking brightness and shoot them out of the sky one by one. "Do you play with our lives for your own amusement?"

The weapon weighed heavily in her arm, yet seemed feather light next to the sinking in her heart. She ran her finger across the point of the arrow, wondering if he'd feel it, or if death would take him before he could.

TODAY...

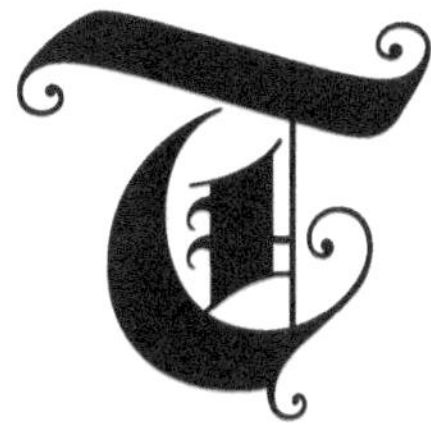

HE AYR OF BRIGHT AFTERNOON MUST HAVE been shaking their golden head at Arrin. Why else did the air, aglow with sunlight yet lacking any semblance of heat, seem to ripple with disapproval? But that was silly — logically speaking, it was Arrin's own conscience eating at her for having frittered away hours.

She wasn't the type to sit around biting her nails and waiting to hear how things would turn out. But though she'd come within eyeshot of the Sapphire Bastille not long after encountering Kiri and Darien, she had yet to go through with her plan to spy on the Sorci and thwart their efforts. Her goals had been lofty — the stuff of epic tales and dramatic ballads — but reality had sabotaged her plans. Unfortunately, she was only human, and humans had to eat and drink and sleep; the songs never spoke of such inconveniences.

Her few provisions had dwindled to practically nothing the previous day, and the miles of travel had caught up to her, leaving her too dizzy and worn to think straight. Not knowing if she'd be able to steal anything from the magicians and fearful that trying would get her caught, she'd decided to head for the nearest town to resupply. If she'd known in advance that it would take more than three hours to reach, she might have reconsidered.

But at the time, with sunset far behind and nothing resembling dawn on the horizon, the well-traveled, neatly paved Eryu road stretching away from the Bastille had been too tempting. *Just a little detour*, she'd thought. To her dismay, the road had stretched on and on, and by the time she'd reached the small village of Makinit, the sun had been on the verge of rising again.

So she'd found a modest inn—whose owners hadn't been happy with her knocking but who'd become considerably friendlier once she'd handed over half her coins—and awakened refreshed, only to find that the day was already creeping toward noon. With her usual energy restored, the detour had suddenly seemed like an immense waste of time.

I should've just squared my shoulders and gone into the fortress last night. Arrin trudged down the road through the forest, back the way she'd come. But there was no point in regretting what was already done, and she mentally listed the justifications for her decision: Firstly, her stomach had the horrible habit of complaining loudly whenever it was unsatisfied, and given the necessary silence of her mission, obtaining food had been critical. Secondly, she'd been dehydrated and lightheaded, and it would have done her no good if she'd blacked out in the middle of the Bastille. And thirdly, lack of sleep was known to lead to all kinds of mental difficulties, from memory problems to full blown hallucinations. She needed to be sharp in order to face the Sorci.

So even if her decision-making had been a bit cloudy, it was justified.

At the very least, she had been able to use the hours spent walking to memorize the building's layout based on the map Darien had drawn her; wandering around lost and checking it for directions while surrounded by dark magicians hadn't seem like the best idea.

Looking up from the notebook in her hands, she found that the Bastille's high towers of stone were finally visible in the distance. Not wanting the Sorci to see her coming, she stepped into the trees and continued under the cover of the woods. An inch or so of slushy snow, which had probably fallen a few days ago, mottled the ground with white and soaked through her boots.

What am I supposed to do when I get reach the gates? Knock and ask to enter? Even Darien hadn't possessed the magic to open the doors.

She sighed at the reminder of just how unsuited she was for this mission. Perhaps she should have gone with Kiri and Darien after all.

I wonder how close they are to Kristakai. If it turned out that they'd already reached the domain by some miracle—or, more likely, magic—then everything she was doing at present would be moot. At a loss for what else she could do, she stopped walking and pulled the crystal fragment from her bag, regarding it with some skepticism. Darien had made activating it look so simple, but he had been training with the Sorci for months. Would she be able to do as he had?

Only one way to find out. She looked into the small, clear stone and whispered, "*Link.*"

The fragment glowed, and white mist swirled around it. A thrill shot up Arrin's spine; this was the first time she'd used anything magical before. It was beautiful, like a piece of starlight glimmering in her hand. What must the world have been like sixteen centuries ago, when such items were as commonplace as the bag on her shoulder? Since history was written by the victors, all the books cast the Age of Magic as a dark era of tyrants, but there must have been wonder as well. What a pity, then, that spells and enchantments had been purged from the land. Though laws criminalizing them had been lifted in recent years, too much had been lost already, and the world had moved on from caring whether anyone brought them back.

The mist curved through the air before her, taking the shape of Kiri's face. The nymph's slim eyebrows gathered. "Arrin, are you all right?"

"I'm not calling for help," Arrin grumbled, though it was a fair assumption to make. "I just wanted to check in and see where you were."

"Yessalem." Kiri bit her lip. "They arrested Darien because he's wanted by Eryu on official criminal charges. The Sorci must influence the kingdom—or at least the courts."

"There's a surprise," Arrin said sarcastically. "But you're still free, right? So you're continuing on your own?"

The other shook her head. "I'm not leaving this city without him."

"What?" Arrin scowled. "You have to get back to Kristakai, you dunce! Why the blazes are you wasting time on some lovesick foolishness when your life is draining away as we speak? And it's not just you—fate of the world, remember? Or have you forgotten that the Sorci are planning to invade your homeland?"

"They'll kill him." Tears glistened in Kiri's eyes, but instead of garnering sympathy, they sent a burst of annoyance through Arrin.

"The Fiend will kill a lot more than one pretty boy if he triumphs!" Her conscience pricked her, telling her that she should care more about someone's life being in danger. But the horror of her visions shone too clearly in her memory, and they might come to pass because one girl decided that saving her blighted lover was more important than everything else. How the blazes did that make any kind of sense?

Arrin started to say more, but then an ominous feeling struck her to the core, sending shivers down her spine. The world around her darkened, and the sensation of having made a colossal mistake crept into her mind. But why? She hadn't said anything *wrong…*

The trees vanished, and a raging fire appeared in their place. But it was no ordinary blaze — it was a forest of flames, crawling with guié and other monsters. Columns rose from a ground of lava, over which creatures with glowing eyes and gleaming fangs ran in packs. She stood on a cliff overlooking the place, which she recognized instantly, having seen it depicted a hundred times in paintings and illustrations.

The Infernal Realm.

This is a vision, she told herself, yet she almost didn't believe it. The hot, thick air pressed down against her skin, filled with the stench of sulfur. *What does it mean?*

A man materialized not far from her, watching the scene below. Glaring flares of red and yellow silhouetted him, and for a moment, she wondered who he was. Then, a burst of fire erupted from the pit, throwing a harsh light across his face.

Darien. Except there was something different about him: Whereas the boy she'd met had been as full of life as she was, the figure before her appeared hollow, as if someone had carved the soul from his body. The fires of Inferno churned below as monster armies gathered, and he watched, still as stone. *What's wrong with him?*

Though she knew none of what she experienced was real, she wondered if she should interfere with the scene playing out before her. The sight of so many evil creatures filled her with both fear and disgust, for these were beings that delighted in the suffering of others. She wanted to stamp them out, all of them.

A gust of wind blasted her, so strong it nearly blew her over. But it was no ordinary gale; it shimmered with faint blue light. Kiri appeared as

a ghostly vision of colored wisps, her hair flowing behind her as she flew toward Darien.

She landed beside him, and as he turned to her, the life returned to his eyes. "What do you want?" he asked, but despite the harshness of his tone, the look on his face was of fear and anguish. Something terrible must have happened, and Arrin wondered what.

"Come with me." Kiri held out her hand to him.

He hesitated, but finally accepted it, and both dissolved into the air.

The vision dissolved as well—the flames, the guié, the lava—it all vanished so quickly, Arrin jumped, startled by the sight of the real world. Everything was normal again—or, as normal as it could get when one was hiding in the trees by the side of a road leading to the Sorci fortress. Green leaves and gnarled branches surrounded her, and sunlight peeked through the treetops.

"Arrin?" Kiri's image still shimmered in the mist of the crystal fragment.

"What?" Arrin blinked, disoriented. What had this latest vision meant? Had it been an actual glimpse into the future? Or did it hold some other meaning?

"I'm sorry, Arrin," the nymph said. "I tried to leave… I even boarded a ship that would have taken me across the gulf. But I couldn't abandon him, and so I ran back ashore."

"Good for you." Arrin was hardly aware of her own words, for her head was elsewhere, pondering the possible meanings behind the prophecy. Then, she remembered that she'd been in the middle of yelling at the girl before the vision interrupted her tirade. The anger that had driven her temper previously no longer burned within her, though, and she wondered whether her own words had somehow triggered her vision. It couldn't have been a coincidence that she'd seen the air nymph and the magician's apprentice right as she'd been talking about them. Maybe Kiri's life wasn't the only one tied to the Age of Fire.

A flash of light brought her attention back to her surroundings, and she glanced at the road. A cloaked figure materialized in middle of the path, and the intricate patterns of embroidery decorating the black and blue garment were symbols only the Sorci used.

"I have to go," Arrin whispered. "*Cease.*"

Kiri's image vanished, and the crystal's glow disappeared, leaving

Arrin with what looked like a shard of glass. She tucked it back in her bag, keeping her eyes on the stranger, who appeared to be waiting for something.

An idea struck her: The person's cloak hid their form so thoroughly, Arrin couldn't even make out a sliver of their face. Such a cloak would surely conceal her as well… Maybe she could fool the Sorci into thinking she was one of them. If so, *then* she might be able to walk up to the door and ask to enter.

It's the only idea I've had so far that might work. No time for wavering.

She had to make her move now, before the magician vanished or someone else joined them. So she slipped her hand into her bag, pulled out her throwing crescent, and crept closer to the road. The crunch of the leaves beneath her feet seemed frightfully loud, despite her best efforts to tiptoe in silence, but the magician didn't appear to notice.

She paused briefly, wondering if it would be wiser to remain hidden, but quickly pushed the idea away. Too much was at stake for her to hesitate, especially since she couldn't count on Kiri warning Kristakai in time.

Upon reaching the edge of the woods, Arrin narrowed her eyes and visualized the angle she'd need to throw her crescent at to knock out the magician. Drawing a breath, she took careful aim, whipped out her arm, and sent the crescent flying.

The blow struck the other in the back of the head, and the magician fell with a grunt. Worried that the rest of the Sorci would somehow sense that their comrade had fallen, she looked up and down the road for any sign of movement. The crescent came flying back at her, and she caught it.

Time to go! Banishing her fears, she stuffed the crescent into her bag and rushed toward the unconscious Sorci. Kneeling beside the prone figure, she carefully pulled back the hood just to make sure the eyes were shut. To her relief, the magician didn't stir. And it was a woman, which was also good, because Arrin would have an easier time impersonating a fellow female. The other's brown complexion was even similar to Arrin's own, which meant that if her hands peeked out from under the cloak's long sleeves, she might still be able to fool the rest of the order.

Her blood rushed with a mix of excitement and terror as she pulled the garment off its owner.

This will work, she reassured herself, but she couldn't shake the feeling that something was terribly, terribly wrong.

The cavernous stone corridor yawned over Arrin with its grand arches. Though the sun filled the sky outside with brilliant light, not one ray made it into the vast recesses of the Sapphire Bastille. Were a gale to blow out the flaming torches along the walls, she would have been left in utter darkness, despite it being golden afternoon.

She strode forward at a brisk pace, keeping her footsteps steady despite tension trying to stiffen her body into a board. Why couldn't she accept that her plan had been a good one and continue her quest in confidence? It was hardly unbelievable that the Sorci, upon seeing one of their own draw near, would open the door to let their comrade in. The great gates of the Bastille had swung wide like a pair of welcoming arms when Arrin approached; she hadn't even needed to ask for entry. The large man who had admitted her had given only a brief nod of acknowledgement before shutting the doors again and going on his way without a word.

No one had confronted her in the ten or fifteen minutes she'd spent inside so far. Yet her heart kept whispering, *Something's wrong.*

Ignoring it, Arrin continued on her way. She'd gone up to the library first, thinking that if the Sorci were searching for ways to break a unicorn's enchantment, they'd might seek answers within the ancient tomes. But the room had been empty; in fact, much of the fortress seemed unoccupied.

Discomfort sent goosebumps prickling down her arms, and the self-preservation part of her mind told her to run. But she was no craven. *Fate of the world, Arrin*, she told herself for the millionth time. *Fate of the world…*

A low voice in the distance caught her attention: "What news, Limali?"

She walked toward the sound, hoping to learn something about the magicians' plans. Or perhaps she could find a way to ask. Reminding herself that, in their eyes, she was a Sorci, she strode with as much confidence as she could muster, trying to act like she belonged.

"The transfer will take place tomorrow," came a woman's voice.

Ahead, an open doorway gaped in an otherwise featureless hall. Two magicians stood near it: a man whose hood was thrown back to reveal his

bald head and harsh face, and a woman whose visage was obscured but for her hard mouth.

"Why the delay?" The man scowled. "Even without magic, it shouldn't take that long to bring our former apprentice back here!"

Arrin drew closer, keeping her head slightly bowed to ensure that the hood's shadow hid her features.

"Sihan!" The man pointed at her, his gaze fixed in her direction.

She stopped in her tracks. Clearly, the man was calling for her—or rather, the woman she was impersonating—but should she respond and risk him realizing her voice was different? Or remain quiet and risk him realizing something was wrong?

"Come, I need your assistance." The man twitched his hand in a beckoning motion.

Praying that her disguise would hold up, Arrin obeyed but decided that it was better to keep her mouth shut as long as possible.

The man gestured at the inside of the room, which was a large rectangular space with walls covered in battered wooden drawers and a single window near the high ceiling. Strange glass apparatuses embedded with crystals sat on long, stone-topped tables. They reminded Arrin of something a scientist might use, but while she was familiar with those set-ups, the ones before her were entirely unfamiliar. Several magicians were at work; this had to be a magical laboratory. One woman, whose hood rested against her back, examined the glittering red contents of a small bottle. Two others, whose faces Arrin couldn't see, sat hunched over large tomes, one of them scribbling notes in the margin. And a fourth was casting a spell of some kind, sending bolts of blue magic from his fingertips into an opaque cup.

So this is where everyone is. She tensed at the thought of having to join them; how was she going to fake knowing anything about magic?

At the end of one table, two bronze bowls glinted under the brilliant white disc—an enchanted light source as bright as a chandelier—that covered much of the ceiling.

Nodding at them, the man who had summoned her said, "Please separate out the firegems over there. But use caution—the Fiend's power is not to be trifled with. In fact, I recommend avoiding magic if possible."

"Pity we don't have an apprentice to do such menial work anymore, isn't it, Worak?" the woman beside him said.

The man called Worak let out a sigh. "Indeed. You don't mind, do you, Sihan?"

Arrin shook her head and, wanting to get away from those two before they tried to engage her in further conversation, sped toward the bowls. Fortunately, she knew what firegems were: red crystals transmogrified from ordinary rocks when the Fiend's power touched them before that final battle millennia ago. While they were said to contain great power, they also backfired easily, and they could only be used once before dissolving into dust.

Glad that her assigned task was simple enough that even someone with no experience could do it, Arrin stuck her fingers into the bowl to her right, which was filled with gravel, and sifted through it in search of the ruby-like stone fragments. Though the terror of being discovered coursed through her blood, she was somewhat glad that she'd been called in, for it gave her an excuse to remain near the two as they continued their conversation.

Worak turned back to Limali. "Now, tell me the reason behind the delay."

"Bureaucracy, sir," the other replied. "Transferring a prisoner from one kingdom to another requires approvals from many levels of officials."

"Fiend take them all! This is why the Terrestrial Realm is doomed — the opinions of the many stand in the way of action. I suppose that, as long as Nikhilim remains too powerful to challenge, we must go through the motions of cooperating, but no matter. Darien will be in our hands soon enough. As for the king of Eryu — he remains under our spell?"

"I checked on him myself, sir. The enchantments we placed on him and those closest to him remain strong, though I reinforced them just in case."

"It's a pity we haven't anything as potent as what the nymphs possess," Worak grumbled. "What we've taken from enchanted creatures so far may be enough to hold a few key people, but even then, we can merely plant suggestions. Only a nymph can control another's thoughts."

Evil blackguards. Arrin scowled beneath the shadow of her hood. While she wasn't surprised that the Sorci held the real power in Eryu, hearing them speak of it with such a cavalier attitude made her blood boil.

Especially since Worak had implied that he'd stolen the abilities of others before Kiri. She didn't want to think about what might have become of the others who had fallen into the magician's clutches.

"We'll have it soon enough," Limali said with confidence. "Perhaps our magic didn't work on the one air nymph, but with all of them in our grasp, we can experiment as much as we want until we find a way."

"Indeed." Worak shot a glance at Arrin, and she pretended to examine one of the tiny firegems. "Are you *certain* that the Nikhilim will hand Darien over? They've been known to make exceptions for their own before."

"True, but remember, the princess and her husband disowned him. He no longer counts among the royals."

No wonder I recognized him! Darien's face flashed through Arrin's mind, alongside that of another she was familiar with: Princess Brisyas of Nikhilim, sister to the king, whose striking black eyes, perfectly sculpted cheekbones, and stern mouth adorned almost as many paintings, stamps, and coins as her brother's did. Arrin must have seen it a million times, and, given a moment to think about it, Darien was the very image of his regal mother.

"As long as they can hold him," Limali went on, "there shouldn't be a problem."

Worak stroked his chin contemplatively. "We are fortunate that he is so young and unfamiliar with his own potential. If he realized how much power he holds… he could destroy everything we've been working for."

Who, Darien? Really? Arrin thought back to her brief encounter with the apprentice, but the only thing that had stood out about him had been his oddly familiar face. *Just who is he? Or perhaps the real question is: What is he?*

"We are close enough that even he cannot stop us." Limali swept her arm, gesturing at the bustling magic laboratory. "Our efforts here have paid off. Come tomorrow, our spell will be complete, and Kristakai will be ours."

Tomorrow?! Arrin froze, her fingers stuck in the bowl of gravel. If she understood that last statement correctly—and she was sure she had, since there weren't exactly multiple ways to interpret it—then the Sorci already possessed what they needed to infiltrate the unicorn domain. With the power to travel instantaneously, they could attack Kristakai the moment their magical preparations were complete. Even if Kiri had raced to her

homeland instead of lingering in Yessalem, she still couldn't have warned them in time. *But that doesn't make sense…*

Arrin had been so sure that Kiri had been right about the vision's meaning. But that had been under the assumption that the Sorci were still a whiles away from being ready. Based on what she'd heard, though, the attack would happen days before the windborn one could warn the unicorns. Which meant it didn't matter whether she arrived ahead of the midnight hour on her magical clock; Kristakai was already doomed. What, then, did the prophecy mean?

Never mind. There would be time enough to ruminate on such matters later; her immediate concern was the fact that an order of wickedness stood to gain great power before the sun set the next day. And, perversely enough, she was helping them by obeying Worak's order to separate out the firegems. *I have to stop them somehow…*

Glancing around, she took note of the delicate-looking glass apparatuses, through which glowing liquids sparkled and flowed, that ran across each table. Maybe if she smashed them, she could take away some vital ingredient to their potion. Or perhaps there was another, more critical device she could sabotage.

"At last, our years of research have paid off." Worak's voice, malicious and gleeful, cut through Arrin's thoughts.

An uneasy feeling, like she was being watched, overcame her, and she struggled to keep her eyes on her task.

"We only need one more piece to complete the magic," he went on. "Do you know what that is, Sihan?"

Why is he talking to me? Arrin wondered.

Suddenly, a great force sent her flying across the room. She smashed into the wall and fell to the ground, pain flaring through her entire body.

Blazes, they know! As she started to get up, a great shadow appeared overhead. Something landed with a resounding *thud* right next to her, and she instinctively threw up her arms, thinking she was about to be smashed.

But when nothing came, she looked around and found metal bars surrounding her. Worak walked toward her with narrowed eyes and a venomous grin on his lips.

"A sacrifice of human blood," he said, looking down at Arrin. "And fortunately, one came to us right when we needed it."

She jumped to her feet and gripped the bars, but they were completely solid. A dark sheet of iron stared down at her. It was a cage—small and sturdy and utterly unyielding.

"Let me go!" she yelled, furious at both the magician for capturing her and herself for walking into his clutches.

"Now, my girl, did you really think it would be so simple to sneak into the Sapphire Bastille?" He spun toward the door. "Sihan!"

The woman Arrin had knocked out entered with a bored look on her face. "I believe you owe me a cloak." She thrust her hand out to the cage.

The garment flew off Arrin's shoulders and squeezed through the narrow space between the bars, flying back to its original owner.

"Thank you for being our bait," Worak said as Sihan caught the dark cloth in her outstretched hand. He arched his brows at Arrin. "It's so much easier to have a victim that no one will miss, seeing as most think she's dead, come to us. Capturing one from a nearby town would have stirred more attention than necessary. So thank you, my girl, for making the task simpler. Rest assured that your death will be in service to a greater cause."

Blades of fear pierced her heart like sharp icicles, sending shivers down her spine. No wonder her entrance into the Bastille had seemed so easy—it had been a trap, and now, she was right where they wanted her. The Sorci must have seen her prowling near their fortress and sent someone who vaguely resembled her so she'd think she had a chance at her deception. Armed with false confidence, she'd walked right into their ambush.

I'm such a dunce! Arrin's eyes darted around for any chance for escape. But the ceiling and floor were solid, and the bars of the cage, by the looks of it, were only about four or five inches apart. With the average human head diameter closer to seven—and her own somewhat larger than that—there was no chance she could squeeze through. Were there any bolts she could unscrew? Hinges she could break? Weaknesses she could exploit?

But no matter which way she looked, she saw only solid metal, which looked as if it had been created from one piece rather than assembled from disparate materials. And no wonder—it was built by the magical and probably fortified with spells.

A plea for mercy rose up her throat, but she stopped herself, unwilling to give her captors that kind of satisfaction. If they were evil enough to work for the Fiend, then nothing she said would change their minds. Pleading hadn't helped Kiri, after all.

Though the windborn one still lived, the Fiend would triumph nonetheless. The agents of Inferno would kill Arrin and use her blood for their spell to infiltrate Kristakai, and the guardians of Terra would fall. The ayri made no mistakes, and so her visions must have been true, but she must have misinterpreted them, leading to disaster.

The intelligence she'd once prided herself on suddenly seemed like nothing more than an arrogant ruse. Who cared if she could draft magnificent buildings on paper when she was stupid enough to walk into an obvious trap? Perhaps she'd never been more than a lowly, ignorant servant after all, and all her dreams of greatness were mere delusions.

She was nothing. And because of that, the world would burn.

Overwhelmed by the gravity of her failure, Arrin collapsed to her knees and buried her face into her hands.

ELSEWHERE...

"The reason, oh Fiend, is that the human girl matters little. The Sorci were watching her well enough, and she is not close enough to our boy to be of much consequence in the shaping of his fate. So what if she possesses a few gifts? They do not give her the power to interfere with what she sees, no matter what her stubborn little mind believes. And yet… And yet I wonder… Could I find a use for her after all?"

14

To blazes with prophecies

Worse tortures she'd endured, harsher torments she'd faced, and yet that reminder brought Kiri little comfort under the battering of this new fate. She'd asked the world what she'd have to give to escape her destiny, and this was its reply.

But beyond the anguish lay a brighter tomorrow and the freedom she'd always desired. It could be hers—if she survived.

TODAY...

IF RETURNING TO THE CITY HAD BEEN A MISTAKE, THEN it was one Kiri refused to regret. Though Nythen had kept his promise to help her by supplying her with everything she'd need—money, food, maps, names of allies—and taking her to a ship bound for the coast near Kristakai, she'd found herself unable to accept the situation. How could she run off and save herself when Darien was in danger? She'd reminded herself of Arrin's vision over and over, trying to convince her heart to leave him behind. But a strange force within had pulled at her as the boat prepared to raise anchor, and she'd ultimately surrendered to it.

To blazes with prophecies. She would not allow a vision of a possible future dictate her actions anymore.

The large cloth bag Nythen had given her tugged down at her shoulder as she wound through Yessalem's crowded streets. Though he'd volunteered to accompany her on the journey, she'd seen the hesitation in his eyes. He was, as he'd said, a Prince of Nikhilim and Captain of the Yessalem Guard, after all, and therefore couldn't leave so abruptly. She was glad it hadn't taken much to persuade him she'd be fine on her own.

While Arrin's anger at her had been justified, Kiri couldn't believe that she was meant to leave Darien to his death. As for warning Kristakai—the idea that her quest was bigger than her had been the reason she'd gone as far as she had. But there were other ways to alert the unicorns to the Sorci's plans even if she didn't make it back in time; there had to be a way for Darien to continue without her.

Perhaps she hadn't made the most intelligent of choices, and Arrin's accusations still rang in her head. Yet if she'd journeyed on while Darien died at the hands of the Sorci, she would never have forgiven herself.

Regardless of the twistings of fate and the fickleness of fortune, her heart was set. The future was never certain, despite what people said about destinies. Hers had been to remain within Kristakai forever, and she'd defied it.

Reaching the end of the road, she stopped in front of a wide, flat area stretching before a grand wall decorated with mosaics depicting geometric patterns in bright hues. At least twenty feet in height, it ringed a grand castle made of red and white stone, from which cylindrical towers capped with pointed red domes overlooked the city. Arched windows, ornamented with scale-shaped tiles, stared down at her, and she wondered whether Darien might see her from one of them.

The grandeur of the Yessalem Citadel, as the structure was called, took her breath way, and yet for all its beauty, there was something menacing about it. Her pleading inquiries to members of the populace had led her here; she hadn't dared question the Guard, fearing that they might remember her from the incident with the magicians and lock her away as well. Her initial assumption had been that there must be some kind of central prison for wrongdoers, and that Darien had been sent to it. While the place did indeed exist, she'd learned — only after spending hours finding it — that higher-profile captives, especially ones pending international transfer, were kept someplace else: within the majestic castle she now gazed at.

From what she'd heard, it had been a royal residency in the waning years of the Age of Magic, but because the tyrannous Sorci king had used it as his seat of power, the revolutionaries who'd overthrown him had turned it into a prison and a hall of justice. The ballrooms had been converted into court rooms, and the private chambers into cells. Furthermore, the last Sorci king, fearful of assassination attempts by fellow magicians, had embedded enchantments within the Citadel's walls that would negate any supernatural powers that crossed its threshold.

But hopefully, they only affected human magic, for Kiri knew her only way in was to break through her curse and fly over the wall. It would cost her, but she didn't care anymore. She'd made her decision.

Vendor stalls and carts of wares littered the area, and rivers of people whisked about. If any of them saw a girl vanish into wind, that might cause a commotion, which could impede her efforts. So, upon spotting a tall pile of crates next to a nondescript building, she ducked into the narrow space between the boxes and the wall.

Hidden from sight, Kiri drew a breath and closed her eyes, preparing herself for the worst. She hoped the power would come easier now that she'd unleashed it once. Blocking out the bustle of the city, she reached within for the magic she knew resided in her — the lightness of air, the force of wind…

A warm sensation hummed somewhere deep, too deep to identify with her physical being. It her abilities stirring — she knew it as surely as she knew her own breath. And it *did* come faster than previously, as if it were a chained creature that had escaped its binds before, and while its captor had seized it once more, the fetters had been weakened, making them easier to shake. Concentrating, she strained at the ties.

A great heat flared through her chest, and though she had expected the curse's all-too-familiar hotness, its ferocity still brought a cry to her lips. She clapped her hands over her mouth, hoping that no one had noticed, for she was getting close and couldn't afford any distractions, even from a well-meaning stranger. The sharpness of countless searing knives wound through her, cutting away at her with merciless vigor. Her knees buckled, and, with one hand, she grasped the wall beside her, holding on to keep from collapsing.

Not here. The shadow of the crates would only keep her invisible as long as no one looked in her direction. She wanted to scream to the skies and writhe in anguish, but swallowed her cries and resisted the spasms. Through the pain, she still felt her power glowing within, fighting for freedom, and clung to it. As long as she did, she could withstand anything. A surge of flaming blades ripped through her, slicing the fabric of her soul. Through the excruciating lacerations, her energy, her life, bled and bled, until she could barely keep her head up. Biting her lip, she stubbornly refused to let the curse keep her from an ability she rightfully possessed

and kept wrestling the chains of the curse, twisting and toiling against them. Sweat dripped down her face, and the cloak she wore suddenly felt stifling. She tasted her own blood, hot and metallic.

Then, a breeze stirred, blowing her hair into her face. She almost laughed aloud with relief and joy, for it was *her* breeze. The tips of her fingers dissolved into the air, freeing her from the earthly burdens of weight and mass. The sensation crept through her hands and up her arms, and she felt herself lifting off the ground while a gale swirled around her. As she melted into its caress, her heart danced.

This was who she was meant to be: the windborn one, a creature of air with the freedom to soar through the sky. *This* was her true form, her natural state, and she wondered how she'd ever forgotten.

The flames were still raging, and her strength was still draining, but she would rather die trying than let go when she was so close. For it was no longer only about gaining an ability or rescuing another — it was about *justice*. The unicorns may have created her, but it was the Divinity who had granted her this life and this condition, and no one had the right to take it away. For herself, for Darien, and for the eternal Mother, she *would* succeed.

An abrupt burst of energy coursed through her, and her magic shattered the curse's bonds and stretched its wings in triumph. Her whole body vanished into the whirling gust, until she no longer knew where she ended and it began.

The curse still burned in her, but she denied it the attention it clamored for. Though she no longer felt the ground beneath her feet, her instincts told her to leap up, and she listened. As she took off for the sky, she opened her eyes, no longer needing to shut out the world to focus, for her magic was back in her hands, and she would not let it go.

The first thing she saw was the azure sky, bright with clouds. Holding out her hand before her, she found it no longer the crude thing of flesh she'd grown accustomed to seeing, but a translucent luminance, blurred and vaguely glowing. Excitement rushed through her, and an uncontainable grin spread across her face. She looked down at the scuttling crowd beneath her, almost expecting to hear shouts of astonishment, but she must have been too ghostly against the blazing afternoon sun for the human eye to spot.

She wanted to dive and tumble through the air, to revel in her ability and delight in its power, but a sharp pain reminded her that the curse burned on, threatening to rebind her. Already, she could feel the broken chain mending. Any moment, what remained of her strength might fade, and if it did, she'd lose her grip on the magic and plummet to the ground.

Seeing the high wall around the Yessalem Citadel, Kiri rushed toward it, but she'd barely flown over it when an explosion of fire tore through her. Its pain was so great, she couldn't stop her scream. The curse's chains wrapped around her, and a great force yanked the magic from her grip. She fought with all her might to hold on but no longer had the strength to succeed.

She felt herself sinking and quickly realized that if she didn't descend, she might fall to her death, smashing against the blue-and-white tiles.

"Did you see that?" a woman shouted below, though Kiri couldn't tell from which direction.

Someone must have spotted her. Kiri looked around frantically for a place she could hide, trying not to think about all the armored guards and colorfully dressed nobles dotting the area below. There *had* to be someplace private… Someplace she could disappear into…

Her eyes fell on a lonely courtyard beneath the shadow of a tower. Square in shape and lined with statues — and, most importantly, devoid of people. It was her best chance.

She dove toward it. As the ground drew closer, she barely noticed the bright gardens or the covered walkway ringing the courtyard. All she knew was the unbearable pain, and only the thought that she would smash into the ground kept her from releasing what little hold she had left on her power.

She lowered herself past the rooftop and, unable to continue any longer, lost the last of her control. Her body seemed to turn to stone, becoming heavy and clumsy, as she plunged the last several feet. With a crash, she landed on her back in a bed of red flowers. Vague buzzing filled her ears, and she struggled to regain her breath. With tears tumbling down her cheeks, she pressed her hands against her mouth, trying to smother the sobs wracking her body. Though she knew she should get up and hide before someone came across her, she couldn't find the strength to move.

Every bone in her body sank into the ground, which was cool and damp around her skin.

I made it. Despite her pain, the joy of victory swelled in her heart. She'd defeated the curse again, and for a few, bittersweet moments, the sky had belonged to her.

The contents of her bag dug into her back, for she had landed on top of it, but she didn't have the energy to move off. She hadn't thought about it at all since deciding to take flight, but its presence confirmed that any object she carried could transform into wind along with her.

Could I carry a person? Perhaps she could fly into the place holding Darien through some crack in the door, and then transform him into air along with her.

"Don't change the subject!" A young man's voice shot through the air. It sounded familiar, though Kiri couldn't be sure through the murmur of her shaken ears.

Realizing that someone was close, she pressed her hand into the ground and tried to lift herself up, but her arm collapsed beneath her. Turning her head to the right, she found herself facing a white stone wall. She followed the vertical lines of its cracks upward, and her eyes met a twisting column that resembled two intertwined ropes. Tiny red and blue tiles, flecked with gold, wound up the pillar in flower-like patterns, until they reached the arched ceiling of a covered walkway. The wall she lay next to wasn't very tall, but she was flat on the ground, and it was high enough to hide her from anyone standing on the other side. Luckily, that was the direction the voice had come from; to a person looking across the courtyard, she would have been in plain sight.

"Did you not hear that commotion?" A woman's rich contralto voice came from the same direction as the boy's had, and the patter of approaching footsteps accompanied its melodious cadence. "There was a cry from somewhere, and I could have sworn that something stirred out here."

She heard me! Kiri held her breath and inched closer to the wall, pushing through the crushing weight of her own body. Pressing herself into the edge between the stone and the dirt, she hoped against hope that the two would come no closer.

"Listen to me!" the young man cried, and this time, Kiri was certain that she knew who it was, for the humming in her head had mostly subsided. *Nythen!* "Did you hear me? *Stop!*"

The footsteps ceased, and she exhaled.

The woman sighed loudly—a breath of exasperation, of annoyance, of patience pushed to its limits. "You're talking in hysterics, and it's not like you. Are you feeling all right?"

"Of course I'm not." Though Nythen's voice was quieter, the same anger simmered beneath it. "How can you abandon Darien like he means nothing? You're *his* mother too, in case you forgot!"

He's talking to Princess Brisyas. Kiri was glad to know that she wasn't the only one still determined to keep Darien out of the Sorci's hands. Praying that Nythen would convince his powerful mother to intercede, she waited breathlessly for the princess's response.

But it was Nythen's words that came next, as he continued, "Can you really tell me that striking his name from a piece of paper erases your blood from his veins? Wipes from existence the years he spent as a child of this house? Does family mean *nothing* to you?"

"Oh, my son." Brisyas sounded weary, and Kiri could almost hear the woman shaking her head. "None of this is personal, to you, to me, or to him. It's the law, and there can be no exceptions—*especially* for one related to the king. Imagine how terrible it would look to the people, if a treaty were broken or a pardon delivered simply because the offending criminal was born in a palace."

"And that's what always matters, isn't it?" Nythen spat. "*Appearances.* You're sending my brother to his death just to—"

"Why do you insist that his life is in danger?" The princess's tone was as smooth as silk, yet there was a tightness to its edges, as if her well-maintained calm would not last much longer.

"You must have seen the wounds on his back! The blood! They already tried killing him!"

"Flogging is a common and nonlethal punishment in many nations, including Eryu. I'm sure a quick look at their court records would reveal that he was previously convicted of some petty offense—theft, most likely, given his current charges. Or possibly hooliganism. Even trespassing carries the weight of lashes—but I digress. My point is: The Eryu are foreigners, not barbarians. None of the crimes he's been accused of are capital offenses—how many times must I remind you of this?"

"And now many times must I remind *you* that it's the *Sorci* who want him dead? They clearly have some kind of influence over the Eryu government to engineer—"

"Nythen, enough." The interruption was gentle, yet firm, somehow both soft-spoken and powerful enough to silence a room. "I don't know what rumors you've been listening to, but the Eryu have been amicable allies for generations, and the Sorci are nothing more than peaceful scholars of magic. Lest you forget, they saved your life."

"Did you not see what they did in the Heart of Yessalem?"

"As I recall, it was Darien's wayward magic that caused the panic."

"So hold him *here* on charges of disorderly conduct or something." Nythen's tone grew desperate. "Keep him in the Citadel and tell the Eryu he'll concurrently serve whatever term they see fit within the borders of his homeland. There must be a legal route by which to keep him away from them."

"Seek a loophole for the king's nephew and face accusations of favoritism? Justice only works if it is dispensed to all parties equally, regardless of how loudly their brothers protest. Fear not, my son. Darien will be granted a fair trial, the same as anyone else. As we do not wish to offend the Eryu, neither would they risk offending us by treating one of our citizens poorly. Now, I'm done speaking about this. The transfer will take place tomorrow as scheduled."

"Mother, please! The Sorci—"

"I said, *enough.* We have real problems to deal with. Since reports of the ayr's fall spread, the people have been in a panic about Inferno possibly growing stronger, and I don't need rumors of dark magic further sewing chaos. Now, return to your duties." The woman's clacking footsteps marched away.

Kiri's heart sank. If only she had some proof of the Sorci's corruption! How could the princess believe that yesterday's frenzy had been all Darien's doing? Had there not been witnesses who could identify the cloaked magicians as the culprits?

The lack of argument on Nythen's part meant he must have already tried — and failed — to persuade her of that. *He'd* certainly seen them — he'd even sent the guards to find them. What explanation did Brisyas have for that? Unless… the Sorci could have cast a spell to make people forget what they'd witnessed.

Of course… If their magic could make me forget who I am, then erasing a brief memory is well within their abilities. She clenched her fists. Someday, Worak and his followers would pay for their treachery. If not in this realm, then the next.

Quick footsteps paced back and forth on the other side of the wall; Nythen must have shared in her vexation. If he was so determined to free Darien, perhaps he might help her break him out.

She hesitated. Though he had shown her great generosity, she barely knew him, and it was possible that his mother's words had swayed him. If that were so, then he might expel her from the Citadel if she revealed herself. Yet from what she'd seen of him, he'd shown nothing but loyalty to his brother.

Her chances of succeeding alone were slim, and she wasn't sure if she could break through the curse again. Though she'd been lying still for several minutes, she remained as weak as she had been when she'd landed. That she hadn't lost consciousness was something to be grateful for.

Deciding to place her faith in Nythen as she once had with his brother, Kiri pushed off the ground. Her wrists buckled, but she managed to keep them from slipping this time. While she was able to sit up, though, that effort drained her too much to continue. She drooped forward and grabbed the wall.

The footsteps started moving away, and, afraid that Nythen would leave, she whispered, "Nythen!"

He stopped. There was a moment's pause, and then he continued; he must not have heard her clearly and perhaps mistaken her voice for a breeze.

"Nythen!" she repeated, slightly louder.

He paused again. "Is someone there?"

"Yes, it's me, Kiri. I'm… I'm down here." Her voice faltered.

Nythen walked into view with a look of confusion in his brown eyes. The expression deepened as he spotted her. "What are you doing here?" he

hissed. He glanced around, then hopped over the wall and landed in the garden beside her, crouching to her level. "How did you get in? You could have picked a better hiding spot!"

"I boarded the ship as you instructed." Kiri tightened her grip on the wall as her back threatened to fall into the ground. "But when they made their last call to go ashore… I *couldn't*, Nythen. I… I *couldn't*." She didn't dare try to express the intense pull urging her to return, as if by leaving Darien, she was leaving a piece of herself behind. "I don't know if I have a chance at saving him, but I have to try. As for how I got in here… Well, walls mean nothing to the wind." She attempted a smile, but only managed a slight quirk. "I'm sorry… I'm afraid breaking through the curse has…"

A wave of weariness dragged her down, and she felt herself falling forward.

"Whoa!" Nythen caught her shoulders. "Easy, there. You flew in here to save Darien? That's quite something, my lady." He started to grin, but it faded before it reached his eyes, replaced by an expression of worry. "But what about your clock? You don't have time for this!"

"It's fine. I'll be fine. I… I have longer than I thought." That was a lie, especially since her efforts to fly must have cost her time. But it didn't matter anymore—she was here, and there was no sense in regret. "I'm a bit weary, but I'll recover in a moment. Nythen, we have to get him out."

"I've tried." Nythen released her and leaned back against the wall, staring at the sky with a look of defeat. "Everything and anything I could think of—I've attempted it. I went straight to the courts to appeal the transfer, called in every favor I had, but Eryu's request is airtight. And no one would believe me when I told them the Sorci designed this whole situation. They think I've gone mad. No one but me seems to remember that the magicians were ever here; they say I sent the guards after two innocent travelers."

I was right about the spell, then. Kiri briefly wondered why it hadn't affected Nythen. She peered into his face, searching. "Why do you believe us when no one else does?"

"He's my brother." Nythen shrugged, as if that were the most obvious answer in the world. "He wouldn't lie to me about something so serious. Even if this does turn out to be a giant misunderstanding… I would rather risk looking like a fool than turning away when Darien's in trouble. Though

I'll say this: If I find out this was all a practical joke, I'll knock him silly for scaring me so."

His earnestness warmed Kiri's heart. "He's lucky to have you."

"Eh." Nythen grimaced and waved his hand dismissively. After a moment, he looked her straight in the eye. "If he goes to Eryu tomorrow… Are they really going to kill him?"

She nodded solemnly.

"Then I have no choice." Steely resolve filled his eyes. "I'll break him out. I'll bribe whoever I need to bribe, steal whatever I need to steal… I'll find a way." He moved to get up, but Kiri grabbed his arm.

"Wait." She'd been so eager to free Darien that she hadn't stopped to think of what consequences his brother might face for helping. But the mentions of bribing and stealing had brought to light the fact that Nythen would be risking his livelihood and everything he'd worked for. "I'll do it—just tell me where they're keeping him."

"Noble of you, trying to save me from being branded a criminal too." He angled his mouth. "But you're not talking me out of it, so save your strength for helping me. I'll need an extra pair of eyes to keep a lookout."

"Nythen—"

"You couldn't leave him, no matter what it cost you. And you've known him for, what, a few days? I've known him my whole *life*. What makes you think I wouldn't do the same?"

The defensive glint in his eyes spoke to the strength of his conviction, and she banished any further protestations from her tongue. Honestly, she was glad, for though she would have stopped at nothing to find a way on her own, she was relieved that she wouldn't have to.

He stood, looked around, and held out a hand to her. "Come, let's get you out of here before someone else wanders by. You're fortunate you chose the Royal Quarter to land in—it's one of the few areas in the Citadel not crawling with people."

She let him help her up, and, to her relief, her legs had regained enough stability to hold her upright.

The ticking of the silver clock beat against her chest, demanding to be heard. *What have you done?* it whispered accusingly. *How much time have you lost, both from lingering here and from using your powers?*

A chill engulfed her, spreading through every vein and penetrating her bones, and she bit her lip to hold back a surge of tears.

She wasn't going to make it—she knew that now. But she refused to feel sorry for herself when it was her own decisions that had pushed her so near the edge. And she refused to give up. Once Darien was free, she would run to Kristakai, even if it was only to die trying.

And so, she squared her shoulders and stepped onto the walkway.

ELSEWHERE…

"Come, come my infernal brethren! Rise from your realm and into this one! Gather! Stretch your black wings—you are now unleashed! Before you ask, yes, I have possessed the power to open this portal for some time now and simply refrained. Do not hold it against me that I did not free you sooner. You and I are all part of our master's greater plans. Now, listen well, and behold. See this pretty pair? A windborn girl and an errant boy—they are not together now, as they are in this image, but they will be again soon. Once they are, then you need not hold back any longer."

15

They are not the enemy

Everywhere. It was everywhere—the crimson liquid running over Darien's skin and soaking his clothes.

Her blood burned him more than any flame—more, even, than the curses of the Sorci once had. Yet, he would never be rid of it. He could strip himself of the stained cloth and dive into the depths of the sea, but he would remain forever tainted.

Nothing would ever be clean again. Nothing would ever be right again.

TODAY...

I T DIDN'T MATTER HOW MANY TIMES THE EFFORT failed; he only needed to succeed once. Or so Darien kept telling himself, for hours of escape attempts had brought him nothing but the agony and fatigue of vain efforts. Whether it was as great a feat as transporting himself out of the prison—which a Sorci master could have done in a heartbeat—or as simple a trick as removing one of the bars in the window—which he'd done before, albeit with a clarion stone's help—his power simply would not surface.

A fiery ember smoldered in his chest, though he couldn't tell if it was the lingering pain of using magic or his irate frustration manifesting.

While he'd always known that the Yessalem Citadel had been fortified specifically to keep magicians from using their powers within its walls, he couldn't resign himself to his fate. Especially since he was familiar with this castle, as he'd spent quite a bit of time observing court proceedings as part of his education. Finding a way out was immeasurably preferable to battling the Sorci again.

At least here, no one wanted him dead.

The blackness of night beckoned outside the window, which looked out onto the wide, paved area between the Citadel and the wall surrounding it.

He yearned for a way to disappear into its shadows and vanish from sight and from memory.

Exhausted from his last endeavor, in which he'd once again tried to make the bars vanish, he approached the bed in the corner and collapsed onto it. The soft mattress caved beneath him as he stared up at the stone ceiling, wondering whether it hid whatever magical devices or enchantments kept him from calling upon his powers.

As far as prisons go, this place isn't so bad. Why, it's practically a palace compared to the Sorci's dungeon. Once upon a time, the room he occupied had been someone's sleeping chambers, before the castle had been converted into a hall of justice. He could hardly complain about how he'd been treated; perhaps the guards had been rude, but they'd given him food, clean clothes, and a chance to wash up. A physician had even been sent to examine the wounds on his back. Nikhilim had always prided itself on being a moral beacon, and treating prisoners humanely was part of that.

Not that any of their good intentions would mean anything once they sent him to his death. Worse still, his own parents were behind his impending doom.

No, they're not my parents anymore. Any previous ties they might have shared were as meaningless as dead leaves. Still, their unconditional support for sending him to Eryu, to Worak, felt like a betrayal.

The ember burned hotter, and he clenched his jaw.

They're not trying to be cruel, he reminded himself. *They are not the enemy.*

They thought that any talk of the Sorci's true nature was malicious rumor, and he couldn't blame them. It was just days ago that he, too, believed in the magician's benevolence—enough to dedicate his life to them.

They are not the enemy, he repeated in his head.

But the ember would not fade. Come morning, someone would shackle his wrists and drag him into a transport bound for Eryu. Worak might not even wait for him to cross the border before attacking with his army of followers. Unless whatever mysterious, miraculous power had saved him previously returned, he wouldn't stand a chance.

What was that? He almost didn't dare to think about it, the strange force dwelling inside him. Though he wished he could believe that it was his own magic, unleashed by desperation, it had been more of a force possessing him than an ability he could control. A strange, compelling power that felt easy and natural when it slipped into his hands, yet foreign in retrospect.

Try again now, a part of him whispered.

As if summoned by his thoughts, an otherworldly tremor stirred within, filling him with a rush of energy.

Take it. Use it to destroy these walls and anyone who stands in your way. If you do not, you will die tomorrow.

At that thought, the ember in his heart ignited into a blaze of anger, fueling the stirring force. It all deserved to fall into Inferno—the entire Yessalem Citadel and everyone in it. To maintain their façades of justice, they would throw him to the wicked. And his parents condoned it. He'd loved them with the pure devotion of the innocent child he'd once been, yet they'd never wanted him. And now, they'd finally found a way to be rid of him once and for all.

Kill them. A dark voice reverberated through his head—his own, yet distant. *Kill them all.*

Energy pulsed through him, and he jumped to his feet, ready to carry out the order. Shaking, he clenched his fists to channel the crackling force blossoming within. He would take it and destroy the walls confining him, then seek out Princess Brisyas and Lord Hidrith to exact his revenge.

Kill them all…

It struck him that he was contemplating murdering those who had given him life. *What am I doing?* Horror rushed through him like a cold wave, dousing the anger. Those thoughts—they had been in his head, but they weren't his. But whose were they? And how could they have entered?

You cannot trust anyone, the voice growled. *Just watch—they will all betray you someday.*

An ominous shudder ran down his spine. Those thoughts may not have been his conscious ideas, but neither were they completely foreign. They were… like an instinct, something he simply *knew*.

Out of nowhere, a wall of flames erupted before him. Startled, he jumped back, wondering why he felt no heat. From the red and yellow flares, a pattern emerged: a circle with a pattern of lines slashed across it.

The mark of the Fiend.

He stared at it, shocked. Where had it come from? Why was he seeing it? What was happening?

Then, as suddenly as it had appeared, everything vanished—the fire, the power, even the rage.

A clinking sound caught his attention, and he whirled toward the door, his head still spinning. It was the dead of night—they couldn't be transferring him already.

The door swung open, and his eyes widened. "Kiri? What are you doing here?"

The flickering light from the room's lone candle made her appear as golden as sunlight. She waved her arm in a beckoning gesture, face tight with worry.

"Come with me," she whispered. "The coast is clear—Nythen bribed the guards into taking a break, but he's keeping a lookout just in case. We don't have much time before they return."

For a moment, he was too startled to react.

She reached inside and grabbed his hand, giving it a slight tug. "Let's go!"

Darien followed her out the door, letting his legs carry him as his mind struggled to catch up. Gratitude washed over him, and the warmth of a thousand summer dawns filled his heart. They'd come for him—Kiri and Nythen had come for him. *But at what cost?*

Relief turned to fear as the consequences became clear. "You're supposed to be halfway to Kristakai," he said, rushing down the empty hallway. "What—"

"It's fine," she said quickly.

"*Fine?* You barely had enough time as it was, and now you're here—in what world is that 'fine'?"

"Please, don't." Though she was right beside him, she refused to look in his direction. "I've made my choice, and it's too late to change it."

A pang of guilt pierced him. What kind of ingrate was he? She'd risked everything to save him—*again*. And she was right—it was too late to change anything.

The door at the end of the corridor swung open to reveal Nythen standing outside, holding the reins of a black horse. A cloth bag with a long strap was slung over his shoulder.

"Hello, muckhead," he whispered with a lopsided grin.

"You actually broke the rules for once?" Darien halted before his brother.

"I seem to recall breaking the rules several times because of you." Nythen shrugged, but fear glimmered in his eyes. He swung the bag off his shoulder and handed it to Darien. "Here. It's got everything you'll need for a week, assuming you don't rankle any more magicians in public places. Money, food… Oh, and your blighted rock." He pulled the clarion stone out of his pocket and tossed it to Darien.

"Thank you," Darien murmured. What more could he say? His passable grasp on the common language seemed inadequate to express his appreciation, for both his brother and Kiri. He'd never imagined they'd rescue him—or that he'd be worth so much to anyone. His tongue itched with dissatisfaction, yearning to speak further, yet his mind refused to formulate any coherent statements. No words, no gestures, no actions could ever be enough, and his heart hardly seemed sufficient to contain the upwelling of gratitude.

"Take Nighthawk here." Nythen handed him the reins as the horse pawed the ground. "He'll outrun all those basic guard horses if you're spotted, which, given your luck, will probably happen in the next five minutes."

Nighthawk? Darien regarded the horse in a new light. He'd heard this particular horse spoken of as being the fastest stallion in the royal stables. "How did you—"

"Never mind, just listen to me," his brother said urgently. "I'm telling you all this now because even I couldn't get the Outer Wall guards to abandon their posts, and one of them will probably spot you, so you're going to have to make a break for it. Whatever you do, *don't* go to the harbor. That's the first place they'll look, and they'll search every ship if they think a fugitive is on board." Glancing at Kiri, he said, "I know you need to get to Kristakai as quickly as possible, but you've been seen with this dunce"—he jerked his head at Darien—"so even if they don't know you helped him escape, they'll capture and question you to see if you know anything. Your best chance is to ride south along the coast until you reach Port Timonar. The captains there don't care who you are or where you're going, and they'll leave in the dead of night if you ask, as long as you pay

them for their troubles." Turning back to Darien, he said, "Did you get all that?"

Darien gave a single, calm nod, hoping that would hide the anxiety chipping away at his mind. Nighthawk's legendary speed couldn't be sustained over long distances, and Port Timonar was at least half a day away. The boats there weren't exactly known for their quality; they might not be fast enough to make it across the gulf in time. While the plan Nythen had laid out wasn't bad, it might not be enough to save Kiri either. And what would happen to his brother once the escape was discovered?

"They'll know you helped me," Darien said.

"I'm well aware of that." Nythen's nervous eyes betrayed the coolness he tried to exude with his words. "I'll talk my way out of it… You said it yourself: I can get away with anything."

Not this time. All the parental love in the world wouldn't stop the Nikhilim justice system from prosecuting someone who had committed as many offenses as Nythen must have. They would lock him away, blacklist him, destroy any chance he had at the future he'd worked so hard for.

"Come with us," Darien said. "You don't have to—"

"Yes, I do." Nythen gave him a firm look. "I'm not like you, Darien. I can't leave my home behind so easily, not with so many counting on me. Whatever consequences come, I will face them with as much honor as I can and hope to someday earn forgiveness."

"Always the noble prince, aren't you?" Darien said lightly. He knew his brother too well to protest; Nythen would rather wear himself away to nothing than let down his family or his people. Sobering his expression, he nodded with understanding. "Good luck. Nikhilim is fortunate to have someone like you watching over her."

"No need to get sentimental," Nythen grumbled. "That rock of yours is magic, right? Can it unlock things? Such as, for instance—"

"The Citadel's main gates? Of course it can." Despite Darien's attempt at confidence, the truth was that he didn't know. The gate could be warded against magic like the Citadel itself.

"Good. Because I couldn't get my hands on the keys. Robbing the Minister of Justice isn't as easy as you'd think."

"Nythen…" Kiri trailed off, gazing at him with a look of pure admiration.

Darien looked away quickly as a disgruntled weight pressed down on his heart. Where had it come from, and why was it there? Of course she admired Nythen—everyone did.

"Thank you for everything," she murmured, a little too sweetly for Darien's taste.

"Anything for you, my lady," the other said. "You too, muckhead."

Feeling a bump on his shoulder, Darien looked over to see his brother retract his hand.

"Now, it's time for you two to get going." Nythen glanced back at the wide space between the castle and the high wall surrounding it. None of the guards who paced the walkway between watchtowers were currently within sight.

Darien wasn't about to argue. After placing the clarion stone in his pocket, he leaped onto Nighthawk's back and reached down for Kiri.

A distant sound rippled through the night—footsteps. And they were approaching, along with the vague orange light of a torch.

"Someone's coming," Nythen hissed. "Go!"

"Wait!" Kiri walked toward the noise. "Let them see me."

"What?" Darien stared at her.

"Are you daft?" Nythen whispered, evidently just as confused.

She spun toward him. "Tell them you were bewitched by a nymph, and that your will was not your own. It won't make a difference to me—my kind isn't governed by human laws, and besides, I'll be long gone. There's no reason you should give up your life because of all this."

I should have thought of that. Darien pulled out the clarion stone, hoping he wouldn't have to wield its power, for those he would be fighting were not wicked enemies, but his own countrymen. What was more, a quick glance told him that half of the crystal had transformed back into rock, and he might need what power remained if he encountered the Sorci again. But if it all came down to the guards' lives or Kiri's, the choice would not be difficult.

Nythen opened his mouth as if to protest, but before he could say anything, a voice shot through the dark.

"Over there!" a man shouted, coming into view from around the corner.

Two others soon followed, and the guards advanced, the flames of their torches glinting off their chain mail armor and throwing long shadows across the pavement.

"Well, they saw you." Nythen grabbed Kiri's arm and pulled her back. "You can go now."

"Wait," she said again, clenching her fists.

Her eyes closed—Darien knew that coupled with the strained look on her face meant she was summoning her powers again. "Kiri, no!"

"They have to know *what* I am," she whispered, her voice tense.

"Stop!" He jumped off the horse and ran to her. Nothing was worth putting her through the pain of the curse again. But she didn't move when he grabbed her shoulder, or when Nythen, standing on her other side, tried again to pull her toward the horse.

"Leave me!" she shouted, her words startlingly loud against the otherwise still night.

Darien let go at once, surprised by the harshness of her tone, and exchanged a glance with Nythen, who had also released his grip.

"What's she doing?" Nythen asked.

Torturing herself. Darien only shook his head in response.

The guards drew close enough for him to make out their faces. Unable to wait any longer, he reached toward Kiri, aiming to grab her and get her out—to blazes with everything else.

Suddenly, she opened her eyes and punched her hands forward. A gale burst forth from her, blowing the guards into the ground and extinguishing two of their torches. She spun to face Nythen and swept her arm toward him. The ensuing gust sent him flying toward the castle wall, and he barely had time to cry out before the impact knocked him unconscious.

"They can't blame him now," she whispered. "They'll find him hurt and decide he must be a victim…" Trailing off, she dropped her arms by her sides and sank.

"Kiri!" Darien caught her before she fell.

"I'm all right." She met his gaze.

The beauty and intensity of her blue eyes in the vague firelight drew him in, erasing the rest of the world. How were they so bright even if the dimness? Caught in their spell, he momentarily forgot where he was.

But then, she glanced away and said, "They're coming."

Shaken back to reality, Darien looked past her. The guards once again

rushed toward them, and one was shouting for backup. He instinctively aimed the clarion stone in their direction but stopped. *No need to waste the crystal's power here.*

He raced back to Nighthawk, jumped on the stallion's back, and reached down to Kiri. "Come!"

She took his hand, and he pulled her up behind him. Stuffing the stone into his pocket, he tried to ignore the flush of warmth that accompanied her touch when she grabbed his waist. A swift kick sent Nighthawk racing across the pavement, the stallion's clopping footsteps thunderous in the night.

Wind howled in Darien's ears, and the thrill of speed rushed through him. He glanced back at the guards, who were quickly shrinking into the distance. *They'll never catch us.*

Kiri, too, was looking back, and he started to reassure her, but she spoke first. "Nythen will be all right, won't he?"

"Of course," he said shortly, turning his gaze forward and wondering why her apparent concern for his brother triggered such impatience. She had every right to be troubled — he, too, worried about what would become of Nythen, after all — so why did his heart churn with such discontent?

"Halt!" came a sharp voice.

Darien barely had time to register something whooshing before an arrow slammed into the pavement ahead with a sharp *crack*. Kiri gasped, and, jerking back on the reins, he glanced up to see a guard staring down at him from the top of the wall, holding a crossbow.

"Remain where you are!" the man shouted. "Or I'll shoot!"

A bell clanged, low and ominous. *The alarm.* One of the guards must have sounded it — swarms of them would be upon them any minute.

Darien gave Nighthawk a kick to send the horse running once more.

"Careful not to hit the king's favorite horse!" he shouted defiantly. "Nighthawk's worth more than your sorry hide!"

It seemed to work, for no more arrows came, but his anxiety remained. The guards were trained to stop fugitives by any means necessary; it wouldn't be long before someone else fired.

He urged the stallion forward, and, moments later, found himself face-to-face with the grand gate, which towered above him in an intimidating arch. The clattering of approaching hooves clamored in his ears.

Knowing he couldn't take any risks with his pursuers closing in, he grabbed the clarion stone and glanced at Kiri. "Hold on tight."

A part of him wondered if, instead of using more of the crystal's limited magic, he should call upon the power that had been stirring just before Kiri's arrival. It had helped him escape once before—but that was before he'd seen the mark of the Fiend invade his vision. What had that meant?

No time to fret about that, he told himself. With danger chasing him, he had to keep his head in the present, and until the situation became truly desperate, he wouldn't use a weapon he didn't understand. Especially since he wasn't sure if it would respond to his call.

Aided by the crystal's power, he brought his ordinary magic bubbling to the surface. Aiming the stone at the great doors, he murmured, "*Open the gate.*"

He gritted his teeth against the sudden stabbing sensation that filled his body but was actually glad for the swiftness with which the pain descended. There wasn't much time to work the spell; the guard's orders for him to surrender were buzzing behind him.

An explosion of supernatural energy flared down his arm and into the stone. The gates glowed green, trembling as the magic gripped them. Barked orders and clattering armor drew closer, and though Kiri remained silent behind him, he felt her grip tighten. Blocking it all out, he held the crystal steady and let the power flow through him.

The gates burst open.

"*Go!*" he shouted. Nighthawk instantly responded to the order, galloping forward with such sharp acceleration that he nearly slipped. The energy continued rushing through him; it was still connected to the gate. Twisting back, he aimed the glowing crystal at the doors, through which the guards had not yet passed. "*Close the gate.*"

The magic responded instantly, and the gates slammed shut, blocking his pursuers. It wouldn't hold them, but at least it would slow them down.

Kiri was gripping his waist so tightly, she seemed to be squeezing the air out of him.

Glancing at her, he asked, "Are you all right?"

She gave a quick nod. Her face was barely visible in the darkness, but he could have sworn he saw the glint of a tear in her eye. He faced forward and steered Nighthawk into a street, wondering whether he had imagined it.

Something hard bounced against his back, and it took him a moment to realize that it was her clock, dangling from its chain around her neck. Its presence reminded him of what she'd risked by coming back for him — and why she would be so afraid. How many days were left? Three? Unless Nighthawk could miraculously keep up his frantic pace and run across water, it wasn't enough time.

But that's under ordinary circumstances, he reminded himself. *That's assuming people stop for the night and travel on walking mounts. If we keep running, if we find a ship built for speed instead of passengers…*

And there was still the magic. Something would work; he would try again, and again, and again, until it did.

"Don't be afraid," he said as reassuringly as he could. "I swear, Kiri, you'll make it to Kristakai."

"I'm not afraid." Kiri's whisper was almost lost in the rush of wind as they tore through the city.

Darien clenched his jaw, trying to contain the great upwelling that invaded his heart, though he couldn't tell if it was sorrow, guilt, gratitude, or something else entirely. *What is it about you, Kiri? Your courage? Your strength? Your infectious sense of wonder? How is it that you came into my life so fast, yet changed it entirely?*

Her smile held the joy of a million sunrises, and despite the consequences of having stopped at the Heart of Yessalem, he didn't regret having given her a moment of bliss. And he would he have given anything to see her that happy once more.

He didn't know how, but he was certain of one thing: His fate was inexorably linked to hers.

ELSEWHERE…

"Guié! The time has come! You know what to do — and what to make them believe. But wait! A little patience will make our plan even more effective. Let's give it some time, until they are in a place where help cannot come. Remember, the more desperate he is, the more quickly he'll awaken the shadow once more. Steady, for now, then. Steady, steady. The opportunity will arise soon enough."

16
You don't belong here

TOMORROW…

Blinding, burning, biting, blazing—Kiri no longer knew where she ended and the great force of magic began. It swallowed her entire being, reshaping the very fibers of her existence.

What was it doing to her? What would become of her once it finished? What would be left, after it was done tearing her apart?

TODAY…

*HE MIST—THE TORTUROUS HAZE THAT WOULD engulf her in its merciless, searing grasp—filled the space between Kiri and the fire nymph across the grove, but she didn't care. Even obscured by fog, Elaia's radiant beauty shone with the light of a million stars. Her mesmerizing eyes of emerald, her luxurious locks of flame, her luscious lips of rose, curved into a smile that would out-dazzle the sun… The sight filled Kiri's heart with longing.*

Elaia's flowing green dress, which perfectly offset her curving hips, whipped around her knees as she raised her hand toward Kiri in a beckoning motion. The gray expanse between them did nothing to diminish the glow of her bronze complexion.

Unable to resist her call, Kiri steeled herself against the pain she knew would come. Already, the mist's wispy tendrils scorched her skin, but she didn't care. She would walk a hundred miles through this torment if it meant that, in the end, she would finally reach the one she yearned for.

She marched forward. The heat pressed down on her flesh like red-hot coals, and her body screamed at her to turn back, but she refused. More than anything, she wanted to be with Elaia again.

No, not wanted. Needed.

So she pushed on, keeping her eyes fixed on the beautiful fire nymph. What memories she had of Elaia were few, but something deeper than her mind recalled

the other's vivacious nature and infectious energy — traits that filled Kiri with wonder. She would do anything to be with her again — to feel the joy Elaia's presence brought and revel in its splendid light.

But even when Kiri reached the other, the mist failed to disperse. Nevertheless, it hardly mattered, since now, she was at last with the object of her desires.

Smiling, she met the fire nymph's gaze and took her hand.

"Oh, Kiri." Elaia pulled away, wrinkling her nose. "We've been through this before."

"What?" Kiri tilted her head, puzzled.

"I'm sorry." The fire nymph's eyes hardened. "It can never be."

A tremendous ache filled Kiri's heart. All she knew was how much delight Elaia brought her and how much she missed her when they were apart. Did the other not return her affections? "What do you mean? Do you — "

"No." Elaia turned sharply and started walking away. "It will never be you."

"Wait!" Kiri grabbed the other's arm. Daggers pierced her heart, and she barely felt the heat of the mist through the terrible pain in her chest. "Please — "

"You don't belong here." The fire nymph spun to face Kiri, tearing free from the grasp. Her gaze bore into Kiri's like a pair of green fires. "You've never belonged here."

"What?"

"Was I not clear? You don't belong here!"

Round lumps rose from Elaia's flesh and undulated across her face, distorting her features into a shapeless mass.

Kiri backed away, frightened and confused. "Elaia?"

Elaia's previously alluring visage became a featureless blur, then abruptly shifted into a new one. Sky blue eyes and snowy complexion… her own. Almost a reflection but for the intensity in her gaze.

"You don't belong here," the other said, and even her voice matched Kiri's. "You will never belong here…"

A sharp jolt roused Kiri, and she opened her eyes with a gasp. For a moment, she wondered where she was — why the surface she sat on was rocking side-to-side, why the sound of clopping filled her ears, why the dark landscape kept shifting. She was sitting upright, but leaning her head on something that was at once soft and firm, with her arms wrapped around a warm and sturdy presence.

Reality rushed back into her mind, and she realized that she must have fallen asleep on the back of Nighthawk, the stolen royal stallion, while leaning on Darien's back. She was glad that she hadn't lost her grip when she'd drifted off.

How long has it been? The night sky stretched overhead, but its blackness had faded into a deep, gray-tinted blue. The colored Estal Magora still winked against the dark canvas as their lesser companions disappeared, swallowed by the encroaching dawn. She marveled at how they remained so bright… The blue-green Honesty Star, the pink Kindness Star, the purple Temperance Star, the green Charity Star…

Green. The color brought Kiri's dream crashing back into her mind, and she turned her thoughts to what she'd seen. The mist, as she knew well by now, must have been the Sorci's curse trying to keep her from her memories. But she'd fought through it, and what had her efforts revealed? No new truths had been unveiled…

The feeling of deep longing struck her, the same one that had tormented her in the dream. Then she realized — it hadn't been the memory of a setting or situation the curse had attacked. It had been the memory of something that meant much, much more.

Love.

I loved her. Kiri gasped, wondering how she could have forgotten. *We were more than friends… Or, at least, I wanted us to be more…*

But Elaia hadn't shared the desire. At that memory, Kiri's chest ached, and tears assaulted her eyes. She blinked them back furiously. It was all in the past — she was certain of that. None of these emotions had plagued her when she'd recalled plucking the silver clock from the tree, and so she must have recovered before leaving Kristakai in search of wonders in another world. And the fire nymph had been with her the day she'd made the fateful decision, even encouraging her rash choice. They'd remained close friends, and the rejection was nothing but an old wound, a scar that had healed over long ago.

Though the dream had brought Kiri no revelations that might help her current situation, she was glad she'd experienced it. Who one loved shaped who one became, and she'd been the type of person who could fall for another and remain friends with her after the sting of heartbreak. For that, she was glad. Perhaps, shortly after being rebuffed, she'd held some

grudge or resentment, but no longer. Her memories of Elaia were few, yet she nevertheless cherished each one—even this latest. An unscarred life was a meaningless one, and she was glad to have rediscovered this part of her.

If she made it back to Kristakai, she would rush to see the fire nymph again and rekindle their friendship, with the understanding that her unrequited love was a thing of the past.

If... A rush of coldness interrupted her train of thought, and she suddenly became aware of the soft ticking of the silver clock pressed against her skin. She loosened her grasp around Darien with one hand, aiming to check the timepiece, but stopped when she realized she would not see its face in the darkness.

Using her powers to enter the Yessalem Citadel had must have cost her hours from what little time she had left. And then she'd unleashed the force again, costing herself even more. Both Darien and Nythen had tried to stop her, which had annoyed her, for what she did with her powers and life was her own business. Still, it made her smile to think about how they both cared about her. However many hours or days she'd expended in the endeavor to free Darien and protect Nythen, she refused to lament them.

Still weary despite having slept, she leaned her head on Darien's back. The warmth of his body filled her with comfort, and she relished the soft hum of his pulse in her ear. Whatever she'd lost in her effort to save him, it was worth the price. Despite Arrin's prophecy, she couldn't believe that she was meant to abandon him. The future was ever-moving and unpredictable; all she could control was what she did in the present.

A strange tugging—the same one that had pulled her back to Yessalem just when she'd been about to depart for her home—yanked at her heart, pulling her closer to the one she held. And then the realization hit her: It was the same yearning that had drawn her toward Elaia in her dream.

But nymphs were meant to love other nymphs; that was the way of the world. They did not fall in love with humans—it was unheard of. The reverse occurring—humans, usually men, falling in love with nymphs— was common knowledge. But for one of her kind to reciprocate? That was simply foolishness. More than foolishness; it was unnatural.

She tried tossing the notion away, but it clung stubbornly to every part of her—heart, mind, soul, and body… all.

Seeking a distraction, she turned her gaze to her surroundings, wondering how far they'd come and how far they had yet to go. A mountainous terrain, visible only as shadows in the dark, rushed by. Though they were only silhouettes, the tangled branches and riotous leaves formed impressive, jagged shapes. The road wound along a high cliff, below which gentle waves rippled under the dim yet brightening sky.

The first rays of dawn peeked out from the horizon as the Ayr of Daybreak stretched their colorful arms across the sky. Layers of deep hues rose from the gleaming sea—rich crimson and burnished copper and flaxen yellow all blending into the lingering indigo of the passing night. The effect took Kiri's breath away, and a smile crept on to her lips. She allowed herself to savor the bliss of this quiet, peaceful moment, casting away the dangers of the Sorci, the silver clock, the prophecy.

For now, the sunrise was beautiful, the pursuers were far behind, and the one she rode with… the touch of her body against his made her heart glow. And she savored the happiness, for it wouldn't last long.

The ticking of the clock once again called her attention. Realizing that there was now enough light to see by, she drew one hand toward her chest and looped her finger around the delicate chain. Perhaps some wise elder would have advised her to journey on in ignorant bliss, until the specter of death swept her away, but she yearned for knowledge. So she pulled the clock out from under her top and cast her eyes upon its delicate face.

The hands pointed at two-thirty. Two and a half days left, no more. If she'd never unleashed her powers, she would have four full cycles of the sun by which to reach safety. But also, she'd have wandered on with no idea of who she was—and no inkling of how much the one she held meant to her. If she'd let the curse bind her, she'd have remained a prisoner until her death and lost one worth everything to her before she'd had a chance to know him. Her enemies would have used her own powers against her homeland—and Terra would have lost a budding hero.

The horse came to an abrupt stop, startling her. With a gasp, she tightened her grip around Darien to keep from falling.

He started to face her, and she hurriedly dropped the clock back under her collar, where it could remain hidden. If he knew how slim her chances of surviving were, it would send him into a frenzy, and she'd caused him enough pain. He would certainly feel guilty if he knew what she had given up to help him escape, and she didn't want to burden him… not yet.

So she met his gaze, and the very sight of his face brought a smile to her lips. "Good morning."

"Good morning," he replied, an incredulous look in his eyes. "You seem cheerful."

Suddenly conscious of how close they were, she released him and gripped the back of the saddle. "It's the sunrise," she said with a shrug. "No matter what's happening, it brings me joy. Why did we stop?"

"Nighthawk needs a break." He jumped off the horse and patted the creature's nose. "If I hadn't made him run the first several miles, he might have walked further, but I've pushed him far enough for now. This seemed like as good a place as any to give him a moment to breathe."

Deciding that dismounting couldn't be too difficult, Kiri tried to imitate the movement, grabbing the saddle and swinging one leg behind her. But she must have done something wrong, for the next moment, she was sliding uncontrollably toward the ground. An involuntary yelp escaped as she tumbled off the horse's back.

Instead of the rough impact from the ground, two strong arms caught her, and she found herself staring up at Darien's worried face.

"Are you all right?" he asked.

Her heart pounded, though she wasn't sure if it was from her near-fall or from his proximity. "Of course," she answered with a sheepish smile.

He put her down. Realizing that the clock had slipped out of her top, she hurriedly tucked it back into its place.

"How much time?" Darien asked, evidently having seen her.

Kiri bit her lip. She didn't want to lie, but neither did she want him to fret, especially when there was nothing he could do to change the situation. He couldn't reverse time, or restore her life force, or make miles and miles of distance vanish. What magic he could work, he'd already tried, and there was no sense in asking him to attempt those spells again when their outcome was known.

"Three and a half," she said, keeping her eyes on the ground.

He remained silent for a moment, and she knew he had to be calculating ways to reach the unicorn domain in that time.

"You'll make it," he muttered. "One way or another."

Kiri nodded, avoiding his gaze. Shivering in the early-morning coolness, she pulled the cloak tighter around her.

As he led the horse to the side of the road and poured water from the canteen into a bowl-like cavity in the rocky ground, she wandered to the edge of the cliff. Looking down, she realized she wasn't as high up as she'd thought, and that the edge didn't actually lead to a drop. Instead, large stones, varying shades of brown in color, sat layered upon one another, cascading into the water. While the sea was mostly calm, every so often, a particularly ambitious wave would crash against the rocks, sending white spume flying. The smell of salt permeated the air, and she inhaled its freshness.

Though she was missing vast swaths of her memory, she was certain she'd never been so close to the ocean before. Kristakai lay mere miles from the shoreline and was home to rivers that flowed into the briny deep, but no part of the coast lay within the forest's enchanted borders.

Unable to resist the lure of newness, she climbed down toward the rippling surf. The rocks were so rough that she had no fear of slipping, even with the cloak hindering her movements.

"Where are you going?" Darien called.

"Getting a closer look." The sea's spray tickled her bare legs, cold yet gentle. It wasn't long before she'd reached the wide, flat stone at the bottom, which sloped at a shallow angle from dry land into the unknown depths below.

Hearing a movement, she turned to see Darien climbing down after her, his bag bumping up against the rocks. He jumped the last several feet and landed beside her.

"Magnificent, isn't it?" he said, his eyes filling with wonder as he looked into the horizon. "I've heard it said that if you travel far enough, you'll find the gates to Celeste. Other tales say it's the gates to Inferno. And still others claim it's the Ether between realms. Whatever the case, I wouldn't care to find out. But I've wondered what it might be like to try."

"Have any attempted the journey?" Kiri glanced up at him. The emerging sun threw golden rays across his dark amber complexion, highlighting his prominent cheekbones and angular jaw. The effect was breathtaking, and she quickly averted her glance, troubled by how her pulse quickened.

"A few, but none have ever returned successfully." He scanned the coast and pointed. "Do you see that?"

Following his gaze, Kiri caught sight of a lumpy mass against the shoreline, distant and dark, yet distinct from the mountainous, tree-covered land that surrounded it. "What is it?"

"Port Timonar—the place we're heading."

Hope illuminated her mind through the shadows of defeat; if the port was close enough to see, then it couldn't take too long to reach, could it? Perhaps there was a chance she'd survive after all.

"We should be there by noon." Despite his optimistic tone, doubt clouded his expression. "Though curving roads can be deceitful. I could try—"

"No," she interrupted, knowing what he was about to propose. The previous attempt to transport her to Kristakai had cost her hours from the clock and weakened them both. For her, with what little life she had left, another attempt could be fatal. Yet she didn't fear the prospect of death—it was the manner she wished to control. She refused to die screaming—if her end were to come, it would be on her own terms. "I would rather take my chances on the road."

His mouth firmed into a harsh line. "You're going to make it," he murmured.

Kiri nodded again, not knowing how else to respond. Her thoughts skittered about like frenzied flies, some fearful, some hopeful, some woeful. There was a chance she'd survive, and yet it was so slight, it barely existed. Hope, like the sun, could burn as easily as warm, could blind as easily as brighten. No matter how many times she'd told herself to accept her fate, she couldn't banish it.

A strong wind blew her long hair into her face, whispering in her ears. *You were born from me,* it seemed to say. *And when you die, your spirit will ascend to the Celestial Realm, and your body will return to me. As I am eternal, so will you be.*

The idea was comforting, but couldn't chase away the sense of loss at everything she would never do if she left this realm forever. Sixteen years were hardly enough.

A red light caught her eye. Darien raised the clarion stone, which glowed scarlet, and aimed the crystal out to sea.

"What are you doing?" she asked.

"Calling a ship." He closed his eyes. "Or trying to, at least. If I can get this blighted spell to work, we'll save half a day."

"Are you sure you should be using it for this?"

"Yes," he said, his voice strained. A powerful wind swirled around him, swallowing the words of the spell he spoke. Moments later, a bright ray shot out of the crystal, hit the water, and disappeared into its unknowable fathoms. Waves of glowing energy pulsed through the air with a low drone as glittering sparks danced around the source of the power.

An explosion of scarlet flashed upon the water before them, sending a gust of hot air blasting toward her. Glittering smoke whirled in a vaguely spherical shape, right where the soft waves kissed the rocky shore.

"What did you do?" she asked.

"I don't know—what *did* I do?" Darien opened his eyes, lowering his arms and staring bemusedly at the enchanted fog, which sparkled and churned with a radius of several feet.

It vanished abruptly, and where once had been empty air, a young woman now stood in the waist-deep water. Long black hair tumbled over her shoulders, which were bare but for the thin straps of a shirt made from gleaming, richly woven blue fabric that reached her naval. The way she stretched her long neck and kept her pointed chin tilted upward gave her a regal appearance, and though her eyes—black and tilted at a beguiling angle—revealed a hint of confusion, it was mostly anger that filled her sharp face.

Then, Kiri noticed what lay beneath the water—not two legs, but a shimmering purple-and-green tail, only slightly obscured by the sea. From its curving end, grand fins billowed in gleaming emerald, catching the light.

A mermaid! Why had the spell, meant to call a ship, brought her here?

"How *dare* you?" the young woman exclaimed, glaring at Darien. "What gives you the right to summon me like this?"

Darien blinked in bewilderment. "Uncontrollable magic, apparently." He gave Kiri a sheepish look. "That's clearly *not* a ship… I really should have paid more attention to those magic books." The smile faded. "Skies, how can I transport others to me, but I can't transport myself?"

The mermaid narrowed her eyes, turning her gaze to Kiri. "Do you have any idea who I am?"

Kiri shook her head, guessing that the young woman must hold some office of importance in her underwater domain.

The girl's demanding eyes then shifted to Darien.

He shrugged. "Evidently, you're a mermaid with a grudge against me, for which, I cannot blame you. But other than that, I'm afraid I don't recall ever seeing you before."

The other gave him a disdainful look, angling her slim black eyebrows into the hint of a scowl. "I could have you killed for your insolence. Does that jog your memory?"

"You'll have to queue up and beat my rotting corpse, given how many people want me dead." He tucked the clarion stone into his pocket. "I honestly don't know who you are, or why my spell brought you here, but I apologize for my error."

"What words did you use to channel your powers?"

"'*Bring me one who can take us to the opposite shore with the greatest speed.*' Inelegant, I know, but I'm rather new at all this."

"Obviously." The young woman reached behind her and pulled something that sent silver fabric tumbling down from the bottom edge of her top. The cloth spilled into the water, covering the upper half of her tail. Her mouth was set in a no-nonsense manner as she glanced down at the skirt. A moment later, her tail glowed and transformed into a pair of human legs, complete with knees and toes.

Kiri watched agape as the girl strode out of the water with an assured stride; she'd never heard of one being transforming into another with such ease before. The girl's damp dress clung to her thighs, and Kiri understood now why she'd modified the garment before turning.

The mermaid—for that was her nature, even though she now looked human—stepped onto the rough rocks. Her smooth complexion appeared as gold as the rising sun, and her posture exuded authority. Though she was about the same height as Kiri and barely reached Darien's chin, she still managed to look down at him.

His eyes widened. "You're the Queen of Marae. Only the reigning sovereign of the merpeople can walk on land at will."

"That's right." The girl brushed one stray strand of gleaming black hair out of her face. "I came of age and ascended to the throne a month ago. You must be very out of touch."

"I won't argue with that." He dropped to one knee and bowed his head. "It's an honor, Your Majesty."

She's the undersea queen? Kiri started to lower herself, but the mermaid waved a dismissive hand.

"No need for that." The girl tilted her head at Kiri. "My name is Ilaerii. And you… You're not human. Who are you?"

"Kiriall Amdyth of Kristakai." Kiri stared at the young woman in a new light. The familiarity of the mermaid led her to believe that she'd come across the marine dwellers before, in the life she could barely remember. But certainly, as an ordinary resident of Kristakai, she would never have dealt with royalty. "I'm an air nymph."

"What in the name of Celeste are you doing so far from the unicorn domain?" Ilaerii turned sharply toward Darien. "Is this why you called me here? To bring her back?"

"Yes." Darien stood. "She only has three days before—"

"I know what happens to nymphs when they leave their lands." Ilaerii walked up to Kiri. "I can help you, but I won't do so without a reason. What possessed you to put yourself in danger in the first place?"

Kiri quickly explained what she could—how she'd awakened in the Sorci's cell, how her powers and memories were bound by a curse, how she was racing against time, both to save herself and to warn her people of the magicians' impending attack. Ilaerii's expression didn't change as the tale progressed, but the tightness of her jaw revealed that she must have been holding back her true emotions.

"And there's one other thing," Kiri said, after completing her tale. "We came across a girl who can see into the future, and her vision said that if I die, the Fiend will triumph."

"Your fate is tied to the Fiend's rise?" Alarm filled Ilaerii's face, shaking her cool countenance. "Who is this prophet?"

"Arrin Velindale."

The other's eyes widened. "I ran into Arrin not long ago… She seems connected to all this Inferno business." Turning to Darien, she said, "I know why your spell worked the way it did. You didn't specify that it was a *ship* you sought; only that you wanted the fastest way to reach the opposite shore. I command a fleet of transports several times faster than any boat." She spun toward Kiri. "I can get you within twenty miles of Kristakai by sundown. I'll also send a Marae messenger upriver as a precaution, but the journey is arduous—winding, full of obstacles, and too narrow for mounts. Your journey will be much faster."

"Thank you," Kiri said, overwhelmed by gratitude. The light of hope glowed brighter as she calculated how long it would take to walk twenty miles… It would be close, but enough. She bit her lip to contain the flood of emotion that overcame her. Yes, with Ilaerii's help and thanks to Darien's efforts, she *would* make it.

"And *you*." The young queen raised her eyebrows at Darien. "You look a great deal like Princess Brisyas of Nikhilim. You're her younger son, Darien Jekh Zakar, aren't you?"

"You recognize me?" Darien tilted his head with a look between confusion and amusement. "Didn't think I was famous enough for that."

"You're not," Ilaerii said bluntly. "But since my kingdom borders yours, I make it my business to know everything I can about your king and his relatives, and you count among them, even if you are insignificant."

He gave her a humorless half-smile. "My family shares that view with you. I think your relations with Nikhilim will be just fine."

"I'll be sure to mention my favor to you the next time I see them. Having Nikhilim owe me would be a bonus to thwarting an apocalyptic prophecy."

"I'm sure they'll be thrilled to know you helped a fugitive escape."

"Excuse me?"

Kiri took a step toward the mermaid. "He was bound to the Sorci but broke his oath to save my life, and for that, the magicians would see him dead. They have some kind of control over the Eryu courts—they sent word to Nikhilim that he's a wanted criminal, and so Nikhilim is obligated to send him back to them… and the Sorci."

Ilaerii shook her head. "Blazes! How did you two cretins get yourselves into so much sludge?"

"That's not a very queenly thing to say," Darien quipped.

"Fiend take you!" The other shot him a venomous look. "Do you want me to bring you across the gulf or not? It's only the air nymph I care about, after all. I'd be happy to leave you to your execution."

"No!" Kiri cried. "Please—"

"His fate is not my problem." Ilaerii's eyes flashed. "And lest you forget, I am a *queen*. I cannot go around helping criminals. The Gattalo Accords may not officially apply to Marae, but we have a longstanding understanding with Nikhilim to uphold many of its tenets nonetheless."

A humorless smile curved Darien's mouth. "And nothing matters more than keeping the peace." He turned to Kiri. "It's all right. You—"

"*No.* No, it's not all right." A sudden storm of fury roared through Kiri. "Darien, you should know better by now than to try persuading me to go on alone. As for you." She spun to face the mermaid. "I do not know enough about your politics to give you a compelling reason to help him, but you should know—you *must* know—what I've done to bring him this far." Emotion surged up her chest—passion and fury and desperation all at once. "I tortured myself to break through the Sorci's bonds, unleash my powers, and keep them from killing him. I could have boarded a ship across the gulf already, but I stayed in Yessalem because he was captured, and I couldn't let them send him to his death. I even bewitched Nythen into helping me break him out. And so I'm leaving here with him—or not at all."

The young queen scowled. "What about Arrin's prophecy?"

"It can burn in the Firelands. This is *my* life." Her own vehemence startled her, and an unexpected upwelling of tears filled her eyes.

Darien started to speak, but she held up her hand.

"You cannot change my mind." Her voice broke. "After everything we have been through, how could you believe I'd abandon you? If I did, I'd spend the rest of my life, however long or short it may be, wondering what became of you, tormented by nightmares, hating myself for that decision… would you inflict that upon me?"

"Kiri…" He wrapped his arms around her, and she fell into his embrace.

Feeling his breath against her hair, she tightened her arms around his waist and buried her face into his shoulder. *I won't let you go, Darien. I won't leave you behind.*

"All right, I'll do it!" Ilaerii's sharp voice sliced through Kiri's ears.

Kiri released Darien and faced her.

"Enough tears already." The mermaid rolled her eyes. "You may be willing to ignore the Ayr of Tomorrow and risk the world burning over

his sorry hide, but I'm not. If his life is tied to yours and yours is tied to the Age of Fire, then I shall simply have to save you both to prevent the Fiend's triumph." She let out an aggravated sigh. "Politically speaking, this is a terrible move. But I also caught the part where Prince Nythen was involved. You couldn't have bewitched him—you said yourself your powers were bound."

Kiri shook her head, scrambling for an answer. "I can access them when—"

"Don't lie. You're terrible at it." An amused glint lit Ilaerii's eyes. "Breaking a criminal out of prison is a grave offense, even for royalty. It sounds to me like Prince Nythen was willing to give up everything to see his darling brother freed. That could come in handy someday."

Darien gave a mock bow. "Your Majesty, you'd make an excellent mercenary."

The other huffed. "I'm only trying to parse out the advantages to this lightforsaken situation. If I'm going to help someone, I need to see if there's any way my actions can benefit my kingdom."

The great stone that had been sitting in Kiri's chest dissolved as she realized what Ilaerii meant. "You'll take us both across the gulf, then?"

"You've left me little choice," the young queen replied, a miffed note ringing in every syllable. "I'm risking my kingdom's reputation because of you. But I'm in no mood to hear more of your plaintive pleas, and we've wasted enough time. As far as I'm concerned, the situation is settled. Until Nythen comes into a position of significant power, it *cannot* be known that Marae helped an outlaw escape Nikhilim. Understand?"

"Yes, of course," Kiri said quickly.

Ilaerii turned her gaze to Darien, who gave a single, sharp nod. "Thank you," he said. "I—"

"You owe me." Ilaerii pointed one commanding finger at him. "And so does your beloved-by-all prince of a brother. Now, wait here while I summon a transport. I'll be back soon."

With that, she marched into the sea. As soon as she was deep enough for the water to reach her waist, her legs glowed and transformed back into a green-and-purple tail. She plunged into the depths, not bothering to retract the skirt she'd let loose in order to come ashore. Kiri watched with fascination as the mermaid sped through the water, her long fins swishing. Within seconds, Ilaerii had disappeared entirely from sight.

"She's rude for a queen," Darien commented. "But a far better person, it seems, than most other sovereigns combined. It's probably because she's new to her position, though I'm surprised she wasn't corrupted by ministers and advisors since her father passed into Celeste."

Kiri released a breath. "I don't know how I'll ever repay her."

"Me neither. Though I'm sure my brother and your unicorns will receive the bill soon enough." An amused glint lighted his eyes, then shifted into something brighter. "I told you I'd find a way. It may have been an accident, but I kept my word, didn't I?" A halo of hope radiated around him.

"Yes. Yes, you did." She smiled, basking in the warmth emanating from him even if she couldn't quite feel it within herself. "Wait... what about Nighthawk?"

"Palace horses are trained to find their ways back to Yessalem if their riders don't return. He also bears the royal insignia, so any passersby will know not to touch him. He'll be fine, especially since my uncle will surely spoil him upon his return. The king loves that blighted stallion." Darien took her hand. "It looks like fortune has finally favored us. By this time tomorrow, you'll be within a stone's throw of Kristakai."

The joyous look on his face warmed Kiri's heart.

Still, she couldn't shake the shadow of dread looming over her, telling her that this situation was merely a false promise to tantalize her, while her ultimate fate remained as sure as the ticking clock.

The brightening day cast a rose-gold hue upon the sea, which rippled beneath a sky streaked with wispy clouds. Kiri felt that she could never grow tired of watching the endless waves, especially under the light of dawn. Though she'd been gazing at it in silence for at least an hour, her eyes seemed inadequate vessels for drinking in all the beauty before her; no matter how long she stared, she wanted more.

Beside her, Darien leaned back against one of the large stones, his eyes shut and his chest moving placidly to the rhythm of his breath. The bag

of supplies rested on the ground beside him. How he'd managed to go as long as he did without sleep was beyond her, and she was glad that he'd found a few moments of respite.

The drumming of the sea beat against the rocks, hushed and mellow. In the tide's murmur, she thought she detected a familiar melody—one that had been in the background of one of her dreams. Then, she realized that the song was in her head, blooming from the depths of her mind. Too busy had she been observing the forefront before that she hadn't realized what she'd heard, yet she must have absorbed it subconsciously, for now, its slow, mournful melody echoed in her head, over and over. Lovely as it was, it haunted her, almost like a warning, and she wondered what it—if anything—her heart was trying to tell her through its words:

In the darkness she flies, singing
She'll take all the pain and sorrow
For her whispers, you give and wait
Amid fields of thorn and yarrow

Cry, poor heart
Cry, pour soul
Love holds you fast
Yet breaks the promise of tomorrow

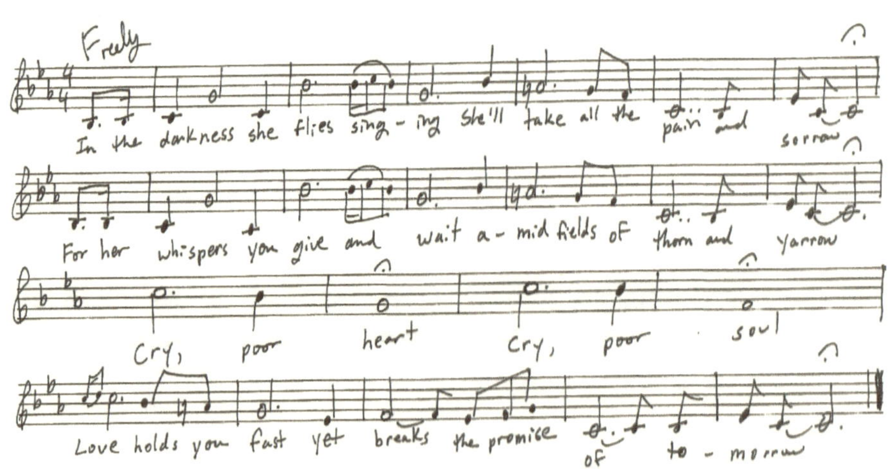

"That was… beautiful."

She whirled to see Darien gazing up at her and suddenly realized that she'd sung aloud. Embarrassed, she bit her lip. "I didn't mean to wake you."

"I wondered for a moment if I was still asleep." The corner of his mouth lifted. "If I didn't know better, I'd think you were trying to bewitch me."

Flattered, she returned his smile. "I wouldn't do that."

The humor left his expression, which became something serious, something meaningful. "You wouldn't need to," he said softly.

Kiri held his gaze, drinking in the wonder behind it. Her frantic pulse could have rivaled the beating wings of a thousand birds all flying off at once.

Before she could respond, the previously serene seawater burbled and sloshed, sending salty spray flying, and a large transparent sphere, about six feet in diameter and as iridescent as a soap bubble, rose to the surface. Gold filigree decorated the top with intricate designs of curling kelp and blooming coral, and two long chains extended from either side, trailing into the water. Inside, a plush blue bench, wide enough for at least three or four people, sat facing away from the shoreline on a glass floor.

"Look!" she exclaimed.

"Glad Ilaerii returned after all." Unsure of whether he was being sarcastic or serious, Kiri gave him a questioning look, to which he responded, "I didn't *really* doubt her, since a royal promise is worth something, but… it wouldn't be the first time one was broken."

The water stilled but for a few stray bubbles and unruly ripples. Ilaerii emerged beside the sphere, wearing what must have been her full queenly regalia, and walked to shore. Her hair still flowed freely down her back like an obsidian waterfall, but she had adorned it with a jeweled diadem that glittered on her forehead in brilliant shades of purple and green. From the headpiece, ribbons strung with gleaming blue stones cascaded down her back. Dressed in a gown of luxurious emerald that hugged her shoulders, she looked every bit a sovereign. On her throat, secured by a lustrous silver collar, a round jewel glowed, outshining the rest of her resplendent attire. The stone itself was dark, but sparkled with red, gold, green, blue—every color imaginable—and Kiri recognized it as a precious stargem, an item so rare, it was almost mythology.

"I hope you know who I am this time," Ilaerii said, stepping onto dry land. Though the rest of her was opulently dressed, her feet remained bare. "I'm handling this situation myself, since I can't have anyone else learning who *he* is." She jerked her head at Darien. "As far as everyone else is concerned, I am helping two residents of our ally Kristakai return home as a favor to the unicorns. Understand?"

"Yes, Your Majesty," Kiri replied, awestruck.

"Come. The elephants don't like being this close to land and will grow restless if we don't leave soon."

"Elephants?"

"Yes, Marae elephants." The mermaid raised her eyebrows. "What did you think I was summoning, dolphins?"

Kiri looked away, unsure of whether she was more embarrassed or irritated.

The young queen pointed at the transparent sphere bouncing gently on the tide. "You two will ride in that pod. I'll be in the front to steer. Now, let's go." She strode into the water.

Kiri bunched up her cloak to keep it from trailing into the water and followed, examining the pod for a door or an opening. No matter which angle she observed it at, she found no break in the shimmering surface. She turned to Darien and whispered, "Where's the door?"

"I was hoping you'd spotted one," he muttered, lifting the sack of supplies to keep it from getting wet as he waded into the sea beside her. Drawing his eyes down the seemingly featureless pod, he twisted his face into a quizzical expression. "Are we both daft, or is something missing?"

The water was already waist-deep around Ilaerii, whose long skirt floated around her. She raised her arms as if to dive.

"Your Majesty!" Darien called.

Ilaerii put her hands on her hips. "Is there a problem?"

He nodded at the pod. "There doesn't seem to be an entrance."

"Any part can serve as an entrance." Though she didn't add the words "you cretin," her tone and expression conveyed them clearly. "Just walk right through. I'd suggest using the back, because it's floating at the edge of a drop-off, and if you go any further, you'll find yourself treading water. Now go on, I haven't got all day!" Without that, she plunged into the sea, leaving behind an angry pattern of white froth.

Darien laughed. "She's about as friendly as the Port Timonar captains would have been. Actually, I'm pretty sure the rogue seafarers would have had better manners."

"At least she's helping us," Kiri said, shaking her head. She approached the pod and tentatively pressed her hand against it. Though it looked as solid as glass, the glimmering surface, smooth and warm beneath her touch, gave way at once. She stepped through as if melting into a wall of butter. When she reached the other side, she found, to her surprise, that her skin was dry, and no dampness clung to her dress or her cloak. Apparently, she'd left the seawater behind. She placed a hand on the back of the blue bench and traced its soft contours as she walked around it, fascinated.

Darien entered behind her, a look of wonderment in his eyes.

A hollow knocking sounded from below, and Kiri turn her attention downward. Ilaerii, back in mermaid form, looked up at her through the transparent floor with an expression of impatience. The flowing green skirt of her gown was gone; only the upper half remained, beneath which her glimmering tail swayed. Kiri wondered if all the queen's clothing were enchanted to convert into dresses when she wanted to shift.

"Sit!" Ilaerii pointed her finger down for emphasis. "Or you'll go flying out the back the moment we start moving." Though the pod muffled her voice, she sounded as sharp as ever.

Kiri obeyed, plopping onto the bench's cushions. Trying to catch a glimpse of the Marae elephants, she leaned down but saw only the two long golden chains and the rocky ground.

Darien took a seat beside her, placing the bag on the floor. "They're probably too far out to view from this angle," he said, apparently noticing her searching. "But as soon as we start moving, I'm sure you'll see them."

"Have you ever been to their kingdom?" she asked.

He shook his head. "The Marae aren't exactly welcoming to visitors; as far as I know, only rulers and a few very important diplomats have ever visited their underwater city. But that's more than the number of merpeople who have seen Nikhilim; other than the reigning sovereign, none of them have the means to travel on land. So the only interactions their kind have with ours is out at sea, and most of those encounters are unpleasant."

"How come?"

"Well, the merpeople consider it an intrusion whenever human ships pass over their territory, and they can become quite rankled. Meanwhile, the captains couldn't care less about what's going on underwater as long as they get to where they need to go. And there have been disputes over island and shoreline territories, since the merpeople don't like it when human settlements get too close to their waters. Not to mention resources—they're unhappy about how much fishing has increased due to our growing population. Suffice it to say, Nikhilim and Marae don't exactly like each other."

"Is that why Ilaerii's so…" Kiri searched for the right word. "Disagreeable?"

"Possibly. Or perhaps that's just the temperament that comes with handling politicians all day. Still, I'd rather deal with a person who is disagreeable but honest than one who always knows the right thing to say." He angled his mouth. "I find myself liking her quite a lot."

The transport lurched forward and skidded across the water's surface for a few seconds before plunging into the water at a dizzying speed. Kiri's stomach leaped into her throat, and she gripped the armrest but soon forgot her anxiety as she beheld what lay before her.

Shimmering shafts of sunlight streaked through the clear blue water surrounding the pod, spotlighting what looked like a golden chariot without wheels that lay at the end of the two chains. In it sat Ilaerii, holding a pair of pearlescent reins. Before her, two great elephants, each with long ivory tusks curving over their gray trunks, swam with elegant movements. Each wore a lustrous white shell on its forehead, secured by beaded red bands. It seemed extraordinary that such heavy-looking animals could move so swiftly—and without sinking. Of course, these were no ordinary beasts. Though she must have encountered enchanted creatures of all kinds back in Kristakai, without access to the sea, she could not have beheld any like these.

"They're wonderful," she murmured.

"They really are." Darien stared out the pod. "This whole transport is. I wonder what kind of spell the Marae used to create it. It's a pity so much magical knowledge was lost in the dark years after the fall of the Sorci's rule. If we humans had held on to some, we might have achieved something like this."

"From what I've seen of your world, your kind has achieved plenty."

Kiri thought back to the marvels of Yessalem, regretting that those few memories were all she had left of the resplendent city. "Nikhilim seems like a fantastic place."

"To some, it is. To others, it's a blighted sludgehole filled with pettiness and greed."

Surprised by the bitterness in his voice, she faced him. "Why did you leave?" she asked tentatively, longing to understand the dark fire kindling behind his ebony eyes. "Nythen told me some, but I want to hear it from you."

He glared out into the deep blue expanse. "I never belonged there. Everyone else had their place, and they all fit together, weaving a flawless fabric of society. Yet, I was always a stranger at best, a burden at worst. I thought that perhaps, somewhere beyond the world I knew, I'd find a place where I, too, could be a part of something. But I was wrong… I'm beginning to think I don't belong anywhere." He shook his head with a wry smile. "You wouldn't understand… You're fighting to return to your homeland. Meanwhile, I would do anything to stay away from mine."

Kiri thought back to the few memories she had of Kristakai. Almost every one of them held the recollection of her either trying to leave or dreaming about what she'd find outside the forest's borders. "You're wrong. I never really belonged either."

He furrowed his brow. "What do you mean? I thought you couldn't remember your past."

"I remember some. I remember wondering how all the other nymphs could be so content when we were trapped through no fault of our own… and longing to see the world outside. And so I, too, left my home, hoping to catch a glimpse of wonders like this." She arced her arm, indicating the pod. "If nothing else, at least that wish came true."

"Do you wish you'd stayed?" His voice was soft, contemplative.

Kiri shook her head. Despite everything she'd endured, and despite the ever-looming specter of death, she'd never once desired to take back the actions that had led her here. If she'd remained in Kristakai, she would never have known what lay beyond, and her days would have been spent in mundane repetition. Though she couldn't have imagined that dark magicians waited in ambush for her, she'd known that danger lurked ahead. Yet she'd taken the leap anyway.

If she hadn't done so, if she'd contented herself with dreaming and accepting the way things were, she would never have experienced the beautiful world surrounding her… or met the beautiful boy beside her.

She met Darien's gaze and answered, "No. Not once. I left Kristakai in hopes of finding a world beyond what I knew, and despite what it cost me, I would do it again. I wanted a purpose to my life, beyond mere existing. The others were content to remain within the borders, but I wanted more."

"I guess we're more alike than I thought." His eyes warmed, and a flush rushed into her cheeks.

"Yes, I… suppose we are."

Why did her heart mutiny in his presence, fluttering uncontrollably against the chastisements of her mind? Why did a piece of him dwell in her very soul, both comforting her and tormenting her at once?

You know the answer, a part of her accused. *Why deny what is so clear?*

Only the absurdity of love could explain her follies. The emotion was like a soft light glowing all around her. While she could ignore it, shun it, or pretend it didn't exist, it would always be there, reaching toward her and beckoning her to follow it.

Did he feel the same? She had to know — even if the answer was no, and any connection she'd sensed between them a mere illusion brought on by her own foolish heart. If this love were to become another scar, like the one Elaia had left, so be it. She would rather know than continue wondering.

"Darien," she began.

The transport lurched to a halt. Grabbing the armrest, Kiri glanced outside to see what was going on. The edge of a grand underwater city stretched below, and undulating ribbons of white sunlight frolicked across sloping rooftops with curling tips.

"There it is: Marae." An awestruck note clung to Darien's voice. "I never thought I'd see it with my own eyes."

Mesmerized, Kiri found her voice stuck in her throat as she tried to reply. The transport moved slowly over the sprawling metropolis, with the elephants trotting steadily. Below, merpeople with gleaming tails in every color swam down streets paved with white stones. Blazing reds and skipping blues, grinning greens and laughing yellows, careening purples and flitting oranges, all swaying, swishing, swirling between stone houses with gilded edges and red doors. Each one was intricately carved, though it was difficult to make out the details from this distance. Statues of roaring lions and undulating dragons stood at the center of city squares, and rotundas with layers of roofs stacked to high peaks rose above the rest of the buildings. Kiri guessed that the tower-like structures must have held some importance, and as they passed over one, she saw the symbol of the Divinity—a gold star with multitudes of rays stretching from a round center—painted over the top. *They're temples*, she realized.

Every direction she turned in held new wonders, and she was tempted to ask Ilaerii to stop the elephants entirely. She yearned to jump out of the bubble-like sphere and dive down to see Marae as the merpeople lived it, rather than looking below like a bird passing over treetops. But that kind of foolishness crossed into idiocy, for not only would it be a waste of time, but she wouldn't be able to breathe, and likely would suffer ill effects from the pressure of deep waters.

"It's a shame we're only passing over," she said with a sigh. "If only we could join it and be a part of it, just for a moment, like we did in Yessalem."

"That was fun, wasn't it?" Darien leaned back against the bench. "It was worth fighting the Sorci and getting captured for three minutes of dancing." His eyes twinkled.

She gave his arm a light smack. "Must you ruin the memory, you… What did your brother call you? Muckhead!"

He laughed. "I meant it! These past few days have been the worst of both our lives. I knew it was a risk going to the Heart of Yessalem, but after everything you've been through… I just wanted to give you a moment of joy."

Her heart fluttered at the look he gave her, and a grin crept onto her lips. She glanced away before the silly giggle teetering on her throat could find its way out and turned her eyes back to Marae, watching the merpeople come and go, apparently oblivious to what a gift their lives were in this delightful place. Leaning forward, she observed the bustle of busy vendors and street performers, whose music, blown through instruments of shell, penetrated the water and the walls. Though muffled, she could make out a lively melody and vivacious beat with similar sounds to those of Yessalem. The city's bright energy reminded her of the aura she'd experienced in the human metropolis, and she wondered whether they were all that different.

"Nikhilim and Marae seem to have a lot in common for two kingdoms that dislike each other," she commented.

"That's true." Darien whisked a stray lock out of his eyes with a toss of his head. "They once existed so separately, each thought the other to be almost mythical. But then both kingdoms grew—Nikhilim toward the sea and Marae toward the land. The humans sought to conquer the waters while the merpeople sought to expand, and they can't reside too deep, for they need sunlight like the rest of us. And so, they ran into each other, and relations have been strained ever since. I sometimes wonder if it would be better if we just united with them, shared the gulf, and brought our two worlds together, rather than endlessly debating what belongs to whom."

"That makes sense to me." The mention of two worlds brought her mind back to how different hers was from his—and how, if she made it home, an enchanted border would stand between them. Melancholy descended as she thought about the impossibility of what her heart desired, making her wonder if there was any point to pursuing it.

Apparently noticing her shift in mood, Darien asked, "What's wrong?"

"I wish our worlds could unite as well," she confessed. "Or, at least, that we could return to the days when my kind wandered freely among yours, before the unicorns retreated into their domain and erected barriers to keep humans out. I know they did it to protect us, but… I was trapped." She bowed her head. "Once I return, I'll be trapped again. I'll probably never see you again, and…" What did she mean to say? That the thought of being separated forever hurt as much as the Sorci's curse? That she didn't know how such a wound would ever heal?

"I don't want to lose you either." He gently put his hand under her chin, lifting it, and looked intently into her eyes. "If I can't enter your land, I'll wait by the border. Come see me when you can."

She shook her head. "Don't tie your destiny to mine. Especially since it seems to be my fate to fall into danger."

"I'd follow you anywhere, even into the darkness." His mouth lifted into a wistful smile, and the light in his eyes told her he meant every word.

Overwhelmed by a rush of desire, she reached toward him and placed her hand on his face, drawing nearer to him. All her previous hesitations no longer mattered; never mind what rules she was breaking. *I am who I am, and I love who I love. What's wrong with that?*

Pulling him close, she pressed her lips against his in one daring, eager kiss. To her delight, he returned it. The rest of the world vanished in the whirlwind of racing hearts and quickening breaths. His lips, his touch, his warmth—she wanted it all, and she was no longer afraid to take it. Whatever darkness or dangers pursued her, she'd left them far behind. For now, the world was perfect.

Perhaps she'd experienced the very worst of her life over the past few days, but she'd also found the very best. The light she'd tried to block out spilled through every corner of her mind, enveloping her in its power, and she let it take her whole. Lost in his kiss, she drifted in a cloud of sheer bliss, illuminated by shooting stars of ecstasy.

The transport lurched again, and she fell into him, grabbing his shoulder for support. Thrown back into reality, she looked around in confusion, then saw that the elephants were running again, and the city beneath them had retreated into the distance. Only the dark ocean floor lay below now, with silvery fish rushing all around.

"Do you think Ilaerii did that on purpose?" Darien asked with a slight laugh.

"I wouldn't be surprised." Still caught in the flush of joy, she leaned toward him again, but froze when a flash in the distance caught her eye. Red and yellow and bright as daylight—it looked like fire. But how was that possible when they were flying through the depths of the ocean? An ominous feeling overcame her, wiping away all trace of her previous euphoria. "Do you see that?" she asked, pointing.

Knitting his eyebrows, he followed her gaze. "What is it?"

Ilaerii seemed to notice as well, for her head was turned in the direction the flash had come from, and the expression on her profile was one of confusion and worry.

An explosion ripped through the water, so close the flames licked the sphere. Two screams buzzed in Kiri's ears—Ilaerii's, piercing through the distance, and her own, torn from her throat by terror. A creature appeared out of the blaze—a monster of fire with the outline of a human but a blank shadow where its face should have been and two burning holes in place of eyes. Grotesque black wings extended from its back and knife-like talons from its fingers… *A gui.*

It opened its mouth, revealing rows of sharp teeth, and let out an earth-shattering screech.

Gripped by horror and fear, Kiri looked around desperately. How could she fight or run when she was so far underwater? Would her powers, if she could unleash them again, do her any good down here?

Darien tensed. "The Sorci must have sent the servants of the Fiend to track us down."

Kiri shuddered. "How did they find us?"

Another explosion bloomed beside the first, followed by another, and then another, and then another, until it seemed the entire ocean would be consumed by the supernatural conflagration. From each, another gui emerged, screeching wildly through the depths.

Inferno was here. And more were coming.

ELSEWHERE...

"Watch them go, my Lord! Are they not magnificent? Soon, legions of guié such as the one we see here will be commonplace in the Terrestrial Realm. Ah, it is wonderful to have such compliant henchmen, those that will obey without question. And even better is knowing that we have Terrestrial servants who are just as deferential, though they believe themselves to be in control. Poor Worak, who thinks he wields such power. He really isn't much different from them, is he?"

17

Reason is beyond him

TOMORROW...

Arrin steeled herself against the inevitable, finally accepting the truth she'd known the entire time. As all rivers led to the ocean, all actions and choices led to the same terrible outcome.

It would happen again. But she would not make the same mistake twice.

TODAY...

INFERNO YAWNED BEFORE ARRIN. THE REALM'S ground of embers smoked around her feet as furious guié flew past, black wings stirring a feverish gust, toward a distant wall of blazing columns. But there was something different about those flames; they glowed with a quality wholly different from the rest of her surroundings. Whereas everything else burned yellow and red, these were pale blue, almost white, and dazzling in their brightness. The luminance evinced a sense of calm amid the chaos.

Then, she realized what they were: The gates to the Firelands, put in place by the Divinity to trap Her wicked brother. Behind them, the Fiend lay imprisoned, stewing in boundless hatred for all things living, and all things good.

The guié clawed hungrily at the columns with their pointed talons, trying to free their master, but to no avail. They screeched in frustration and climbed over each other, trying to reach their lord, until Arrin could no longer tell where one creature began and another ended.

Though heat should have seared her, she felt nothing against her skin, for she was a ghost in this world, existing out of space and out of time.

A great voice thundered through the air, enveloping her in its menacing power. "Though you and your kind will enjoy thousands of years of peace, it will be no more than a flicker of light in the eyes of the universe."

The Fiend.

Shuddering, Arrin looked around, but saw nothing other than a scorched wasteland, barren but for the coruscating gates and the rampageous guié.

A black shadow appeared halfway between them and Arrin, taking the vague shape of a man.

"Before the Age of Thrones reaches its sixteenth century, a human child will be born with the power of Inferno." The Fiend's voice resonated in her bones, sending an ominous chill through her. "Though the child's Terrestrial parents will be human, his soul will belong to his true father, the Fiend. He will be known as the Starless Prince, for none of the virtues of the stars will glow within this being of pure evil."

The man's form solidified, and he headed toward the Firelands, his movements eerily slow, as if wading through water, or perhaps sleepwalking. This had to be the Starless Prince — what other human would enter in this cursed place?

From where she stood, Arrin was only able to make out the man's shape, for the brilliant gates ahead silhouetted him. Wondering who he was, she ran toward the starless one, and though she moved with the same swiftness as she would have on Terra, she felt nothing beneath her feet. She soon drew close enough to see his profile, and the sight made her stop in her tracks. The sharp angles of his cheeks and chin, the hair so dark that not even the divine light reflecting off it revealed any color — it couldn't be… Could it?

She dashed in his direction, surpassing him and whirling to get a look at his face straight-on. There was no mistake.

"Darien?" She stared in shock.

But there was something wrong with him — he appeared empty, as if someone had stolen the spirit from his body and reanimated it, like a puppet with invisible strings. Oblivious to her presence, he passed through her if she were made of mist. The feeling was unnerving, but not nearly as unnerving as seeing someone she'd met, spoken to, and considered an ally cast in this cursed role.

"He will release the Fiend, and together, they will conquer not only the Terrestrial Realm, but the Celestial as well." The Fiend's voice, disembodied yet overpowering, lifted with glee. "And this will be the Age of Fire, which will last for all eternity."

The guié abruptly ceased their rabid attempts to claw open the gates to the Firelands and backed away, their glowing eyes fixed on Darien. The young man raised one hand toward the Fiend's prison, continuing his steady advance.

"Darien!" Arrin cried, rushing toward him.

Out of nowhere, an older woman appeared before her. A tangle of ebony hair cascaded down her shoulders, framing a wide face with bold features. The brown dress covering her full figure looked to be of an ancient style not seen since the Age of Unicorns — a crudely woven garment cut from a single piece of cloth and secured by knots. A white veil, bound to her head by a woven blue band, flowed down her back.

"Who are you?" Arrin demanded.

"The future is never absolute, for the slightest flicker in the present can illuminate a path that would otherwise remain unexplored." The woman's voice, soft and deep, rang with authority. "Yet the inevitable cannot be stopped." She vanished as abruptly as she had appeared.

"Wait!" Arrin reached out but grabbed only empty air where the woman had stood. "Who are you? What did you mean?"

A swirl of colored wind appeared in front of Darien, its serene tints of azure and lilac starkly contrasting the hot hues around it. Then, a girl with silvery blond hair materialized from it.

Kiri stood between Darien and the Firelands, her blue eyes fixed on him with an expression that was somewhere between sorrow and defiance. But he didn't seem to see her, for he continued forward with his hand extended toward the gates, looking past her like she was invisible. As he neared, she raised her own hand, touching her fingertips to his, and he stopped. His gaze met hers, and the life returned to his expression.

"Kiri?" He closed his hand around hers.

A red explosion ripped through the gates, its fiery blooms consuming the divine light and tearing past the prison bars.

Arrin screamed in terror as Kiri and Darien disappeared into the infernal blaze, swallowed by its merciless flames. The fire took the shape of an enormous man with a circular symbol burning yellow on his chest.

Recognizing the mark at once, she stared, horrified, as the Fiend raised his eyes to Celeste.

"Listen well, Sister!" he shouted. "Everything You created, everything You love, will be mine! This is the Age of Fire!"

"No!" Arrin cried. Her heart hammered with panic as she tried to think of a way to stop him... Anything... Anything... Anything...

A scream pierced Arrin's ears, and it took her a moment to realize that it had been her own. The drumming of her desperate heartbeat filled her ears, and sweat covered her panicked body.

She sat up, but the iron bars surrounding her did little to still her furious pulse. The sunlight spilling through the small window in the Sorci's laboratory, where she'd been trapped since the previous day, brought her no solace. Her leather bag sat in the corner of her cage; the Sorci had neither searched nor taken her belongings, probably thinking they were too worthless to bother with. Noticing that the tables, previously covered in apparatuses and spell ingredients, were now completely bare, a stab of panic pierced her. If they'd cleared everything out—not just tidied, but taken down all their equipment and put away the items needed to create what they sought—that meant they'd finished their work.

Come tomorrow, our spell will be complete, and Kristakai will be ours. The echo of the Sorci's words sent icy shards racing down her back.

Arrin's head throbbed, and she rubbed it absentmindedly, wondering how long she had been asleep. She remembered yanking at the bars in a vain attempt to break them, examining their structure in a useless effort to find a weakness, and then, when all else failed, shouting at the top of her lungs for her captors to release her. One of them must have decided they'd heard enough, since the aching in her skull and the lack of distinct memory told her she hadn't fallen asleep, but had been knocked out by something. Probably a curse, given who her captors were.

The daylight had been fading when she last recalled being awake, but now, the sun shone brightly, which meant she must have been unconscious for at least fifteen hours, if not more. That couldn't have been natural, no matter how weary she'd been.

And it meant that the spell would be completed *today*. Any moment, the magicians might burst in to take her to the "nexus of power" they'd spoken of and sacrifice her to the dark magic. There was no chance she could escape the cage before they returned; she'd spent hours the previous day trying to concoct a plan, but the bars conjured by magic had no lock— only solid, solid iron in every direction.

Despite having been locked up for almost a full day, she felt neither hunger nor thirst, which was odd considering how far she'd walked to reach the Sapphire Bastille. She'd heard of spells that froze people entirely—locked them into whatever state of being they'd been in before the magic overcame them, so that a hundred years could pass and they'd awaken as if they'd only blinked—and guessed that something similar had been used on her. But clearly it had worn off, for she wouldn't have dreamed if that were so.

It wasn't a dream…

That vision had been no nightmare, but another prophecy. She knew it as instinctively as she knew she needed to breathe. The Fiend's threats still rang in her head, and she hugged her knees to her chest. Her one comfort—if it could even be called that—in her seemingly hopeless situation was that if she died at the hands of the Sorci, she would never have to see the Age of Fire rise or witness the unspeakable horrors the Fiend and his followers would wreak upon the world she knew, the world she loved.

Images of her family suffering at the hands of the guié rampaged through her mind, and she pressed her hands to eyes. If that was the future she faced, she would rather be dead.

But all was *not* lost, she reminded herself. Though her failure to sabotage the magicians weighed on her heart, she was not the only player in this game of fate. There was still the original object of her quest: the windborn one. If Kiri warned the unicorns, then the great creatures could protect their land. But was there any chance she could reach the domain in time? The last time Arrin had spoken to the air nymph, the girl had been halfway toward a foolish attempt to break Darien out of a Nikhilim prison.

If she dies because of that, I'll throttle her when we meet in Celeste. The blighted, lovesick idiot!

Yet another feeling nagged at her, saying that Kiri's actions had been right. Not only because the girl had risked herself to save someone else—a noble, if rather stupid, action—but because of the other visions she'd witnessed. Twice now, Arrin had seen the nymph intervene when Darien, breathing but otherwise devoid of anything resembling life, seemed ready to step into the abyss.

Is he really the Starless Prince? Upon seeing his figure appear out of shadow, that had been Arrin's immediate assumption, before she'd seen his face. But that was only because the Fiend's voice had surrounded her with words about his prophesied son, and she'd assumed that any human approaching the Firelands had to be the child of darkness. Yet she could easily have been mistaken.

The more she thought about it, the more ridiculous she found the notion. Besides, the Sorci were working for the Fiend, which meant they would seek to *protect* their master's supernatural descendent, not chase him across kingdoms.

How, then, did Darien fit into all this? And what about Kiri?

I should have gone with them. Not only would Arrin have avoided her current predicament, but she could have learned more about them, which would have helped her piece together what her prophecies were trying to say. *Of course, I would have had to put up with their moon-eyes and syrupy talk…* She made a face, recalling the dulcet tones with which the lovers — and they *were* lovers, whether they admitted it or not — had spoken to each other. *Skies, I hope no one ever speaks that way to me. It's kind of sweet to witness, I suppose, and I like a good love story as much as the next person, but I want no part of one.*

The creak of an opening door pulled her attention back to her surroundings, and she jumped to her feet.

Worak strode into the laboratory, his fingers steepled and his face obscured by his hood. Yet she recognized him by the gold pendant he wore across his chest and the distinctive patterns embroidered in rich metallic threads upon his black cloak. When he lifted his chin, his eyes caught the sunlight, glinting beneath the shadow, and they reminded her of an infernal gui.

"A convergence of magic such as the one I detected from here is quite unusual," he said, approaching. "Tell me, are you practiced in the magical arts?"

"Fiend take you!" Arrin spat, the curse spewing from her lips before she realized how idiotic it sounded when the one she faced served Inferno.

"I'll take that as a no." His eyes swept across her, probing.

Scowling, she recoiled. "You're an idiot. The Fiend seeks to make *all* the Divinity's creations suffer, and, despicable as you are, you still count as human. Barely."

"What would *you* know of the Fiend's intentions?" The magician glared down at her.

"It's common sense, you benighted ignoramus! He's the source of all evil, isn't he? What makes you think he would treat *anyone* fairly? You could dedicate your life to him, dance on his command and satisfy each demand he makes, but he would dispose of you the moment you ceased to be useful." She tilted her head with a mocking grin. "No, that would be too rational of him. He would dispose of you simply because it amused him." Angling her mouth, she pretended to ponder the words. "No, still too judicious. He is the Fiend, after all. Reason is beyond him; he'd destroy you just because he felt like it, on nothing more than a frivolous whim."

Worak swept a hand in her direction, she flinched. A warm breeze emanated from his spell, whirling about her. Glittering yellow sparks flew from his fingers, and she gasped as one brushed her hand, for it stung the way an open wound did when touched. More blew toward her, and she turned away, covering her face. Her whole body tensed as she wondered what this magic was intended for, but, knowing the magician would only laugh at any pleas she made, she focused only on shielding herself. What felt like a thousand tiny needles pricked her back, and she clenched her teeth.

"No wonder," Worak murmured. The breeze vanished, along with the stings.

Arrin spun to face him. "What do you mean?"

"I was only seeking a blood sacrifice when I found you lurking, but it looks like I have found far more. I take it you think you know the Fiend because of your prophecies."

Her eyes widened. *How does he know about those? I only told Kiri and Darien... Right, the spell. So that's what it was for.* "It must be convenient to have magic that can figure things out for you. Saves you the trouble of using that worthless brain of yours."

"An uncut gemstone." Apparently choosing to ignore her retort, Worak pushed his hood back and observed her. "Perhaps you would be more valuable alive. It's been a generation since the last Sibyl walked the Terrestrial Realm, and the power to see into the future could be valuable."

I'm a Sibyl?! Sibyls were chosen by the Ayr of Tomorrow and possessed the ability not only to see into the future, but to communicate with Celeste. They were more than prophetesses, more than psychics—they were conduits to the Divinity's own realm. According to the legends, the first

Sibyl, Nameed, had only learned how to open a channel to the heavens shortly before her death, but she had taught the ability to her apprentice, and since then, it had been passed along the generations. But the last Sibyl had died fifty years before Arrin's birth, and without choosing a successor. It was said their order was finished. *Is this some kind of trick?*

"I see this news surprises you." Worak sounded smug. "Yes, my girl, you are more than you appear to be. Your visions will reveal the fate of the world, not just the petty comings and goings of ordinary folk. What have you seen so far?"

"Eat sludge." Arrin crossed her arms.

The other grabbed a bar with one hand and leaned down with a glare. "I have no patience for your childish antics. You have one chance, and one chance only, to preserve your little life. Swear yourself to the Sorci, and I shall choose another victim for the sacrifice. Refuse, and you will die a torturous death this afternoon, as we drain your body of every drop of blood it holds and peel the flesh from your bones."

Arrin hugged her arms, a chill engulfing her from the inside out. The prospect of facing so much pain was more than she could bear. It hit her, truly hit her, that she was going to die screaming before the sky darkened. Everything she'd hoped for vanished into the winds of doom as she realized she'd never get the chance to achieve the life she'd worked so hard for. That notebook full of designs contained nothing more than the dashed dreams of a doomed soul. Tears surged into her eyes, and she tried not to think about what horrors she would endure before the evil magicians let her die.

Nevertheless, the idea of joining the monsters made her gut twist. Every fiber of her being revolted at the idea, and she knew better than to hope she might escape after they claimed her. Darien had been one of their own, after all, and now they hunted him like an animal. And who knew what they'd force her to do before she found the opportunity to try?

I won't do it. She strode up to Worak and spat in his face.

"Fool!" he shouted.

A sudden gale sent her flying back into the bars, and she grabbed one to keep from falling. The impact sent bolts of pain shooting through her, yet despite the bruises, she managed a satisfied smirk.

A second magician entered, holding a tray. Three small bottles full of

glimmering liquids sat upon it, one red, one green, and one gold. "Am I interrupting?" she asked, and Arrin recognized her voice as belonging to Limali.

"No." Worak drew his sleeve across his cheek. "Our little sacrifice is quite ready to have her blood spilled."

"Then we should leave for the Ashen Plains." Limali nodded at the tray. "The potions are ready, and the others are prepared to journey to the nexus on your command."

"Let me see." The leader strode to the woman, eyeing the colorful liquids.

An idea flashed through Arrin's mind. Those bottles looked as if they were made of glass…

Deciding to act before fear could stop her, she seized the wooden crescent from her bag and hurled it through the bars.

"*Forth!*" Worak punched his hand toward it, but the blast of red magic missed its target, and the crescent hurtled into Limali's tray, shattering the bottles. The woman let out a dismayed cry, staring down at the spilled liquids in disbelief.

Take that, curbrains. Arrin lifted her head in triumph. The crescent clattered against the bars and fell to the floor.

Worak incinerated it with a fiery blast then sent a green spell flying toward her. The next think she knew, pain ravaged every iota of her being, exploding through her stomach and shooting down her limbs. She screamed in anguish and found herself balled up on the floor, tears streaming down her face. Agony filled her, and no matter how she writhed, she could find no respite. She grabbed her hair and yanked at it, not even knowing why, as her legs kicked on their own volition against the unyielding metal bars.

"We have spares, yes?" Worak's voice cut through the buzzing of Arrin's cries, and she tried to focus on listening for information to take her mind away from the ripping, raging torture.

"Of course, sir," Limali answered quickly. "Except…"

"Except *what*?"

"This one requires a firegem touched by the first rays of dawn. And it must be the dawn of the day the spell is to be cast, for the magic becomes moot the moment the sun sets. Since the stones are so precious, we only left one out this morning."

They can't perform the ritual until tomorrow! That one thought shone through the ocean of agony.

The curse vanished, leaving Arrin a sobbing heap on the ground. She tried to stop her tears, hating that someone—especially the one who had inflicted her pain—would see her so vulnerable and picked herself up. If only she could set fire to the monster and watch him burn until he was nothing more than smoldering bone.

To her disappointment, Worak was on his way out, his back to her, so he didn't even see the venomous glare she shot in his direction. The woman was already gone. Furious, Arrin strode up to the bars, holding her head as high as she could.

"Listen, you curborn blackguard!" she yelled at the Sorci master's retreating form. "You know I can see the future, so let me tell you your destiny. You will die, alone and hated, by the hand of the one you serve so faithfully. The Fiend will rip the flesh from your bones and slice what remains into bloody chunks he'll feed to the guié. And then your filthy, worthless soul will writhe in the fires of Inferno for all eternity while I look down from Celeste and laugh!"

Though she had no way of knowing if anything she spoke was true, it made her feel good to say it and brought a malicious grin to her lips. She had no qualms about being cruel toward the wicked, and she hoped her words struck fear into his black heart.

"Silence!" Worak thrust his hand at her, and a spell flung her back into the bars so hard, her ears rang.

She wasn't quick enough to catch herself, and she fell to the ground. But though the world spun, that grin remained on the corner of her mouth. Deciding she'd had enough of his curses, she closed her eyes and pretended to be unconscious. She'd had her last word, and it left her satisfied.

Not only that, but she'd bought herself an extra day. It was a small triumph, but at least it gave her a chance. Perhaps the extra time would give Kiri a chance to return to her homeland and the unicorns an opportunity to reinforce Kristakai's defenses. And it was one more day to live, which Arrin wasn't about to spend waiting for either her doom or a miracle.

After hearing Worak's footsteps fade away, she sat up and panned her gaze across the cage. *Think, Arrin, think!* The bars looked as solid as ever, but there had to be something she could do. Her eyes landed on her bag, and she suddenly recalled the clarion stone fragment inside. *Skies, how did I forget about that? Well, I suppose I've been a little distracted. Couldn't have used it yesterday anyway, since this place was crawling with Sorci.*

But now, the room was empty.

After double-checking to make sure no one was around, she scrambled to retrieve the crystal shard. The chance remained that the Sorci had some magical way of keeping an eye on her, but that was a risk she'd have to take. *Better to get caught trying than do nothing at all.*

Arirn held the fragment to her lips and whispered the word to activate it, praying that someone would answer her call.

ELSEWHERE...

"Everything is going according to plan, great Fiend. Whatever disturbances these Terrestrial players think they've made, they only serve to bring us further toward our goal. I must admit, I was surprised when you revealed how the things into which I put so much effort will ultimately be of such little consequence. But I understand how the ebb and flow of destiny matter more than immediate gains and losses, for I am not unknowing, as the Terrestrial are."

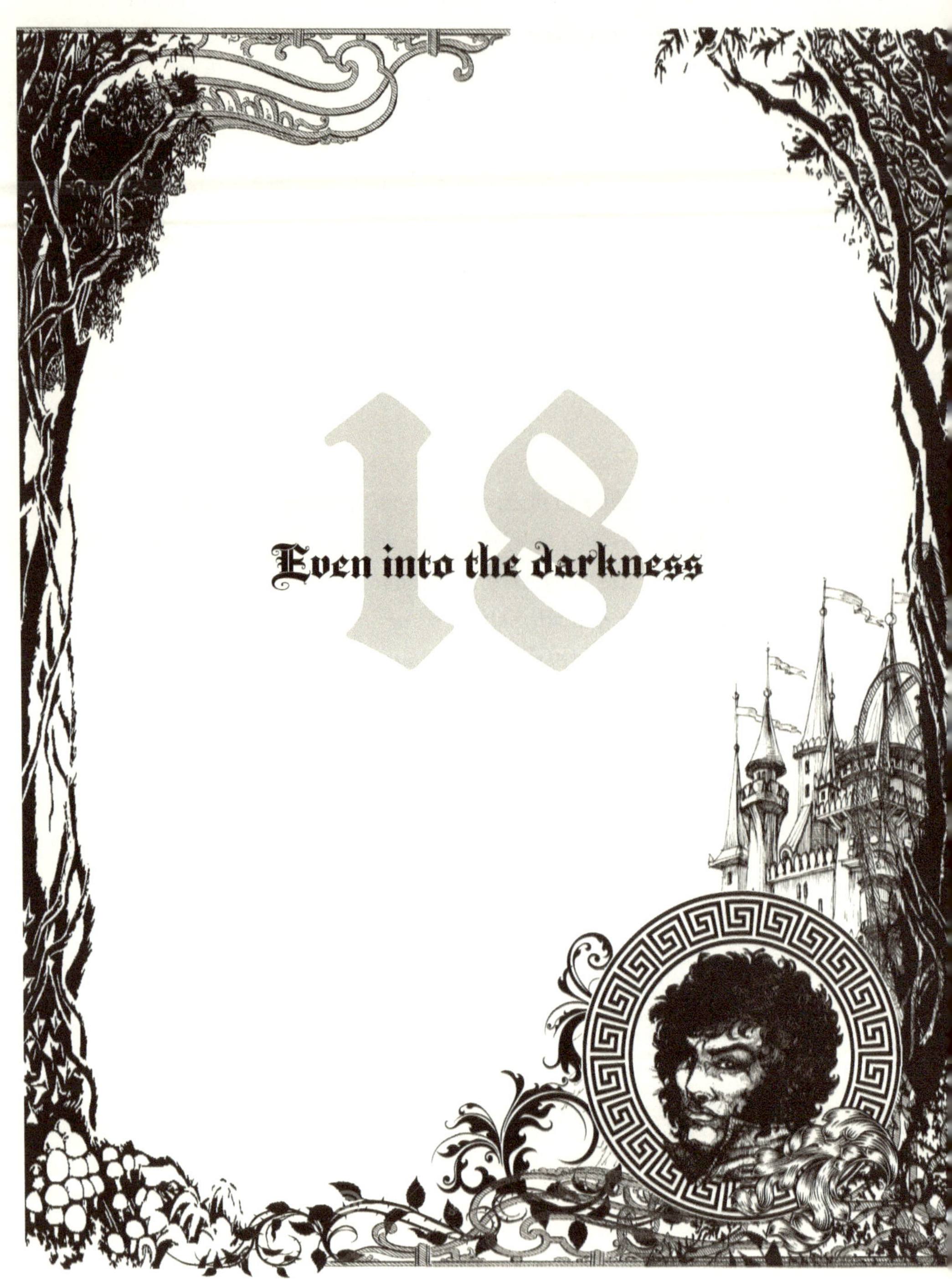

18

Even into the darkness

The Fiend spread his fiery mouth into a wicked grin, and the Starless Prince smiled back. Blackness filled the hollow where once his heart had been, blissful in its emptiness, for everything he'd once been was gone, no more.

Yet something tainted the darkness, a memory that refused to die. A secret light, a hidden lure, an intimate flame that not even the master of Inferno could blow out.

TODAY...

**EVERYTHING BECAME A BLUR OF RED FIRE AGAINST** the dark sea outside. Facing the back of the transport, Darien gripped the bench as the floor beneath him lurched. The sound of Ilaerii yelling for the elephants to go faster was loud enough for him to hear even with all the water between them. The guié pursued, a trail of fiery figures and blazing eyes flying underwater on jagged black wings. Though their speed was no match for the beasts of Marae, they kept appearing in nearby explosions, and each time the elephants sped past them, they'd materialize again.

With the clarion stone glowing in his fist, Darien summoned yet another spell, hoping this time it would do more than briefly slow them down. Only a sliver of the crystal remained usable, but if ever there were a moment to wield what remained, this was it. The stirring magic sent bolts of pain through him, but he barely felt them anymore. The urge to fight blazed in his heart, sending energy rippling through his muscles.

Flaming darts, whizzing by in brilliant yellows, shot from the taloned hands of the guié. Whatever magic held the transport together also deflected the projectiles, but Ilaerii appeared exposed in her chariot, and the elephants certainly had no shield. One gui lifted its claws toward her.

Fearing that it was aiming for the mermaid queen, Darien flung his arm out, reaching through the enchanted sphere and into the water.

"*Forth!*" he exclaimed, channeling the magic through the crystal.

The green bolt of a destroyer spell exploded from the stone. Its force should have shattered anything it hit, but the gui hardly seemed to notice despite the magic striking it square in the chest. The creature whirled to face him, spewing darts. Darien withdrew into the safety of the transport, but not before a projectile struck his outstretched hand.

A spike of pain shot up his arm, and he cursed.

Frustrated, he glared at the clarion stone, wondering why the magic had failed—again. Though his hand stung where the gui had hit him, no visible sign of injury marred his skin. He frowned. Entire libraries could be filled with accounts of the guié's horrors—how each could incinerate people, tear them to pieces, or shatter their bones, with a flick of its hand. He should have been hurt a lot worse… Were all the projectiles so mild? Was that why he, Kiri, and Ilaerii had managed to remain unharmed so far?

It did seem incredibly fortunate that they'd made it so far with dozens of monsters in such close pursuit. An ominous thought clouded his mind: that the guié were holding back, seeking not to destroy them but to drive them to a darker fate that lay at the end of the chase. *Perhaps Worak still hopes to kill me himself. He must have called the Fiend for aid to send guié after us. I suppose I should be flattered by all the attention.*

That the master of Inferno's gaze had turned to him sent a shiver through Darien. Whatever strange power dwelled within him, the one that frightened even Worak, must have drawn the Fiend's attention, and he dared not wonder why.

Perhaps the reason why his spells hadn't worked was because the guié were of the Infernal Realm—perhaps his Terrestrial magic lacked the power to affect them. But he'd rather try and fail a thousand times than stand idly while the enemy attacked. Red sparks flashed against the sphere as dart after dart impacted against its transparent surface. Itching for action, he raised the clarion stone again.

"Darien, don't." Kiri looked up at him from her place on the bench. "You're only hurting yourself."

"I have to do *something*," he replied, though he knew she was right. What if he was just wasting the stone's powers for nothing?

The sound of a horn, high and piercing, rang out. Darien caught sight of the mermaid queen holding a large, curved shell to her lips. White in color, the instrument was so bright it seemed to glow against the darkness. She blew into it again, sending out a second burst of noise, and this time, he glimpsed water rippling around it. *Is she calling for help? But if she had that the whole time, why wait until now to use it?*

His question was answered by the sight of a glimmering triple-gabled building hovering between the sea's surface and the incalculable depths below. "A Marae outpost," he muttered.

Kiri glanced at him. "Can they help us?"

"I don't know."

The elephants barreled toward it, drawing close enough for him to make out the two dragon statues guarding the enormous red gate. After a third horn blast, the doors flew open, and several merpeople, each wearing a bronze helmets and breastplates, swam out, armed with swords and shields that glowed with enchantments.

"Destroy the guié!" Ilaerii pointed emphatically at the creatures behind them.

A gui exploded into being right beside her chariot, clinging to its side, and she screamed.

"*Ilaerii!*" Without thinking, Darien leaped from the sphere, passing through the enchanted wall and into the water.

It wasn't until after he was outside the transport, floating in the cold, dark mass of liquid, that he realized how foolishly he'd acted. Unable to breathe and barely able to see, and with the pressure of the ocean crushing him, he found himself drifting in an undersea abyss. His eyes stung as he tried to reorient himself, but everything was blurred, and all he could make out were the vague shapes and lights around him.

A sharp-taloned hand gripped his shoulder from behind, burning like a brand. He whipped his head back and found himself staring into the blazing eyes of a gui. Clenching the clarion stone, he held it up.

But before he could attempt a spell, the crystal glowed without his instruction, and a white cloud of light appeared around it. A

communication—Arrin must have been sending a message through her shard.

Perfect timing. He briefly considered refusing to answer but feared she might have something important to say. Knowing he wouldn't be able to use the crystal while the link was being made, he kicked at the creature instead. Slowed by the water, the blow didn't have much effect. The creature grinned, then released him and opened its mouth into a wide yawn.

A blast of heat struck him in the face. He opened his mouth to cry out, only to have water fill his mouth, and his hands flew up to shield himself from a second assault.

"Kiri? Darien?" Arrin's voice rang out, and he suddenly realized he wasn't holding the stone anymore.

Looking around frantically, he glimpsed the glowing crystal tumbling into the depths.

"Are you there?" Her voice was clear even through the water, but he could barely hear it.

He started to dive after the stone, but the gui gripped his shoulder again, drawing blood this time.

Meanwhile, Arrin continued speaking: "If you can hear me... The Sorci have almost finished their spell. They'll be ready to invade Kristakai *tomorrow.* They're heading for the Ashen Plains, where they'll complete the magic and add the final ingredient... me. They're going to sacrifice me..." Her voice faded as the crystal vanished from sight.

Darien's mind raced, and he wasn't sure which piece of news he found more disturbing—the imminence of the Sorci's assault on Kristakai or the danger Arrin had encountered. *I shouldn't have let her go to the Bastille...*

His lungs felt like they were collapsing, and both the transport and the water's surface appeared a million miles away. Desperate for air, he gripped the blazing claw still gripping his shoulder and tried to yank it off, but the creature held him tight. Water rushed around him, and blackness invaded his vision, blotting out even the blurred lights of the world around him.

A familiar yet still-strange sensation stirred at his core, urging him to release it—

Someone seized his arm and jerked him back. Pain ripped through his shoulder as razor-like talons slashed his skin. But he hardly cared, for air surrounded him once more. Coughing up water, he found himself staring at the transport's floor, which appeared to spin beneath him. He inhaled sharply, drawing in as much as his lungs could carry.

"Darien!" Seated beside him, Kiri stared down at him with a worried expression.

Confused, he blinked. "What happened?"

"The gui dragged you near enough that I was able to reach through the transport and grab you. Are you all right?"

He nodded. Then, remembering why he'd gone into the water in the first place, he managed, "Ilaerii?"

"She's fine. Her chariot must be enchanted too—the gui couldn't touch her."

Upon hearing that, he realized just how stupidly he'd acted. Of course a queen would not travel unprotected! That whole ordeal had been for nothing—not that he could have defended her if she'd been in danger.

Realizing that Kiri had just saved his life *again*, he started to thank her, but then, the transport lurched. Startled, he looked outside. The water was growing lighter; they must have been nearing the shallows. Marae soldiers, rallying to defend their queen, struck at the fiery attackers with blades that glowed yellow. One sliced through a gui's wing, and, to his surprise, the monster screeched and vanished.

Bursts of red appeared before the sphere, and the chains connecting the transport to Ilaerii's chariot burst into flames, which crawled toward the pod like snakes.

The mermaid twisted back in her seat and yelled, "*Get out!* If the chain is severed, the pod will collapse!"

Darien jumped up. "Can you swim?" he asked Kiri.

Worry filled her eyes. "I don't know…"

"Take off your cloak, and hold your breath."

Kiri ripped off the heavy black garment and grabbed his outstretched hand. Pulling her along, he leaped through the pod's wall once more, but this time, he was prepared. He kicked against the water and swam for the surface, blocking out the chaos around him.

An explosion erupted before him, bringing forth one of the infernal monsters. The gui swiped at him, and he raised his arm to block the blow. But before it could land, a sudden wave knocked into the creature and sent it hurtling backward through the water, which swirled around Darien in a powerful whirlpool.

Though bewildered, he didn't have time to contemplate what had happened. Still holding Kiri's hand, he fought the mysterious current and swam upward with all the strength he could muster. All around, infernal flames clashed against Marae swords, a wild blur of mad light spinning through the stinging, swirling sea. The glow of sunlight brightened as he neared the rippling surface.

A burst of red assaulted his vision. Raising his hand, he prepared to blast the gui back to its dark realm with whatever magic he could summon, but before he could make his move, he felt himself being dragged away by the hand that held Kiri's.

Water rushed around him, and the next thing he knew, it was wind that surrounded him instead of waves. Blue sky filled his vision in place of the dark ocean, and a powerful gust roared in his ears. His eyes soon found Kiri, but though her hand remained solid in his, she was no longer a humanlike girl, but a translucent being gliding through the atmosphere, ethereal and beautiful as dawn's first light.

"Don't worry," she said with a smile. "I have you."

She soared over the ocean, carrying him along with her powers. Under any other circumstances, he would have grinned at the thrill of gliding across the sky with an ease only known to those with wings. But he couldn't take his mind away from Kiri and how much she suffered each time she defied the Sorci's curse. He wished he could tell her to stop, but what was she supposed to do, drop them both back into the underwater fray?

A strip of green sparkled on the horizon ahead—they were closer to land than he'd thought. Kiri headed toward it, her mouth pursed in concentration. With her speed, it would not take long to reach. Darien looked around for any sign of the guié, but the creatures must have been too engaged in the battle to have noticed the escape. Red lights continued flashing beneath the ocean, and he dreaded what might be going on beneath the surface. It was foolishness to think the merpeople could cut down or drive back the creatures without sustaining any casualties, but he hoped nevertheless.

A fierce anger burned in his chest. He should never have spared Worak's life; if he'd struck down the Sorci master when he'd had the chance, swarms of guié would not be attacking the brave soldiers of Marae. Not only had his failure to act endangered himself and Kiri, but he'd dragged Nythen, Arrin, Ilaerii, and several bystanders into the mess.

Kiri's hand tightened, and her face contorted in pain.

"Kiri?"

"I'm fine." Her voice was so strained, it was almost a sob.

"It's the curse, isn't it?" The anger grew. He couldn't bear to see her suffer, especially when it was because of him—because he'd listened to whatever instinct had told him to spare Worak in an idiotic attempt to hold some moral high ground. "Let it go. We're close enough to swim from here."

She shook her head. "I can make it."

"Kiri—"

A scream burst from her lips. The wind buoying them vanished, and they both plunged into the sea. The impact knocked the breath from Darien's lungs, and saltwater stung his injured shoulder. But he was able to surface quickly enough, yanking her up beside him. She gasped for air, shaking.

He pulled her close. "Hold on to me."

She grabbed his shoulder but wouldn't meet his gaze. "I'm sorry. I don't know what happened."

"It's not your fault." Then, trying to lighten the mood, he said, "That's the third time you've saved my life. According to one of the ancient tribal cultures, this means you own me."

The vaguest hint of a smile tugged at her lips. "If you count the time I pulled you back into the pod, it's the fourth."

"You're right. I'm definitely bound to serve you for the rest of your life, then." Too late, he realized how terrible that comment was, given that she might not have much longer to live. "I only meant—"

"It's okay," she said with a weak smile.

Cursing his clumsy words, he swam toward the shore. Kiri seemed

weightless in the water, hardly slowing him down at all, and he barely felt the gui's scratches beneath her grip. His mind rattled with all the things he could have said instead, from the clever to the mundane. He'd wanted to tell her that he would have stood by her forever had she asked, for she'd become the light his heart yearned for, and he didn't know how he could ever let her go.

For a moment, he dared believe that his words about staying by the borders of Kristakai could become truth; it would have been worthwhile to wait for the precious moments when she could cross into his world. But with Worak so hellbent on his death, he would have to defeat his enemy before he could go chasing dreams.

The water became shallow enough to stand in, but she was still shaking so hard, he wasn't sure if she had the strength to walk. So he scooped her up and carried her toward land. Without a word, she rested her head against his shoulder. Her body became limp in his arms, and her eyelids drooped, as if she were struggling to remain awake.

Instead of a rocky shoreline like the one they had departed from, he now stood on a slender strip of sand running along the coast, just a few steps from a dense green forest. It wasn't until he emerged from the water that he realized how exhausted he was.

Where are we? Still within Nikhilim's borders for sure — the gulf's entire coastline belonged to the kingdom — but he had no idea which part of it they were on. Hoping to find some clue, Darien approached the woods. But he'd scarcely taken two steps when a menacing red light flickered between the trees. A hot breeze — too hot for the otherwise crisp air — surrounded him, carrying the smell of smoke.

"Put me down," Kiri said, her voice tense.

He complied, an ominous feeling looming over his thoughts.

A gui stepped into view, black wings spreading behind it. Even though it was still several yards away, he could see its sharp-toothed grin glowing against its shadowy face. More lights flickered into view, until a line of them stretched between the tall trunks.

The monsters advanced slowly, as if relishing the terror they caused.

An ambush. No wonder why the underwater guié had driven the transport in this direction. Yet they didn't attack. *What are they waiting for?*

He briefly thought about fleeing, but he wouldn't have gotten very far when his enemies could materialize wherever they pleased. And there was nowhere to run to but back into the sea.

Their only choice was to fight. But with Kiri weakened and the clarion stone gone, they didn't stand a chance.

Something hummed and sizzled in his chest—that strange magic once more. Powerful and vigorous, rising and clamoring.

Kill them all…

A warning whispered in the back of his mind, reminding him that he still knew nothing about the nature of this power or even whether he could control it. But with the army of beasts drawing closer step by step and Kiri vulnerable beside him, he chose to take a chance.

"Stay back," he murmured, the latent energy sparking in his blood. "I'll handle this."

"Darien—"

"Stay back."

He strode toward the guié, magic coursing through his veins and strengthening with each breath. A strange haze filled his head, and an abrupt surge of energy quickened his steps into a sprint. He barely felt the ground beneath him as an immense sense of power raced through him, swirling and crackling and demanding to be released. It came upon him so quickly, it was alarming, but he couldn't hesitate—not now. His hands tingled with unreleased spells, and his bones rattled with their latent force.

Kill them all…

The guié suddenly took flight and swarmed him, surrounding him in red blazes and black shadows. Kiri's scream tore through the air, but he couldn't see her through the tangle of infernal bodies.

Kill them all…

He thrust his arms out and let loose the monstrous force. Red light exploded all around him, and thunderous booms shook the ground, yet he felt nothing but the exhilarating rush of power, unconditional and unrestrained. How it worked, he didn't know. Nor did it matter, as long as it took down his enemies. Wherever it had come from, it belonged to him now, and he wielded it without hesitation. High-pitched screeches shredded the air, and earsplitting cracks shattered the sky.

Silence descended, and the power vanished, as if he'd been a cannon from which a single great shot had fired, but now, all the ammunition was spent.

His head cleared, and he blinked. Without the strange force urging him on, he suddenly realized how wholly it had taken over his mind—how it had blotted out his thoughts until he was nothing but the power.

The scorched bodies of guié lay scattered on the ground, their wings burned to ash and smoke still rising from their incinerated forms. Yet the sight of his fallen enemies brought him no sense of triumph, no joy of accomplishment. Instead, a deep well of fear opened in his core, and it was with a sense of foreboding that he took in the rest of his surroundings.

Dead seabirds lay among the ashes, white feathers charred and broken eyes staring lifelessly. An entire flock, scattered between the gui. They must have been passing over and been caught in his blast. The trees, once lush with life and rich in thriving greens, now teetered as bare, blackened trunks. Not only them, but all the foliage that surrounded them as well— bushes and grasses and vines. Lying amid the smoldering ruins of the forest were the corpses of countless animals and insects. Most were small, barely big enough to see—a butterfly, a squirrel, a songbird. But there was also a king-cat—a magnificent feline that stood as tall as a man, with stripes of black and yellow. A rare, precious animal almost never seen by human eyes.

All around him was death, death, death, death, death. He hadn't just destroyed the gui… He'd destroyed *everything*. An innocent stretch of coastline, a pristine piece of his homeland, lay shattered by his hands. *What have I done?*

He swept his gaze, unable to believe how much devastation he'd wrought. His one solace was that the area appeared unpopulated, and that no bystanders had been near… except one.

"*Kiri!*"

Cold dread engulfed him. He whirled toward the shoreline, where he'd last seen her, his pulse hammering erratically, but she was nowhere in sight. Then, the waves retreated, revealing a still form lying in the wet sand, pale hair covering her face. Hardly able to breathe through the panic, he sprinted toward her. *No… Please, no…*

Darien stumbled to his knees and gathered her into his arms. Brushing the hair out of her face, he pressed his ear to her chest and searched for a sign of life. But instead of a pulse, he found only the ticking of her clock.

His heart shattered, and a pain more potent than anything he'd faced before—sharper than a blade in his stomach, rawer than Worak's punishing whip, harsher than all the torments of spell-casting combined—sliced through him. He'd sworn to protect her, to save her. He would have given his life to ensure her safety, and yet there she lay, gone because of him.

What cursed stars had filled him with an unknown magic and tempted him with a glimpse of what it could do, only to have him lose control and destroy what he cared about most?

Raising his eyes to the skies, he screamed, "*What do you want from me?*"

Sobbing, he held her close and buried his face into her hair. *I'd follow you anywhere, even into the darkness.*

A soft sea breeze wafted by, and only the quiet rush of waves disturbed the silence. His tears subsided, but the agony remained, and, anchored by the weight of grief, he was sure he would remain still where he sat until his breaths ran out.

"Darien?" A soft voice—a miracle blooming—floated toward him.

He looked up with a start. To his shock, Kiri blinked up at him. It had to be a dream—he'd been so sure he'd lost her. To make sure he wasn't hallucinating, he touched her lips. They were warm with life, and he felt her breath against his fingers.

Joy, confusion, relief, astonishment—drowning in a torrent of emotion, he momentarily found himself unable to speak.

"You… You're alive," he managed. "What happened?"

She placed one hand on his face, brushing away a stray tear. "I tried to summon the wind again, but something blew me into the sea… I must have fainted."

"I-I thought…" *I thought I killed you.*

"I'm all right, I promise." As if to prove it, she sat up, but though her lips curved into a smile, a deep sorrow glimmered in her eyes.

"What's wrong?"

She didn't answer, instead gazing out into the horizon.

"Kiri?"

"I'm worried about Ilaerii," she said, a little too quickly. "I hope her soldiers fought off the guié."

"I think they were all here."

He turned back toward the blasted, blackened forest and the charred bodies strewn across the ground. It seemed impossible that he could have been the cause of all that when just days ago, he hadn't even had the power to open the doors of the Sorci's fortress.

The magic that had caused this—it was not a power he wielded, but a dark force that dwelled inside him. Not an ability or gift, but a monster asleep within him that grew stronger each time it stirred. Whatever its origin, he could never trust himself to call upon it again. Yet a foreboding instinct warned that he might have little say.

What dark forces of fate had chosen him for this burden, this curse? Recalling how the mark of the Fiend had flashed before him, he shuddered as an ominous thought loomed… that the answers he sought lay in the Firelands, and that his destiny would be forever tied to Inferno.

ELSEWHERE…

"Oh, poor child, you may fear your own power for now, but it is who you are, and soon, you will learn to relish it. You must have noticed now how every time you loose the shadow, it gets a little easier. Though what you do not know is that with each wielding, the darkness consumes a little more of your starlight, and you lose a little more of the boy you are. Then will you become Starless, and you will belong to us: the Infernal."

19

For the sake of all living

TOMORROW...

Kiri almost wished she could fall into eternal sleep, and yet, with the Age of Fire rising, not even the Celestial Realm was safe. But what was it all for? Why should she endure the raging storms of fate? Like all others living in this broken world, she'd strived and stormed and longed and loved, yet all her travails were mere shadows upon the face of Terra.

Nothing but noise, screaming in vain to the unhearing, uncaring stars.

TODAY...

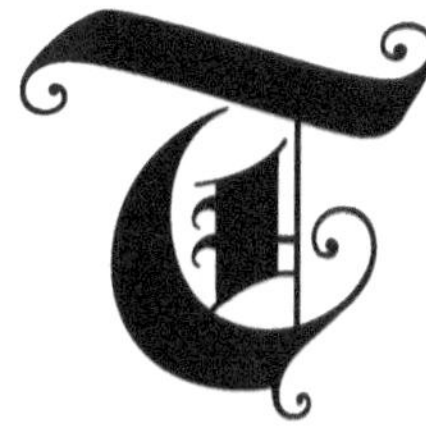

HE BRIGHT SUN WARMED KIRI'S BACK YET DID little to dry out her sodden clothing, which clung to her skin and sent shivers down her spine. Clutching her skirt, she twisted to wring out the water, but her eyes drifted back to Darien, who walked among the ashes of death, surveying the consequences of his spell.

Though she didn't regret the demise of the guié, her heart wept for the fallen forest, once a magnificent jewel of Terra, now a blasted shadow. She recalled how Darien had run toward the infernal creatures, faster than she'd imagined possible, and vanished into the blur of snapping jaws, flapping wings, and swiping talons. Certain that she was about to witness his death, she'd sought to unleash her powers once more to save him. Then, a great force had sent her crashing into the waves.

That was the last thing she remembered before waking up in his tearful embrace. His hurried confession, his profuse apologies, his palpable guilt—they all told her that though he'd been the cause of the destruction, he'd never meant for it to happen. Whether some force beyond his ordinary magic had possessed him or whether he'd wielded a kind of power he hadn't known before, she believed that he'd only meant to destroy the guié. He'd more than earned her trust, and his was the kind of spirit that desired to protect all life, to help and uplift wherever he could. There had to be some other power at work. But what it was, and why it would target him, neither of them could answer.

An image flashed through her head: Elaia's face, laughing with merriment. Since breaking through the curse to escape the underwater fray, snippets of her past had torn through her mind at unexpected intervals — she must have loosed a few memories along with her magic.

"Isn't it a wonder?" Elaia had said with a giggle, tossing her flaming hair over her shoulder as she held up a leatherbound book with gilt lettering that read: *Tales of Issalar.* "All these far-off adventures and worlds unseen… Heroic quests! Passionate love! Magnificent lands! Oh, wouldn't it be amazing if we could witness them?"

"It would," Kiri had replied, gazing longingly past the safe trees of Kristakai and picturing what lay beyond the forbidden perimeter. "I'd do anything to see what lies outside."

The homeland that had once been a mysterious blur now seemed so clear, Kiri wondered how she'd ever forgotten it. As she twisted her dress again, sending droplets of water into the sand, she thought back to the place that had once been her entire world.

Tall trees so thick with leaves, only the greenery was visible. Colorful unicorns brilliant enough to illuminate the shadows of nightfall, each awe-inspiring in their power and grace. Fellow nymphs dancing through their forest realm, glowing with beauty. Here, a flower nymph, from whose footprints pink buds sprung to life. There, a light nymph, who glittered with brightness from every angle. And, of course, the fire nymph, whose smile burned brighter than all the flames she cast.

Elaia.

Was it her beauty — the perfection of her swan-like neck and curving cheeks? Or her laugh — the melodious pitches joyous enough to blow all gloom away? Or her boldness — the daring bravado courageous enough to challenge traditions long adhered?

"Why should we remain imprisoned here?" Elaia had said, her brilliant eyes flashing. "Why are the curiosities of the human world barred from us?"

The desire to defy the unjust rules had burned in Kiri's heart. "It is no fault of ours," she'd replied bitterly. "We're bound for being natureborn,

but we didn't choose this. We are the way we are because the stars deemed it so, and we should not be punished for that." Emboldened by the eager agreement in the fire nymph's expression, she'd said, "Let's fly away from here."

Thinking back to all she'd witnessed, Kiri knew she'd rather be where she was, even amid the ashes of Darien's spell, than still safe within Kristakai. It seemed she'd lived a lifetime in a few days, having witnessed the dark grandeur of the Sorci's fortress, the bustling vibrancy of Yessalem, and the astounding majesty of Marae.

The silver clock ticked against her chest. She glanced at Darien to make sure his back was turned, then pulled the timepiece out by its chain. Its face greeted her with ominous numbers: one o'clock.

Her efforts to unleash her magic had drained so much of her life, only one day remained. Tucking the clock back under her top, she squeezed her eyes and held tight to the precious memories her struggles had unlocked.

I've lived my life. I remember a beautiful world, protected and perfect. I remember a wonderful girl, who stole my heart but whose love I couldn't earn. And I remember choosing to leave, against all advisement, for a chance to learn more. That is my story, and I accept it.

Though she recalled how, after Elaia's rejection, she'd thought could never love another again, the world had proved her wrong, in the very best of ways.

She caught sight of Darien, still wandering through the burned forest. She ached for him, knowing how pained and guilt-stricken he was, yet, at the same time, admired him for the courage he'd displayed when he'd faced an entire legion of infernal creatures alone. Though part of her feared his power, a greater part believed in his virtue. Unconditionally, for she *knew* him, on a level earthbound rationalizations could never explain.

Her love was true, and it was real, sure as the stars and the sun. Though it would end tomorrow, when the enchanted clock struck midnight, at least it had lived. She would happily ascend to the Celestial Realm and join the spirits of the fallen, knowing she'd found him, if only for a few, stolen moments.

But what would become of Darien? The memory of his tear-stained face, filled with all the anguish of the world, haunted her. The way he'd brightened when he'd realized she lived still — how could she tell him this

joy would last only a day? She'd thus far hidden the cost of her abilities, hoping to spare him the pressure and the grief, but come tomorrow, the truth would be revealed.

I have to tell him. Her conscience nagged at her for having kept her secret for so long. And yet, she couldn't, for he'd surely blame himself, or try something foolish in hopes of returning to Kristakai in time.

Standing amid the ashes, Darien collapsed to his knees and buried his face in his hands.

Kiri approached and placed a hand on his shoulder. "You couldn't have known what would happen," she murmured.

He placed his hand over hers and wrapped his fingers around it. "I keep telling myself that if I hadn't acted, we would both be dead. Yet..." He trailed off, staring at the ground. "All my life, I wanted only to do what was right, and yet my folly has led to disaster after disaster."

She knelt beside him. "Worak is the one behind this; *he* sent the guié, and you had no choice but to defend us."

"He's a monster." Darien drew away. "Maybe I'm a monster, too."

"You're *not.*" She placed her hand on his cheek and turned his face toward her. "Worak only desires power for himself, even if it means allying himself with the Fiend. I've seen you fight for others without thought for your own safety. You are *nothing* like him." She lowered her hand, thinking about how the magician intended to break into her homeland—and how she'd have to ask Darien to continue the journey alone once she was gone. "Kristakai must be warned—"

"Kristakai!" Darien stood suddenly, running his hand through his dark locks. "I'd nearly forgotten in all this chaos but... Arrin sent a message, right before I lost the clarion stone."

Kiri rose. "What did she say?"

"That the Sorci will invade Kristakai tomorrow." His words rushed. "Blazes, what am I doing, wasting time here? She said they're heading for the Ashen Plains, and that they're going to kill her there as a sacrifice to the magic."

"*What?*" Horror flooded Kiri. "We have to stop it."

"The Ashen Plains are only half a day's journey from Kristakai. If we can make it there by tomorrow, you'd still have time to return to your forest." Darien paced, a frenetic energy pouring from him. "If only we

could go to Kristakai first… ensure your safety, warn the unicorns, and maybe gather help… but I fear we're still too far. We wouldn't make it in time to stop the sacrifice."

Kiri pursed her lips. She couldn't confess the truth about the clock now—he might see in it a false choice between saving her or saving Arrin. *I've accepted that I'm going to die, but Arrin shouldn't have to.* She briefly wondered if she could use her powers of flight to bring them to Kristakai faster, but she'd barely been able to hold onto them for more than a few minutes. She knew better than to believe she had the strength to carry them both for miles.

"You're right," she said to Darien. "What are the Ashen Plains?"

"They're the home to the Blood Tree, a nexus of magic. Any spell cast there grows in power, some say up to a thousand times in strength… I could find it on a map, but I don't know where we are." Darien shook his head in frustration. "Perhaps—"

A great splashing noise erupted. Kiri spun toward the water in time to see a transparent sphere—similar to the pod Ilaerii had transported them in but with slightly different decor—rise out of the sea some distance from the shore. Marae soldiers emerged around it, visible only from the waist up, their helmets and breastplates glittering under the sun.

Kiri ran toward them, hoping perhaps one of them could point her toward the Ashen Plains. She'd only made it ankle-deep into the surf before Ilaerii rose from the ocean, her green-and-purple tail swishing beneath its clear surface.

"Are the guié still here?" she demanded, her eyes darting around.

"They're dead." Darien approached, his voice flat.

The mermaid gave him a skeptical look, and then her eyes moved past him and onto the death-strewn beach. "What happened?"

"They met their match."

With an apprehensive look, Ilaerii turned to Kiri. "He did this, didn't he?"

Kiri nodded. There was no sense in hiding the truth. "It was an accident… he cast a spell to destroy the guié but lost control."

"At least the minions of Inferno are gone. Whatever collateral damage occurred, it's better than letting them terrorize our realm." A disturbed look filled her expression as she surveyed the damage. "I didn't know a

novice magician could do all this," she muttered, looking suspiciously at Darien. "But only *outcomes* matter to a queen, and the fact is, all of Terra is safer now that those creatures are destroyed."

Her tone puzzled Kiri for a moment, but then her eyes fell on the soldiers. *She can't let them know how worried she is.*

"I made you a promise," the mermaid went on. "And an honorable sovereign always keeps her word. Come, let's continue to Kristakai."

"No, we need to go to the Ashen Plains." Seeing the confusion on the other's face, Kiri explained, "We've just learned that the Sorci plan to cast their spell to invade the unicorn domain tomorrow, from that spot. We have to stop them."

"Your destination is inland, which means I can't help you." Ilaerii pursed her lips. "Even with this detour, you'll still reach Kristakai before the messenger I sent upriver. You're currently on the coast of Sihtah — that should mean something to the Nikhilim here." She nodded at Darien. "If you travel southwest and follow the golden Justice Star by night, you should reach it, but I don't know how long it will take."

"Half a day." Darien sounded relieved. "If we're in Sihtah… I know this region. We can make it before dawn tomorrow."

"Your next words will be to ask for help, won't they?" The queen raised her eyebrows, lifting her chin with a look that exuded arrogance yet lacked disdain. "You don't need to justify your request. I understand perfectly well what's at stake. I'll give you what I can, but you're on your own after that. I am the only one among my kind who can walk on land, and I've lost enough time because of your predicament."

Darien arched his brows. "If the Sorci succeed, the Fiend will come after your kind as well."

"Ingrate!" Ilaerii spat. "My nation needs my attention, and I've already abandoned my duties for half a day to aid you, based on your word alone! Because of you, I was nearly killed by those who pursued you!"

"We're immensely grateful for your help," Kiri said quickly, hoping to diffuse the argument. "Thank you."

"And what about you, boor?" The mermaid gave Darien a pointed look. "If your brother ever reaches a position of influence, I'll be sure to hold this over his head."

"Poor Nythen." A smile flickered across Darien's lips. "I understand that you've gone as far as you can. Thank you, truly, for everything you've done."

Ilaerii narrowed her eyes at him, then threw a proud look across her face as she turned to Kiri. "I will gather what I can for you and be back soon." Her expression softened. "I hope you succeed."

She dove into the water, her long tail flashing as it breached the surface, and the other merpeople soon followed suit. Kiri watched them leave, admiring the grace with which they swam.

"A day and a half." Darien stared into the murmuring tide, contemplative. "That's how long it will take to reach Kristakai, including the detour to the Ashen Plains. Ilaerii brought us pretty close to where we want to be." He looked up at her. "You have three days on your clock right?"

She nodded, hoping he wouldn't read the lie on her face. But this was her choice to make. Protecting her homeland and all who resided there—not to mention thwarting Inferno's plans—was far more important than her own life. She'd already chosen to forfeit it, yet the unconquerable hope for survival had lingered. Now, the simple truths of time killed even that faint glimmer.

For the sake of all living, it has to end like this. She couldn't grieve for the life she'd never live, or mourn the things she'd leave undone. Her last act in this world would be to save others.

That was how her story would end, and she'd chosen it. And she no longer feared it.

Dawn spread its warm rays across the brightening sky, visible as colored flecks between the multitudes of branches beneath which Kiri lay. She wished she could have viewed it from the unobscured coast and taken in all its hues in their full glory, for it was to be her last sunrise. The ticking clock against her chest reminded her that only a few hours remained. Exactly how many, she didn't know, for she couldn't bear to look at the shrinking sliver between the hour and minute hands again. But it would

be enough to reach the Ashen Plains, and as long as she stopped the Sorci, what happened to her mattered not.

She sat up, pushing the blanket she'd wrapped herself in, and regarded the lush greenery around her—an explosion of plant life all clamoring for sunlight and climbing on top of one another. If this was her last morning, then at least it was a beauteous one. Dew clung to green brush, and soft white mist swirled above rich flora. Crossing the low forested land between the coast and her destination had been more difficult than the journey to Yessalem had been, for the foliage here was much denser. Though she and Darien had walked along a manmade road, it was evidently one rarely traveled, for vegetation had begun retaking the strip of land. So certain were they that no one would come this way, they'd made their camp right alongside it. Enough plants surrounded them to hide them from anyone more than a few feet away, and she wasn't looking forward to pushing her way through the tangle.

But the end was in sight; hints of blue and white peeked through the tangled branches before her. Those were the colors of the Ashen Plains—a swath of land on which nothing but two types of grasses could grow, one snowy and tall, the other cerulean and short.

Asleep beside her, Darien stirred. He looked so beautiful and placid, she almost wished she could preserve him like this forever. The first fingers of light falling from the sky highlighted the perfect angles of his face in glowing amber, and she found it charming how his hair, tousled in the night, fell across his forehead. But only strife awaited when he awoke, and she was partly to blame.

He'd mourn her when she was gone. That was her greatest regret in leaving this world early—and that she'd spent so little time with him.

The last traces of darkness melted into the morning glow, telling her that she'd rested long enough; it was time to go. Hopefully, she and Darien would arrive at the magical nexus before the Sorci and catch them by surprise.

The pack Ilaerii had given them sat on the ground nearby. The mermaid had been very generous, and Kiri had been surprised at how much food, clothing, and other travel necessities one could shove into a bag woven of kelp fibers. Beside it lay a small cluster of Marae weapons—swords, shields, daggers—each of which would glow with magic the moment someone wielded it.

She folded her blanket and shoved it into the bag, then glanced at Darien again. Once she roused him, another day's travails would begin, and she wanted to spend a while longer savoring this peace before throwing herself back into the fear and pain ahead. This might well be her last moment of bliss, for there was a good chance she'd die at the hands of the Sorci before she had a chance to worry about what it would feel like to have the last of her life force drain away.

Leaning back, she breathed in the scents of the forest, subtle and crisp and sweet. The touch of the ground beneath her hands, the damp coolness of the air, the chirping of insects and birds… Terra was indeed a magnificent place. If only the Ayr of Passing Time would freeze her in this moment instead of letting the minutes roll on.

But the Sorci could begin there spell any moment, and there was no more time to waste.

ELSEWHERE…

"She won't be a problem much longer, oh Fiend, and even she knows it. Look, those eyes shining with unshed tears! But whatever becomes of her, she's already wreaked the damage we need. And I will not hesitate to exploit those bruises, those wounds, those scars. Were I Terrestrial, I would thank the stars for sending her our way, for she has turned out to be advantageous indeed."

20

All is not lost

Arrin's mind was set, but her heart trembled and kept reaching for a way out. *Any* way out. No reason in the world could quiet its riotous screams, which pulled her back from every step she took.

She'd never thought it would come to this: The moment when she would cross over from the light of goodness to the abyss of evil. And she'd never imagined it could happen this way — that in doing the right thing, she'd become the wicked one.

LUE AND WHITE GRASS RIPPLED UNDER A COLD gust, which ripped a flurry of red leaves from the lone tree standing amid the flatness of the Ashen Plains. The Blood Tree — that was what the Sorci had called it. Arrin vaguely remembered of having read about it, probably in a book concerning the Age of Magic.

Behind the bars of the cage, which the Sorci had transported to the spot along with the other enchanted items and ingredients in a blaze of yellow light, she searched for any opportunity for sabotage. Maybe Kiri and Darien had received her message, even though, when she'd sent it through the crystal fragment, she'd seen only an indistinct swirl of mist with strange rumbling noises emitting from it. And when she'd tried again earlier that morning, the mist had been still and silent. She refused to imagine the worst — that the two were dead and the clarion stone lying at the bottom of a pit somewhere. If the Sorci had caught up to them, surely she would have overheard something about it. They'd had no qualms about discussing their matters in front of her, evidently thinking her no more dangerous than a slab of slaughtered meat.

In any case, more important than her own survival was that she keep

the wicked ones from carrying out their plan. There were only three of them here: Limali, Sihan, and, of course, their dear and evil leader, Worak. The spell apparently called for the power of that precise number—no more, no less.

Good thing it didn't require the power of twenty, she thought, trying to find optimism wherever she could. Were she free from her prison, she might have stood a chance against them. But as it was, she couldn't even throw anything else from her bag, for they'd sealed the spaces between the bars with a magical force field, which was invisible but for the occasional white bolt reminding her it was there. Though she could see and hear through it, any attempt to break past it had been met with a mass as solid as stone.

Try as she might, she couldn't shake away her fear. It was all she could do to keep her face stoic when her heart trembled at the thought of the horrors awaiting her.

Arrin, my child, do not be afraid. A voice floated through her head—one she recognized from her previous dream. It belonged to the strange, veiled woman who had as good as told her the Age of Fire was inevitable. *Who is she?* Arrin wondered if the voice was part of another vision, only one unattached to images.

She wanted to believe the woman's words; she needed every shred of hope she could get. Each was a precious arrow with which she shot at the shadow of despair. She looked to the mountains in the distance, which, shadowed by the early light, appeared purplish-gray, and then the green forest along the edge of the field, hoping someone—anyone—would emerge.

As long as her heart still beat, she could keep fighting, and idea after crazy idea whirled through her mind. The Sorci would have to let her out at some point to kill her. Perhaps she could use that window strategically and inflict as much damage as possible before they struck her down.

"Erect the mirror," Worak said to his two followers.

Limali and Sihan nodded in acknowledgement, then each grabbed the end of a large rectangular object lying flat by Arrin's cage. A black cloth so dark, it absorbed all the light of the brightening day, covered the item, and she recalled what she'd heard the magicians say about it.

A mirror touched only by starlight from the moment of its creation to the moment of its use... That was why it was so carefully wrapped. The two magicians placed it vertically on its stand by the Blood Tree. If she tore off the covering before the rest of the spell was ready, its power would be rendered moot.

Worak reached into a large wooden trunk and retrieved a long, bleached skull. Even in death, the creature looked ferocious, with its pointed teeth and angry eye sockets frozen in an eternal glare. Sharp horns extended from the top of its head and the tip of its protruding snout—it was the skull of a dragon, a Great One, a powerful being of magic not seen by human eyes since the Age of Unicorns. Arrin stared in amazement. Such creatures were so rare, even their bones had become things of legend. Though it was somewhat morbid to admire the remnants of a life lost, she found a strange, haunting beauty in the skull's sharp contours, and she tried to imagine what the magnificent beast must have looked like when it was alive.

Gleaming green scales, blazing yellow eyes, flaring nostrils billowing smoke… Her imagination ran wild.

Worak muttered something, and a blue mist appeared beneath the skull, forming a column under it. Then, he released it, and it remained hovering in the air.

Nice relic, she thought, trying to determine how thick it was—and whether it would shatter under her step. *Too bad I'll have to destroy it.*

Under different circumstances, she might have delighted at the chance to learn more about the mysterious ways of the Sorci, especially given this chance to see magic so rare and powerful. Now, she observed with the intention of finding weaknesses. While great forces worked against her, she had one important advantage: The magic they sought required precision, and upsetting one piece would undo all their work.

Worak shot a glance in her direction, and she quickly looked away, hoping her gaze hadn't betrayed her intentions.

"Sihan! Limali!" he shouted. "Prepare the sacrifice."

Arrin's blood ran cold as the two magicians approached, and sweat beaded on her forehead.

Limali held one hand out to the cage. *"Away with the barrier."*

This was it—her chance. The bars before her crackled and glowed, then dissolved into the air. Arrin dashed forward as fast as she could but had barely taken a step before she found herself floating, caught in a red haze.

She flailed uselessly in the air, unable to touch the ground or grip anything solid.

Sihan held out one hand, controlling the spell with a smirk on her lips. With a sweep of her arm, she sent Arrin flying into the tree.

Arrin's back slammed against the trunk, and the impact knocked the wind from her lungs. A powerful force yanked her hands behind her.

"*Let me go!*" she screamed, struggling to break free. But no matter how she kicked and twisted, she couldn't escape. Ropes wound around her wrists, so tight, her hands went cold.

"Poor child," Sihan said mockingly. "Did you really think we'd give you another chance after the trouble you caused yesterday?"

Realizing her movements were pointless, Arrin stopped. She was bound so tightly, she might as well have been frozen. Her chest clenched, and she battled a surge of panicked tears.

All is not lost. The voice floated through her head again. *Your story has already been written, Arrin, and this is not how it ends. When the time comes, trust in my voice, and follow me to your salvation — and your destiny.*

She looked up at the sky, still marbled with the rosiness of sunrise, and prayed to the Divinity that this phantom woman could be believed.

Sihan and Limali moved to the other side of the tree, standing on either side of the covered mirror, as their leader guided the dragon skull toward her. He brought it to a halt. Unable to resist a last-ditch effort, Arrin kicked up a leg, hoping to knock it off its mist-made pedestal, but couldn't reach it.

"Your energy will make this a most lively spell." Worak sneered, uncapping a small green bottle. Tipping it over one of the dragon's eye sockets, he muttered, "*Water from a celestial spring, corrupted by the blood of a gui and poured over a firegem touched by the first rays of dawn. The first ingredient, ignite.*"

Emerald flames erupted within the skull, throwing light and smoke upward.

Arrin could hardly breathe through her fear, yet anger lay beneath it. This *couldn't* be how things ended… There had to be *something* more she could do.

A sharp gale blew against her face, and she closed her eyes against its sting. Grass whipped around her ankles. The wind's roar and the clattering of the disturbed leaves seemed as loud as cannon fire. But it died away seconds later, leaving the air as still as it had been previously. An uncanny feeling trickled into her senses, though she couldn't define it.

The Sorci appeared unperturbed by the gust. As Worak returned to the trunk, presumably to gather the second ingredient, Arrin's eyes fell on a figure rapidly approaching from the direction of the forest.

Who is that? She squinted in attempt to get a better look.

"Worak!" Darien's voice rang out across the plain.

They got my message after all! Relief and gratitude poured through her. *But where's Kiri?*

Arrin looked around wildly, wondering what the plan was. With a sword in one hand and a shield in the other, both of which glowed with supernatural light, Darien was clearly aiming to fight. She hoped those weapons held some powerful magic, because it was foolishness for him to face three Sorci alone.

"Worak!" Darien repeated, drawing closer. "Are you such a coward, you would send your master's minions to kill me instead of facing me yourself?"

From the look on the Sorci master's face, he was as surprised by the boy's return as she was. Hidden beneath a glower, a trace of shock—and possibly fear—flashed through his eyes.

"Limali! Sihan!" He beckoned them with a twitch of his fingers, and the two stepped away from the mirror and joined him.

"Just as I thought!" Darien continued his charge, swinging the sword by his side. "You're nothing without your mindless lackeys!"

Fury poured off Worak's scowling form. He glanced at his followers, who stood to either side of him, and raised his arm toward the advancing youth. The others did the same, until all three pointed at him.

Darien halted and gave a scornful grin. "You craven curbrains! I wiped out an entire legion of guié singlehandedly. Do you really think your petty charms can defeat me?"

What the blazes is he doing? It seemed he had no strategy other than to charge at her captors—which was not a strategy at all. *Must I come up with all the solutions?* She was about to tell him to destroy the Sorci's equipment when something soft clamped over her mouth.

Startled, she couldn't stop the squeak that rose up her throat.

"*Sh!*" came a sharp whisper behind her. "It's me, Kiri!"

Kiri? Arrin twisted her neck and caught sight of the air nymph, ducked up against the tree, and she realized why that gale had felt so different from an ordinary gust. It had been *her*, the windborn one, passing over. With one arm, she gripped a glowing shield identical to the one Darien held; her other was angled out of sight.

A faint sawing noise wafted up, and the bonds around her wrists moved; Kiri must have been cutting the ropes.

The pieces clicked into place. So that was why Darien was acting so brazenly; he was distracting the Sorci so Kiri could free her, and it was working — perhaps too well.

"*Forth!*" all three magicians shouted at once, sending red lightning spewing toward him.

He threw up his shield and ducked behind it. Kiri gasped, but whatever worry she had did not slow her progress.

"Is *this* the great power I was so concerned about?" Worak strode toward his former apprentice, bolts still shooting from his fingertips. "I wonder what will happen once we wear down that shield."

"You don't want to find out," Darien growled. "I possess a kind of magic greater than anything you could imagine, and you, old man, are no match for me."

Something felt different about those words — they were more than taunts meant to provoke and distract. A dark rage simmered beneath them, and something about it seemed almost… Arrin didn't want to think the word, but there truly was no other… It was almost… *evil*. It wasn't his words or actions — it was something about *him*, an energy rolling off his being that she hadn't detected before. Maybe it was her psychic power, or maybe it was nonsense, but either way, had Arrin not met him before and known him to be among her allies, she would have feared him. Actually — she *did* fear him, or this version of him. This was not the aspiring hero she'd encountered before, but a creature of pure wrath.

The luminous sword twitched in his hand, and she sensed him itching to take a swing.

Don't do it! The moment he lowered his shield, one of the three magicians might hit him. He might have been terrifying in his anger, but that didn't make him invincible.

His expression darkened, and she could almost see the flames of rage snapping behind his glare. She shook her head rapidly, trying to tell him to keep up his defenses, but didn't dare speak aloud, for she didn't want to call the Sorci's attention to Kiri.

Darien's gaze shifted past Worak, though she couldn't tell whether he was looking at her or at the air nymph. Something changed in his eyes, and the cloud of rage dispersed. Suddenly, there he was again—the boy she'd met halfway through an impossible quest, foolish but brave, flawed but genuine.

A snapping sound rang out behind her, and the ropes fell from her wrists. Free at last, Arrin wasted no time and dashed for the mirror, since it was the easiest thing to attack.

"*Ignite!*" Worak hollered.

Something whizzed toward her, and an explosion rattled the ground. Though it knocked her off her feet, she didn't look around to see what had happened—she had a task to fulfill.

Springing up, she grabbed the black cloth covering the mirror and yanked it as hard as she could. But it was wrapped too tight and didn't budge. More explosions boomed in her ears, and, realizing she wouldn't be able to tear the thick cloth with her bare hands, she spun, looking for anything she could use.

Her eyes fell on Kiri, who stood behind her up holding her shield. No wonder Worak's spell had missed. Noticing a glowing knife in the nymph's hand—likely the one used to cut the bonds—Arrin exclaimed, "Give me the blade!"

Kiri handed it to her, then swung the shield to block another spell.

"Over here, you dastards!" came Darien's infuriated voice, accompanied by the sounds of blasting and clanging metal.

Arrin dug the blade into the black cloth covering the mirror and slashed down with all her strength.

"No!" cried a woman, though whether it was Limali or Sihan, she couldn't tell.

Glee rose up her chest as she tore open the covering, exposing the mirror to the raw daylight. All the Sorci's work, all their careful planning, had been undone by that one, simple movement. But just to be sure, she

smashed the blade into the gleaming glass, fracturing it, and kicked hard, sending it toppling to the ground, where it shattered.

Beside her, Kiri held up the shield and blocked a spell. Gratitude poured through Arrin, but this was no time for thank-yous, for the job wasn't finished yet. She whisked her gaze toward the dragon skull, still hovering on its enchanted pedestal. If they destroyed it, the Sorci could not attempt their spell to infiltrate Kristakai again, at least not for some time. A mirror could be recreated and a potion re-brewed, but the skull of a Great One could not easily be replaced. Darien was a few feet from it, alternating between swinging the sword at the magicians and throwing up his shield to block their spells.

"Darien!" she exclaimed. "The skull! Destroy it!"

She would have done so herself, but his blade seemed more suited for the job than the much smaller one she'd taken from Kiri. His eyes flicked to the enchanted object, and he managed a quick nod before disappearing behind his shield once more.

Knowing he'd need help, Arrin rushed at the magicians, Kiri close by her side.

"You don't have another one of those handy shields, do you?" she said.

"No, but I do have more blades." The other reached into a fabric belt around her waist and pulled out a second dagger.

Seeing that there were several more, Arrin yanked one from its sheath, and it blazed with supernatural light the moment it entered her grip. She wondered when the nymph had found the time to become a walking arsenal.

Light whizzed past her, and she jumped out of the way. Searching for its source, she saw Limali raising her hand for another spell. Arrin hurled a dagger in the magician's direction. The throw wasn't precise—knives weren't anything like the throwing crescent she'd been so familiar with— but it had the desired effect; the woman vanished to avoid getting hit.

Arrin, come to me. That mysterious woman's voice floated through her head again, seeming to come from behind. But she couldn't obey; she was in the middle of something important.

Looking over at Darien, she found him struggling to advance toward the skull, only to be thwarted by exploding magic. His tactics seemed limited to the sword and shield—where was the great magic he'd mentioned?

Kiri ran at Sihan, who stood not far from Worak. Catching a flash in the corner of her eye, Arrin spun in time to see Limali reappear behind her. Before the magician had a chance to cast a spell, Arrin launched herself at the woman, knife in hand. The magician vanished, and she landed with a stumble.

Come, my child! Follow my voice! The ghostly woman called out again.

Not yet! Arrin mentally called back. It was three against three; the magicians had more power, but she and her allies were decently matched. And they didn't have to *win* the fight—just to destroy one critical piece of equipment. *After that, we can run.*

But Darien seemed to have forgotten what she'd asked of him, for he continued swinging at Worak, moving away from the hovering skull. From his wrath-filled movements and the black fire in his eyes, revenge had moved to the forefront of his mind, crowding out the bigger picture.

Curbrain! she thought, irritated. *I'll do it myself, then!*

At least he seemed to be doing a good job of keeping Worak's attention. Meanwhile, Kiri had Sihan locked in battle. Though the nymph's attempts at using her knife were clumsy at best, she seemed able to transition in and out of her wind form, making herself a difficult target.

A fiery pain shot through Arrin's back, sending her flying, and she screamed. After landing in a heap, she scrambled to turn around. Limali approached with arms outstretched. But Arrin also noticed something else: The skull was just within reach.

Thanks for the ride, she thought with a smirk. Ignoring whatever else might come, she grabbed the enchanted object, dropped to the ground, and thrust her blade into it, piercing the bone. Pain shot through her as a spell hit, but she ignored the fiery daggers and continued stabbing. She wondered how she was still alive, then noticed the ground quaking. A sudden feeling of doom surrounded her; a magic darker than anything she'd known before crackled in the air. But she kept her focus on destroying the skull. The pain faded, and she hacked away until all that remained were white shards.

"Darien!" Kiri shouted, her voice tinged with panic.

Arrin glanced up to see all three Sorci closing in around the young magician, who had dropped both sword and shield by his sides and glared unblinkingly at Worak. A strange red glow colored his eyes, though

she couldn't tell whether it came from within him or whether it was the reflection of Worak's magic, which flamed around his clenched fist.

What's happening to him? Arrin wondered with alarm. Then, she realized that Limali must have released her from the curse of pain and left her to do what she would with the skull. What was it about Darien that could have drawn the Sorci away from something so important?

Kiri threw her knife at Worak with a desperate look in her eyes. Though the effort missed, it called Darien's attention to her, and a look of horror descended upon his expression. The ground stopped shaking, and Arrin wondered if he'd been the one causing the tremors. Maybe this was the power he'd spoken of. He raised his shield in time to block a combined spell from the magicians but stumbled back from the force.

We can't keep fighting them, Arrin thought. She and the other two had made a good effort, but they didn't stand a chance at winning. Especially since Worak still had the option of calling more Sorci to aid him. *We have to run.*

She glanced back at her bag, which remained in the cage. In it lay her notebook—it would only take a few seconds to run over and get it. Yet a practical voice warned that their window for escape was barely a sliver, and those few seconds could be enough to slam it shut.

Her eyes stung as she turned away, though it seemed like such a petty, foolish thing to worry about at a time like this. Still, she was leaving behind her life's work, the closest thing she had to a manifestation of her dreams. *It doesn't matter. Anything I wrote in there, I can write again.*

"The spell is destroyed!" she yelled at Kiri and Darien. "We can run for our lives now!" The two glanced at her, and she gestured for them to follow her. "This way!"

All right, mysterious lady from my vision, she thought, hoping she hadn't misplaced her faith in the phantom woman. *I can come to you now. Where do you want me to go?*

She bolted in the direction she'd last heard the voice come from, glancing back to make sure Kiri and Darien followed as she sprinted past the Blood Tree and the broken remnants of the mirror. A moment of panic gripped her when the woman didn't immediately respond, but, luckily, it was short-lived.

This way, my child. The sound came from ahead, and she knew she was heading in the right direction.

Skies, I hope my instincts are right about this. With nothing but open plain surrounding her, she didn't have much choice other than to trust in the voice.

The three magicians appeared in a flash of yellow before her, and she cried out in surprise. A glowing blade slashed the air, and it took Arrin a second to realize it was Darien's. Knowing she had to go in *that* specific direction for safety, Arrin thrust her knife at Sihan while Kiri threw up her shield to block Worak's spell.

Just a little further, Arrin. Come, come to me…

A white light glittered above the blue grass before her. Rectangular in shape, it appeared about the size of a large door. Where it led, she didn't care—*anywhere* was better than this cursed place. And it was just a few sprints away, if she could get past the Sorci.

I'm waiting for you… Right through that door…

With a feral cry, she lunged at Worak, brandishing her knife. The madness of that move must have alarmed the other, for he vanished in a burst of light. This was her chance; it was now or never. The door was right in front of her, but she wouldn't go through alone. Dropping the dagger, the last defense she had, she reached for Kiri, who was closer, and grabbed the nymph's arm. Pulling the other along behind her, she ran to Darien and clasped his wrist.

Ignoring their frenzied questions, she yelled, "Just trust me!" and yanked them toward the otherworldly door.

As soon as she stepped through it, a wash of light filled her vision, and she squeezed her eyes. The air swirled and crackled, hotter than the hottest sun.

Then, it stilled, and the temperature cooled. Blinking away the swaths of blackness resulting from having looked into something so bright, Arrin took in her surroundings. The golden star-shaped symbol of the Divinity gleamed in the center of a round floor paved with red, blue, and green tiles arranged in dancing swirls. Images of the celestial ayri—beautiful, humanlike creatures with great feathered wings stretching from their backs—decorated the round walls. The paint was chipped from years of neglect, and yet the sight nevertheless filled her heart with awe. *A temple…*

"What happened?" Kiri asked. "How… How are we here?"

"Didn't you see the door?" Arrin said, too busy staring at the temple's décor to look at her. The grandeur made her want to weep with amazement and reverence. It was ancient, very ancient. That much was clear from the faded colors, as well as the outdated architectural style. Its age only added to its unmatched majesty, and she admired every twisting stone column leading up to the domed, gilded ceiling. She'd always dreamed of designing noble buildings like this one, of showing her love for the Divinity through her work. If ever she might dream up something that could equal this place in dignity, then she could die the very next day with no regrets.

"Arrin?" Kiri's voice drifted past her ears, and she realized she'd been too caught up in her wonderment to catch the nymph's previous words.

"Sorry, what was that?"

"Can you please let us go now?"

Realizing she was still grasping the other two, Arrin released her grip with a sheepish grin. "Sorry." Catching sight of the temple's door, she was surprised to see the Ashen Plains on the other side. Worak stormed across the grass, shouting at the other two.

"They can't have vanished!" he yelled. "Gather the others! *Now!*"

He was glaring right in her direction, yet seemed oblivious to her presence.

"Isn't that something," she murmured. "I guess he can't see it."

"See what?" Kiri knitted her eyebrows. "Arrin, what did you *do?*"

It hit her that she'd been the only one who'd seen the door, though given a moment to think about it, Arrin realized she shouldn't have been surprised. After all, she'd gone that way because of a voice she alone could hear. Part of her must have known it too, for she'd grabbed the others in order to lead them through; her subconscious must have understood that they wouldn't have found the entrance without her.

"You know how I get visions?" she said. "Well, it turns out I have other psychic abilities as well. I saw a door glimmering over the grass and a voice telling me to go toward it. So I listened and… here we are."

"Where's 'here'?" Darien wandered toward the golden star in the center.

"No idea," she confessed. "But while we're asking questions… What the blazes happened to you out there?"

"No idea," he echoed, his gaze fixed on the emblem of the Divinity.

There's an evasion if I ever saw one. An uncomfortable feeling rattled her, one akin to fear. A profound darkness had overtaken him during the fight, descending like the shadow of a storm. She couldn't help thinking about her visions of him standing amid Inferno's flames, but though it was irrational, she refused to consider what it all added up to when he'd just saved her life.

"My child, you've come." A voice reverberated through the temple.

The woman from her vision approached, her broad, curving figure garbed in a brown dress that glowed against her deep amber skin. A ghostly white veil, secured by a beaded blue band, draped down her back over her voluminous black curls, and black eyes pierced from a bold, regal face. Though she was barely taller than Arrin, she held a presence that filled the space, more so than any towering giant could have.

"Who are you?" Arrin felt herself drawn toward the woman, despite the other being a total stranger.

"You do not recognize me?" The woman's eyes crinkled. "Perhaps you are not as well-read as you claim you are."

Arrin huffed, not sure whether she was more irritated or embarrassed.

"You're Nameed, the first Sibyl." Darien's voice was hushed with reverence. "Are you… Are we in the Ether?"

"Indeed," the other said softly.

Nameed? That seemed impossible—the first Sybil had lived thousands upon thousands of years ago. But the Ether existed between realms, and it was said the spirits of the restless dead dwelled there, instead of ascending to Celeste as they should have. The living and lost alike could move through these shadows, though to cross over into the opposite realm was a thing not yet written of. If this temple, which felt as firm as Terrestrial earth beneath Arrin's feet, was indeed part of that undefined space, then she'd just entered a world she could hardly imagine. A place where past and present met, where boundaries between the living and the dead blurred.

Nameed approached Darien, her gaze boring into him. "If you know of me, then you know that I can see into the very nature of a person and understand his true heart. What do you think I see in you?"

His eyes dropped, and he took a step back, his sword and shield clattering to the ground as if some force compelled his hands to release

them. Clutching his arms, he shook his head and trembled. Arrin had never seen someone so afraid before.

"I… I don't know," he whispered, his voice quivering.

The Sibyl turned to Arrin and raised her brows. "What do you see in him, my child?"

Images of Inferno whirled through Arrin's mind, but that was not her answer. "Someone who faced his darkest enemies to save a girl he barely knows," she replied.

Darien caught her gaze, and a faint smiled flickered across his lips. He turned his eyes to Nameed and whispered, "Please, tell me… what's happening to me?"

"You will find out in due time." The Sibyl placed her hand on his shoulder. "But right now, I see the same thing your friends here see." She swept her hand toward Arrin and Kiri. "I beg you, be that person, and not the one your master would applaud."

"Worak is no longer my master," he growled.

"Perhaps not, but in time, you may serve another." Nameed sighed. "The future is never absolute, for the slightest flicker in the present can illuminate a path that would otherwise remain unexplored. Yet the inevitable cannot be stopped."

She snapped her gaze toward Arrin, who felt a sudden shiver run through her, for she recognized those words from her vision. *What's she trying to tell me?*

"I have been waiting for you, my child." Nameed approached, obsidian eyes fixed on her. "You must be wondering how you came to be here. This"—she swept her arm to indicate the temple—"is one of the few areas of the Ether grounded enough for the Terrestrial to enter. Only my kind can see its portals, and only we can enter, though we can bring others if we desire." She smiled, yet her gaze was too eager—hungry, even—to be considered friendly. "Do you know now what you are?"

"A Sibyl." Even as she spoke the word, Arrin's mind spun. Her heart knew its truth, even though it still seemed bizarre to her that the Ayr of Tomorrow would choose her to be not only a conduit for prophecies, but a connection to the Celestial.

"Yes," Nameed replied. "Since the last of our order died, years before you were born, I have searched and waited. I have watched over the Sibyls

since my own death millennia ago, and I have watched over you since you were born. Now that you are old enough that the Ayr of Tomorrow has seen fit to let your gift manifest, I have come for you."

"What?"

Though Arrin had suspected something greater at work since her first prophecy, she'd refused to acknowledge it fully, secretly hoping that once the windborn one was rescued, she could leave the visions behind. She'd never *wanted* to be chosen. Her dreams lay elsewhere—in magnificent castles, in glorious machines, in spectacular inventions that would shape the world long after she'd left it. She wanted to create, to build, to make, to imagine, but the world didn't care. It had spurred her along a path driven by mystical powers that had nothing to do with the skills she'd worked so hard to cultivate.

"Come with me." Nameed reached a hand toward Arrin. "I will teach you how to use your power, how to call upon it when you wish. The fate of the world will depend upon your ability to commune with the stars and the ayri—to see that which ordinary human minds cannot."

What if I don't want this? Arrin bit her lip. From the way the Sibyl spoke, she had no right to refuse, but this was *her* life, and it seemed unfair that she should have to sacrifice everything she wanted because of a fluke of destiny. If she obeyed, she'd never have a chance to live out her dreams. Her chances had always been slight, but becoming the next Sibyl would destroy them entirely. Perhaps she hadn't known enough about their order to recognize Nameed, but the daughters of Tomorrow had been known to devote their entire selves to their duties. Nothing else mattered to them, and she couldn't make that same promise when her heart desired so much more.

Yet... The Age of Fire was coming. She'd seen that with all certainty, and though she'd thwarted the first threat by disrupting the Sorci's attempt to steal Kristakai's powers, she knew there was more to come. Perhaps this was the Ayr of Tomorrow telling her so, perhaps it was her own instincts telling her the Sorci wouldn't abandon their efforts, or perhaps it was because there were other forces at work—the magicians, the unicorns, the windborn one that stood between them.

If Inferno triumphed and the Fiend conquered the Terrestrial Realm, then all she wanted would be in vain. What sense was there in designing,

conceiving, or inventing when there would be no one left to experience her creations? And then there was her family—some part of her had still hoped that she would see them again soon, but that would do no good if they perished at the Fiend's hands. The last breaths of resistance died in her heart, and the walls of destiny closed in around her. Terra needed the next Sibyl, and the only rational answer to her situation was to accept the mantel.

"Fine." Arrin didn't care that her voice emerged as a disgruntled groan. She glanced at Kiri and Darien. "What about them?"

Nameed walked up to Kiri. "You wish to return to your homeland?"

"Yes," the air nymph replied, gazing in awe at the other.

The Sibyl gestured at one of the temple's columns. "Beneath this lies a passage back to Terra, one far from where the Sorci seek you now. It lets out in a place just half a day's journey from Kristakai." Her eyes took on a strange expression. "One of the stones in this floor conceals a handle. Pull it up, and you will discover what you seek." She waved her hand. "Go, show me you can find it."

Kiri scrambled toward the column, and Darien followed. They felt along the lines between tiles, then Kiri's fingers hit something that made her gasp. She pulled up at the tile, revealing a stained metal handle concealed beneath the floor.

"You will have to remove a few more," Nameed said. "But the passageway *is* there." She turned back to Arrin. "Well, my child, your friends are set. Why does your heart still hesitate?"

Because you're killing my dreams. But that was an incredibly selfish answer considering all that was at stake, so she kept it to herself. "If I become a Sibyl, will I stop the Age of Fire?"

"Even the Ayr of Tomorrow doesn't know that answer," Nameed replied with a cynical laugh. "The line between the inevitable and the changeable is as indistinct as the wind. But I can say this: If you become a Sibyl, you will do more to battle the Fiend than your human capabilities can allow."

Fate of the world, Arrin thought with a slight smile. The words had become old in just a few days, embedded in her mind. Yet they hadn't lost their effect, for she had a duty. If the world as a whole was too large and abstract for her to envision, then her family was what mattered—Mahtim,

Tahtih, Myla, Tam. The people she loved most in the world, for whom she would do anything. She'd seen what would become of them if the Fiend triumphed, and she could not allow that to pass. *She* didn't matter anymore; only their future did.

Squaring her shoulders, Arrin lifted her chin. "Where do we begin?"

The Sibyl extended her hand toward Arrin once again, and she took it. Her body melted into the air as a brilliant force wrapped her in its cool embrace, carrying her off into the bright unknown.

ELSEWHERE...

"Rage on, Worak. I understand your wrath, for you are not privy to the greater happenings, to which you are merely a pawn. I will admit, I am sorry that we will not be harnessing the powers of the unicorns — not yet, at least. But though this small plan was thwarted, a much bigger victory will soon be won. The Age of Fire is coming, and no power of Celeste or Terra can stop it now."

21

This is my choice

TOMORROW...

Kiri raced through the darkness, searching for the telltale red glow of the Infernal Realm. The wind swirled around her as she flew, seeming to whisper, "Turn away, go back, accept what's come to pass."

If only she could listen! If only she could see things the way everyone else did—here was good, there was evil, and in between was the line, solid and impenetrable.

But her heart refused, and so she journeyed on. Beneath the starfall, she reached… and reached… and reached…

TODAY...

AS KIRI WATCHED ARRIN AND NAMEED VANISH IN a swirl of white light, a strange feeling struck her, telling her that their paths would cross again. Yet that seemed impossible. The clock ticked still against her chest, and she doubted if more than a few stray minutes remained after all the times she'd used her powers to battle the Sorci.

"Where did they go?" she asked, though she didn't expect Darien to know the answer.

He shook his head. "All I know is that Sibyls train in some far-off place unknowable by other humans. Perhaps it lies within the bounds of a unicorn domain… But I can only guess."

"I hope she finds what she's looking for." Her eyes fell on the glowing door through which they'd entered the temple. On the other side, the Sorci congregated around Worak, who held out his arms beside him, likely summoning a spell. Despite what Nameed had said about only Sibyls and those they chose being able to enter, Kiri would not have been surprised if the Sorci had found a way to bypass that magic.

Darien must have had the same thought, for he tore up the next tile, revealing more of the hidden door. "We shouldn't linger here."

She nodded and dug her fingers into the floor, but cold descended upon her. What was the point? The clock seemed to tick faster and faster, and she'd barely had half a day left before she'd used her powers. What remained now? Minutes? Seconds?

She glanced at Darien to make sure he was busy, then lifted the chain around her neck, just enough to catch a glimpse of the little timepiece. What she saw made her eyes well, and she hurriedly dropped it. The hands were nearly at the midnight hour.

It was over. How many times could she tell herself that, yet still shatter each time?

Enough. She'd allowed herself plenty of self-pity before, and she'd known what she'd been giving up by saving others. No more dwelling — the only thing to do was to make the most of the moments she had left. At the very least, she could see Darien to the other side of the passageway, where he'd be safe. And then she'd finally confess what she'd hidden — just in time to say goodbye.

She watched as he pulled up another tile, revealing the edge of the wooden door beneath them. Before, it had seemed kinder to keep him ignorant of the truth, but faced with the prospect of telling him right before she expired, she suddenly wished he already knew.

"Are you wondering what happened out there, why the ground shook?" His tone carried a hint of accusation.

Though that wasn't the reason why she'd been staring, she could not deny that the question had entered her mind. Still, she hesitated to ask, for he'd been reluctant to speak of his strange powers before. The first Sibyl had seemed to sense them, as if she'd detected a force within him.

He spoke before she could answer, his voice tight. "I don't know either. After what happened on the coast, I swore I would not use that magic again. But when I saw Worak, all I could think about was his cruelty and corruption. At first, it was just anger. Then... There was something else. It was in my head, but it wasn't a part of me. I could feel it eating away at my will, pushing me to obey its power, and I *wanted* to listen... I don't know how to explain it." He looked up at her. "And then I saw you, and I remembered how I... how close I came to..." Trailing off, he turned his

attention back to the tiles. "I pushed it down. But I still don't know why it affects me so."

"I'm sure you'll learn in time." Though possibilities entered her mind, it seemed pointless to let empty speculations churn on. "Arrin did not understand her gift either, but then Nameed found her and explained everything. The same will happen for you, I'm sure. Celeste does everything for a reason."

"I'm not sure Celeste is behind this. But I hope you're right."

Kiri pulled at the rest of the tiles in silence. Too many thoughts wrestled in her head, all contending for the honor of being her last. What would she spend her last moments doing, aside from seeing him to safety? Would she allow her past to reenter her mind — or, at least, what pieces of it she'd uncovered? Contemplate and appreciate all she'd been and all she'd gone through, so that she might have as whole a picture of her life as she could when she departed?

No.

If she followed that line of thought, then surely she would find only regret. The past was unchangeable, and there was so much she wished she could have done, and so much that remained locked behind the Sorci's curse. *I will know it all once I reach Celeste.*

This was not the time to ponder the greater world. Teetering on the brink of death, this was the time to be selfish and indulge what she truly wanted.

Darien. There was so much she wanted to know about him, to share with him, to learn about — and learn with — him. And she would savor as much of it as she could before her last breath.

She grabbed the door's metal ring and yanked it up. The hinges creaked loudly as cold air wafted up from below. Resting the wooden plank against the ground, she gazed into the darkness. All she could see was a ladder leading downward, and she hesitated. But then she glimpsed Worak's advancing form through the enchanted doorway and forgot her reservations.

"Come!" She grabbed the last of the Marae daggers in her belt, and its blade glowed white. Using it to light the way, she descended into the passage.

Nothing but rough stone walls surrounded her. A slamming sound resounded from behind, and, whirling, she saw that Darien had shut the door above them. But instead of following her down, he stared upward.

"What's the matter?" she asked.

"I should cast a spell to put those tiles back in place in case the Sorci find a way into the temple. But… I don't know what the magic will do."

"Leave it. We have to go."

Nodding, he scurried down the ladder but stopped at the bottom. "Worak doesn't know the doorway is there, so he wouldn't see anyone emerge until it was too late. Perhaps I could—"

"Darien, no." She seized his hand. "No more fighting. Just come with me, I beg you."

He twisted his head back one more time then faced her. "Wherever you go, I'll follow." A smile flashed across his lips but didn't reach his eyes.

Anger still burned in him; she could sense it through the tension in his grasp. Yet he didn't act on it, instead dashing through the corridor alongside her.

Once they emerged from the other side… What then? She dreaded the moment when she would have to reveal the truth about the silver clock.

But until then, it was just the two of them, and they didn't need to speak a word, for his presence was enough.

Light glowed at the end of the passageway, and beyond that lay a plush carpet of green and purple flora. The fresh scents of sweet flowers and crisp leaves brought a smile to Kiri's lips. She had scarcely spent a quarter hour in that passageway, yet her legs were ready to dissolve beneath her. Not from the weariness of running, or even from the battle she'd fought before then, but because her life was running out, and soon, there would be nothing left.

She stepped onto the grass and halted, admiring the colorful blooms sprouting among the blades. Enough racing away—she wanted to absorb her surroundings instead of letting them pass her by as meaningless blurs. Ahead, tall trees reached toward the sky, spreading their regal branches toward the azure sheath, and sapphire-colored vines with broad, gleaming leaves braided their ways up their proud trunks.

"Nonara," Darien said, regarding the cave from which they'd emerged.

Following her gaze, she found the word carved in tall, proud letters into the jagged rock. "What does that mean?"

"It's the name of the region." He looked around, his eyes bright with excitement. "Depending on what part of it we're in, Kristakai is only a five- to eight-hour hike away. I don't see any roads, but it should not take long to find one. You'll make it back with almost two whole days to spare."

Kiri bit her lip. She didn't want to tell him that she'd been lying for days, and that even this close, no effort of his could save her now. But the final hour was upon her, and she could put off the inevitable no longer.

"Less than that," she muttered.

"What?"

"I don't have two days."

"How is that possible?" Alarm filled his expression, and he grabbed her hand. "Never mind—we have no time to lose, then. Come!" He raced forward, pulling her along behind him.

"Stop!" She planted her feet into the ground.

"What—"

"Please, Darien…" Her legs trembled, and she sank to the ground.

"What's wrong?" He knelt down beside her. "Are you too weary? I'll carry you, then." He placed one arm behind her back, but she grabbed his other before he could continue.

"Just stop!" A sob rose up her throat. "I'm sorry. I… I lied to you."

"What do you mean?" His eyes bored into hers, seeking meaning.

She pulled the clock out and turned it to face him. "Breaking through the curse and unleashing my magic made the clock run faster. I don't have very long left."

He took the timepiece from her, and dismay filled his face. "Why… Why didn't you tell me?"

In those words lay so many unspoken questions: *Why did you use your powers so many times, then? Did you know when you did? How many times did you drain your own life to save those of others—including mine?*

"This is my choice." She gave him a firm look. "There were things that mattered more to me than surviving."

His jaw trembled, and a look of anguish filled his eyes. The sight made her own well, for she hated how much pain she had brought him. She opened her mouth to speak again, but before she could, he scooped her up and started running with a wild, panicked look on his face. It was a kind of delirium, a madness, a battle against reality, and she couldn't stand it.

"*Stop!*" she screamed, and he froze. To the stricken, questioning look he gave her, she replied, "I don't want to spend my last moments running."

At that, something within him broke, and tears streamed from his eyes. He collapsed to his knees and whispering, "I'm sorry… I'm so sorry…"

She placed her hand on his face. Though tears flowed down her own cheeks, she managed to keep her expression firm. "Darien, look at me."

His glistening eyes met hers. "Forgive me, Kiri… I failed you."

"No. *I* made the choices that led to this moment, and I do not regret a single one."

"How could you, when you knew they led to certain death?"

"All death is certain." She brushed her hand across his cheek. "I'll see you again among the stars."

He shook his head but seemed unable to summon any words.

Whatever energy had remained within her no longer seemed present, and she sank into the soft ground, the grass cool against her legs. But she wasn't finished—there were more words she had to speak before the shadows claimed her.

"Listen, Darien." She meant for those words to be as firm as her previous ones, but they emerged as a feeble whisper. "The Sorci will not abandon their quest. They will attempt their assault on Kristakai again, and you must warn the unicorns. Ilaerii's messenger may reach them first, but you have more knowledge. Though you cannot enter, others wander in and out of the border—sprites, fairies… You must ask for the unicorn Amdyth. Tell them I sent you… And take this as your proof." She removed the clock from around her neck. Her hand trembled as she held it out to him.

He took it slowly, staring and shaking his head. Then, he clenched his fists around the timepiece. "No. This cannot be the end."

Frustration curled through her at the denial, and she wanted to shake it out of him. False hope would do them no good now. But she did not want her final words to be ones of anger.

"Look at me." She pressed her hand against his face, turning him back toward her. "Forget everything else—just look at me."

He obeyed, leaning down toward her with his gaze fixed.

"I love you," she murmured. "I thought it might be kinder to leave without telling you, but… my heart wouldn't let me." Despite the weakness pulling her toward the ground, she wrapped her arm around his neck and pulled herself closer. "It was worth having lived through everything I faced to have loved you for even a few days."

She pressed her lips against his and kissed him deeply. Bittersweet joy flooded her at the passion returned, and she wanted to vanish inside the sweetness of his mouth, the warmth of his breath, the wonder of his touch.

"I love you too," he whispered.

She sank into his arms, smiling with absolute happiness. Yes, she would face the torments of the Sorci all over again, just to be here, now. In the arms of someone she loved, who loved her in return. And that was the most wondrous thing anyone could ever know. On that, no doubt could be shed.

"Stay with me." She leaned against his shoulder, and her eyelids drooped. "Just hold me, and let me rest in the comfort of your embrace. It will not be long until I'm sleeping. And don't weep for me… I feel only peace."

"I love you," he repeated. "I love you…"

He pressed his forehead against hers and fell into silence. She let her eyes shut. Any moment, the darkness would fall. This was as much of a happy ending as she could ask for: dying in the arms her beloved, having thwarted her enemies and saved a friend, amid a beautiful bed of flowers.

The air trembled, shaking away the bliss, and the heat of magic raced through her, burning and tearing its way down her limbs. Darien's arms tightened around her, quivering against her body.

Opening her eyes in alarm, she saw his face tense with concentration. "What are you doing?"

"Bring us to Kristakai," he muttered.

The fire lanced through her again, bringing a cry of pain to her lips. "No!" she exclaimed. "Darien, don't! It's no use!"

"I won't let you die."

Sweat beaded on his forehead, and his face contorted with effort. The heat of magic kept swirling around her, piercing her with its invisible daggers and tearing her apart from the inside out. It had to be hurting him, too, but he wouldn't listen, no matter how she screamed.

"Darien, please! I don't want this! Please, *stop!*"

But the pain kept hacking through her chest and head and stomach, drawing cry after cry of anguish to her throat. Why wouldn't he listen? She struggled against his grasp and pounded his arms with her fists, hoping to shake him out of the spell, but he remained as firm as stone, oblivious to her protests.

The ground quaked, rumbling with anger. The low growl of shaking earth filled the air, alongside a strange gust that rose out of the ground and whirled around them. Her hair whipped into her face, stinging her cheeks, and glittering yellow sparks tumbled madly across her vision.

A burst of light exploded before her, and agony surged through her, ripping a new scream from her throat. But then, everything abruptly went still—no more wind, no more quakes, no more pain. Yet the light remained, surrounding her in its brightness.

When it faded away, a white unicorn stared down at her with gentle, violet eyes.

Recognizing her at once, Kiri tried to sit up. "Amdyth!"

But she wasn't strong enough, and she found herself falling back into Darien, who scooped her up as he stood. Confusion clouded his expression, but before he could speak, a piercing thought floated though her head.

Why have you called me here? It was the unicorn, communicating to both of them through their minds.

"I didn't mean to." Darien said quickly, striding toward her. "I was trying to transport us to your domain… But it doesn't matter. She is one of yours, and she needs to return *now*. Can you help her?"

Kiriall, my daughter. Amdyth bent her knees and sank to the ground. *I have been so worried about you. Yes, come, you are safe now.* She lifted her gaze to Darien. *Place her on my back. I will take her home.*

Kiri felt Darien's muscles loosen as he exhaled in relief. She tried to move on her own as he lowered her onto the unicorn's back but could barely lift her head.

Amdyth turned back to look at her. *Everything will be all right, my child.*

I will not let you fall. She turned to Darien. *You, I'm afraid, cannot come with us, for you are human, and therefore forbidden from our borders.*

"I understand," he said.

For a moment, her violet gaze fixed on him, penetrating and stern.

He recoiled. "Why do you look at me that way?"

The unicorn shook her head. *Your choice may have saved Kiriall, but it was unwise.*

"She will live—that's all that matters." He turned to Kiri, his expression somehow mournful and joyful at once.

Though she disliked that he'd ignored what should have been her final wish, she could not deny that she was glad that she would live on. Knowing this could be her last glimpse of him, she let her eyes linger, drinking in every beautiful angle, every perfect curve, and reached out one weak hand to him.

He took it and kissed it gently. "Will I see you again?"

"Yes," she replied, without hesitating.

No, Amdyth said sternly. *If you leave again, you will not survive next time.*

Kiri tried not to let the warning sink into her head. No matter what, she would find a way to return to her love—never mind the laws of her kind.

He is not what you think he is. Amdyth's voice cut through her mind, startling in their loudness.

What does that mean? she wondered, but no response came.

The unicorn's words must have been to her alone, for Darien did not react to them. With one hand still wrapped around hers, he held up the silver clock with the other. "This is yours."

Kiri shook her head. "Keep it."

Feeling a shift beneath her, she grabbed a fistful of silky mane just before the unicorn took off into the air, ripping her hand from Darien's. An invisible force held her safe against Amdyth's back as the unicorn ran across the sky.

Startled by the quickness of the departure, Kiri looked back. Darien, still clutching the silver clock, watched her from the ground. Soon, he shrank into the distance, until she could glimpse him no more.

What would become of him, with the Sorci still out for his blood? Why did such strange power surround him, dark and frightening even to him? How could she leave him alone to face all that lay before him?

I will find you again, Darien. I promise.

Considering how many powers and wonders she had encountered on her journey, she refused to believe she could be chained to her homeland forever. Somewhere, there had to exist the magic to liberate her for good. And she would find it. Not only to be with him, but for herself. No more would she be imprisoned by the circumstances into which she had been born.

To blazes with destiny. To blazes with fate. To blazes with all the laws binding her.

Tomorrow was hers, and hers alone.

ELSEWHERE…

"Cry, poor heart. Cry, poor soul. Love holds you fast, yet breaks the promise of tomorrow."

Trickery—first released of the Three Blazes, general of the Infernal Realm, and loyal follower of the Fiend—echoed the nymph's song with laughter and wondered if she knew how prescient that ditty would truly be. The words rang through his mind, as vibrant as if he'd spoken them with his own voice. Not the human voice he had adopted, but that of his true self, a being who had long ago been forgotten even to mythology.

Though his sisters, Misery and Enmity, remained dormant still, they, too would rise soon. His very awakening and ascent out of Inferno—brought on not by any power of his own, but a shift in the stars—was a sign of the Fiend's imminent return, though the world did not know it yet. Soon, his deceit would bring the Starless Prince into his clutches.

And more importantly, the Infernal Father's embrace.

"Great Fiend, my Master! Are you not pleased? Isolated and desperate—the boy's soul is ours for the taking, and he will come to us soon enough. He may hold some petty suspicions, but I shall wipe them away quickly enough, and before long, he will think me the only guiding light he has. Then, oh then, the Age of Fire will truly begin."

Though his dark master did not answer with words, he sensed approval. Pleased with himself, he reached out with his psychic powers, seeking the windborn one. The unicorns' borders might have kept out the manmade

magic of the Sorci, but they were no match for his ancient force. Wherever deceit dwelled, he could see.

In his vision, Kiriall Amdyth lay amid a bed of white flowers at the center of a grove. Colorful unicorns surrounded her and aimed their radiant horns at her, sending forth their healing magic in glittering blue and purple swirls. The nymph's eyes were closed, but through his powers of sensation, he detected the life force returning to her body.

"Good, good. 'Twould be a shame if we lost our greatest weapon before we had a chance to wield it in full force. You swear your allegiance now, but your feeble mortal heart is no match for the winds of destiny. You will reach for him with the noblest of intentions, yet once you learn what he truly is, not even the Ayr of Loyalty will be able to keep you by his side. Your Terrestrial fears will lead you to betrayal, yes, yes. You'll break the promise of tomorrow."

Acknowledgements

Special thanks to my writing buddy Elizabeth Corrigan, who has been there for *Windborn*'s whole half-decade-long saga from idea to published book, and who is the one who came up with the title of the series, *Fated Stars*. Thank you for listening to all my wild brainstorms and frustrated rants, and for beta reading the manuscript.

Thank you to Karissa Laurel for being generally awesome and for always being there when I need an ear.

Thank you to the Snowy Wings Publishing family, especially Lyssa Chiavari and Jane Watson, for giving *Windborn* a perch from which to fly.

Thanks as well to everyone who supported my novella "Tell Me My Name," which was originally published in 2014 and served as the springboard for the *Fated Stars* series. In particular, thank you to Tash McAdam, George Ebey, William Herr, Jacqueline Simonds, and Carrie White-Parrish.

Finally, and most importantly, thank you to all the readers who've been willing to take a chance on my books, to step into unfamiliar new worlds and meet fictional strangers.

Other Books by Mary Fan

THE STARSWEPT TRILOGY

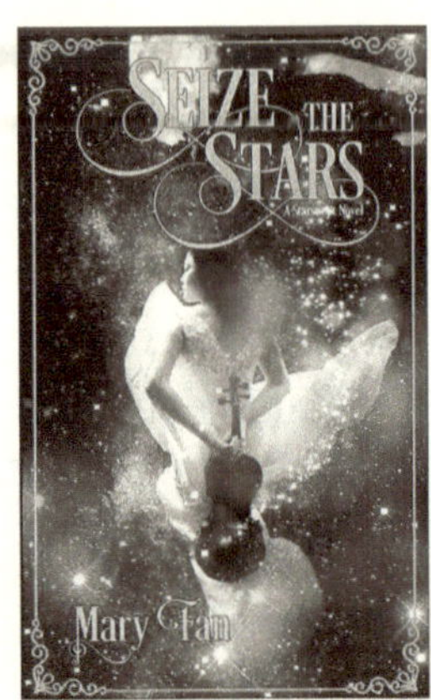

"...a sophisticated commentary on art, society, and how we perceive our own worth. The beginning of an elegant, spirited rebellion saga."

- Kirkus Reviews, review of Starswept (Book 1)

IN THE SERIES:

Starswept (Book 1)

Wayward Stars (Book 2)

Seize the Stars (Book 3)

STRONGER THAN A BRONZE DRAGON

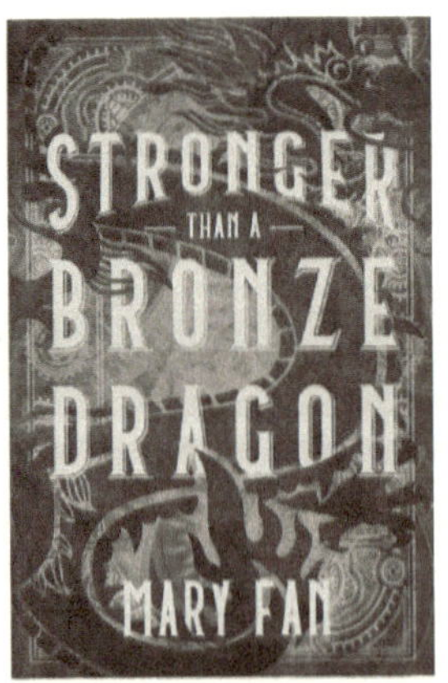

"In this Asian-inspired, steampunk-flavored fantasy, Fan creates a spitfire heroine who is memorable."

– Booklist

THE JANE COLT TRILOGY

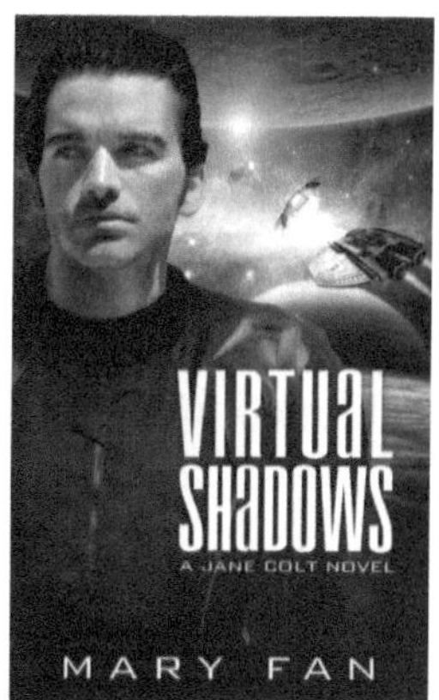

"[A] thrilling science fiction-adventure series launch... [T]he fast-paced action is balanced by thoughtful meditations on what it means to be human."

- Publishers Weekly, starred review of Artificial Absolutes (Book 1)

IN THE SERIES:

Artificial Absolutes (Book 1)
Synthetic Illusions (Book 2)
Virtual Shadows (Book 3)

THE FLYNN NIGHTSIDER SERIES

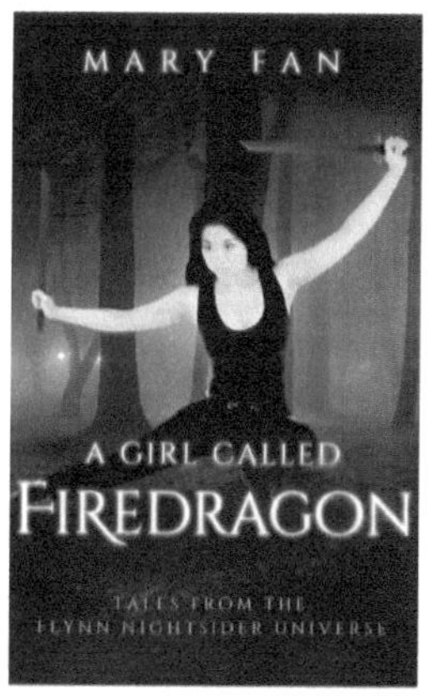

Break the enchantments. Find the truth. Ignite the revolution.

IN THE SERIES:

Flynn Nightsider and the Edge of Evil (Book 1)
A Girl Called Firedragon: Tales from the Flynn Nightsider Universe

Mary Fan is a Jersey City-based writer specializing in young adult, sci-fi, and fantasy books. Her works include *Stronger Than A Bronze Dragon*, *Flynn Nightsider and the Edge of Evil*, the *Jane Colt* trilogy, and the critically acclaimed *Starswept* trilogy. Her short works have been featured in several anthologies, including *Thrilling Adventure Yarns*, *Love, Murder & Mayhem*, *Keep Faith*, and *Mine!: A Celebration of Liberty and Freedom for All Benefitting Planned Parenthood*.

She is also the co-editor, along with fellow sci-fi author Paige Daniels, of the *Brave New Girls* young adult sci-fi anthology series, which seek to encourage more girls to explore STEM careers and raise money for the Society of Women Engineers scholarship fund.

When she's not writing, Mary can usually be found tackling harmonies at choir rehearsal, tearing up bags at the kickboxing gym, getting tangled up in aerial silks, or falling off a flying trapeze.